DEAD ON ARRIVAL

Mike Lawson is a former nuclear engineer who turned to full-time writing in May 2003. He lives with his family in the United States. *Dead on Arrival* is his third novel featuring Joe DeMarco.

Visit www.mikelawsonbooks.com for more information on Mike Lawson

Praise for Mike Lawson

'This assured first novel shows Michael Lawson to be a talented storyteller, and DeMarco makes a likeable hero as he follows an intricate trail through some typically murky American politics'   *Sunday Telegraph*

'Mike Lawson shows every understanding of the skills required of a thriller writer to keep a reader fully engaged and utterly thrilled'   *Guardian*

'Mike Lawson writes a mean thriller and has a sense of humour that hurts. I love this one'
Independent on Sunday

'*The Inside Ring* is the kind of whodunnit thriller you can't stop thinking about while you're reading and can't stop thinking about once you're alone'
Vince Flynn, bestselling author of *Memorial Day*

Visit www.AuthorTracker.co.uk for exclusive updates on Mike Lawson.

D0709781

Also by Mike Lawson

The Inside Ring
The Payback

MIKE LAWSON

Dead on Arrival

HARPER

Harper
An Imprint of HarperCollins*Publishers*
77–85 Fulham Palace Road,
Hammersmith, London W6 8JB

www.harpercollins.co.uk

A Paperback Original 2008
1
First published as *House Rules* in the USA 2008

Copyright © Mike Lawson 2008

Mike Lawson asserts the moral right to
be identified as the author of this work

A catalogue record for this book
is available from the British Library

ISBN: 978-0-00725629-7

Set in Meridien by Palimpsest Book Production Limited
Grangemouth, Stirlingshire

Printed and bound in Great Britain by
Clays Ltd, St Ives plc

To Keith – the best birthday present ever.
We're so very proud.

Acknowledgements

I wish to thank a number of people: Frank Horton for proofreading and fact-checking all my books before anyone else sees them; Bob Koch for his editorial comments and his technical advice on bizarre things like hiding meth labs and plastic weapons; Jerry Main for counsel on guns and bullets; Joe Smaldore, brother-in-law extraordinaire, for driving me all over D.C. to look at locations in the book, and in particular the trip to West Virginia to locate the home of Jubal Pugh; Bill Harman for introducing me to a man who will remain nameless but who provided an insider's insight on the F-16s guarding the nofly zone around D.C.

I am grateful to everyone at Grove/Atlantic who helped with the production of this book, but particularly to my editor Jamison Stoltz who improved the book tremendously and to Morgan Entrekin, president of Grove/Atlantic, for giving me the opportunity to publish this novel.

Lastly, and as always, to David Gernert and everyone at The Gernert Company. David, I just can't thank you enough for the work you did to find the right home for this book.

Prologue

They had no idea how big the blast might be.

The techs, those useless dorks, said the bomb could take out just the garage or just the surrounding homes – or it could flatten structures as far as a quarter mile away. It all depends, they said. It depended on how the bomb was constructed, if it was shaped to blow in a particular direction. It obviously depended on how much ammonium nitrate the bombers had. It all depends.

No shit, had been Merchant's response, *and thanks for all your help*.

But Merchant knew, no matter how big the bomb might be, that he couldn't evacuate the nearby homes. If he started an evacuation, the two guys inside the garage might notice all the lights going on at three in the morning and then would see people running like hell, dressed in their pajamas. Or, with his luck, one of the good citizens they were trying to protect would call a radio station, and the bombers would hear that they were surrounded by fifty FBI agents. And once they knew that, they'd probably blow the thing right where it was, and Merchant and his guys, hiding less than twenty yards from the garage . . . well, they'd be toast. Literally.

If the bomb did explode and a bunch of civilians were killed, the media weenies and the politicians would naturally second-guess the hell out of his decision not to evacuate. They'd call him reckless and irresponsible, and his bosses would blame it all on him to save their bureaucratic butts. But then what did he care? He'd be dead. No, the smart thing to do was to forget evacuating anybody and go in now. And as for trying to negotiate with the guys in the garage. . . . Hell, even the suits at the Hoover Building agreed that would be useless. You can't negotiate with people who are willing to kill themselves in order to kill you.

What a way to spend Labor Day.

He spoke softly into his mike: 'Alpha to Bravo Team Leader. Any sign of a third man yet?'

'No, sir.'

The two men assembling the bomb were in a garage that was fifty feet from a two-story house. Merchant had overall tactical command of the operation and command of the five-man squad that made up Alpha Team. Another senior agent commanded Bravo Team, also a five-man squad. Bravo was on the opposite side of the garage from Alpha. Charlie Team, which consisted of almost forty agents, was protecting the perimeter, making sure no one entered or left the site. Charlie also had the snipers. The snipers would shoot anyone they thought needed shooting – and they wouldn't miss.

Merchant and his men were dressed in SWAT gear: combat helmets with face shields, black fatigues and body armor, headsets so they could hear and talk to Merchant, night-vision goggles, and an assortment of assault rifles, shotguns, and .40-caliber pistols. They were dressed for war, a war they were going to start.

'Alpha to Charlie Team Leader. What about you? Any sign of the third man?'

'No, sir.'

The reports they'd received said three guys were involved, but there might not even *be* a third guy. The intelligence on him was weak. Maybe the third guy was in the house sleeping, or maybe he'd left to get something. Whatever the case, it was time to move. They had to move before daylight and the longer he waited the higher the likelihood that the guys in the garage would see his men or, even worse, drive the truck out of the garage. If that happened he'd be dealing with a *mobile* bomb, and that would be no fun at all.

'Alpha Team Leader to all personnel. We're going in. Bravo, are you ready?'

'Yes, sir.'

'Charlie, are you ready?'

'Yes, sir.'

Merchant nodded, although no one could see the gesture. He couldn't rely on the intelligence and he couldn't rely on the techs – but he could rely on his guys. He spoke into his mike again. 'Remember, we want these assholes alive but I don't want any of you people dyin' to keep them that way.'

Merchant took a breath, flipped the safety on his weapon, and felt the adrenaline start to squirt into his bloodstream. 'On my go,' he said. 'Three. Two. One. Go!'

The garage had two doors: a normal door, like the door to a house, and a slide-up garage door operated by an electric garage door opener. There were also two small windows. On Merchant's *go*! the men from both teams belly-crawled forward until all ten agents were pressed up against the walls of the garage. Merchant tapped one of his men on the shoulder, and the agent placed four small C-4 charges on the large garage door, each charge at the corner of an imaginary six-foot square. A fifth charge was placed in the center of the square. Merchant took a breath and whispered into his mike a second time. 'On my go. Three. Two. One. Go!'

Three things happened simultaneously: flash-bang

grenades that produced a horrific amount of noise and light were shot in through the two windows; a door knocker – a heavy piece of pipe with a plate welded on one end and equipped with handles – was slammed into the small door, ripping it open; and a button was pushed on a remote control and the five small charges on the garage door exploded, blowing a hole in the door. Merchant's men were inside the garage in less than three seconds, screaming like banshees out of some urban nightmare.

It went down perfectly, like a training exercise at Quantico. The two men inside the garage were both on the floor, knocked down by the concussion of the door being blown open. They'd been blinded by the flash-bangs, had their fists pressed against their eyes, and were wondering why their ears didn't work. Merchant's guys had handcuffs on the mutts less than a minute after they breached the building.

Jesus, Merchant thought, they're just kids. Then he looked inside the truck. Holy shit! That was a *lot* of fertilizer. There had to be at least a ton, maybe two.

'Merchant to Charlie Team Leader. Garage secure. Perps in custody. Get the bomb techs in here now, *right* now, to tell me if this goddamned thing is armed.' Turning to the agent in charge of Bravo Team, he said, 'Harris, take your people and do a quick sweep of the house and make sure the third guy's not in there. Clemens, you take these bastards to the command vehicle and stand by. I'll wait here until the bomb techs show.'

Merchant looked into the truck again. Man, that was one big bomb! He wondered what – or who – these guys had been planning to blow up.

He was two blocks away when he saw all the flashing red and blue lights. He stopped the car and took the binoculars from the glove box. There were so many lights that he could see the scene as clearly as if it were noon instead of 4 a.m. He could see a fire truck, two ambulances, and more than a dozen marked and unmarked police vehicles. There were also two armored trucks, one truck looking like something a bomb disposal squad might use. The other truck, with the satellite dishes on the roof, was probably a command and communications center. There were uniformed men milling about and men wearing windbreakers over white shirts and ties. FBI, he assumed. Standing off to one side was a group of men dressed in helmets and black clothes, shaking hands, patting each other on the back, acting like athletes who'd just won a game. There were also a lot of people standing outside their homes wearing robes or clothes they'd just thrown on, wondering what was happening in their peaceful American neighborhood.

What had those fools done wrong?

He had to leave immediately; he was particularly vulnerable now. He hoped he hadn't left anything inside the house or the garage that would identify him, but if he had there was nothing he could do about it. They could have cars patrolling the area and if they stopped him he had no doubt they'd detain him because of the way he looked. He made a slow turn into a driveway, backed up, and began driving in the direction from which he'd come, forcing himself to drive slowly.

His right leg was on fire; it always hurt when he'd been sitting for a long time. He needed to get out of the car and walk around a bit, but he couldn't do that. He would bear the pain – as he'd always borne the pain – until it was safe to stop.

He headed in the direction of the freeway. With God's blessing, he'd be in Philadelphia in two hours. There he had a place to go, a place set up in advance. There he *might* be safe.

What had those fools done?

Myron Clark was good at his job because he was smart and because he was patient, but most of all because he was tireless. He was absolutely indefatigable.

He always looked fresh whenever he conducted an interrogation: his shirt wrinkle-free, his tie in place, face clean-shaven, hair carefully combed. He looked as if he'd just stepped from a shower after a full eight hours of peaceful sleep. The truth was that he was surviving on catnaps, but he would never allow the prisoners to see this. They had to think that Clark could go forever, that he'd never stop. And he wouldn't.

Clark was interrogating the two men captured in the garage in Baltimore. He'd been interrogating them for twenty-six straight hours, and he could tell that the one named Omar al-Assad was going to break first. In fact, he was going to break the next time Clark talked to him.

Clark was an ordinary-looking man in his forties, five-nine, receding hairline, carrying twenty pounds he ought to lose. He wasn't physically intimidating and he knew it – that's why he had Warren Knox for an assistant. Knox was six-four, heavily muscled, and kept his hair cut close to his big knobby skull. He had a particularly brutal face, the kind you'd expect to see on a tattooed felon, and he always looked like he was just barely suppressing an incredible amount of rage. The truth was that Warren Knox was hardly violent at all; Clark had killed more men than Knox.

Omar had asked for a lawyer when the interrogation first began, and Clark had nodded to Knox and Knox had grabbed Omar by the throat and slammed him up against the wall of the interrogation room. As Omar was pinned against the wall, choking, his feet no longer touching the floor, Knox said, 'If you say *lawyer* one more time I'm gonna kick your teeth out.'

That's when Omar began to fully appreciate his situation. This wasn't like TV. It wasn't like all those *Law and Order* shows where the cops yelled at the prisoners but never touched them – and stopped yelling as soon as they asked for a mouthpiece. No, Clark and Knox had made it clear to Omar that he had no rights. He wasn't going to be allowed to see anyone. Not a lawyer, not his partner, not his mother. He was completely alone.

If they took these clowns to trial, the fact that they'd trampled all over their rights as citizens could be a problem. The government's lawyers would spout legal gibberish to minimize the damage, but *convicting* these guys wasn't a priority, not at this point. In London, in Spain, in India, the subway attacks hadn't involved just a single bomb; the terrorists had set off four or five bombs simultaneously. Clark needed to know if Omar and his pal had accomplices, and if he had to cause Omar a little discomfort to find this out . . . well, too bad for Omar.

So for twenty-six hours Omar wasn't allowed to sleep. He'd be allowed to almost fall asleep, but just as his head would hit his chest, Knox would slam open the door to the interrogation room, cuff him on the back of the head, and tell him to go stand in the corner as if he were a truculent five-year-old.

And Omar was given no food and a lot of coffee. The coffee not only kept him awake but the caffeine in his empty stomach compounded the condition of his already jangling nerves. Yes, Omar was ready. Omar's partner – who was just a bit dumber than Omar and didn't have Omar's imagination – would last a bit longer, but not much.

Clark checked his appearance in the mirror near the interrogation room door and entered the room. He took a seat across the table from the prisoner and looked for a moment into his bloodshot eyes, his terrified young face. 'Well, you've beaten me, Omar,' he said, shaking his head in mock disappointment. 'My boss says we gotta send you someplace else, to see if some other guys can do better than me. We used to send people like you to Gitmo, Guantánamo Bay, down there in Cuba. But Gitmo became a fishbowl, Omar. Too many pussy liberals always watchin' over our shoulders, always tryin' to make us play by the rules. Well, my friend, we've gotten a lot smarter since Gitmo. Now we use an island off the coast of Maine.'

Clark smiled sadly at Omar, as if he truly pitied him.

'The army used to use the island for testing biological weapons. They have a facility there, and they have cages in the facility. The cages don't have a lot of headroom because they used to keep monkeys in them – you know, the monkeys they used for the experiments. The monkeys are all dead now, but the cages are still there. But the best part isn't the cages, Omar. The best part is that nobody knows about the island. And nobody knows what happens there.'

Omar al-Assad stared at Clark for a moment, maybe looking for mercy, but knowing by now that there was nothing merciful about Myron Clark.

'We were going to explode the bomb in the Baltimore Harbor Tunnel,' Omar said.

In the next hour, Clark had the whole story. Omar al-Assad and his friend Bashar Hariri were American-born Muslims. They were eighteen years of age, from low-income families, high school dropouts, and unemployed. Neither young man was particularly religious, and their tastes and style of dress were typical of Americans their age.

One Saturday evening, they attended a lecture at a local mosque. The main reason they attended was because it was cold outside, and free food and coffee came with the speech. The title of the lecture, which neither young man could remember exactly, was 'The Impact of American Imperialism on the Muslim World.' Something like that, they said.

The lecturer told the two Americans that his name was Muhammad – he might as well have said John Smith – and he was from Yemen, was an imam, and was traveling around America preaching to the faithful. He instantly became the two young Americans' new best friend, spending hours with them, buying them dinners and hammering into their weak brains a message of hate. After a month he convinced them that blowing a hole in the Baltimore Harbor Tunnel, killing several hundred people, and disrupting commerce up and down the eastern seaboard would be a good and noble thing to do. *And* they'd each be given ten thousand dollars after the job was done.

Muhammad gave the young men the money to purchase a truck and the other ingredients they needed to make the bomb. He had been helping them assemble the bomb until just before Omar and Bashar were captured. All Omar knew – and ultimately, three hours later, Myron Clark believed him – was that Muhammad had to leave the garage to call someone, but Omar didn't know who.

But the most important thing Omar told Clark was that Muhammad had an artificial leg. That's what allowed the Bureau to find Muhammad in their files and determine who he really was – an honest-to-God al-Qaeda operative.

'How did you catch us?' an exhausted Omar asked.

Clark didn't tell him, but they'd caught Omar and his buddy because a fertilizer seller hadn't liked their looks.

They had needed two major ingredients for their bomb: ammonium nitrate fertilizer and a racing fuel composed primarily of nitromethane. At one of the places they'd purchased the ammonium nitrate, the fertilizer supplier had asked the young men why they needed it and Omar had said that they operated a landscaping business. The supplier was used to dealing with beefy white farmers, and the two men purchasing the fertilizer were obviously of Middle Eastern ancestry, too young to be likely principals in any business and visibly nervous during the purchase. He was on the phone to the FBI before the young men and their truck had exited his parking lot.

But instead of answering Omar's question, Clark asked one of his own. 'Why did you and Bashar decide to become martyrs? I mean, do you guys really believe all that virgins-in-paradise bullshit?'

'Martyrs?' Omar said. 'We weren't going to be martyrs.'

Then Omar explained. Their plan had been to drive the truck and another car – the car Muhammad had escaped in – into the tunnel, punch out the tires on the truck so it couldn't be easily moved, and flee the scene in the second vehicle. They would have been miles away when the bomb exploded.

That's when Clark unveiled the part of Muhammad's plan that Omar obviously didn't know.

'Omar,' he said, 'your pal Muhammad had set the timer to detonate the bomb two seconds after you armed it.'

Senator William Davis Broderick, Republican, the junior senator from Virginia, waited impatiently for his turn to speak.

In the two weeks since those Muslim boys had tried to explode a bomb in the Baltimore Harbor

Tunnel, Broderick had listened to his colleagues say all the usual and expected things. Some senators grumbled that controls for bomb-making materials like ammonium nitrate were still lacking. Yada yada yada, Broderick said to himself.

Others complained that our borders were still too porous, that terrorists could obviously enter and leave the country at will. Shake-ups at Homeland Security were coming, they promised. Hearings would soon be held, they warned.

Yeah, like *that* was gonna help.

But what Broderick really liked was that the senator currently speaking had just given him the perfect lead-in to his speech. Patty Moran, the senior senator from Oregon, had just said that the federal government was continuing to underfund those poor cops and medics who would be first on the scene the next time al-Qaeda attacked. And then she said the magic words. She said them as if she'd been given an advance copy of Broderick's speech. She said, 'We *must* adequately fund our first responders, senators, because, as we all know, it's not a matter of if there will be another attack, it's only a matter of when.'

Oh, Patty, if you weren't a Democrat I'd kiss you.

Finally, Broderick was at the podium. He went through the obligatory will-the-senator-yield litany and then took his speech from the inside pocket of his suit, knowing he would never look at it. He had this one nailed.

'My friends,' he said, 'we just heard the good gentlewoman from the great state of Oregon say what we've all heard so many times before. In fact, I've heard it said so many times I'm sick of it. She said that another terrorist attack is not a matter of *if* but *when*. Well, ladies and gentlemen, I'm here to tell you it's only a matter of if – *if* nothing changes.'

Broderick's aide, Nick Fine, had written the speech, and Broderick had to admit the man had done a good job. He knew Nick didn't like him – hell, the man hated him – but when writing this particular speech ol' Nick had really put his heart into it.

'Senators,' Broderick said, 'I'm here today to propose changes, real changes, changes that will make this great country safer. It's time to stop being politically correct. It's time to stop being afraid to speak the truth because someone will be offended. It is instead time for *somebody* in this body, this body chosen to represent and protect the people, to stand up and say what needs to be said. And I'm gonna say it.

'The first thing I propose to change is that we quit calling this a war on terrorism. We're not at war with terrorists. We're at war with *Muslim* terrorists. It's time to quit making redheaded schoolchildren and their grandmothers take off their shoes at airports when we all know the most likely terrorist is a young Muslim man.'

Broderick could almost hear the redheads cheering.

'And as the near miss in Baltimore clearly showed, the threat isn't solely from outsiders, from foreigners from across the sea. My friends, even though we don't like to say it out loud, the fact is that we are at risk from some of our own citizens because some of them – hopefully a very small number – have more allegiance to Islam than they do to their own country.'

Broderick looked around the Senate chamber. It was half empty, and most of the senators in attendance were busy talking to their aides or reading e-mail on their BlackBerries. That's the way it usually went. Politicians didn't give speeches to change the minds of other politicians; they gave speeches to get their faces on C-SPAN and their names in the papers. And Broderick's name *was* going to be in the papers. As he was speaking, Nick Fine was e-mailing the text of his speech to everyone, friend and enemy alike, and Broderick figured that on this occasion his enemies were going to be at least as much help as his friends.

'My fellow Americans, I'm going to introduce a bill that contains three provisions that will make this country safer. Some of you will be shocked, some of you will be angered, but as I said before it's time for us to start doing something other than *praying* that we don't have another nine-eleven. Yes, it's time for somebody in the United States Senate to do something other than hold a bunch of daggone hearings after we finish mopping up the blood from the latest Muslim attack.'

And lay out his bill he did. He noticed that as he spoke a few senators actually began to pay attention – or, to be accurate, he could see them chuckling and shaking their heads. But they'd see who had the last laugh.

His first proposal was to eliminate a large part of the threat by shipping every Muslim who was not an American out of the country. And he wasn't kidding, he said. Students, visitors, immigrants with green cards . . . Well, adios, or whatever the Arabic word was for goodbye. He noted that Prime Minister Tony Blair had had a similar reaction toward foreign Muslims when the London subways were bombed. Blair, however, had wanted to deport only the rabble-rousers and agitators; Broderick wanted to take Tony's good idea one large step further.

His second proposal was that future visits by people from Muslim countries would be significantly limited, carefully controlled, and primarily allowed only for business purposes. Being a good Republican he knew that business mattered, but Muslims could send their children to Europe for school and if they wanted to take a vacation they could visit the Fijis. He knew some would argue that education and tourism *were* businesses, but hey, you had to draw the line somewhere.

Muslims desiring to enter the country would have

to apply for entry months in advance to permit time for background checks. Upon arrival they would be photographed, fingerprinted, and DNA-sampled, *and* they would have to have an American sponsor who would be responsible for their conduct. Naturally, these people would be carefully monitored while they were in the States.

But Broderick knew it was his last proposal that would draw the most attention: he proposed that background checks be performed on all Muslim Americans. These background checks would identify if a Muslim belonged to a radical group or supported radical causes and, most importantly, would identify who these people knew and were related to overseas.

'The near demolition of the Baltimore Harbor Tunnel – God only knows how many would have died – showed that radical Muslims in this country, American citizens, can be proselytized and turned into weapons of mass destruction. We *must* take steps to guard against this very real threat.'

Later, he wished that he hadn't used the word *registry*, but he did. He said that all Muslims who successfully passed the background checks he was proposing would then be entered into a registry, one of the benefits of this being that airport travel for these folks would become less bothersome. He wasn't saying they wouldn't have to go through the metal detectors, just that they were less likely to be pulled off to the side and patted down. He noted that the idea of travelers having some sort of special identification to speed up airport screening was nothing new.

'I'm just saying let's start with the Muslims,' Broderick said.

Joe DeMarco saw Mahoney sitting on the warped wooden bleachers with five black women and a couple of toddlers. The football players they were watching appeared to be ten or eleven years of age, their helmets too big for their heads. The team in the hand-me-down, washfaded orange jerseys was called the Tigers; the other team, their color blue, their uniforms just as worn, were the Cougars. Just as DeMarco reached the bleachers, the Cougars' quarterback threw a perfect tenyard spiral to a kid who was about three feet tall and who was immediately buried under a sea of orange shirts.

'Good hands, son!' Mahoney yelled out. 'Way to stick. Way to hang on to that ball.'

DeMarco had no idea why Mahoney did this – the stress of the job, a need for some time alone – but whatever the reason, every once in a while he'd leave his office and sneak over to southeast D.C. and watch the kids play. He'd sit there on the sidelines with the mothers, completely out of place, a big white-haired white man dressed in a topcoat and a suit in a part of Washington that was predominantly black. The other odd thing was that he wasn't usually recognized; this was odd because John Fitzpatrick Mahoney was the Speaker of the U.S. House of Representatives. It seemed as if folks who lived in this section of the city had lost their faith in politicians a long time ago and no longer paid all that much attention to the players, including those at the top of the roster.

DeMarco took a seat on the bleachers next to Mahoney. Mahoney glanced over at him – clearly irritated that he was there – and turned his attention back to the game. DeMarco took an envelope out of his jacket pocket and handed it to Mahoney. 'I ran into Martin Born up in Boston,' he said. 'He asked me to pass this on to you.'

Born was a Boston developer, one of Mahoney's wealthier constituents, and he had his small avaricious heart set on a wetland area known to be home to some variety of slow-breeding duck. Mahoney, at least for the moment, was siding with the ducks.

Mahoney started to open the envelope, but the Cougars' quarterback was sacked just then by a ten-year-old who looked big enough to play for Notre Dame. 'You gotta double-team that guy, boys. Protect your quarterback!' he yelled.

One of the mothers, a woman as big as Mahoney, turned to him and said, 'They gotta *triple*-team that one. That chile, he must weigh a hundred fifty pounds.'

'Yeah,' Mahoney said, 'but that kid playin' right guard, he's stoppin' him by himself about half the time. That kid's got game.'

'You got that right,' the woman said. 'That's my sister's boy, Jamal.'

When the Cougars took a time-out, Mahoney ripped open the envelope and fanned out a number of hundred-dollar bills, maybe ten of them. 'What the hell's this?' he said. 'A *tip*?'

DeMarco just shook his head. He was a lawyer, although he'd never practiced law, and he occupied an unusual position on Mahoney's staff. If asked his job, he would have said he was the speaker's personal troubleshooter, but one of his duties was bringing Mahoney envelopes like the one he'd just delivered. There were times DeMarco didn't like his job.

'Mavis sent me over here to get you,' DeMarco said. Mavis was Mahoney's secretary. He didn't bother to add: *Which I wouldn't have had to do if you'd ever turn on your goddamn cell phone!* 'You got a roomful of people waiting to talk to you about Broderick's bill.'

Mahoney shook his head. 'What a waste of time. That bill's not goin' anywhere. Broderick's a fruit-cake.'

DeMarco shrugged. 'I dunno. People are scared.'

'So what?' Mahoney said. 'Just because – ' Mahoney leaped to his feet. 'Offside! Number eight, he was offside!'

'Yeah, Lionel,' the big woman said. 'You shoulda seen that, for cryin' out loud. Them glasses you got, they thick enough to see stuff on the *moon*.'

Mahoney whooped.

Lionel, a man in his sixties, a good guy who had volunteered his time to ref the game, glared over at the woman – and the speaker.

'What are you lookin' over here for?' the woman yelled. 'If you wasn't always lookin' at the women in the stands, you'da seen that boy was offside too.'

Mahoney sat back down, happy. Nothing he liked better than starting a ruckus.

'Mavis said the meeting was supposed to start half an hour ago,' DeMarco said.

'Aw, goddammit,' Mahoney said, but he rose from the bench. He started to walk away, then turned back to the woman. 'Hey, you got some kind of fund for uniforms and stuff ?'

'Yeah,' she said, suspicious now, not sure what Mahoney was up to.

'Well, here,' Mahoney said, and handed her the envelope that Mr. Born had stuffed with cash. 'Get those boys some new jerseys – and football shoes too. You know the kind with little rubber cleats on the bottom, so they won't be slippin' all the time.'

1

The two F-16 Falcons screamed down the runway at Andrews Air Force Base.

Pete Dalton – Lieutenant Colonel Dalton – *lived* for this. There was absolutely no other experience on the planet like flying an armed-to-the-teeth air force fighter.

It was the week before Thanksgiving, and when the klaxon went off, Dalton and his wingman had been sitting in the ready trailer at Andrews, bitching that they'd been assigned to work the holiday, although Dalton didn't really care that much. Then the klaxon blared and they were out of the trailer, into their planes, and tearing down the runway five minutes later.

As they were ascending into the skies over Washington, they were briefed on the situation. Some idiot in a small slow-moving plane had just taken off from an airfield in Stafford, Virginia. The guy was at three thousand feet and doing eighty-six knots, almost a hundred miles an hour. He had flown briefly to the south, then turned northeast and crossed into the outer zone and was not responding to air traffic controllers at Dulles.

There are two air defense zones around the nation's capital, an inner and an outer zone. The outer zone has a ragged, roughly circular boundary that extends thirty to fifty miles outward from the Washington Monument. This zone is called the ADIZ – the Air Defense Identification Zone. To enter the ADIZ a pilot has to identify himself, must have an operating transponder that broadcasts a signal identifying his aircraft, and must remain in continuous two-way communication with FAA controllers. The second zone, the inner zone, is the no-fly zone. The no-fly zone is a perfect circle extending out sixteen miles from the Washington Monument. The only aircraft allowed to enter this area aside from commercial traffic going in and out of Reagan National Airport have to be specially cleared.

The fool in question hadn't identified himself, his transponder was either malfunctioning or disabled, and he wasn't responding to queries from FAA controllers. He was doing *everything* wrong. When the unidentified aircraft was two miles inside the ADIZ, thirty-three miles and approximately twenty minutes from all the government buildings in D.C., a whole bunch of things began to happen.

An air force colonel in Rome, New York – the officer commanding NORAD's Northeast Air Defense Sector – scrambled the F-16s out of Andrews; Blackhawk helicopters under the control of Homeland Security lifted off from Reagan National; the Secret Service and the U.S. Capitol Police were alerted and told to be prepared to evacuate the White House, the Capitol, and the Supreme Court; and men in secret locations throughout Washington who are qualified to fire surface-to-air missiles were notified and told to stand by.

At the same time, four people were paged: the secretary of defense, his deputy, a navy admiral located at Peterson Air Force Base in Colorado who had overall command of NORAD, and an air force major general located at Tyndall Air Force Base in Florida who was responsible for NORAD's operations in the continental United States. These four people were paged because they had been delegated the authority by the president of the United States to shoot down a plane entering the no-fly zone.

Dalton was fairly certain, however, that it wouldn't come to that; it never had in the past. He expected that within the next two minutes the dummy from Stafford would be on his radio saying, 'Oh, shit,

sorry,' about sixteen times and then get headed in
the right direction, and Dalton would be ordered
back to Andrews before he could have any fun.

But these incidents, pilots breaching the ADIZ,
occurred two or three times a week, and once Dalton
had been on duty when it happened three times in
one day. These muttonheads who couldn't read a
map or a compass, who had their radios turned off
or set to the wrong frequency, would blunder into
the ADIZ and then have the livin' shit scared out of
'em when two F-16s went roaring past them at six
hundred miles an hour.

'Huntress. Hawk Flight. Bogey still not responding.
Snap vector three-twenty for thirty. Intercept and ID.
Noses cold.'

Huntress was the call sign for the colonel commanding the Northeastern Air Defense Sector. He
had tactical command of the F-16s. *Hawk Flight* was
the two F-16s: Hawk One was Pete Dalton; Hawk
Two was his wingman, Major Jeff Fields. *Snap vector
320 for 30* meant the bogey was on a bearing of 320
degrees and 30 miles from the Hawk Flight's position. *Noses cold* meant they were to approach with
their weapons systems unarmed – which was a damn
good thing for the bogey.

Dalton responded. 'Hawk One. Huntress. Copy
that. Proceeding to intercept.'

The unidentified aircraft was now twenty-four
miles and fourteen minutes from Washington, D.C.

Dalton could see the bogey on his radar, and a minute later he could make out a dot in the sky that had to be it. He and Fields headed directly at the dot, and when they were half a mile away, and the bogey was clearly visible – and they were visible to it – Dalton split to the right and Fields to the left, and they blasted past the plane, coming within a hundred yards of its wingtips. Dalton looked over his shoulder and saw the bogey wobble in the jet wash caused by the F-16s, and he figured that whoever was flying that baby was sitting there right now in a puddle of his own piss.

Dalton and Fields made tight loops in the sky and came in behind the plane, slowing down to match its speed.

The bogey was now twenty miles and twelve minutes from Washington.

'Hawk One. Huntress. Bogey is a Cessna One-fifty, tail number N3459J. Repeat N3459J.'

'Huntress. Hawk One. Copy that. Attempt contact.'

'Hawk One. Huntress. Roger that.' Dalton switched frequencies on his radio. 'Cessna 3459, Cessna 3459. This is the Air National Guard. Respond. Respond. You are approaching the no-fly zone. Respond.'

Nothing came back from the Cessna. Shit.

'Cessna 3459. Cessna 3459. Respond or you will be fired upon. You are *entering* the no-fly zone.'

Nothing. It was possible, of course, that the Cessna's radio wasn't working or that the pilot was unconscious and the plane was flying itself. That had happened before, though not this close to the capital.

'Hawk One. Huntress. Cessna 3459 is not responding. Going alongside for visual.'

'Huntress. Hawk One. Copy that and proceed.'

While his wingman stayed behind the Cessna, Dalton pulled up next to it, the tip of his starboard wing less than fifty feet from the other plane. He waved his right hand at the pilot, signaling for him to get the hell out of the air and down on the ground, but the Cessna pilot, the damn guy, was staring straight ahead, not even looking over at Dalton's jet. He looked like he was in a trance.

Jesus, Dalton thought. *The pilot looks like an Arab.*

The Cessna was seventeen miles and ten minutes from D.C.

'Hawk One. Huntress. Cessna not responding. Pilot ignoring visual contact.'

'Huntress. Hawk Flight. Fire flares.'

'Hawk One. Huntress. Roger that. Firing flares.'

Dalton and his wingman shot ahead of the Cessna and made tight turns in the sky to come back at it. This was the sort of maneuver they practiced a dozen times a month. Each pilot fired two flares. The flares missed the Cessna, but not by much, the closest one coming within thirty feet of the Cessna's cockpit. There was no way the Cessna pilot didn't see those flares – or the F-16s coming directly at him once again.

But the guy just kept going, never deviating from his original course.

The Cessna was now ten miles – six minutes – from Washington.

Dalton shot past the Cessna again, turned, and pulled up alongside it a second time. He waggled his wings and waved an arm at the pilot. No response. The bastard just sat there like he was made of stone. Dalton reached out to – aw, shit! The Cessna had assumed a downward angle. It was going to cut right across one of the approaches to Reagan National. Beyond the airport, across the Potomac, Dalton could see the White House.

This son of a bitch was headed directly at the White House – and the Cessna was now less than three minutes away from it.

Dalton wasn't concerned about his F-16 or the Cessna colliding with commercial airplanes going in and out of Reagan National. He knew that by now every plane within a hundred miles either was on the ground or had been diverted away from D.C. Dalton also knew that at this point the White House was being evacuated: guards screaming, people running and tripping and falling, images of 9/11 burned into their brains. Dalton didn't know if the president was in town, but if he was, two big Secret Service guys had him by the arms and were running him to the bunker, the president's feet not even hitting the ground.

The Cessna was now four miles – less than two and a half minutes – from the White House.

Dalton spoke into his radio. 'Hawk One. Huntress. Cessna not responding. I repeat. Cessna ignoring all attempts at contact.' Dalton knew that he *sounded* calm – he'd been trained to sound calm – but his heart was hammering in his chest like it was going to blow through his breastbone. He also knew he didn't have to tell anybody where the guy in the Cessna was headed.

There was no immediate response from Huntress. *Oh, shit!* Dalton thought. *Please, God, don't let somebody's goddamn radio go out now.* Then his radio squawked.

'Huntress. Hawk One. Bogey declared hostile. Arm hot. You are cleared to fire. Repeat. Arm hot. Cleared to fire.'

Now Dalton understood the pause. The word had gone up and back down the chain of command. One of those four men who had the authority to give that order had just given it.

Dalton knew this was his mission. This was the reason they'd spent all those years and all that money training him. This was the reason he was flying an F-16 Falcon. But he had never *really* expected to have to execute the command he'd just been given.

Dalton hesitated, he hesitated too long – he hesitated long enough to end his career.

'Huntress. Hawk One. Did you copy that order?'

'Hawk One. Huntress. Roger that. Arm hot. Cleared to fire.'

And then Lieutenant Colonel Peter Dalton did what he'd been trained to do. He reached down and toggled the master arm switch in the cockpit to ON, slowed down to increase the distance between him and the smaller plane, and just as the Cessna was crossing over the Potomac River – less than two miles from the White House – he fired.

NORAD and the Air National Guard refused to tell the media what sort of weapon had been used to destroy the Cessna. Ordnance and armament used to protect the capital from aerial assault are classified. But whatever Dalton fired, it struck the Cessna and a ball of flame fifty yards in diameter bloomed in the sky over the Potomac. Pieces seemed to rain down onto the river for a solid minute after the Cessna had been obliterated.

2

Danny let Vince take the lead going up the stairs.

Charlie Logan lived on the fifth floor of an ancient apartment building in Flushing, not too far from Shea Stadium. It was a crummy, stinky place, the elevator broken, the stairway barely lit, the rug on the steps so dirty and worn that it was impossible to tell what color it had originally been. They found Charlie's apartment, and Vince took a snub-nosed .38 out of his jacket pocket. *Oh, shit*, Danny thought.

Vince used the butt of the .38 to rap on Logan's door. He waited a minute and then slammed the gun butt three times against the wooden door, the sound echoing down the hallway. Danny figured whoever was in the apartment across the hall from Charlie had to have heard the noise. But fuckin' Vince, he

didn't think about things like that. He didn't care
about things like that.

Vince Merlino didn't look like a tough guy. He was
five-eight, wiry, not heavily muscled. At forty-five
his hair was getting thin right on the top, like he
was going to have a little skin circle up there in a
couple of years. Yeah, if you saw Vince from the back
you wouldn't be scared at all, a half-pint guy in a
cheap leather coat and jeans and high-top Nike
knockoffs. But from the front, he'd give you pause.
His face looked like it didn't know what a smile was,
lips so thin they practically weren't there at all, but
it was his eyes that got you. He had these flat don't-
give-a-fuck eyes, eyes that said he'd go off on you
no matter how big you were.

Vince hit the door again, practically splintering the
wood. 'Jesus,' Danny said. 'You're gonna wake up
everybody in the fuckin' building. Maybe he's not
home.'

'He's home,' Vince said. He raised the .38 to hit
the door again, but before he did they heard a bellow
from inside the apartment and the door flung open.
'What the hell do . . . oh, hey, it's you,' Charlie said
when he saw Vince, and he stepped back so Vince
and Danny could enter the apartment.

Charlie Logan was a fat guy, six-foot-four, two
hundred and eighty pounds. Maybe it was because
of Charlie's size that Mr B had told Danny to go
with Vince. Danny didn't normally do this sort of

stuff, but he'd been hanging around Mr B's office when Vince said he was going to see Charlie, and that's when Mr B had told him to go too. Danny had said he didn't think Vince needed any help – it wasn't like Charlie was gonna wrestle with him or something – but Mr B had said to shut up and do what he was told.

Charlie was wearing a white sleeveless T-shirt and white boxer shorts with blue stripes. The T-shirt was the ribbed kind, clinging to Charlie's love handles ballooning out around his waist. His shoulders were hairy and his arms were heavy and flabby looking. His legs were surprisingly thin compared to his frame and his feet . . . *Christ*, he had ugly feet, the toenails yellow and cracked, big corns on some of the toes, nasty blue veins running all over the place. Danny wished he'd never looked down at the guy's feet.

'Hey,' Charlie said again. 'Can I get you some coffee? It's not made, but I can make some. Or a beer maybe.'

Then Charlie saw the gun in Vince's hand.

'Hey,' Charlie said a third time, and pointed at the gun. 'Come on, guys, what's with that?'

Vince looked at Charlie for a moment, his eyes as warm as a snake's. 'You owe twelve grand. I told you two weeks ago to pay it. I told you last week to pay it. Now you're gonna either pay it today, right now, or you're gonna give me the keys to your Lincoln.'

'I can't give you the Lincoln,' Charlie said. 'How would I get to work?'

'I don't give a *shit* how you get to work,' Vince said. 'Gimme the money or gimme the keys.'

'Let me have until Saturday night,' Charlie said. 'Oklahoma's playin' Nebraska. I got it nailed.'

Danny would have laughed if he hadn't been trying to look tough. Fuckin' gamblers. Charlie had borrowed money from some *other* shark, hoping he'd win enough to pay back the *first* shark. These guys should just kill themselves.

'Go get the keys,' Vince said.

'Come on, just till Saturday,' Charlie said. When Vince just stared at him, Charlie looked over at Danny, his eyes begging.

Then Vince hit Charlie with the gun, whacked him right across the side of the face, high up near his left eye. Danny thought Charlie would collapse to the floor or hold his hands up to his head and start moaning – but he didn't. Instead he let out a yell and grabbed Vince's throat.

The crazy bastard. He ignored the gun like it wasn't even there, put two big hands around Vince's throat, and began to strangle him. Danny thought later that that was why Mr B had made him go with Vince. Mr B had known Charlie was the kind of nutcase who would do something dumb like this.

As Charlie was choking Vince, Vince banged his gun ineffectually on the top of Charlie's head, but

Charlie, the maniac, was oblivious to the blows. Danny tried to pull Charlie away from Vince, and when he couldn't, he jumped on Charlie's back, put his right forearm under the fat man's chin, and began to press his arm against Charlie's windpipe. The faces of both Vince and Charlie were now turning purple as a result of being simultaneously strangled.

And then Danny heard the gun go off.

The first thing that went through Danny's brain was that it was lucky Vince's bullet hadn't passed through Charlie and hit *him*. The second thing he thought was that Vince hadn't really wanted to shoot the guy. You never kill someone who owes you money. No, Vince hadn't meant to shoot him. He'd just panicked, thinking Charlie was going to kill him. Or maybe he didn't panic; maybe he was so goddamn mad at what Charlie had done, so humiliated that Charlie had made him squawk, that he stuck his gun into the guy's gut and pulled the trigger.

'What the hell did you *do*?' Danny said, looking down at Charlie lying on the floor, the front of his white T-shirt turning red.

Vince didn't say anything. He just stood there rubbing his throat, staring at the gun in his hand as if he was surprised at what *it* had done.

And then Danny saw Charlie give a little shudder and die.

Vince hadn't shot him in the gut, he'd shot him in the heart.

'Let's get out of here,' Vince said.

'Oh, Jesus,' Danny said, still looking down at Charlie.

'Come on. Let's go!' Vince said. He turned toward the door and started running.

By the time Danny got to the door, Vince had almost reached the fourth floor landing, one flight down. Danny started to follow him, then for some reason, for some fuckin' reason, he pulled out a handkerchief so he wouldn't leave prints and started to close the door to Charlie's apartment. That was his big mistake.

Just as he was shutting Charlie's door, the door across the hall opened. He and the woman stared at each other for about two seconds. She was a short, heavy old broad with a fat nose and gray hair tied up in a bun. Polish or German, Danny thought, and she looked tougher than elephant hide.

'Danny!' Vince cried out from the stairwell. 'Come on!'

Great, just call out my fuckin' name, Danny thought, as he tore his eyes away from the old Polish woman and started to run. But Vince wasn't through. Just as Danny reached the stairs – the woman now standing in the hall looking at his back as he ran – Vince yelled again.

'DeMarco!' Vince screamed. 'Move your ass!'

3

Joe DeMarco's hand was on the doorknob when the phone rang again.

Mahoney's secretary had called twenty minutes ago, waking DeMarco and telling him to get to Mahoney's office right away. He took a quick shower, skipped shaving, and dressed in a white shirt and a dark suit. He'd put on his tie and shave in the cab on the way to the Capitol.

When the phone rang the second time he thought about not answering it, but maybe it was Mahoney's secretary calling back, telling him the meeting with Mahoney had been canceled. Half the meetings he had with Mahoney were canceled. He picked up the phone.

'Hello.'

'Joe, it's me.'

DeMarco couldn't speak. He could barely breathe.

It was his ex-wife. He hadn't spoken to her in almost two years. He hadn't even thought about her in . . . shit, maybe a week.

'What do you want, Marie?' he finally said. He tried to keep his voice flat, to let her know how much he hated her, but somewhere in the back of his mind was the thought that she was calling because she wanted him to take her back. It was pathetic that he should think such a thing, pathetic that he'd even *consider* such a thing.

'I need your help, Joe,' Marie said.

'My help?' DeMarco said. 'My help with what?'

'It's Danny, Joe. He's in trouble, big trouble. I didn't know who else to call.'

DeMarco couldn't believe this. His ex-wife was one of the vainest, most self-centered people he had ever known. And not all that bright, if he was honest about it. But he couldn't believe she'd ask for his help when it came to Danny.

Danny DeMarco was Joe DeMarco's cousin. Marie had had an affair with him, and then she divorced Joe and married him. She didn't even have to change her last name when she married the asshole.

'You gotta be shittin' me!' he said, and started to slam down the phone.

But he didn't.

DeMarco sat impatiently in Mahoney's office, staring at the photographs on the walls. In them Mahoney was posing with various famous people, mostly politicians, and in the photos all the politicians were smiling – as if they actually liked Mahoney.

The man that DeMarco and Mahoney were waiting to meet was fifteen minutes late, which was almost unheard of. Mahoney kept people waiting all the time because he was rude and inconsiderate – and, yes, busy – but no one kept Mahoney waiting.

DeMarco was five-eleven and Mahoney was the same height, but he always seemed taller than that to DeMarco. Maybe that was because of Mahoney's bulk – or maybe it was because of his personality. The speaker had a big hard gut, a broad back, and a wide butt. His hair was thick and white, his features large and well formed, and his blue eyes were red-veined and watery. Mahoney had the eyes of an alcoholic, which he was. And like DeMarco's ex-wife, Mahoney was vain and self-centered and selfish; he was conniving and manipulative. But, unlike her, he was very, very bright.

As DeMarco sat there, his mind kept drifting back to the call from Marie. He had no idea what he should do. No, that wasn't right; that wasn't right at all. He knew *exactly* what he should do: absolutely nothing.

While DeMarco stewed about his ex, Mahoney sat in the big chair behind his big desk and made phone calls. He was currently talking to someone named Bob. At least that's what he had called the man at the beginning of the conversation, but in the last five minutes, as the phone call had progressed, *Bob* became *Congressman* and finally *you greedy little asshole,* as in: 'Listen to me, you greedy little asshole! You've got four projects in that bill worth more than sixty million, including a fuckin' bridge to nowhere that's gonna have your name on it. Now that's *enough!'*

DeMarco realized that Mahoney was talking about a so-called transportation bill, a bill intended to resurface potholed highways and prop up crumbling bridges that was, in reality, a five-thousand-page pork package. Every member of the House was squeezing into the bill as many pet projects as he or she could, and any link to transportation, no matter how remote, was considered a fair addition. The most outrageous example that DeMarco had heard of was the proposed construction of a velodrome, a stadium for racing bicycles. This was included in the bill under the guise that erecting such a structure would give birth to legions of bicycle-peddling commuters and thus save the country's highways from future wear and tear. At least that was the most outrageous thing he'd heard until Mahoney began his dialogue with Congressman Bob.

'I've been trying for six weeks,' Mahoney was saying, 'to get this thing finished. It's already twenty billion bigger than what we agreed on, and every fuckin' time – my *language*? I don't give a shit about my language, you sanctimonious twit! Now I'm *tired* of this. It's bad enough I can't get the other side to line up, but when the people in my own party start pullin' this crap. . . . Yes, Bob, crap! Why should the taxpayers have to pay for a freeway exit that goes right to your brother-in-law's goddamn furniture store? Tell me that.'

The speaker sat silent for a moment, his large face the color of a boiled beet, as he listened to Bob explain how easy access to a retail store in his home state would improve the flow of goods and services throughout America.

'Okay, Bob,' Mahoney said, 'I give up. I'll leave the exit thing in the bill, but then I'm gonna call up every newspaper in your state and tell 'em it's in there. I'm gonna tell 'em, because no one with a human-sized brain'll be able to spot that little gem in five thousand pages of text. So fine, Bob, you win. Now you better get ready to explain your victory to everybody who's not related to you.' With that, Mahoney slammed down the phone.

'Of all the jackasses on Jenkins Hill,' he muttered.

'Jenkins Hill?' DeMarco said.

'That's what Capitol Hill used to be called,' Mahoney said, 'back before they built this building and started stuffing it with idiots.'

Mahoney sat there fuming a moment longer and then looked at his watch. 'Go see if he's being held up at security,' he said. 'I'll bet that's what happened. If I hadn't been preoccupied with Bob-goddam-Meechum I woulda thought of that sooner.'

As directed, DeMarco left the speaker's office and

traveled to the door that approved visitors, those with appointments, used to enter the Capitol. Normally it took only a couple of minutes to get past security if your name was on the list, but DeMarco suspected, times being what they were, that the U.S. Capitol Police were exercising more diligence than normal – especially with this particular visitor.

The man who was keeping Mahoney waiting was named Hassan Zarif. DeMarco didn't know Hassan, but he figured it was a pretty safe bet that the Arabic-looking guy standing with his arms outstretched as a security guard patted him down was him. On the table next to Zarif was everything that had been in his pockets: wallet, keys, spare change, and a pen. Another guard was now taking the pen apart, a simple ballpoint, to see if there was a surface-to-air missile packed inside it. A briefcase was lying open on the table, emptied of its contents, and next to the briefcase were Hassan's belt and tie and shoes.

Hassan Zarif was a short, slender, handsome man. His hair was black, his nose aquiline, his eyes an odd but attractive caramel color. Clearly embarrassed at the treatment he was receiving, he was restraining himself, saying nothing, but he looked as if he was about to explode.

'Hey, guys, what's going on here?' DeMarco said to the security guards.

The man frisking Hassan looked over at DeMarco, then glanced down at the security badge pinned to the breast pocket of his suit, the badge confirming that DeMarco was permitted to be inside the building. DeMarco had worked in the Capitol for many years, but this particular guard didn't recognize him and DeMarco didn't recognize the guard.

'What do you want, sir?' the guard said.

DeMarco looked at the guard's name tag. McGuire.

'Mr McGuire, would you come here a minute so I can talk to you without everybody hearing?'

'I'm in the middle of—'

'McGuire, a lot of powerful people work in this building. You are not one of them. I'm just trying to save you some pain, m'man. C'mere.'

McGuire turned to the guard dissembling the pen and said, 'Watch this guy,' gesturing with his head toward Hassan, then he stepped over to DeMarco. 'Yeah, so what is it?' he said.

'That guy you're screwin' with, McGuire, was invited here by John Mahoney. The speaker. In fact, he was supposed to be in Mahoney's office fifteen minutes ago.'

'I'm just following procee—'

'McGuire, it feels like it's about twenty degrees outside. Right now you're working indoors, probably a pretty good place to be this time of year. How hard do you think it would be for Mahoney to have you assigned to a less comfortable post? Now, the speaker's waiting to see that man and you've had plenty of time to confirm that he's safe, so quit dickin' with him, put his stuff back in his briefcase, and apologize for hassling him.'

McGuire's face flushed red – not as red as Mahoney's had been a few minutes ago but red enough. But he didn't say all the profane things flashing through his Irish brain. He turned and said to Hassan, 'Sir, you're free to enter the building. And I – uh, I apologize for the inconvenience of our – ah, current security procedures.'

Hassan didn't say anything. He put his belt back through the loops in his pants and shoved his belongings into his pockets. He put on his shoes and started to tie his tie, then just shook his head and stuffed the tie into a pocket in his suit jacket.

'Mr Zarif,' DeMarco said, 'I'll escort you to Mr Mahoney's office.'

'Thank you,' Hassan said, but he didn't look at DeMarco. He just stared straight ahead as they walked toward the staircase, bristling from the embarrassment of what had just happened but too dignified to complain.

As they stepped into the speaker's office, Mahoney got up from his chair and came out from behind his desk. DeMarco thought he would shake Hassan's hand but instead Mahoney pulled the smaller man close, crushing him in a hug.

While Mahoney was greeting Hassan, DeMarco explained what had happened at the security checkpoint.

'Goddamn, Hassie, I'm sorry,' Mahoney said. 'I

should have had someone down there to meet you.' Then he glowered at DeMarco as if DeMarco should have thought of that.

Hassan smiled, but it was a bitter twist of his lips. 'It wasn't as bad as at the airport. I was expecting that they'd give me a hard time, so I left Boston early yesterday morning. I missed my first flight because they spent so long inspecting my luggage and searching me. I was actually *strip*-searched. That's never happened before.'

'I'm sorry,' Mahoney said again. 'Would you like a drink?'

Hassan looked away and his chin began to tremble, and for a moment DeMarco thought the man was going to cry, but then Hassan took in a breath and said, 'Yes, Mr Mahoney, a drink would be good. Bourbon if you have it.'

Hassan Zarif, DeMarco concluded, was not a strict Muslim. Any more than Mahoney and DeMarco were strict Catholics, for that matter.

Mahoney poured drinks for himself and Hassan, Then, realizing that he hadn't bothered to ask if DeMarco wanted one, he said, 'Joe, what about you?'

'No, I'm okay,' DeMarco said. He knew that's what Mahoney expected him to say. Plus – sheesh! – it was only ten in the morning.

'How's your father doing?' Mahoney said.

'Not well, sir. He's in intensive care. It was his second heart attack. We're not sure he's going to make it.'

'But they're taking good care of him?' Mahoney said.

'Yes, the nurses at the hospital, they have souls. And at least, where he is, the press can't bother him.'

Mahoney didn't say anything for a minute. 'So,' he finally said. 'What can I do for you? When you called—'

'Excuse me, Mr Mahoney, but is this gentleman,' Hassan said, looking over at DeMarco, 'one of your assistants?'

DeMarco knew Hassan might have asked the question simply because he wanted to know who DeMarco was before he spoke. But DeMarco also suspected that the question may have had to do with the way he looked. DeMarco had dark hair that he combed straight back, a strong nose, and a big, square, dimpled chin. He was broad-chested and had thick shoulders and heavy, muscular arms. He was a good-looking man, but he looked tough and hard – he didn't look like some congressman's assistant.

Most congressional staffers were eager young kids just a few years out of college. Or, if not kids, they looked like crafty old negotiators, wheeler-dealers who spend all their time in dimly lit bars making the trade-offs that pass the laws. DeMarco didn't look like someone from either of those groups. He looked instead like the guy a casino boss might assign to have a word with a card counter or a man the Teamsters might deploy to talk to a trucker who was behind on his dues. He looked, in other words, a lot like his father – and DeMarco's father had been a hit man for the Italian Mafia.

In response to Hassan's question, Mahoney made a motion with his head – a little bit of a shake, a little bit of a nod – a motion that could have meant anything, and said, 'Sorta. When you called, I figured it might be good if Joe sat in on this meeting. He's a guy who helps out with things around here.'

That was *sorta* clear as mud, DeMarco thought, and Hassan seemed to think so too.

'I only ask because—'

'Joe's okay, Hassan. Now tell me why you're here. Is it because the FBI's hassling your family?'

'No. I mean we are being hassled – the FBI's questioned me and my sister and searched our houses – but I don't need your help with that.'

'So what is it, son?' Mahoney said.

'I want some answers!' Hassan said, his voice rising. 'This thing is killing my father. I want to know what really happened.'

'Answers?' Mahoney said. Then he added, in a surprisingly gentle voice, 'Reza *was* flying the plane, son. There's no doubt about that.'

'Sir, I know he flew the plane, but nothing makes any sense. The FBI claims they found links between Reza and al-Qaeda, but they won't say what they are. The information's classified, they say. At the same time they're implying that Reza was working with al-Qaeda, they're saying he just went crazy because of all the pressure he'd been under lately. And he *was* under pressure, but he wouldn't have tried to crash a plane into the White House because money was tight or because he'd lost a few cases in court. And no matter what kind of pressure he was under, he wouldn't have killed his family! You knew Reza, Mr Mahoney. Can you imagine my brother killing his own children?'

'Not unless he went off the deep end like the Bureau's saying,' Mahoney said.

But DeMarco was thinking, *This guy's the pilot's brother!*

Hassan shook his head. 'I talked to Reza three days before he . . . before he died. He was angry about everything going on – this bill of Broderick's and what happened on *Meet the Press* – but he didn't have some kind of nervous breakdown. I don't care what the FBI says.'

Mahoney just sat there for a moment, not sure what to say. 'What do you want me to do, Hassie? You know how I feel about your dad, but I can't change what happened. And you might not like what the Bureau's saying, but those guys are pretty sharp. And for something this big . . . well, you know they didn't do some half-assed investigation.'

'The Bureau's wrong!' Hassan said. Before Mahoney could debate the point, he added, 'Mr Mahoney, all I want are some answers that make sense. I want to know why this happened. I want to know about these so-called links to al-Qaeda. I want to know why my brother killed his wife and kids. The FBI won't talk to me, sir – but they'll talk to you.'

Hassan Zarif left Mahoney's office a few minutes later, after extracting from the speaker a promise that he would look into Reza's death. As Hassan was departing to fly back to Boston, Mahoney tried desperately to think of something to say to comfort the man. The best he could come up with was, 'If that hospital's not treating your dad right, you let me know.'

And Hassan's response had been, 'The doctors can't do anything for my father, sir. He's lost his will to live. You're the only one who can help him.'

After the door had closed behind Hassan, DeMarco said, 'What do you want me to do?'

'Shit, I don't know,' Mahoney said. He poured more bourbon into his glass and took a deep swallow. 'But I sorta agree with him on a couple things.'

'Like what?' DeMarco said.

'Reza was always a hothead, but I can't imagine him getting hooked up with terrorists. So I'd like to know myself what this supposed connection is between him and al-Qaeda. And as for killing his family – I mean, you read all the time about some fruitcake deciding he wants to end it all but instead of just shooting himself he takes his whole family or a bunch of strangers with him. Like that wacko down at Virginia Tech. But those kind of people, they usually have a history of mental illness or they're loners and losers. Reza wasn't like that.'

DeMarco wasn't too sure about Reza Zarif's sanity, but he didn't say so. Instead he said, 'But he *did* kill his family, boss. And it's like you told Hassan. The FBI's not staffed with fools, and from everything I've read they did a pretty thorough—'

'Yeah, yeah, I know,' Mahoney said, sounding tired.

'So what do you want me to do?' DeMarco asked again. 'Go talk to somebody at the Bureau?'

'I guess. Poke around a little, but keep my name out of it.'

'Aw, come on,' DeMarco said. 'You know the Bureau's not going to talk to me unless you tell them to.'

Mahoney shook his big head. 'I go back a long way with Hassan's father, but the press doesn't know that yet – and I don't want 'em to know. I don't feel like dealing with a bunch of goddamn reporters asking me how come I'm such good pals with a guy whose kid tried to park a plane on the president's desk. And if I talk to the Bureau, the press'll find out. So you do some diggin', but keep my name out of it.'

'Just how am I supposed to—'

But Mahoney wasn't listening. He'd already picked up the phone and was punching buttons. It was time for him to make someone else's life miserable.

4

Mahoney tried to get back to work, to get everybody moving in the right direction on the damn transportation bill, but he couldn't concentrate. He couldn't stop thinking about Hassan Zarif's visit. The other thing nagging at him was he couldn't help but wonder what impact Reza Zarif's act would have on Bill Broderick's cockamamie bill. He finally decided he had to get out of the office to clear his head.

He put on his topcoat, muttered something to his secretary that she didn't hear, and left the Capitol. He'd been thinking about going for a walk on the National Mall, but when he got outside he realized it was *way* too cold to be doing that. He'd freeze his fat ass off. Then he saw a U.S. Capitol police car, the cop inside it drinking coffee and reading the *Post*.

Mahoney rapped a big knuckle on the passenger-side window of the patrol car and the cop jerked in surprise, almost spilling his coffee. Then he saw it was Mahoney, and his lips moved in a silent *Oh, shit!*

The cop powered down the window. 'Yes, sir, Mr Speaker,' he said.

'Hey,' Mahoney said, 'how 'bout givin' me a lift someplace?'

Now the cop knew he wasn't supposed to be Mahoney's chauffeur, and Mahoney knew he wasn't supposed to ask the cop to drive him – but the cop was afraid to say no and Mahoney wasn't afraid to impose on anyone.

'Uh, sure,' the cop said, and Mahoney got into the front seat of the patrol car.

'Where to, sir?' the cop asked, transitioning effortlessly into his new job.

'Tell you what,' Mahoney said. 'How 'bout takin' a slow spin around the Mall? I just gotta clear my head. Politicians . . . shit, they make my brain *ache* some days.'

'You got it, sir,' the cop said.

Mahoney lit a cigar, was kind enough to crack a window in deference to the other man's lungs, and then sat back and reflected on the political phenomenon named William Broderick.

A year ago, it would have been difficult to find a dozen Americans outside the state of Virginia who'd ever heard of the damn guy. And even three months ago, only 23 percent of all Virginians could name their newly elected representative to the U.S. Senate. But in the last two months, since Broderick had introduced his dumb-ass bill on the Senate floor, his name had become known to virtually every American who could read a paper or turn on a television.

It was a fluke that Broderick was even in the Senate. His predecessor had been a flamboyant egomaniac by the name of John Wingate whom Mahoney had sometimes admired but more frequently detested. Wingate had served in the Senate for forty-one years and then died suddenly and unexpectedly six weeks before the last election. At the time of Wingate's death, Broderick had been running for a seat in the House, and there was considerable doubt that he would have been able to beat the incumbent. But when God created a senate vacancy by way of a well-timed stroke, the Republican bosses put Broderick's name on the ballot – and he won. As there had been little time for his constituents to get to know him, all Mahoney could figure was that the majority of Virginians preferred a Republican they'd barely heard of to *any* Democrat running.

Mahoney glanced out the window to his right, at the Federal Court House, and saw two cameras pointed at a guy in a suit. Someone was holding a press conference. He wondered which lawyer, prosecutor or defender, was telling lies today.

Why Broderick had been chosen by his party was not totally clear to Mahoney. He knew Broderick had served briefly as an aide to that gasbag Wingate, he'd spent some time in the Virginia state legislature, and eight years ago he'd been a largely invisible one-term lieutenant governor. But that was about it, as far as Mahoney knew. The man certainly hadn't cast an impressive shadow on the political landscape.

But Broderick did have money, and quite a bit of it. His granddaddy had owned coal mines at a time when those pesky unions hadn't been strong enough to insist that miners be paid a living wage for their dangerous labors. When Grandpa died he passed on his loot to his only son, and then Broderick's father died at an early age and passed it on to Bill and his two brothers.

The car was passing the National Archives. Mahoney was aware that on the other side of the building was a statue of a lady seated in a chair, and chiseled into stone at the base of the statue were the words WHAT IS PAST IS PROLOGUE. The sentiment was Shakespeare's, from *The Tempest*. Mahoney had no idea what the words meant in relationship to the play, but they were certainly appropriate to the seat of government.

Broderick had gotten considerable ink the last couple of months, so Mahoney knew something about the man's family, and he concluded that Bill Broderick had been the runt of the litter. He was the middle brother. Brother number one was a doctor, a neurosurgeon, no less, and brother number three was a real estate baron on the West Coast whose net worth would soon surpass Grandpa's. Bill, by comparison, was just a minor party hack, a guy trying and largely failing to ascend the political ladder. Until recently, nobody had even noticed that he was *on* the ladder.

So maybe it was his money that caused the Republican czars to place Broderick in the Senate, but the cynics on the Hill, Mahoney included, didn't think that was the whole story. The cynics thought Broderick had been chosen because of his *malleability*, meaning that the Republican pooh-bahs would be able to make young Bill dance to whatever tune they felt like playing. Well, it looked like they'd all been wrong about that.

The cop had almost reached the end of the Mall and was about to make the turn to pass behind the Lincoln Memorial. Just before he did, Mahoney saw the Einstein statue on the grounds of the National Academy of Sciences. The statue is bronze and twelve feet tall, and Einstein is seated on a bench in rumpled suit. Children like to climb the statue and sit on Albert's lap. In the statue, and every picture of Einstein that Mahoney had ever seen, the genius always looked relaxed, like a man who had all the answers – and maybe he did. Mahoney wished he could say the same about himself.

Radical Muslims – al-Qaeda and its spawn – scared the hell out of people. Governments didn't seem to be able to stop them. They were always blowing up something, and, when they did, old ladies and little kids were killed. Broderick's bill, flawed as it was, appealed to a lot of folks because it sounded as if it might make them somewhat safer. And he'd timed it perfectly, coming out with it right after those two pea brains tried to blow up the tunnel.

The reaction to the bill had been as predictable as old men dying. Hard-core right-wingers thought the man was making good sense. Radical Muslims were indeed a threat, they were the enemy, and they, the non-Muslims, were sick and tired of the government dancing around the issue. At the other extreme were the liberals. The ACLU rose up en masse against Broderick, as if its entire roster had been goosed with a four-foot cattle prod. Broderick, for them, was the most energizing thing to come along since caffeine had been discovered.

The reaction of Broderick's fellow politicians was equally predictable. Mahoney and the Democrats denounced him for the devil he was; comparisons to Hitler, McCarthy, and lesser-known demagogues were frequent and loud. Broderick's own party had to walk a finer line. They couldn't just scream that the man was a friggin' nut! They said instead that he had a good point – action was indeed needed, not mere rhetoric – but maybe young Bill, in the heat of the moment, had gone just a little too far. All these politicians, both Republican *and* Democrat, were surprised when they returned to their offices to find hundreds of e-mails from their constituents telling them to quit being such wimps and get on board Bill Broderick's train.

Because his bill was so controversial, Broderick had become a frequent guest on radio and television. Mahoney had noticed that the senator preferred shows where he just got to talk and didn't have to defend his position, but the producers liked it better when they could pair him up with a liberal opponent. Watching Broderick and a liberal go at it was a lot better than watching two fat girls fighting over an ugly boyfriend on the Maury Povich show.

One of Broderick's opponents, on two different telecasts, had been Reza Zarif, a prominent Muslim attorney and now the most famous terrorist in America.

But *still*, Mahoney thought, Broderick's friggin' bill would have eventually died a quiet death in a Senate committee. People would have calmed down and come to their senses, realizing that the thing was not only horribly xenophobic but fraught with a number of practical problems. Broderick wasn't just proposing to kick out visiting foreign Muslims. He was also proposing to do background checks on Muslim Americans but had yet to address exactly how one defined such a person. What about ex-Muslims who no longer practiced their faith? What about people married to Muslims? And what about Christians who'd converted to Islam, a category that included a number of high-profile African Americans like the boxer Muhammad Ali, to name one. Not only hadn't Broderick addressed these small points, he also hadn't explained to anyone's satisfaction how his proposal would be paid for or the economic impact on universities and tourism or the likelihood of retaliation from countries who sold us oil. None of these issues had been adequately addressed. But these were just *details*, Broderick said, and to a degree Mahoney had to admit the man was right. Once Broderick's proposal had been accepted in concept, the details were small matters for lawyers and accountants and other nitpickers to resolve.

They were on Independence Avenue now, headed back toward the Capitol, and on the right was the Tidal Basin. Mahoney could never look at the lagoon in front of Jefferson's memorial without thinking of Ohio Congressman Wilbur Mills, who, in 1974, got drunk one fine night and went frolicking in the Tidal Basin with a stripper named Fanne Foxe. Mahoney had done some dumb things in his cups, but nothing quite that bad.

Yeah, Broderick and his bill *should* have faded into the woodwork, but Broderick had two things going for him. The first was that he had supporters and the number was growing. Ads, similar to campaign ads, were now appearing on television, and the most frequent one showed Broderick on the Senate floor making his now famous statement: *I'm here to tell you it's only a matter of if* – if *nothing changes*. One thing Mahoney thought he'd have DeMarco do was find out who was paying for the ads.

But it was the second thing that was the real problem. When Reza Zarif, son of Mahoney's old friend, decided to crash a plane into the White House, Broderick became a damn *prophet*. *He* was the one who had warned that all Muslims were a threat, including American citizens, and Reza had proven him right.

'Mr Speaker – uh, sir, we're almost back to the Capitol. Was there anyplace else you wanted to go?'

'No. In fact, drop me off right here, by that hot dog cart over there.' The cop stopped the car and Mahoney reached out and placed a big paw on the cop's shoulder. 'What's your name, son?'

'Dolan, Mr Speaker.'

'You like watchin' the Redskins get their asses kicked, Dolan?'

'No, sir. I mean, yes, sir.'

'Well, you sneak on up to my office later today. There'll be two tickets waiting for you with a nice lady named Mavis. Being a fan of the Patriots, I'm frankly used to a higher standard of play, but maybe you and the missus will enjoy the view from the owner's box.'

5

He had been in Philadelphia for more than two months, and then two days ago, when he was finally on his way to Cleveland, on to the next target, that man tried to crash his plane into the White House. He'd been walking toward the bus depot when it happened, and he'd just passed a crowd gathered around the window of an electronics store when he heard a woman say, 'Oh, my God! Not again.'

He should not have stopped, it was foolish to have done so, but he did. He looked at the enormous television in the window of the store and saw a small plane flying; then, an instant later, he saw the plane explode and a military jet fly through the ball of flame and smoke where the plane had been. The caption at the bottom of the television screen read, 'Katie, we don't know who was flying the plane at this time. One high-ranking official at the Pentagon, who we can't name, said the pilot was a well-known Muslim attorney, but we have not been able to confirm that. What we do know is that the man appeared to be trying to crash his plane, a Cessna, into the White House. The Cessna was shot down by Air National Guard pilots flying F-Sixteen Falcons, and the president was evacuated from the White House only minutes before the plane was destroyed.'

As he had stood there looking at the huge television set, he became aware that people were turning and beginning to stare at him, so he had lowered his head and continued on his way, trying to remain calm. Someone in the crowd had called out to him, but he'd kept walking.

He had decided immediately that it would be too risky to go to the bus depot that day. People would be too vigilant. So he had returned to the safe house where he'd been staying since the debacle of the Baltimore tunnel. Once inside, he had turned on the television and listened to the news reports, realizing as he listened that he was going to have to postpone going to Cleveland for a few days, maybe longer, because of what had just happened.

He had only God to thank that he was not at that moment in a jail cell being tortured. He had left the garage in Baltimore that night to make a phone call, a call from a public phone booth, and had difficulty finding a working phone in a country inhabited by animals. And then he had gotten lost because he didn't know the city very well. Had it not been for making a wrong turn, he too would have been in the garage when the FBI blasted their way in. But God saved him. Praise be to God.

He knew from subsequent news reports how the two fools had been caught. He'd told them to buy the ammonium nitrate in small batches, very small batches, but for whatever reason – laziness, recklessness, stupidity – they had purchased enough fertilizer in one place to draw suspicion upon themselves. Worse yet, *he* had been identified.

When he had fled Baltimore he had gone to the home of a devout couple in Philadelphia. His intent had been to stay there only a week, two at the most, by which time he thought it would be safe to travel. But then the fools told the FBI about his artificial leg, and the next thing he knew there was a grainy, barely recognizable photograph of him in the newspapers. So he had cut his hair and shaved his beard and stayed in the basement for two months. But it hadn't been a total waste of time; while he was in hiding he learned more about the boy in Cleveland and about another boy, this one in Sante Fe. And he learned *much* more about the next objective.

The Internet truly would set the world free.

The amazing thing about the incident in Baltimore had been the reaction of this senator, this William Broderick. It was exactly the sort of reaction they had wanted, but he had never expected it when the attack on the tunnel had failed. But now, because of what this lawyer had done, there was talk of some law being passed that would cause even more discontent among the faithful in this country.

They were truly blessed.

What he didn't know was if any of his brethren had helped the lawyer. He knew he was not the only one of his kind in this country, so it was possible that the leader of another cell had recruited the man. But the lawyer was not the type he himself would have selected; he was too old, too well educated, and, most important, he seemed too entrenched in American society, not a devout Muslim at all. So maybe it was as their FBI had said – the man had just gone insane because of all that had happened to him – but that didn't strike him as sounding right either.

Whatever the case, the lawyer had helped them, and this senator – he was helping them even more.

6

DeMarco had learned long ago that working for John Mahoney was never simple.

The simple thing would have been for Mahoney to call the FBI, ask his questions about Reza Zarif, and then swear the Bureau to secrecy if he was worried about the press. But no, that would have been simple. And straightforward.

Mahoney had never done anything straightforward in his life.

But if Mahoney's character had been different he wouldn't have employed DeMarco, a man with an office in the subbasement of the Capitol, a space a long way from the speaker's realm in terms of both distance and stature. DeMarco's family history – the fact that his father had worked for the mob – was not something a politician preferred on an employee's résumé. DeMarco's lineage, however, was not the only reason he worked where he did. The other reason was that Mahoney liked having a man on his staff who wasn't really on his staff.

No organizational chart showed that the speaker employed DeMarco, because this provided Mahoney that ever-important political advantage known as *deniability*. For example, because it was DeMarco who brought Mahoney envelopes stuffed with cash, Mahoney could honestly deny ever having met with the envelope stuffer, should the need arise. DeMarco was the guy, in other words, that Mahoney used when he wanted something done but didn't want his fat fingerprints, literally or otherwise, found at the scene. And if DeMarco was ever caught doing something illegal, John Mahoney could, and would, deny that DeMarco worked for him.

DeMarco could understand, of course, why Mahoney had no desire for the press to know of his relationship to the Zarif family – that he was, as Mahoney had phrased it, a lifelong friend of a man whose son 'tried to park a plane on the president's desk.' DeMarco figured, however, that the news guys would have to dig pretty hard to connect Mahoney to Ali Zarif.

Ali was an Iranian immigrant who had come to this country when he was ten and had known Mahoney from the time they were teenagers. Mahoney had been the catcher on his high school baseball team, and Ali Zarif had pitched. How the young Iranian had learned to throw a curve ball was but another legend of the American melting pot.

In his twenties, Ali leased a space near Boston's Quincy Market and began to sell rugs. Persian rugs, Chinese rugs, Indian rugs. He sold beautiful, expensive rugs. Forty years later, he owned two other stores in the Boston area. When his friend John Mahoney made his first run for Congress those many years ago, Ali helped with the young politician's campaign, registered his fellow Muslims to vote – and they *all* voted for John Mahoney. But Ali was just a successful businessman and not a big-name donor or a guy who craved the spotlight. Unless the press discovered that Hassan Zarif had visited Mahoney – or became aware that the floors of Mahoney's Boston home were covered with Ali's rugs – Mahoney's friendship with Ali would most likely remain hidden from the media.

Regarding Reza Zarif, DeMarco decided that before he talked to the Bureau or anyone else, he needed to do a little preliminary research. And this meant bending over and picking from the stack of newspapers on the floor next to his desk the last two days' editions of *The New York Times* and *The Washington Post*. He'd read the articles about Reza before, but when he'd read them the first time he'd just been another shocked citizen and not a man assigned to uncover the reasons behind a terrorist act.

As he hated to work in his windowless office,

DeMarco decided to accomplish his research on Reza in more pleasant surroundings: the Hawk and Dove, a Capitol Hill bar that had been in business almost as long as politicians had been taking bribes. He plopped down onto a bar stool, greeted the barman, and ordered a martini. He had discovered that the first martini of the day sharpened his mental powers; the martinis that followed tended to have the opposite effect. Drink in hand, he then spread open the papers to read for a second time what all the Pulitzer Prize winners had to say about Reza.

There was no question that he was flying the plane that the Air National Guard had blown out of the sky two days ago. The plane had been co-owned by Reza and three other lawyers, the other men all white Christians. The morning he attacked the White House, Reza had been seen by two people at the Stafford airfield who had known him for five and seven years respectively, and one of those men had seen Reza climb into the cockpit of the Cessna.

Ten minutes after the F-16 pilot had identified the tail numbers on the Cessna, FBI agents had been dispatched to Reza's home in Arlington. Inside the house they found Reza's wife and two children – a boy of eight and a girl of eleven – all dead. They'd each been shot once in the head with a .9mm automatic that had been found sitting in the middle of the Zarifs' dining room table like some sort of ugly lethal centerpiece. Reza's fingerprints were on the gun.

One sentence in the article said that the FBI had found a document in Reza's house that indicated he had ties to al-Qaeda, but that's all the FBI would tell the press. The Bureau claimed that the specifics of the document were classified because disclosing them could affect other ongoing operations, which was a fairly standard explanation used by the feds when they wanted to keep something from the media. Whether the explanation was true or not was a different issue.

Had Reza Zarif been an Iranian national who had slipped into the country using a false passport, his actions might have made some sense: just another radical Muslim who had decided to strike a blow for his brethren in the jihad and sacrificed himself and his family in the process. But that's not who Reza Zarif had been.

Reza and his brother, Hassan, were Americans, born and raised in Boston. They attended public schools, and then Reza went to Boston College where he obtained a law degree. After law school, he moved to Washington, worked briefly for the Department of Justice, then established a small private practice near his home in Arlington, Virginia. A large number of his clients had been of Middle Eastern descent and he dealt mostly with mundane matters related to wills, taxes, and property. And he prospered.

But all this changed with 9/11. Reza became a fervent advocate for American Muslims. He was concerned that, in the backlash following the attacks, Muslims would suffer the same fate as Japanese Americans had following Pearl Harbor. He objected loudly and publicly to the Patriot Act and defended several Muslims, all American citizens, who had been detained or incarcerated for allegedly having terrorist connections.

Reza was handsome and articulate and passionate. He became an occasional guest on *NOW* and *The News Hour with Jim Lehrer,* and when Senator William Broderick made his famous speech, Reza became one of his most vocal opponents. Two weeks before his death, Reza appeared with Broderick on *Meet the Press* – and he lost it. He absolutely lost it.

The morning of the show he'd flown in from New York, where he had been defending a client, and had received disproportionate attention from airport security personnel. So when he arrived on Russert's set he was already angry. For a while he maintained his composure with Broderick, but then Broderick made a remark about how performing background checks on American Muslims seemed like a pretty sensible thing to do, them being the people most likely to be terrorists. It wasn't so much what Broderick said as the way he said it, as if it was no big deal – and Reza just went nuts. He rose up from his chair, pointed his finger at Broderick's pale face, and screamed at him for several minutes, spittle flying from his mouth. Russert cut to a commercial when the fireworks died down, and when the show resumed Reza had left the set – which was too bad, as Broderick was then able to use the remaining air time to give his standard pitch.

Unfortunately, one of the things Reza said to Broderick was that 9/11 had occurred in part because of people like Broderick, people who made absolutely no attempt to understand the struggles of Muslims throughout the world. And maybe, Reza had said, it would take another 9/11 before Broderick and his kind would wake up.

Using less technical jargon than they normally did, the FBI concluded that Reza Zarif had just plain *snapped*. In the last seven years, he had dug himself into a deep financial pit because he had neglected his law practice, and he was perpetually resentful because the government's lawyers usually kicked his ass in court. He'd lost weight, his hair had turned prematurely gray, and, always an emotional man, he'd become downright volatile, flying into rages on the slightest provocation. To help make the FBI's point, *The New York Times* showed a still picture of Reza berating Broderick on *Meet the Press*, his eyes bugging out, his face twisted with fury, looking in general like an escapee from a mental institution. He just snapped, the FBI spokesman said.

So who should DeMarco believe: Hassan Zarif, a man who claimed his brother was not only sane but patriotic, or a legion of qualified FBI agents who had gathered a mountain of evidence and had guys with doctorates in psychology backing up their claims?

DeMarco decided that the answer to that question would have to wait until tomorrow.

He ordered a second martini.

7

As the cab cruised down Main Street at precisely thirty miles per hour, Jeremy Potter took in the neat shops, the old-fashioned lampposts, the courthouse that had been the background for a Rockwell cover on *The Saturday Evening Post* – and he immediately begin to relax. The last two months had been very hectic. He was so glad to be home.

For two months, he'd worked like an absolute slave. He'd spent hours on the Internet and had taken trips to Washington, New York, Philadelphia, and Trenton to observe people who often lived in minority neighborhoods and where, being a small white man of fifty-three, he'd felt quite vulnerable. And then there'd been the meetings with the two government people. Those meetings hadn't taken long, but they'd been extremely stressful, by far the riskiest part of his assignment. But now it was finally over and he'd been successful, and Mr Lincoln had been very pleased.

He didn't know why Mr Lincoln had asked him to do what he did, but that wasn't at all unusual. He would be given a task – typically research, sometimes surveillance, frequently duties as a courier – but he would rarely know how his role fit into Mr Lincoln's grand design. Come to think of it, it seemed as if this time he knew much more than he normally did. He was certainly able to see a pattern in his research, and the government men – well, in order to bribe them, although *bribe* may not be the correct term, he had to be very specific regarding Mr Lincoln's expectations.

Yes, he could definitely see the outline of Mr Lincoln's plan. He couldn't see every detail – not how it would be executed, or why or when or by whom – but he could see enough that it made him feel uncomfortable.

In most respects, Mr Lincoln was an ideal employer. He paid well, he was invariably pleasant in conversation, and his directions were always perfectly clear. But he had always suspected that knowing too much of Mr Lincoln's plans could be dangerous – terminally dangerous – and right now he had this little mental itch, this tickling sensation at the back of his brain, that said maybe, just maybe . . . ?

Oh, quit being such a nervous Nelly, he told himself. He'd worked for Mr Lincoln for years. He was a trusted employee. A *valued* employee. And he'd been paid. He patted his chest and felt the reassuring lump of cash in the envelope in the inside pocket of his blazer. Mr Lincoln certainly wouldn't have paid him if his plan was to harm him. That would be illogical, and Mr Lincoln was never illogical.

The cab stopped at his address. He tipped the driver exactly fifteen percent and stood for a moment on the sidewalk admiring his home. He privately thought of it as a *cottage* – loved his small patch of lawn, the ivy crawling up the chimney, the daisies that grew near the door – and he didn't care one whit that his white picket fence was considered by some a cliché.

He unlocked his front door, dropped his suitcase in the foyer, and silenced the alarm. It was so, so good to be home. His only disappointment was that Mabel wasn't there. But he'd pick her up from the kennel later, and then he and his cat would spend the next week reading, relaxing, and cooking – and thinking about how they'd spend the money in the envelope. Maybe they'd take a trip to Martha's Vineyard; they hadn't been there in years.

He walked into the living room. The first thing he thought when he saw the woman sitting on the loveseat holding a silenced automatic in her hand was not *How did she get in without setting off the alarm?* No, his mind leaped right past that question.

His first thought – and his last thought – was that the person Mr Lincoln had sent to kill him was very beautiful.

8

DeMarco figured the best way to get in to see the secretary of Homeland Security was to get up at 4:45 A.M. and be waiting outside the man's office at 5:30.

DeMarco was not a willing early riser. Regardless of what time he went to bed the night before, he found that if he woke up any time before 7 A.M. his head felt as if it were stuffed with barley. His brain didn't work; his fingers couldn't button his shirt; he couldn't find his wallet or watch or keys or anything else that he needed. And his stomach just recoiled at the thought of food.

But rise he did. He knew that General Andrew Banks, secretary of Homeland Security, arrived at work early, usually before 6 A.M., and once at work the man's calendar would be completely full. DeMarco also knew he would never get an appointment to see

Banks unless Mahoney made the appointment for him, and Mahoney had made it clear that he didn't want to be connected with this assignment.

So DeMarco drove to Banks's office and convinced the security guards that he was a messenger from Congress. He showed them his congressional ID, looked humble and messenger-like, and held up a manila envelope on which he'd written in Magic Marker: GENERAL BANKS, EYES ONLY. He had underlined EYES ONLY. The guards made him walk through the metal detectors, copied down the information on his ID, and then allowed him to stand outside Banks's office door.

At five-forty-five, DeMarco saw Banks striding down the hall like a man who could hardly wait to get to work and start kicking ass. He had a gray crew cut, a prominent nose, and wore wire-rimmed glasses over a pair of hostile gray eyes. He was tall and, though in his sixties, his stomach was still hard and flat. DeMarco suspected the maniac rose every morning at daybreak and performed those same masochistic exercises that he had once done as a midshipman at Annapolis. His first words of cheery greeting to DeMarco were, 'What the hell are *you* doing here?'

Banks wasn't particularly fond of DeMarco, although DeMarco wasn't sure why. It may have been because Banks was an ex-marine, a retired three-star general, and considered that DeMarco would never have met the marines' few-good-men standard. Or it could have been because DeMarco had once done some work for Banks. The case had been a complicated one involving an assassination attempt on the president in which the Secret Service had been involved, and it had concluded with Banks, Mahoney, and DeMarco knowing a secret they should not have kept from the public but which they did. This, DeMarco figured, gave him a certain amount of leverage over the general, which was why he had decided to talk to him instead of to the FBI. He knew the FBI wouldn't tell him anything unless Mahoney made them, but because the Zarif incident was terrorist-related, he figured Homeland Security would know almost as much as the Bureau.

'I need a favor,' DeMarco said, answering Banks's question.

'What kinda favor?' Banks said, his eyes narrowing into suspicious slits. But then he would have been suspicious if DeMarco had asked him the date.

'I need to talk to one of your guys about the Reza Zarif thing.'

'Why?' Banks asked.

'I can't tell you.'

'Are you out of your goddamn mind?' Banks said. 'Do you have any idea how much heat I'm under because of everything that's happened lately?'

'I think so,' DeMarco said.

'But you still think I'll let you waltz in here and start poking around without telling me why?'

'General, I swear I'm not going to do anything to cause you a problem,' DeMarco said. 'I just want—'

'Forget it,' Banks said, and started to unlock his office door. So much for prior association.

DeMarco had to say something to get Banks to help him, and he was pretty sure Banks wouldn't talk to the press because he hated reporters. At least DeMarco hoped he still hated them.

'Okay, look,' DeMarco said. 'Mahoney grew up with Reza Zarif's father, and he's known Reza since he was born. He just wants to know a little more about what happened, something so maybe he can understand why the guy did what he did, but he doesn't want to ask the Bureau because they blab too much.'

Banks stopped turning the key in the lock and DeMarco watched as he mulled things over. He knew Banks didn't particularly like Mahoney either, but he also knew that Mahoney had been helpful to Banks and his department in the past.

'And I swear, General,' DeMarco said, 'if I learn anything that reflects poorly on Homeland Security, I'll tell you and no one else.'

'Shit,' Banks said. 'These days *everything* reflects poorly on Homeland Security: FEMA fuckin' up recovery after those tornadoes in Kansas. Those two kids tryin' to blow up the tunnel in Baltimore. That one-legged al-Qaeda bozo gettin' into the country and then gettin' away. I mean, Jesus – it's like there's no end to it. All I can say is I'm glad I've already got a pension from the corps, because it's damn unlikely I'm gonna be in this job much longer.' Banks felt sorry for himself a couple of seconds more and then said, 'Okay. The guy you wanna talk to is Jerry Hansen. He's my liaison guy with the Bureau for this kinda stuff. He's not in this early – none of these goddamn people ever are – but I'll leave a message on his voice mail telling him you'll be dropping by.'

'Thank you,' DeMarco said.

'Yeah, right. You fuck me over on this, DeMarco, and I'll run you down with my car.'

The Homeland Security official that DeMarco was supposed to meet wouldn't be in his office until 8 A.M. So since he had time to kill, he found a place to have breakfast and read the morning paper, and, as he usually did, he turned to the sports page first. The gloomy headlines on the front page could always wait.

The Redskins had lost five games, two games in their division. DeMarco couldn't understand it. The team had three receivers that were faster than chee-tahs, a quarterback with an arm like a rocket launcher, a decent offensive line, and a running back who could knock over tanks – and they couldn't score. The *Post*'s sportswriters had already started doing playoff math scenarios. If the Redskins won all their remaining games, and if teams A, B, and C won the next five games, and if Teams D, E, and F lost the next five games, the Skins could get a wild-card spot. Yes, it was *mathematically* possible that Washington would make the playoffs – just like a hole-in-one and a basket from the half-court line are mathematically possible.

Sports news consumed and digested, he turned to the front page but gave up after a few minutes, unable to focus. He couldn't stop thinking about his ex-wife and the conversation they'd had yesterday morning.

Marie DeMarco had been his first love. He'd met her when he was sixteen and she was fourteen. She'd been the first girl he'd kissed, the first woman he'd made love to. They'd dated throughout high school, broke up briefly when DeMarco went off to college, then connected again and married after he had completed law school.

He had wanted kids. She hadn't.

Marie was, without a doubt, the sexiest woman he had ever known. She was pretty, of course, and an absolute knockout when she dressed up. She had big expressive eyes, large wonderful breasts, a trim little butt, and good legs – but it wasn't just her looks that made her so desirable. Some women just *ooze* sex appeal. Take the young Elizabeth Taylor or Sharon Stone: There are dozens of Hollywood starlets just as beautiful as either woman, but nowhere near as sexy. Why? God only knew. Or maybe God had nothing to do with it.

Sex appeal aside, Marie DeMarco was hugely flawed: vain, selfish, shallow – and unfaithful. DeMarco suspected, after the fact, that his cousin wasn't the only man she'd slept with while they were married, but it was the affair with Danny that had hurt the most. Danny had been his best friend when they were kids, and Marie's infidelity had shredded his ego and pierced his heart and almost destroyed him financially – and yet here the damn woman was asking for his help. She was unbelievable.

She'd told DeMarco what had happened. Danny and a leg-breaker named Vince Merlino who worked for Tony Benedetto had been assigned to collect an overdue debt from a gambling junkie – and Vince had killed the junkie. Danny had been seen fleeing the scene by a witness and was now residing in a cell on Riker's Island. The police knew Danny hadn't killed the gambler; they knew it, but they wouldn't admit it. Danny was primarily a fence, a man who was very good at moving stolen goods, more like a charming retail salesman than a thug. The cops knew he didn't carry a gun, and he didn't have any violence on his sheet. But Danny refused to give up his partner, so the cops had no choice: Danny was going to swing for the gambler's murder.

'So why the hell doesn't he just tell them this Vince guy did it?' DeMarco had asked his ex.

'Because he'd be a rat,' Marie had said.

'He *is* a rat,' DeMarco said.

'And because Vince is Mr Benedetto's nephew.'

Oh, man, that wasn't good.

'So what in the hell do you want from me, Marie?' he had asked her. 'If you're expecting me to pay for his lawyer or put up his bail, you're out of your mind.'

'I don't expect you to pay for anything. They won't give him bail and Mr Benedetto's springing for the lawyer.'

'So then what's the problem?'

'The problem is Mr Benedetto expects him to do the time, that's what the damn problem is. The lawyer will get him the best deal he can, but if Danny gives up anybody, Vince or anyone else in Tony's crew, Tony will have him killed.' She had started crying. 'They're gonna put him away for fifteen years, Joe, maybe longer.'

'But what do you want *me* to do, Marie?'

'I want you to get Mr Mahoney to get him a pardon.'

DeMarco had laughed out loud. He hadn't been able to stop himself. 'Marie' – he almost added *you fuckin' moron* – 'first of all, the speaker of the House can't give pardons to convicted criminals in the State of New York. And second, there's no way in hell he's going to ask the president to give Danny one.'

'But—'

'Marie, I hate you and I hate Danny, but even if I didn't, you gotta believe me when I tell you there's no way he's gonna get a pardon, not from anyone, and there's nothing I can do to make such a thing happen.'

When he hung up, she was crying, and for some damn reason *he* felt bad. To hell with her, he said to himself – a phrase he'd used many times since she'd left him.

At 8:30 A.M., burping a bit from his corned beef hash and eggs – calories and cholesterol be damned – DeMarco strolled back into Homeland Security and five minutes later was sitting in Jerry Hansen's office.

Hansen looked so much like Andy Banks physically – short gray hair, trim and in good condition, wire-rimmed glasses – that DeMarco figured he was probably an ex-marine, just like his boss. Maybe a retired colonel, DeMarco thought, Banks's trusted right-hand guy when they had served together in the corps.

DeMarco decided to see if his instincts were on the mark. 'Were you in the marines with General Banks, Mr Hansen?' DeMarco asked.

'Call me Jerry, and hell, no,' Hansen said. 'I was never in the service and never wanted to be. When they formed up Homeland Security they pulled all these government departments together. I was a supervisor over in ICE, that's Immigration and

Customs Enforcement, but in this job I got now I just keep track of things. This terrorist shit, you've got the FBI involved, local cops, and sometimes CIA, NSA, and DIA. And internal to Homeland Security, you got ICE, TSA, Coast Guard, and maybe Secret Service. You need a damn spreadsheet – I can show you one – just to keep track of who's who and who's doing what. So that's my job. I try to make sure I know what all the players are doing and keep the general informed. And man, what a hard-ass he is.'

'Got it,' DeMarco said.

'So,' Hansen said. 'The general left me a message saying you worked for Congress and I'm supposed to fill you in on Reza Zarif.'

The 'worked for Congress' part was good, DeMarco thought. That made it sound like whatever he was doing had been officially sanctioned.

'So what do you wanna know?' Hansen said. 'Most everything's been reported in the papers, and for the most part the news guys got it right.'

'One thing I'm curious about is this link to al-Qaeda the Bureau says they found.'

'Well, that's classified,' Hansen said.

'Come on, Hansen. I've got a security clearance and I'm from Congress. And your boss told you to talk to me.'

Hansen screwed up his face as he debated giving up national secrets to a complete stranger, but he finally relented.

'They found a letter in Zarif's house that came from a mosque in Atlanta. The letter was thanking Zarif for a donation he sent them.'

'So?'

'Well – and this is the classified part – this particular mosque funnels money to al-Qaeda and the FBI follows the money. But they don't want any mention of this mosque in the papers because this will tell the bad guys what the Bureau's doing in case they haven't figured it out already.'

'And they think because Zarif got a thank-you note from a mosque that he has al-Qaeda connections?'

'*Possible* connections, just like they told the press.'

'Did the Bureau find any evidence that Zarif actually sent these folks money?'

'They didn't find a canceled check or an electronic transfer, anything like that. But he could have mailed them cash.'

'Not exactly a smoking gun,' DeMarco said.

'Hey, you don't need a smoking gun when you find what's left of the guy's body in the plane you shot down.'

DeMarco had to concede that point.

'Another thing I was kinda curious about,' DeMarco said. 'Was there any evidence that Zarif was under psychiatric care or taking antidepressants? You know, Valium, Prozac, anything like that?'

'Why would you be curious about that?' Hansen said.

'Well, according to the Bureau, the guy just went nuts. I'm wonderin' if there was any prior indication of mental instability.'

Hansen laughed. 'Did you see Zarif on *Meet the Press*?'

'No, but I read about it.'

'Well, you oughta watch a tape of the show. You talk about a guy that was wrapped too tight, that was Reza Zarif. The guy acted like such a maniac when he went off on Broderick, you don't have to be Sigmund-fucking-Freud to know he had some problems. And then, of course, you got the small issue that he wasted his entire family before he decided to take on two F-Sixteens in a Cessna.'

DeMarco had to concede that point too.

'Going back to the al-Qaeda link,' DeMarco said, 'was there any evidence that he had accomplices?'

'The Bureau's still looking into that,' Hansen said. 'Half the people Zarif represented were on the FBI's watch list, but so far there's no evidence that anybody helped him. He didn't need any help to fly that plane, and as for somebody other than family being in his house, there's no indication that there was. The neighbors didn't see anybody around that morning, and there were no strange cars parked in the neighborhood. The only thing is, the Zarif house is right on Sixty-six and one of those noise-suppression walls runs along his backyard line. *Theoretically*, somebody could have parked on the highway, ninja'd over the wall, and gotten into his house that way, but that's pretty unlikely.'

'There were no unidentified fingerprints found in the house?' DeMarco said.

'There was a shitload of unidentified prints,' Hansen said. 'The Bureau matched about eighty percent of them to Zarif's family and their friends and his clients, but they still have a bunch they can't tie to anybody. So far they haven't found a print for anybody that's some kinda radical Muslim al-Qaeda wing nut.'

'But they still have twenty percent of the prints unidentified?'

'Yeah, but it's early.'

'How 'bout the gun Reza used to kill his family. I heard' – DeMarco couldn't tell Hansen that his source was Reza Zarif's brother – 'that Reza Zarif never owned a gun in his life.'

'According to one of his friends,' Hansen said, 'Zarif had talked about buying a gun a couple months ago. There'd been some vandalism at his place, somebody spray-painting anti-Muslim shit on his door, and when those yahoos tried to blow up the Harbor Tunnel, his family started getting threatening phone calls. And that *really* got Zarif upset. So anyway, Zarif's flying buddy said Reza had been thinking about getting a gun.'

'Was the gun registered in Reza's name?' DeMarco asked.

'No, but the Bureau has a pretty good idea where he got it from: a punk named Donny Cray.'

'What are you talking about?'

'The Bureau found a fingerprint on a box of bullets in Reza's house. They found a partial thumbprint on the little flap thing that you use to close the box, and they matched the print to Cray. He's a small-time punk who's into a lot of stuff, mostly gun and drug related. DEA and ATF both have him in their files. Anyway, one of the things Cray has been known to do is steal guns – or buy stolen guns from his friends – and sell 'em at swap meets. So the Bureau thinks there's a good chance Reza got his gun from him. The FBI figured a guy like Reza, an *Arab*-looking guy, wouldn't try to buy a gun legally because he'd be worried that after he filled out the paperwork some redneck gun-shop owner would report him as a potential terrorist.'

'So how does the Bureau know Cray wasn't involved in some way?'

'For a couple of reasons,' Hansen said. 'First, the *only* fingerprint from Cray found in the house was the one partial print on the bullet box, while Reza's prints were all over the gun, on all the bullets in the clip, and on the casings of the bullets that had been fired. It was obvious that Reza had loaded the gun himself.

'The second reason why the Bureau's sure that Cray wasn't involved,' Hansen said, 'is motive. Or, in this case, lack of a motive. Donny Cray was into dope and guns, not radical Muslim causes, and there's no logical reason why some Virginia peckerhead like him would help Zarif try to fly a plane into the White House.'

'Has Cray admitted to selling Reza the gun?' DeMarco said.

'Not yet. The Bureau can't find him.'

'Can't find him?'

'The guy lives in a trailer, and every once in a while he hooks it up to his truck and takes off, especially in the winter. He likes going to Florida; he's got friends down there. The Feebs'll run him down eventually.'

'So why wasn't this in the papers? I mean about Cray's fingerprint on the bullet box.'

'Because the Bureau doesn't want to give rise to a bunch of conspiracy theory nonsense when all they have is one partial print from a guy who's known to sell guns. And the kind of dumb questions you're asking proves they're right.'

9

He couldn't find a position where he was comfortable. Before the woman had sat down next to him, he'd been able to stretch his right leg out, but with her sitting there he was forced to sit with both knees pressed against the seat in front of him. The woman, a heavyset Hispanic, nodded and smiled at him before she sat down, but at the same time it was clear she expected him to move his leg and make room for her. In his country, she would have stood in the aisle of the bus until he permitted her to sit.

And she wasn't even a real American, yet like all women in this country – all women *exposed* to this country – she had an air of confidence about her that infuriated him. The men here were weak and undeservedly arrogant, and the culture as a whole was decadent and wasteful, but the women were the worst. They went about with their heads uncovered and their faces unveiled, the young ones dressing like painted whores, but their lack of modesty was not as infuriating as their presumption – no, not a presumption, their *conviction* – that they were equal to men. And it wasn't even the rich highborn ones who acted this way. This woman, who probably cleaned toilets for a living, had no doubt that she had a right to speak to him, to sit next to him, to intrude into his space and his thoughts as if she were his equal.

He had crossed into the United States from Mexico, and on his way to the East Coast he had stopped at a restaurant in Texas. He ordered coffee and the waitress brought him a cup that was tepid and weak, as if it had been made with yesterday's grounds. He told her this and said, 'Bring me another cup,' and she had said, 'You mean, Bring me another cup *please*, now, don't you, honey?' She was smiling when she said this, but at the same time she was serious, correcting his manners. He looked at her and said, 'I meant what I said. Make me a decent cup of hot coffee.' And she had said, 'You know what, sugar? You can just go fuck yourself.' And then she'd walked away and started talking to another waitress, laughing as she gestured at him with her head. He'd left the restaurant a few minutes later, his face burning with embarrassment. He'd thought about waiting until she left work and cutting off her lips, but of course he didn't. He was too disciplined to permit himself such an indulgence.

He saw a sign on the highway. The bus was still a hundred miles from Cleveland, a hundred more miles of sitting in this cramped seat next to this woman, his right leg on fire. It would have been so much better if he could have flown from Philadelphia to Cleveland, but he could no longer take the risk. So now he traveled by bus and by train and by car, but usually by bus. Security on trains had become tighter since London and Madrid, and he was always worried that in a car he would be pulled over by some country sheriff because of his race.

And the problem with air travel wasn't just that he was an Arab, it was his right leg. Below the knee it was made of metal and plastic and it set off the detectors in airports. Thanks to the two fools in Baltimore, the American security forces knew about his leg, and any foreigner with an artificial leg would be detained until his identity could be confirmed. It wouldn't matter if he shaved his head or put padding in his cheeks or wore a wig and contact lenses; it wouldn't matter if he didn't look anything like the poor picture they had of him in which he wore a beard. They would detain him until the FBI examined him, and the FBI *would* confirm his identity.

So now he traveled on buses with cleaning women, taking seven hours to make a journey that should have taken an hour and a half. But that was all right. He had a lifetime in which to complete his mission.

10

Mahoney was pissed.

That morning in *The Washington Post* there had been an article saying that he'd been visited by Hassan Zarif, brother of the terrorist Reza Zarif. And the reporter had, of course, discovered that Mahoney and Reza's father had been boyhood friends in Boston. The guy had even found a high school yearbook picture of Mahoney and Ali Zarif dressed in baseball uniforms, Mahoney's thick arm around Ali's thin neck.

'How'd the press even know he was here?' Mahoney said to DeMarco. 'I didn't have him down on the damn list as comin' to see *me*.'

DeMarco was fairly sure he knew the answer to that question: McGuire, the U.S. Capitol cop. When DeMarco had threatened McGuire with an outdoor

cold-weather posting for hassling Hassan Zarif, he'd
made the mistake of saying that Hassan was expected
by the speaker. So McGuire, probably recognizing
the Zarif name, decided to exercise a little anonymous payback and informed the *Post* that Mahoney
had been paid a visit by a man with the same last
name as a terrorist. And the *Post* took it from there.

'Geez, I can't imagine,' DeMarco said.

'The bastards – TV guys too – they've been calling
all morning,' Mahoney said, 'asking what Hassie was
doing here.'

'What'd you tell them?'

'The truth, sort of.'

That was Mahoney: a man who told the truth –
sort of.

'I told them,' Mahoney said, 'that I had known
Reza when he was a kid and had known his dad all
my life. I said Hassan had stopped by because he was
here in town for somethin', I didn't know what, but
since he was here and he knew I'd want to know
how his dad was doin' after his heart attack, he
stopped by to tell me. I also told them that Hassan
and his family had gotten a pretty good grilling from
the cops, this maybe being understandable, but that
we had to watch out we didn't ruin their lives because
of what his brother did.'

'But you didn't tell them Hassan thought the FBI's
story had a bunch of holes in it and he wanted you
to get him some answers.'

'No. *Hell,* no!'

Mahoney brooded for a moment over the political liability of having his picture in the paper with the father of a dead terrorist.

'So what'd you find out?' he said to DeMarco.

DeMarco told him.

'You think it means anything, this yahoo's fingerprint on the bullet box?'

DeMarco shrugged. 'If I was placing a bet, I'd put my money on the Bureau's explanation. Reza probably bought the gun from this Cray character like they think, and when the FBI finds Cray he'll admit it.'

'So you think Reza just woke up one day and decided to kill his family and crash a plane into the White House?'

'I guess,' DeMarco said. 'There wasn't anything I learned from Homeland Security that would make me think different.'

'Well, I don't buy it,' Mahoney said, his big stubborn chin jutting outward. 'I've been thinkin' about this a whole lot since his brother was here, and I think Hassan's right. There *has* to be something more goin' on than what the Bureau thinks. In fact, I'm sure there is.'

But DeMarco knew that Mahoney wasn't so sure that he'd say what he'd just said to the press – or the Bureau.

'So what do you want me to do?' DeMarco said. 'I'm going on vacation next week.'

'For now, just keep your ear to the ground. Stay in touch with Homeland Security and make sure the FBI's really looking for this Cray guy.'

DeMarco didn't have the authority to make the FBI do anything, so all he did was nod his head. He wasn't worried about the FBI diligently searching for Donny Cray; he knew that with a case of this magnitude they probably had a couple hundred agents out looking for the man. No, he wasn't worried about any lack of effort on the Bureau's part. What he was worried about was that he wouldn't be able to take the vacation he had scheduled three months ago.

It was difficult for DeMarco to plan vacations, and not because Mahoney always had something urgent for him to do. It was because Mahoney didn't *care* whether DeMarco had made plans or not. DeMarco would ask for permission to take time off, he'd tell Mahoney the days he intended to be gone, and Mahoney would almost always nod his big head in agreement. But Mahoney never bothered to write down the dates when DeMarco would be absent, because from his perspective the dates were unimportant. Then, after having given his permission, after DeMarco had purchased airline tickets and booked hotels and made promises to friends and lovers, Mahoney would force him to cancel his vacation, believing sincerely that *whatever* problem John Mahoney had far outweighed any problems that he might cause his subordinate.

DeMarco bought travel insurance every time he made reservations.

This year DeMarco was planning to spend a week in Key West, sitting in the sun, drinking rum, and ogling women in small bikinis. Now his trip might be in jeopardy. On the other hand, Mahoney had not specifically instructed him to cancel his vacation. He'd just said for DeMarco to keep his ear to the ground, an activity DeMarco figured he could do by phone from a Florida beach, unless otherwise directed.

To change the subject, he asked Mahoney, 'How's Broderick's bill looking?'

Mahoney shook his head in disgust. 'It's still in committee, but with this thing that Reza did, there's a good chance it'll make it to the floor for a vote. I'm gettin' a lot of mail saying that Broderick's got the right idea, and I'll betcha everybody on that Senate committee is too.'

On occasion, when Mahoney would talk to high school kids, he'd ask them if they knew how laws were made. The education system being what it is, the answer was usually no, and Mahoney would give the high schoolers the kindergarten version of the lawmaking process.

A bill could be initiated in either body of Congress, the House or the Senate, or in both bodies simultaneously. Suppose a senator – say, William Broderick – decided that the nation needed a new law. He would draft his proposal in the form of a bill, and the bill would go to the appropriate standing committee in the Senate. Here the bill would be reviewed and discussed and modified and then, if approved by the committee, it would go to the floor of the Senate to be voted upon. If the bill passed by simple majority in the Senate, it would then go to the House, and if the House voted to approve the bill, it would go to the president for his signature, and the bill would become law, unless the president vetoed it, which he rarely did.

That was the kiddy-class version of how a bill became a law.

The actual process was much more complicated. It involved backslapping and backstabbing, compromises and trades. Think tanks would crank out position papers, twisting facts as needed to support or undercut the legislation, depending on who was paying their fee. Lobbyists would take lawmakers on golfing trips and ply them with booze and broads and bucks. Party leaders would bend back arms, making it clear that the partisan way was the only way, and special-interest groups would dance around their bonfires and flood the legislature with threatening mail. The politicians would take all these factors into account, add to the mix the proximity of the next election, listen to a reading of the bones cast by various blind pollsters, and, most important of all, decide how a yea or nay vote could affect their chances of being reelected – and then the politicians would vote.

Laws are a lot like hot dogs: You don't really want to know how they're made.

'What are you going to do if it's approved in the Senate?' DeMarco asked.

'It'll never happen,' Mahoney said.

The speaker was almost always right when he made predictions about how Congress would behave, but he hadn't factored Youseff Ibrahim Khalid into his thinking.

11

Youseff Ibrahim Khalid was so frightened he could hardly walk. He'd already vomited once since arriving at LaGuardia. He would have vomited again, but he had nothing left in his stomach. As he approached the security checkpoint, he could feel the sweat soaking into his shirt and pouring down his forehead. He knew he had to try to appear calm, but he couldn't. He couldn't stop the trembling in his legs. He couldn't stop the sweat rolling down his face.

He was certain the TSA agents at the checkpoint would stop him because of the way he was acting. However, as fate would have it, a snowstorm had hit the Midwest and this had caused a number of flights to be delayed or canceled – although Youseff's flight was not one of them. So it was unusually busy at the airport that morning, there were long lines of upset, impatient people everywhere, and the agents were rushing their inspections to avoid further delays. It was God's will.

Youseff placed his carry-on bag on the conveyor belt and moved slowly forward to walk through the metal detector. He had already made sure he had nothing on him that would set off the detector. His pockets were completely empty; he had even removed his belt and thrown it into the garbage can in the airport restroom. All his possessions were in the carry-on bag. He expected that they would search the bag and pat him down because of his name, but this time they didn't. He simply passed through the metal detector, picked up his carry-on bag, and put on his shoes.

It was all God's will.

The small jet used to shuttle passengers between New York and Washington had twelve rows, two seats on the starboard side of the plane, one seat on the port side. He was in the single seat in row eight. A woman and her child were sitting across the aisle from him, the child a tiny blond-haired girl no more than seven. He couldn't look at the child.

He sat there with his eyes closed as the plane was being prepared for takeoff and thought of his wife and his own children, his beautiful children. Would his wife miss him when he was gone? Probably not, he'd treated her so badly the last two years.

The plane rose into the sky over New York. The

stewardess informed the passengers that they would arrive at Reagan National Airport in less than an hour. When the seat-belt light was extinguished, Youseff sat a minute, tried and failed to remember a prayer from his childhood, and then rose from his seat. He pulled his carry-on bag from the overhead bin and walked back to the restroom. As he walked down the aisle he saw more children. The plane seemed to be *filled* with children.

Inside the restroom, he removed from his bag the pieces that made up the pistol. The pistol was constructed of some sort of plastic, a polymer that was very tough, and the gun's components resembled common objects: the barrel was the handle to a hairbrush; the trigger was the earpiece to a pair of sunglasses; three small-caliber plastic bullets and a spring had been packed into a container that appeared to be a ballpoint pen. Youseff assembled the pistol with trembling hands and loaded it, then looked into the mirror. His face was unshaven, his hair was sticking up, and his eyes seemed to have swelled in their sockets, as if they were about to explode from all the emotions he was trying to suppress. He looked like a madman.

But it was time. It was time to do what he had to do. Then it would all be over.

He left the restroom and walked slowly up the aisle of the plane, the pistol in the pocket of his jacket. He dropped his carry-on bag on the seat where he'd been sitting and continued up the aisle toward the stewardess, who was standing by the coffee mess near the cockpit door. He approached as if he was going to ask for something, then grabbed her by the arm, jerked her in front of him, and placed the barrel of the gun against her head. He heard people start to scream and then he started screaming too, telling the passengers not to move, not to resist. At least that's what he *thought* he said. He wasn't sure, there was such a roar inside his head.

He dragged the stewardess backward until the re-inforced cockpit door was at his back and he began to kick at the door with his right foot, yelling for the pilot to open up. He waved the pistol at the passengers to keep them in their seats, and then placed it again against the stewardess's head. He heard someone inside the cockpit say something and he turned his head slightly, to hear better, to yell again at the pilot, to tell him he would kill the stewardess if he didn't open the door.

Youseff Khalid didn't see, sitting in a single seat in row five, no more than six feet from him, the U.S. air marshal raising his arm. He didn't see the pistol in the man's right hand. He didn't feel the bullet that entered his head and blew his brains all over the cockpit door.

12

Mahoney had not wanted to go to the vice president's sixty-fifth birthday party. He went only because his wife, Mary Pat, was good friends with the VP's wife. And to make matters worse, since his wife was with him, Mahoney couldn't flirt with all the good-looking women who'd been invited – like the new undersecretary from State that he could see talking to the president's chief of staff.

The new undersecretary was not only a looker but Mahoney had heard she was some kinda genius and spoke half a dozen languages. Mahoney thought it almost unfair that God would give a woman an ass like that and brains too. And now she was laughing at something the president's chief had said. As the man was about as funny as a case of the clap, Mahoney figured that in addition to being brilliant she was also polite.

Mahoney turned back to the bartender and asked for another drink. So far he'd spent more time talking to the bartender than anyone else at the party. He glanced over at the new undersecretary again, looked around for his wife, and saw that she was talking to the birthday boy himself. The vice president was nodding his head agreeably and had, as usual, this blissful expression on his face as if he'd swallowed a bottle of Prozac.

Thomas Riley Marshall, who had served as vice president to Woodrow Wilson, once said, 'The vice president of the United States is like a man in a cataleptic state: He cannot speak; he cannot move; he suffers no pain; and yet he is perfectly conscious of everything that is going on about him.' Mahoney agreed completely with that sentiment, particularly as it applied to the current occupant of the office.

Mahoney looked at his watch. Dinner had ended half an hour ago. He wanted to get the hell out of here and go home and go to bed, but it looked as if Mary Pat was having a pretty good time. He was thinking – his wife otherwise occupied – that maybe he should go over and introduce himself to the lady from State. He'd just pushed away from the bar when he heard someone say, 'Good evening, Mr Speaker.'

Mahoney turned. Aw, shit, it was Broderick. Mahoney had managed to avoid the guy all night, but now here he was. Mahoney could understand why the VP had invited a bunch of Republicans to his party, but did he have to invite Broderick?

'How you doin', Bill?' Mahoney said.

Mahoney had always thought that Commie-buster Joe McCarthy, the politician to whom Broderick was most often compared, had *looked* like a bad guy. With McCarthy's five o'clock shadow and his dour face, it was easy to picture him in the role of thug and bully. But Bill Broderick didn't look like that.

Broderick was in his early forties, tall, broad-shouldered, and trim. He had a full head of sandy-brown hair, an engaging smile, and wide blue eyes that made him appear open and honest and sincere. And he had no particular facial feature – big ears, Durante nose, Leno chin, or odd bouffant – that political caricaturists could readily capture. When the cartoonists portrayed Mahoney, they all went after his white hair and his gut.

'Just fine, Mr Speaker,' Broderick said. 'I realize this is a social occasion but . . .'

Then why don't you go socialize.

'. . . but I thought I should take this opportunity to talk to you. As I'm sure you've heard, my bill reported out of committee today.'

The FBI's preliminary report was that Youseff Khalid had planned to crash the New York–D.C. shuttle into the U.S. Capitol. Why they concluded this had not yet been made totally clear, but it didn't matter. After a few senators heard what the Bureau said, Broderick's goddamn bill had practically *squirted* out of committee.

'No, I hadn't heard,' Mahoney said.

'Well, it did, sir, and it's going to the floor in a couple of weeks. Maybe sooner, because after what happened today, the public is demanding we take action.'

Oh, please, spare me the speech, Mahoney thought.

'I'm fairly confident that it's going to pass in the Senate,' Broderick said.

And it just might, Mahoney thought, although it was going to be close, from everything he'd heard. But all Mahoney said was, 'Is that right?'

'Yes, sir. The reason I wanted to speak to you tonight was that I was going to suggest that you might want to fast-track the bill in the House when it comes your way.'

Mahoney gazed over at the new undersecretary again as he took a sip of his drink. Jesus, the woman was built. He swiveled his head around; his wife was nowhere to be seen.

'Well,' Mahoney said to Broderick, 'we've got a lot on our plate at the moment, but I'll—'

'A lot on your plate, sir? The country is *under attack* from a segment of its own population. The plot in Baltimore, two terrorist attacks this month – surely, Mr Speaker—'

Mahoney wasn't sure the country was exactly

under attack, but it was certainly acting that way. National Guard troops armed with automatic weapons were patrolling borders and airports, grim-faced cops were prowling subway stations in packs, and air travel had virtually ground to a halt due to security delays. But there was no point discussing any of that with Broderick.

'Bill, would you excuse me please?' Mahoney said. 'There's a gal over there from the State Department. She's new in the job and I think she needs an old hand to explain to her how things work in this town. I'd give you the lecture, but you seem to have figured things out already.'

As Mahoney walked toward the lady from the State Department, he wondered what the hell that damn DeMarco was doing. He'd call the guy tomorrow, make sure he wasn't goofing off.

13

He stood in an alley where he could see the apartment in which the boy lived. This neighborhood in Cleveland was filled mostly with brown and black people so he blended in, and at this time of day the few people he saw were hurrying off to work and didn't even seem to notice him. He had arrived at six, though he hadn't expected the boy to leave that early, but it was almost eight now, so he should be coming out soon.

It was odd, but his leg hurt less when he stood. He didn't know why but he could stand for hours, yet as soon as he sat or reclined on a bed the pain would come. The doctors had said it had something to do with the way the stump had healed, something about his circulation. It was particularly bad at night, and when he ran out of pills he couldn't sleep for more than an hour at a time. He was addicted to the pills by now, but that was a minor problem.

He had lost his lower leg in Afghanistan. He didn't know if the mine was Russian left over from the eighties or American from the war in which he had fought. It didn't matter. It was an enemy mine and it had killed his best friend, and another man he didn't know, and blown off his leg below the knee.

The doctors said he was lucky that he lost his leg below the knee instead of above it. They said it was much more difficult to learn to walk when the amputation was above the joint. And then they gave him a good French prosthesis, very light, very durable. He couldn't run on it but he could walk and stand and do what he must do. And in a way, he *had* been lucky to lose his leg. It was the amputation that had brought him to Sheikh Osama's attention – or, to be accurate, it was the fact that he didn't go home after he lost his leg that brought him to the sheikh's attention.

Like Osama bin Laden, he was from Arabia. He went to Afghanistan when the Americans had invaded to slaughter the Taliban, and he went there for the same reason that other Saudis did: to serve, to sacrifice, to kill – and, if necessary, to die. Like Sheikh Osama, he was well educated – he spoke English and French and some German – and he came from a wealthy family. He didn't have to go to Afghanistan. He could have stayed in Arabia, done nothing, said nothing, and lived in the lap of luxury like the corrupt royal princes. And he could have returned to Arabia when he lost his leg; his father, after a suitable period of sulking, would have taken him in. But he didn't go back.

Instead, after his leg had healed and he could walk again, he went into the mountains near the Pakistan border to find Sheikh Osama. He never did find him, of course – he had been naive and arrogant to think that he could – but Osama somehow, some way, had found him. He was taken blindfolded to the house where Osama was staying that night – he'd be in a different house or tent or cave the next night – and he had tea with him. He had been shocked at how weak the sheikh had looked and he couldn't help but wonder if he was still alive today, though he would never have said this aloud. He was with him for only an hour, but in that hour Sheikh Osama saw the depths of his belief, the fire of faith blazing in his soul. Osama told him what he must do next, then embraced him, and when Osama's cheek touched his, he was surprised by how hot the man's skin was. He could still feel that burning cheek next to his own. He would feel it for the rest of his life.

Following the meeting with Sheikh Osama, he made his way out of Pakistan and made contact with another Saudi, a man not much older than himself, a man who might one day be the next Osama. This man provided money and passports and equipment and helped him cross borders. They hadn't spoken face-to-face in three years, not since London, but this man, thousands of miles away, was still helping him. He was the one who had given him the name of the couple in Philadelphia that had hidden him for two months, and he was the one who would make sure the couple never talked about him.

Ah, finally, there he was! The boy stood for a long time on the stoop of his building, as if he was reluctant to go wherever he was going. He was holding two or three books in his right hand. The papers had said the boy was fourteen but he looked younger, much younger. And he was small, maybe five-foot-two, less than a hundred pounds. But the boy's size was irrelevant, as was his age. He had worked with martyrs who were as young as nine. All he hoped for was that the boy was ready. That his hatred had made him ready.

14

As DeMarco lay in bed he could hear the shower running – and the voice of a content woman singing in the shower.

Could life possibly get any better than this?

He'd been in Key West for five days, and for once his vacation had been exactly as advertised. The daytime temperature had been a balmy 80 degrees, the breezes had been mild, it hadn't rained once, and the sea was as warm as tepid bath water. His second night in Key West he'd been sitting in a bar on Duval Street, looking out at the ocean. He'd had swordfish for dinner and the bartender had just cleared away his plate when a woman in her late thirties sat down one bar stool over from his.

He had glanced at her and then, because she looked so good, he immediately did a ham actor's double take. *Oh, great,* he'd thought, *that was really suave.* He sat there, staring down into his drink, desperately trying to think of something clever to say, something other than *How do you like Key West? Isn't the view great? Isn't the weather wonderful?* But his brain chose that moment to vapor-lock; he couldn't produce even a passable, much less original, opening line. And then she said, 'Hi, my name's Ellie. Isn't the weather wonderful here?' It didn't sound bad at all when she said it.

Ellie Myers was cute and funny and bright. She had dark hair and bright blue eyes and a light-up-the-room smile that made little dimples in her cheeks. She also had legs that looked very good in shorts, though a bit on the pale side, as if she too resided somewhere far north of Florida. DeMarco soon found out that she was a teacher from Iowa, divorced, no kids, and, like DeMarco, had just decided to escape the grim midwestern winter to enjoy the sun. They wondered together if there was something wrong with them, going on vacation by themselves, and soon concluded that there wasn't. They went to bed together that night and for the three nights that followed. And they still had one night left, thank you, Jesus.

They had been snorkeling and had taken sunset walks on the beach. They had sat naked in a Jacuzzi, even though it had been too hot to do so. They drank too much and ate too much and made love – but not too much. And DeMarco never once thought about John Mahoney or Reza Zarif. He barely thought about his ex-wife and his asshole of a cousin.

He did make one call to New York the day he arrived in Florida and found out that Danny's case wouldn't go to trial for six months. DeMarco wondered if Danny's boss was hoping the witness would die during that time or lose her memory, or maybe he was thinking about *forcing* her to lose her memory. DeMarco wondered – but he didn't care.

Ellie came out of the bathroom. Her hair was uncombed – wet and tangled – but she was already dressed in shorts and a T-shirt that she'd bought in a tourist shop. They'd been living together for three days but she still didn't feel comfortable dressing in front of him. The T-shirt had a grinning alligator and a pink palm tree on it, and there were glittery things on the palm tree's fronds; it was okay to wear T-shirts like that when you were in Key West.

She smiled at him and said good morning. He smiled back and said he'd already called room service, and coffee and croissants were on the way. She turned around to rummage in her purse for her comb, and DeMarco admired her backside and wondered if he could talk her into getting back into bed. He had concluded a long time ago that there should be some way to stop time and cause all relationships to stay forever at the four-day point.

At that moment there was a knock on the door.

Ellie opened it and took the tray from the room service guy and overtipped him because she was feeling so good. She placed the tray on the dresser and handed DeMarco his coffee. Then she glanced down at the paper that had been delivered with the coffee.

'Oh, those bastards!' she said when she saw the headline: TERRORIST SHOT ON D.C. SHUTTLE.

Ellie went shopping, to buy Florida trinkets for her nephews and her sister and all the other poor souls she knew who were freezing back in Iowa. She asked DeMarco if he wanted to go with her but he'd begged off. He enjoyed shopping almost as much as having his teeth extracted. So instead of trailing behind Ellie, walking from store to store, bored out of his skull, he sat in a lounge chair and read the morning paper. It was the first time he'd looked at one since he'd been in Florida.

He read the three articles on the hijacking attempt, skipped the editorials on Broderick's bill, and then, because he hadn't been keeping his ear to the ground as directed, he called Jerry Hansen at Homeland Security to see if there was anything new going on with Reza Zarif. Jerry wasn't in. Too bad. He'd tried – and he wasn't going to try anymore. Hassan Zarif was just going to have to accept that his brother had done what he did for the reasons given by the boys in the Bureau.

So, beach umbrella shading his form, a drink in his hand, he picked up the novel he'd been trying to finish ever since coming to Florida. So far the novel had taken a backseat to sex, but maybe today he'd get past the sixth chapter. He'd just opened the book and started to flip through it to find the last page he'd read when his cell phone rang. He figured it was Ellie. She had said she would call him after she'd jump-started the island's economy and tell him where to meet her for lunch.

'Hel-lo,' he said cheerfully into the phone.

'Where the hell are you?' Mahoney said.

Aw, shit!

'I'm in Florida. Don't you *remember*?' DeMarco said. He could hear the whiny desperation in his voice. 'I told you I had this week off.'

'I don't remember that,' Mahoney said, 'but you need to get your ass back here. I want you to check out this guy that tried to hijack the shuttle. Broderick's goddamn bill reported out of committee yesterday, and the Senate's gonna vote on it in two friggin' weeks.'

'I don't understand,' DeMarco said. 'Is there some connection between the hijacking and Reza Zarif?'

'Goddammit!' Mahoney screamed. 'How the hell would I know? That's what I want *you* to find out.'

Rather than argue with Mahoney, DeMarco said, 'I understand.' *I understand* is a really good noncommittal reply.

DeMarco had asked himself more than once why he still worked for Mahoney. He had graduated from law school the same year his mafia father had been killed, which made employment in any decent law firm on the eastern seaboard problematic. But then his godmother, his dear Aunt Connie, came to his rescue. She and Mahoney had had an affair when they were both fifty pounds lighter, and she pressed the speaker to give DeMarco a job, which he did, and which DeMarco gratefully accepted at the time. But why was he still with the bastard all these years later? The answer to that question, unfortunately, was because he had no marketable skills. When you're a lawyer who's never practiced law, a man who acts part time as a bagman for a politician, and when you can't even put the politician's name down on a résumé as your former boss, your career options become somewhat limited. And at this point, he was heavily invested in a federal pension, possibly the only good thing about working for Mahoney.

But, pension and future career prospects aside, there was no way DeMarco was leaving Florida that day. He'd leave tomorrow, meaning he'd cut his vacation one day short, and the only reason he was doing that was because Ellie was returning to Iowa tomorrow. As far as he was concerned, there was no urgent need to look into this hijacking no matter what Mahoney said. There'd been nothing to indicate that the Bureau was wrong about Reza Zarif, and therefore no rational reason to think that there was any connection between Zarif and this nut who'd tried to hijack the shuttle. Or maybe a better reason for not rushing back to Washington was this: What in hell did Mahoney think DeMarco could do that ten thousand FBI agents weren't already doing?

If Mahoney called later in the day to see if he was back in D.C., DeMarco planned to lie to the inconsiderate shit. He'd tell him he'd been on his way but a massive accident on the bridge from Key West to the mainland had caused him to miss his plane, or that all the flights out of Miami had been delayed because security was so tight, or that . . .

Aw, screw it. He'd make up something when the time came.

15

He watched the boy for three days before he approached him.

The first day that he followed him, he saw the boy enter the public school he attended, but three hours later he left it. He was holding books in his hand when he left the school, just as he had been when he'd left his home that morning. He wondered why the boy was leaving school so early in the day.

The boy walked a block from the school – but not in the direction of his home – put his books down in an alley behind a Dumpster, and covered them with old newspapers. Then he began to walk.

He appeared to walk aimlessly, no destination in mind. He would stop occasionally and sit at a bus stop or on a park bench or on a stoop. But he would just sit, looking down at his feet, not even paying attention to the people around him. The boy was unhappy and something was weighing heavily on his spirit. This was good.

The next day when the boy left his apartment building, he put his schoolbooks down behind another Dumpster, this one right near his apartment, and began walking again. For five hours he either walked or sat. He did nothing, participated in no activity, spoke to no one, ate nothing, then returned to his apartment, picked up the schoolbooks he'd hidden, and went into the building where he and his mother lived. He had obviously decided to stop going to school but didn't want his mother to know.

On his fourth day in Cleveland, two things happened: a man, a Muslim, tried to hijack a plane in New York and that was the day he approached the boy.

He needed to find out more about the hijacking, but from what he'd heard it appeared that his brethren had helped the hijacker. Unfortunately, just as *he* had failed in Baltimore, whoever had assisted the man in New York had also failed. But not completely.

What Sheikh Osama wanted was for the faithful who lived in Western countries to rise up against the infidels. If outsiders attacked, as they had on 9/11, people would die, and the cause would be advanced, but what was happening now was far better. In London, in Madrid, in Paris, all the recent attacks had involved Muslims who *lived* in those countries – and that was important. First, the security forces of those countries, which were already stretched thin, were now forced to spend more time looking inward, at their own citizens. And this provided the second advantage. By investigating their own citizens, they alienated them. People already scorned because of their skin color and their religion were now harassed by the police, detained, their houses searched – and sometimes, as had been the case with the boy's father, their lives were destroyed. The fact that there had been two back-to-back attacks on Washington committed by Americans . . . Well, even though the attacks had failed, they clearly demonstrated that God listened to Sheikh Osama.

When he approached, the boy was sitting on the ground, on a small grassy bluff overlooking the Cuyahoga River. He had come to this place twice before; he seemed to like watching the river as it flowed away from this ugly town. He sat down next to the boy. The boy glanced over at him but didn't say anything, and looked back down at the river. He greeted the boy in the language of the boy's father and wished God's blessings on him. He could tell the boy was surprised to be addressed this way, but still he didn't respond.

He had been thinking for four days about what he would say to the boy during their first meeting. He had been thinking that he would begin by saying how sorry he was for what had happened to the boy's father and then lie to him and tell him how something similar had happened to someone he had loved. But he didn't want to begin with a lie, and he still had not come to a decision when he sat down next to the boy. And then God told him how to begin.

He said, 'What do you think about this man who tried to hijack that airplane this morning?' And the boy, though he was still looking at the river and not at him, said, 'I think it's too bad he was killed before he could do what he planned.'

There are times when you meet someone and you have an instant connection. It was that way between him and the boy. The boy, of course, needed a father – so he would become his father. Also his teacher, his brother, and his friend. He would become whatever he needed to become to make the boy his own.

He had found the boy on the Internet while hiding in Philadelphia. He had searched for tragedy, and there he was. The boy's father had made the mistake of going home to see his dying mother in Pakistan and, through sheer coincidence, through sheer bad luck, he happened to be in his mother's village at the same time that one of Osama's warriors was passing through. The Pakistani spies who worked for the Americans relayed this information to the CIA, and when the man returned home he was detained and questioned. He was detained for three months before the FBI was finally satisfied that he had no connection with al-Qaeda – other than being a Muslim.

The boy's father had had a weak heart to begin with, and the stress caused by his imprisonment worsened his condition. He had also owned a shoe repair business, and in the time he was in jail his business died like a plant that has not been watered. His wife, a simple woman who had never become acclimated to American life, was brought to the brink of a nervous breakdown from being questioned by the police and because of what was happening to her husband. And the boy, of course, was harassed by his schoolmates, all those Christians who had pretended to be his friends. Two months after being released from jail, the boy's father had a heart attack and died. The boy's mother, who now survived on a small Social Security check, had to sell her home and move into a small apartment in a dirty part of a dirty city. The boy told him later that his mother was still so stunned by what had happened that she barely spoke.

He put a hand on the boy's thin shoulder and said, 'You haven't eaten all day. Let's go somewhere and get some tea and some food. Let's go talk about your father. Let's talk about who you are.'

16

'You look like you've been someplace where the sun actually shines,' Hansen said.

'Yeah, Key West,' DeMarco said.

He'd gotten off the plane an hour ago and managed to make it to Jerry Hansen's office at Homeland Security just as Hansen was shutting off his computer and locking up his safe. DeMarco's plane had in fact been delayed leaving Miami because of security. They were searching every carry-on bag going onto every plane because of the attempted hijacking of the New York–D.C. shuttle.

'Key West,' Hansen echoed. 'Man, that sounds good. It must have been ten degrees when I left for work this morning.'

'Is that right?' DeMarco said. He didn't want to talk with Hansen about the weather or his aborted vacation. 'I was just wondering if you could fill me in on that hijacker, like you did before with Reza Zarif.'

'I dunno,' Hansen said. 'The general said I could talk to you about Zarif; he didn't say anything about this other guy. Plus it's kinda late.'

'I cleared it with the general,' DeMarco lied. 'Call him up. He'll tell you.'

DeMarco was betting that Andy Banks's staff hated talking to him, Banks being the unpleasant, unreasonable, demanding bastard that he was.

Hansen studied DeMarco's face, looking for signs that DeMarco was lying.

'Nah, that's okay,' Hansen said, after a moment. 'I'll take your word for it. Anyway, it's just like it was with Zarif. If you read the paper this morning, you got almost everything.'

Hansen then told DeMarco just what he'd already read in the newspaper. Twenty-five years ago Youseff Khalid had left Somalia with his parents, became an American citizen, and eventually earned a degree in computer sciences from Colorado State University. He had worked for IBM in New York City for nine years but was laid off three months ago. According to IBM, Youseff had just been a random casualty of corporate downsizing, meaning there was probably some guy in India who was now doing his job. Youseff, however, didn't accept this explanation. He was convinced that he'd been fired because he was both black and Muslim, and he had filed a discrimination suit. He'd been informed a week ago that it would probably take two or three years before anyone would make a decision on his lawsuit, and in the three months since he'd lost his job the only work he had been able to find involved making coffee drinks for people who didn't need caffeine. Youseff's friends told the FBI that Youseff had been depressed, angry, and absolutely convinced that he was a victim of racial and religious bigotry.

Youseff's congressman, Representative Charles Cantrell from the fourteenth district of New York, came forward about this time and showed the FBI two letters that he'd received from Youseff. The first letter politely asked Cantrell for help. The second letter, written a month later, cursed Cantrell to the heavens for caring more about IBM than he did about a poor constituent – which, of course, Cantrell did: IBM was a major contributor; Youseff was not. Youseff's second letter concluded with the statement that Shakespeare got it only *half* right: We shouldn't just kill all the lawyers, we should kill all the lawmakers too. Then the FBI discovered that Youseff had taken six flying lessons four years earlier but had never obtained a pilot's license.

The FBI added up the facts: a Muslim with a grievance plus flying lessons plus a letter to his congressman saying all lawmakers should be killed, and the Bureau concluded it was very likely that Youseff had planned to crash the shuttle into the

Capitol after he had hijacked it. And because the shuttle was cleared to land at Reagan National, it was possible that Youseff could have entered the no-fly zone and crashed the plane before the Capitol's defenders had time to react and shoot it down.

To DeMarco there was one major difference between Reza Zarif and Youseff Khalid, which was that Khalid's motive seemed more substantial. It appeared that Zarif had just wigged out and turned kamikaze. Khalid, on the other hand, had, at least from his perspective, a more legitimate complaint. He'd lost his job because of what he thought was prejudice and then was ignored after trying to rectify the situation by filing a lawsuit and writing his congressman. It may have been irrational to try to hijack a plane and crash it into the Capitol, but at least DeMarco could somewhat understand his reasoning.

Come to think of it, there was another major difference between Khalid and Zarif: Khalid, thank God, hadn't killed his wife and his three kids.

'Did the FBI uncover any sort of connection between Reza Zarif and this hijacker?' DeMarco asked. 'You know, phone calls to each other, letters from the same mosque, e-mails, common friends, anything like that?'

'No, and they looked hard,' Hansen said.

'Where'd he get the gun he snuck on the plane?' DeMarco asked.

'Now *that's* the sixty-four thousand-dollar question,' Hansen said. 'It's the gun that makes the Bureau think some bad guys – you know, al-Qaeda – may have gone to Youseff and convinced him to do what he did. This weapon was special. The Bureau's lab thinks at least one part came from India, and it took pretty high-tech equipment to make the plastic parts. This weapon definitely wasn't somethin' you could pick up in your average gun shop.'

'How 'bout from someone like Donny Cray?' DeMarco said.

'No way. Cray didn't have the equipment or the know-how to make something like this,' Hansen said, as he put on his coat. 'And in case you're wondering, the Bureau didn't find Cray's fingerprints in Khalid's house or in his car or on the gun.'

'But there's no trail to any specific terrorist group,' DeMarco said.

'Not yet, but Jesus, DeMarco, this thing just happened two days ago. Look, I gotta get—'

'Did the Bureau ever find Donny Cray?' DeMarco said.

'Yeah they found him. His body, anyway.'

Hansen wrapped a bright orange scarf around his neck and started toward the door, but DeMarco remained seated.

'His body?' DeMarco said.

'Yeah. It was just like I told you. The guy hitched his trailer to his pickup, headed south, and drove off the road. And he left the same day the roads were icier than shit. Anyway, some hunter found the pickup and the trailer in a gulch. Cray's neck had snapped and his girlfriend – her head went through the windshield. Neither of them was wearing seat belts, and his truck was so damn old it didn't have air bags. Look, I gotta catch—'

'So the FBI wasn't able to confirm that Cray really sold Reza a gun.'

'No, it's hard to talk to a dead guy, but Cray selling him a gun still makes a hell of a lot more sense than Cray having been to Zarif's house or him being some kind of Muslim convert al-Qaeda operative. Look, I'm outta here.'

DeMarco thanked Hansen and trailed behind him as he left the Homeland Security building. He didn't even try to keep up; he bet that the fastest the guy moved all day was when he was leaving work.

As DeMarco watched Hansen fleeing, he was thinking that maybe now he could report back to Mahoney and tell him that he was through investigating Reza Zarif. He hadn't uncovered any flaws in the FBI's explanation for either event, and there didn't appear to be any connection between Reza and Youseff Khalid.

But one thing did bother him, and the thing just wouldn't go away. It was like a woodpecker rapping on the back of his head.

It bothered him that Donny Cray had died before the FBI could talk to him.

17

The bar was called Mr Days. Flat-screen television sets marched across the walls of the place, one hanging every five feet, and showing on all those screens was nothing but sporting events. The sound on the sets had been muted, and captions ran across the bottom of the pictures so one could read the all-too-familiar clichés of the broadcasters. Everything that could be said about sports had already been said a thousand times over, but apparently *something* had to be said about these events.

DeMarco was waiting for a man named Barry King who worked for the DEA. He wanted to talk to King about Donny Cray. DeMarco felt somewhat guilty about not having followed up on Cray earlier; he probably would have had he not been so anxious to escape D.C. and bask in the sun. But, he rationalized, he really didn't have any reason to investigate Cray more thoroughly until Cray died. Until then, the FBI's explanation that Cray had most likely sold Reza the gun had sounded plausible; now, the coincidence of his dying before the Bureau could confirm the sale was disturbing.

As he waited for King, DeMarco thought about the marvelous time he'd had in Key West with Ellie Myers. He genuinely liked the woman in every way, and had she lived nearby, it was possible the relationship might have developed into something more than five days of sex and piña coladas. But she lived in Iowa, for Christ's sake, a thousand miles away.

DeMarco had promised, as they kissed goodbye at the airport, that if he ever went to Iowa – God only knows why *anyone* ever went to Iowa – he would call her. She in turn had promised that if she ever came to D.C., she would do the same. But they both knew that the wonderful week they'd spent together was almost certainly the last they'd see of each other.

DeMarco was convinced that in some prior life he had done something horrible to women. There had to be some cosmic explanation for his terrible luck with the opposite sex. He married a woman who had cheated on him with his own cousin. A few months ago he met an FBI agent – a pretty lady from his old neighborhood back in New York named Diane Carlucci – and right after he'd fallen in love with her the Bureau reassigned her to Los Angeles, which was even farther from Washington than Iowa. And now he meets a cute schoolteacher with a sense of humor, has a wonderful vacation fling just like he'd always wanted, only to find out he wanted more. God was either testing him or toying with him, one or the other.

Fortunately, before DeMarco could get more depressed, King strolled into the bar. He was a lanky, fidgety guy, one of those people blessed with a metabolism that allowed him to eat like a hog and never gain weight. He and DeMarco played on a softball team composed of men over forty who made up for their lack of youth and skill by being absurdly competitive in games that didn't matter.

King had agreed to pull the DEA's file on Donny Cray, not because DeMarco worked for Congress but because he and King were friends. He knew they were friends because King had once called DeMarco to help him move a sofa into his house, and once DeMarco had called King when he had to get a new washing machine down into his basement. That, DeMarco figured, was a good definition of a friend: someone you called when you had something you couldn't lift on your own.

After DeMarco had told King about Cray's death and his connection to Reza Zarif, King said, 'According to our records, Cray was just a nasty cracker who spent half his life in jail. He'd been caught for using dope, selling dope, making dope, and transporting dope. He was also into guns. He'd modify 'em – you know, turn rifles into machine guns, that sorta thing – then sell 'em. But if you want to know more about the gun stuff, you'll have to talk to somebody at ATF.'

This was typical: To find out about one small-time criminal, DeMarco would have to talk to the DEA, the ATF, the FBI, and God knows how many state and city cop shops.

'The funny thing about Cray was . . .'

At that moment, on the television directly above their heads, one welterweight African American boxer began to pummel the shit out of a Puerto Rican boxer, both men looking as if they weighed maybe eighty pounds. The poundee had been pinned into a corner, his head snapping back with every punch, and just when it looked like the ref was about to stop the fight – which would have really pissed off all the rich white guys who'd paid to see it – the bell rang. DeMarco and King watched as the Puerto Rican's cut man slit the puffy bag of blood beneath the boxer's left eye, so that in the next round he'd be able to see the fist that would turn his brain to mush.

'Oh, yuck,' King said, as blood squirted from the boxer's face.

'You were saying about Cray,' DeMarco said.

'Oh, yeah. The funny thing is that in the last two years this guy wasn't arrested once. He'd been working for a guy named Jubal Pugh.'

'*Jubal?*'

'Yeah. Southerners, go figure. Anyway, Pugh, from what I've heard, is one of the biggest meth distributors in Virginia.'

'From what you've heard?'

'Yeah. He's not in the area I cover.'

Great, more bureaucratic divisions.

'This guy Pugh is supposed to be careful, and apparently Cray had been doing exactly what Pugh told him to do, which explains why he hadn't been nabbed for anything lately. But it makes me wonder what he was doing selling a gun to Zarif.'

'You don't think he would have sold Zarif a gun?' DeMarco said. 'Why not? Because he was a Muslim?'

'No, he wouldn't have cared if Zarif was a Muslim. Donny would have sold a gun to a four-year-old if the four-year-old had the money. What I'm saying is, I'm surprised he was selling guns at the same time he was working for Pugh. Pugh's into dope, not guns, and from what I've heard about Pugh, he wouldn't like it if one of his guys was moonlighting.'

'Huh,' DeMarco said. 'So that's the whole story on Cray? Drugs and guns?'

'No,' King said, 'drugs and guns are the only things he was convicted for. He's probably got some kinda back story – been buggered by an uncle or starved by his foster parents – but whatever the reason, Donny was one mean son of a bitch. He pistol-whipped a neighbor practically to death because the guy told him to keep his dog chained up. He didn't do time for that because the neighbor was afraid to testify. And he smacked a couple of his girlfriends around, bad enough to put one in the hospital for a week. Why in God's name a woman would hook up with someone like him is a mystery to me. I also saw one note on his sheet that said he was suspected of killing another meth dealer when he worked for Pugh but, like I said, I don't know anything about Pugh.'

'Was Cray political at all?' DeMarco said.

.'Political?' King said.

'You know, into radical causes, white-power stuff, anything like that?'

'Not that I know of, but I think Pugh might be. I remember hearing something, but I can't remember what.'

'And to find out, I have to talk to somebody else over at the DEA,' DeMarco said.

'Yeah, Patsy Hall. She's the expert on Pugh. She hates his guts.'

King said he'd get DeMarco in to see Hall if he wanted to talk to her, but it would have to be in a week or so because right now she was out of town.

DeMarco and King watched the rest of the fight, which the ref finally stopped when the Puerto Rican's face resembled a plate of uncooked ground beef. As the cameras were showing a close-up of what used to be the Puerto Rican's nose, DeMarco thought to himself that you'd have to hold a gun to his head to get him to climb into a ring with a professional boxer.

And then DeMarco was no longer seeing what was on the television screen. It was as if his brain had just changed lanes. *You'd have to hold a gun to his head.*

Goddammit. He wanted to be *done* with this thing with Reza Zarif, but now there was something else he needed to do. He was going to have to go to New York and talk to Youseff Khalid's wife.

He told King it was time for him to leave because he had to go home and buy an airline ticket and pack for a trip, but King begged him to stay. King wasn't yet ready to face his wife and three noisy kids. And it wasn't hard to twist DeMarco's arm. It wasn't like he had that much to pack.

So he sat there with King and drank half a dozen more beers and tried to focus on three TV sets simultaneously, one showing another fight, one a hockey game in Toronto, and the third a golf tournament in San Diego. The shots of blue skies and palm trees in California reminded DeMarco of Key West, which in turn reminded him of Ellie.

The next morning DeMarco woke up late and with a terrible hangover. Beer always gave him one, so why did he drink it? The answer came from that great western philosopher John Wayne: *Sometimes a man's gotta do what a man's gotta do.*

He caught a midafternoon shuttle up to New York and spent the night at his mother's place in Queens. The following morning, as he'd consumed no beer and been fawned over and fed by his mom, he woke up bright-eyed and bushy-tailed, ready to conquer the world.

He took a cab to an apartment building in the Astoria section of Queens, where his knock was answered by an enormous scowling black woman in a bright orange and yellow caftan.

'Are you Mrs Khalid?' DeMarco asked.

'No,' the woman said. 'Who are you? A reporter? Police?'

The woman's English was heavily accented but understandable; what her native tongue was DeMarco had no idea.

'No, ma'am,' he said, and showed her his ID and explained that he worked for the U.S. Congress.

The woman glanced at his identification and looked back at DeMarco's face. She had a truly impressive scowl. He bet she scared the hell out of small children.

'What do you want?' she said.

'Just to speak to Mrs Khalid. I want . . . I *need* to ask her a few questions.'

'About what?'

'Is she here?' DeMarco said. This woman may have had him outweighed and intimidated, but she was starting to annoy him.

The woman stood there for a moment longer, like the immovable object she was, and finally stepped back so DeMarco could enter the apartment. Sitting on a couch inside the small apartment was another black woman. This woman was wearing a scarf on her head and a drab gray-colored robe that reached her knees. Beneath the robe she had on jeans. Sitting near the woman were three children, two girls and one boy, ranging in age from maybe two to eight. All the children had enormous luminous dark eyes.

The scowling woman who had opened the door said something in a foreign language that DeMarco couldn't identify, and the children left the room without a murmur of protest. As the children were leaving, DeMarco looked for some sign that Mrs Khalid and her children had been recently abused. This was important, but he couldn't see any marks or bruises or any other indicator that she or her kids had been hurt or restrained in any way. All he could see was that Mrs Khalid was scared to death.

'The reason I'm here,' DeMarco said, 'is I'd like to know if you have any other explanation for why your husband did what he did. I mean, I know he lost his job and he was angry, but hijacking an airplane?' Hell, he might as well spit it out. 'Look, what I'm trying to say is: Did someone *make* Youseff hijack that plane?'

The big woman spoke. 'Mrs Khalid doesn't speak English,' she said.

Oh, great.

'Well, can you tell her what I said?' DeMarco asked.

The big woman talked to Youseff's wife for what seemed an unusually long time for a simple question, and Mrs Khalid's response was equally long. As she spoke, DeMarco could hear the agony in her voice even if he couldn't understand the words. Finally the big woman turned to DeMarco and said, 'She doesn't know.'

All that talk, and he gets a three-word response.

'Then ask her if she or her children were used in any way to force her husband to hijack the plane.' She should at least know *that*, DeMarco was thinking.

The woman looked at DeMarco for a moment as if he were crazy, then had another long conversation with Mrs Khalid. The women must have talked for at least three minutes, and by the time they were done Mrs Khalid was weeping.

'She says no,' the big woman said to DeMarco.

Jesus, this was hopeless. He had no idea what the two women were saying to each other – he didn't even know what language they were speaking – and all he was getting was one-word answers. He told the big woman he didn't have anything else to ask and rose to leave. As he was doing so, Mrs Khalid said something to him.

The big woman said to DeMarco, 'She wants to know what will happen to her and her children. Will they be sent back to Africa?'

'I'm sorry,' DeMarco said, 'but I have no idea.' Then, because he knew his response had just added to the poor woman's anguish, he added, 'But I'm sure that if she wasn't involved in any way with what her husband did she has nothing to fear.'

'Bullshit,' the big woman said. She pronounced the word perfectly.

After his short fruitless meeting with Mrs Khalid, DeMarco had five hours to kill before his flight back to D.C. so he decided to visit a man named Orin Blunt. Blunt was the air marshal who had shot Youseff Khalid in the head from a sitting position in the airplane.

The newspapers said there'd been no interaction between Blunt and Khalid before the shooting, but DeMarco still wanted to talk to him. He wanted to hear directly about the moments leading up to the hijacking and see if Blunt remembered anything Khalid had said that hadn't been reported in the papers. The other thing was – and he didn't know why – DeMarco just wanted to put his eyes on the guy.

About the only thing DeMarco knew about federal air marshals was what he'd seen on a television show, probably *60 Minutes*. At one time the marshals had worked for the FAA in the Department of Transportation, but when the Department of Homeland Security was formed, the air marshals were placed under the Transportation Security Administration. The only other thing he knew was that to be a marshal one had to be able to shoot the eye out of a gnat with a handgun, such a qualification being reasonable if your job entailed shooting hijackers in crowded airplanes flying at thirty-five thousand feet.

Blunt worked out of an office at JFK Airport. DeMarco took a cab to the airport and located the air marshals' office, where he found three men engaged in an intense discussion about the New York Giants. Two of the men were white, the third man black, and none of them was physically impressive. They were all of average height and weight, not muscular but not skinny or fat either. If you saw them seated in the coach section of an airplane dressed in rumpled suits, they'd look like tired salesmen on their way home.

DeMarco showed them his ID and told them he was a lawyer who worked for Congress. If the marshals were impressed, they disguised their awe quite well. He asked where he could find Blunt and was told that the man was on administrative leave. That made sense. DeMarco guessed that when a marshal shot somebody – though he couldn't recall this ever happening before – the bosses would prob-ably conduct some sort of review and take the guy off duty until the review was complete. But he didn't bother to confirm this with the three guys in the bullpen; he could tell they'd be no help at all. When he asked where Blunt lived, they as much as told him to go shit in his hat. If he wanted that sort of information he'd have to talk to their supervisor, who was in D.C. and wouldn't be back for two days.

So DeMarco thanked Blunt's coworkers for all their help, called directory assistance, and got an address and a phone number for Blunt in the town of Commack on Long Island. He called the phone number; nobody answered. He caught another cab, took a long, expensive ride out to Blunt's place, and discovered that Blunt wasn't home.

There's an old mountain man's saying: Some days you eat the bear and some days the bear eats you. The bear, that day, had DeMarco for breakfast, lunch, and dinner.

18

He had spent every day with the boy for the last five days. The boy would come to his motel in the morning and they would pray together and read the Koran for an hour – and then they would begin to talk. He soon found out that he didn't need to fan the boy's hatred. What he did instead was provide a structure for his beliefs, some perspective, and, of course, the history that the boy lacked. Having spent his whole life in America, the boy's concept of reality, of what was happening in the rest of the world, was completely distorted. So he told the boy about his own people, how they'd suffered, how they'd died, how they'd been exploited – and how they would continue to be exploited if good men didn't act. He spoke a lot about how the world would be a better place if everyone followed the true path. And the boy soaked it all up, like he'd been waiting his whole life to have someone explain the things to him that he already felt in his heart but didn't know how to put into words.

The boy was like a nearly finished sculpture. Only a few deft chisel strokes were needed for it to become precisely the form the artist desired.

This boy was different from the young men he had recruited in Baltimore. There was nothing frivolous about him. He paid attention, he didn't fidget, he didn't get bored; he was *focused*, intensely focused. And he had no doubts about the boy's faith. He had never been certain, but he had thought from the very beginning that the two from Baltimore had agreed to help him only because of the money he had promised them – and that was why he'd set the detonator to kill them as soon as they armed the bomb. But this boy was different. He reminded him very much of another boy, one in Indonesia whom he had trained, a boy who had walked onto a bus and praised God as he detonated the bomb strapped to his narrow chest.

Yes, he knew this boy's heart. It was time to take the next step.

'Come with me,' he said, and they took a city bus to a used-car lot. He wanted a pickup truck. He could put things in the back of a truck: old furniture, boxes, maybe grass clippings and a lawn mower – things that would make it look as if he and the boy were just a couple of immigrants engaged in menial manual labor. But the trucks on the lot were either too big – he didn't feel comfortable driving a large vehicle in the city – or too new and expensive. He said this to the salesman, a man whose teeth were so white he must have gargled with bleach.

'I think I have just what you're looking for,' the salesman said, and showed them a type of automobile he'd never seen before. The front part of the vehicle looked like a sedan but the back was a truck. 'It's called an El Camino,' the salesman said. 'It's made by Chevy. Ford used to make one just like it called the Ranchero. It rides like a car, looks classy, good horsepower, *and* you can haul stuff in it. This one's an 'eighty-six and only has ninety thousand miles on it. I can let you have it for twenty-five hundred.'

El Camino. Silly name, he thought, but typical of foolish Americans and their obsession with automobiles. It was an odd color too – a pale green – but the price was acceptable and he liked that it had a low profile and wasn't so big he'd feel uncomfortable driving it. He would have preferred one of the more conventional-looking trucks made by Toyota or Honda, but this – this El Camino – would do.

Then, for the first time, he and the boy made the 120-mile journey to a city that sat on the western edge of Lake Erie. He stopped the car on a hill and pointed. He pointed at the refinery – and at the tanks inside the refinery that contained the chemical.

19

Mahoney sat in his condo at the Watergate, staring out the window holding a glass filled with bourbon and crushed ice against his forehead. He had a headache, and the cool glass made his head feel better. It never occurred to him that the bourbon in the glass had made his head hurt in the first place.

Mary Pat had purchased the condo after his fifth term, maybe thinking that after having served in the House for ten years, her husband's career in politics was secure enough to invest in a permanent D.C. residence. He liked the place mostly because it was a quick drive to his office and because of the view. From where he sat he could see the dome of the Capitol, all lit up at night, looking like a cathedral – a cathedral where the unholy gathered.

Naturally, living at the Watergate made him

occasionally reflect on Richard Nixon. What had always amazed Mahoney most about Nixon was not the cover-up and all that stuff. What had amazed him was that the man hadn't liked people. Mahoney couldn't imagine being a politician and not liking people. Clinton, Kennedy, Truman, Bush – all of them had seemed to genuinely enjoy spending some time with the folks who had elected them. It was certainly that way with Mahoney; it wasn't an act with him. He took real pleasure eatin' barbecue with a bunch of blue-collar guys and their wives. But Nixon, that gloomy bastard, always came across as a man who preferred to hide in his office, the door bolted, having as little contact with the common folk as he possibly could. Hell, even an asshole like Broderick seemed to like people – or at least some of them.

Based on the mail Mahoney had been getting, a lot of folks back home favored Broderick's thinking, which wasn't all that surprising. Not only were people scared, but Mahoney's district included Boston, a city where not that long ago a black man entering certain parts of the town was likely to get an Irish thrashing. There may have been a lot of liberal thinkers at Harvard and MIT, but in places like Southie and in suburbs like Revere and Chelsea, people tended not to be so cerebral.

But Broderick's bill was just *wrong*. To Mahoney this wasn't a matter of constitutional law, although the Supreme Court might have a problem with it. It was instead a matter of fairness. An American citizen had a right to be treated like all other Americans until he did something illegal, something that could be proven to violate the law. And there was something else. It was one thing to think of Muslims in the abstract, faceless strangers practicing their incomprehensible religion, but when you actually knew a good decent Muslim family the way Mahoney knew the Zarifs – well, it changed the way you thought about what Broderick was proposing.

The problem was that Broderick's damn bill just kept gathering momentum. You couldn't turn on a television set without seeing two people debating it, and the editorial pages of every newspaper in the country had been devoted to the topic for the last three months. Oprah, of course, had a show where she dressed in a burka and compared the Muslim registry proposal to the Holocaust and Japanese internment camps and lynchings in the South. God bless Oprah.

And lately, almost assuredly because of all the media attention on the subject, other things were starting to happen. Customs agents on the Canadian–Michigan border riddled a car with bullets and killed the driver – a turban-wearing Sikh, not a Muslim – when he attempted to flee a security checkpoint. It turned out the man had two pounds of hashish hidden in his spare tire. Subway cops in Chicago stopped three

Muslim teenagers who 'looked suspicious,' and when the teenagers sassed the cops, one of them got thumped with a nightstick and was still in a coma. In Kansas City, an Arabic-looking kid was jumped by two college football players because they'd seen the kid shove a parcel into the courthouse mail slot and run away from the building, which in fact the kid had done. He worked for a law firm and was dropping off a transcript that the courthouse clerk had wanted back that night, and he was running to catch his bus. His neck was accidentally broken during the tussle. In Dallas, people stampeded out of a Wal-Mart, screaming their heads off, when a Muslim woman entered the store with a bulge under her coat. It turned out that the woman had not wrapped sticks of dynamite around her torso; she was pregnant.

Mahoney could understand that people were afraid. They were terrified that they or their loved ones might be the victim of the next suicide attack. He could also understand why the Japanese were put in the camps after Pearl Harbor and how McCarthy had been able to whip the country into a Commie-hunting frenzy in the years following World War II when ol' Joe Stalin had the bomb. He didn't like it, but he could understand it. And he also knew that if Broderick's bill passed, people would one day regret what they had done just as they now regretted having interned the Japanese fifty years ago. But what really pissed him off were people like Bill

Broderick, politicians who took advantage of a frightening situation and fanned the flames of hatred and bigotry to get their way.

What he wished was that something else would happen – he didn't know what, but something. Some scandal, some crisis; hell, even some natural disaster. Anything that would take people's minds off the Muslims, anything that would change the current focus and provide some time for people to come to their senses.

Dear Lord, Mahoney prayed, *please let things just quiet down for a while*.

It had been a long time since John Mahoney had prayed.

20

Mustafa Ahmed was praying as he walked slowly across the Capitol's grounds toward the West Terrace. There were tourists everywhere, even as cold as it was. He stopped when he reached the wooden sawhorses barricading the steps leading up to the Capitol and looked up at the building, a building he'd always loved.

Before 9/11, people could simply walk up the steps and stand on the terrace and look back at the National Mall, or they could walk right into the Capitol itself and look around. But no longer; all that had changed. Now, to see the interior of the building, tourists had to go through a visitor's entry and pass through metal detectors and wait while their bags were searched. And the exterior of the building, including the West Terrace, was surrounded by wooden and concrete barricades, and behind the barricades stood uniformed U.S. Capitol policemen. Mustafa could see two of the policemen standing there now, up at the top of the steps, and just as he crossed the barrier a third officer joined the other two men.

'Sir,' one of the policemen called out, 'you can't come up this way. You need to use the tourist entrance.'

Mustafa ignored the cop and slowly continued up the steps.

'Sir!' the cop yelled. 'Did you hear what I said?'

And then Mustafa opened his raincoat.

Beneath his raincoat was a canvas vest, and attached to the vest were twenty small bricks of C-4 explosive. White, red, and blue wires connected the bricks to each other. In Mustafa's right hand was a dead man's switch. The switch was a black tube about four inches long, and wires ran from the switch, up his arm, through his coat sleeve, and connected to a detonator. The switch was called a dead man's switch because if Mustafa took his thumb off the little button on the top of the switch – or if his thumb was to come off because he had been killed – the C-4 would explode.

Mustafa continued to walk up the steps, his pace measured, his arms spread wide. The U.S. Capitol policemen, all three of them, now had their weapons out. They were screaming at Mustafa; they were screaming at the tourists to run away; they were screaming at one another.

Then one of the policemen shot Mustafa three times in the chest.

The last thought Mustafa Ahmed had before he died was: Thank God. They hadn't lied to him when they said the bomb wouldn't explode.

DeMarco and Mahoney had been in their respective offices when Mustafa Ahmed was killed.

Mahoney's office was on the second floor. It was spacious, filled with historically significant furniture, and had a view appropriate for a man of his station. He had been sitting behind his desk, sipping coffee laced with bourbon as he listened to one of his staff brief him on a bill having to do with tax benefits for people who made fuel out of corn, a subject simultaneously so boring and so complex that it made his brain ache.

DeMarco had been in his windowless box in the subbasement, and the only thing historically significant about his office furniture – one wooden desk, two chairs, and an empty file cabinet – was that the items had been purchased when Jimmy Carter was president. When Mustafa Ahmed was killed, he had been on the phone trying once again to contact the air marshal who had shot Youseff Khalid.

According to structural engineers hired by Fox News, had Mustafa been allowed to enter the building, and had his bomb exploded inside, the dome of the building might have collapsed into the rotunda, and then all the rubble would have continued down-ward, squashing DeMarco pancake-flat as he sat in his office.

Mahoney would most likely have died too. But in Mahoney's case, he could have been killed if the bomb had exploded when Mustafa was standing on the West Terrace steps. The walls in Mahoney's office could have imploded and crushed him, or the glass in the windows could have blown out, a million sharp pieces, severing Mahoney's head from his thick neck.

Mahoney had not heard the shots that killed Mustafa but he did hear the sirens. It seemed that every car in Washington equipped with a siren was simultaneously headed toward the Capitol. He was wondering what all the commotion was about when two plain-clothed U.S. Capitol policemen burst into his office and told him he had to leave immediately. As the security guys were hustling Mahoney from his office, he asked what the hell was going on.

'Some Muslim son of a bitch just tried to blow up the Capitol,' one of the cops said. 'We need to get you out of here until we can sweep the building.'

DeMarco left the Capitol along with a few hundred other people like himself – meaning those not suffi-ciently important to warrant personal protection. He was standing on Independence Avenue, watching all the cops milling about, when a woman grabbed his arm. 'Come on, honey,' she said, 'let's go over to Bullfeathers and get us a drink. You know they're not gonna let us back in for a couple of hours.'

The woman – a forty-year-old redhead with a body sculpted by some sadist who taught aerobics – worked for the Majority Whip, and whenever she saw DeMarco she treated him to a smile that was more than just friendly. According to Mahoney's secretary, a woman who could be relied upon for such information, the redhead was recently divorced and was trying to make up for twenty years of monogamy.

DeMarco wanted to know about the dead man lying on the West Terrace steps, but when he saw all the news vans he figured he'd learn more sitting in a bar and watching television than he would by bothering the Capitol cops.

'Sounds good,' he said to the redhead, but he felt leery, like a little kid who'd just been offered a ride by a stranger.

21

DeMarco turned down an offer from the redhead –
to make him a good home-cooked dinner – even
when she winked and said that dessert would be
something special. Two hours later was ringing the
doorbell of a large expensive home in McLean,
Virginia. The home belonged to a lady named Emma.

The door was answered by a young woman in her
thirties. The young woman was tall and willowy and
blond and lovely. Her name was Christine and she
played a cello in the National Symphony. Christine
was Emma's lover.

DeMarco had known Emma for a decade, but
Christine had only been with her the last three years.
During those three years, DeMarco discovered that
he and Christine had absolutely nothing in common.
He thought classical music was a cure for insomnia

and she thought people who liked football were direct descendants of Attila the Hun. So their conversations, most times they met, usually went like this:

DeMarco: 'Hey, how you doin'?'

Christine: 'Fine. How are you?'

DeMarco: 'Good. Is Emma here?'

Christine: 'She's in the kitchen.'

But this day their discourse was slightly different. When Christine answered the door, DeMacro could see she was holding something in her hands. He studied the thing. He knew it was technically a dog, some micro-breed with long hair and bulging wet brown eyes and legs the diameter of a pencil. DeMarco also noticed the critter was trembling even though it was cupped in Christine's graceful hands. Maybe the cold air coming through the door was causing the tremors, but DeMarco suspected the animal shivered whenever a door opened. Each time it was exposed to the outside world anything bigger than a hummingbird could swoop down and carry it off in its talons.

Oh, boy, DeMarco thought. He knew Emma liked dogs, but real dogs, practical dogs – dogs like German shepherds and Doberman pinschers and bloodhounds. She would not like something that looked like a furry hand puppet. And Emma was a neat freak. She wouldn't appreciate canine hair on her upholstery or tiny dog turds on her manicured lawn. DeMarco was guessing that the prissy mutt in

Christine's hands was a source of high tension in her and Emma's shared domain.

'Ah, see you got a dog,' DeMarco said.

'Yes,' Christine said, clutching the animal to her small bosom, looking defensive, looking ready for a fight.

'What's its name?'

Christine blinked once and said, 'I named him Joe. I always wanted a little Joe of my own to boss around.'

He was pretty sure she was pulling his chain, but not completely. 'You're kidding,' he said.

'Maybe,' she said.

Christine not only played the cello at the professional level, she had a master's in mathematics, music and math seeming to go together. She could be a bit of a ditz at times but she probably had an IQ that was in a category of its own. In a verbal sparring match, DeMarco figured he was likely to get a bloody nose.

'Well,' he said, 'it's . . . he's really cute. Is Emma here?'

'She's in the kitchen,' Christine said, and walked away, stroking the dog and cooing to calm its nearly shattered nerves.

DeMarco strolled into the kitchen. Emma was sitting at the table reading the business section of *The Washington Post*. DeMarco knew Emma had money, and he suspected this might have something to do with the fact that she read stock reports instead of box scores.

Like Christine, Emma was tall and slim. She had features that DeMarco always thought of as regal, a profile you'd expect to see on an old coin from some ancient land ruled by queens. She had a perfect straight nose, a broad forehead, and intelligent light-blue eyes the color of faded denim. Her hair was cut short, flawlessly styled, a blondish shade with a little gray streaked in. She was at least ten years older than DeMarco, maybe fifteen, but in much better condition. She played racquetball and ran in marathons but not just to stay in shape. Emma liked to beat the competition.

DeMarco poured himself a cup of coffee. He loved Emma's coffee, and he should – it cost about forty bucks a pound. He sat down across from her but she continued to read, pretending he wasn't there.

'Hey,' DeMarco said. 'Just met your new dog.'

'Don't start,' Emma muttered.

DeMarco grinned. 'What's its name, by the way?'

'What do you want?' she said, still looking down at the paper.

'You wanna hear a conspiracy theory?' he said.

'You bet,' she said, and now she looked at him and smiled. 'I love conspiracy theories. They're almost always wrong, but I like to hear them anyway.'

'You don't believe in conspiracies? *You*, of all people?'

Emma was, without a doubt, the most enigmatic person DeMarco had ever encountered. She refused to discuss her past, and although DeMarco had known her for more than ten years, he knew almost as little about her today as he did when he first met her. She was gay but she had a daughter, yet he didn't know if her daughter was adopted or her natural offspring. He knew she was wealthy but had no idea of the source of her wealth, whether it was inherited or earned. He knew she had worked for the DIA, the Defense Intelligence Agency, but he didn't know if she'd been civilian or military, or if she'd been a spy or a handler of spies or someone who analyzed the intelligence provided by spies. Naturally, everything she had done for the agency was classified Top Secret, but even if it hadn't been she wouldn't have told him anyway.

She also claimed to be fully retired from the agency, but he suspected that this wasn't totally true because there were times when she was gone for extended periods and couldn't be reached and never returned looking relaxed and tanned like a person who had enjoyed a restful vacation. She knew people in virtually every segment of the government, had particularly close ties with people in intelligence and law enforcement, and knew folk with a wide range of illicit skills – skills such as wiretapping and forgery and safe-cracking. And these people she knew always seemed to respond instantly when she asked anything of them, but why they responded – out of past loyalty or because she had some particular authority – he didn't know. But there was one thing he did know: She believed in conspiracies, because she had almost certainly engineered a number of them herself.

DeMarco had met Emma by saving her life. He had just dropped off a friend at Reagan National Airport and was about to leave the terminal when this complete stranger – this elegant middle-aged woman – jumped into his car and told him to drive to the Pentagon. When he'd asked why, she pointed over her shoulder at two men running toward his car and told him the two were armed and were going to kill her – and would probably kill DeMarco as well if he didn't step on the gas. Having no choice he drove, and when the men gave chase and started shooting at them, Emma got on her cell phone, talked to someone at the Pentagon, and five minutes later choppers and SWAT vans intercepted them. And that was his introduction to Emma – just a guy parked in the wrong place at the wrong time who saved her life by giving her a lift.

After that day, she told him if he ever needed a favor to just ask, and he occasionally did, particularly when things got complicated or he needed access to the resources at her disposal. She treated him most times like an aggravated big sister, and why she helped him was not always clear. Sometimes she helped him because she decided that whatever he was doing was sufficiently important to warrant it. At other times, however, he suspected she helped simply because she was bored with retirement – or semiretirement, whichever the case might be.

'It's been my experience,' Emma said, 'that whether or not something's a conspiracy is a matter of perspective. If a bunch of guys are doing something we like, we call it a good organized effort. It's only a conspiracy when we don't like it.'

'Huh?'

'Say the city council of Dirt Water USA wants to tear down kindly Grandma Jones's house to make a convenient highway exit to the local mall. Now that's a conspiracy to all those who side with Grandma, but for all those citizens who want easy access to the mall – which by the way will improve sales and thereby increase tax revenues for the good city of Dirt Water – it's just a city council doing its job by exercising its right of eminent domain.'

'Fine, Emma. Conspiracies are in the eye of the beholder. But I'm not talking about grandma and a freeway exit.'

'So what are you talking about?'

'I think,' DeMarco said, 'there's a chance that Reza Zarif tried to crash a plane into the White House because somebody told him that they were going to kill his wife and kids if he didn't. But then the . . . the bad guys, they killed his family anyway.'

Emma could do two things that DeMarco had

always wanted to be able to do. She could arch a single eyebrow and she could whistle through her teeth to call a cab. She now arched an eyebrow, the left one.

'And what makes you think that Mr Zarif didn't do exactly what the papers – and the Federal Bureau of Investigation – said?'

DeMarco explained. He said the FBI's theory was that Reza had just snapped because of all the pressure he'd been under lately and then decided to commit an irrational act of terrorism that would bring attention to the plight of Muslims worldwide. The problem with that theory was neither Mahoney nor anyone else who knew Reza well could accept that he would do something like that. But what they *really* couldn't accept was that he would kill his wife and two young children.

'So I asked myself,' DeMarco said, 'what if someone held a gun to the heads of Reza's kids and told him to fly the plane? I think if Reza thought that might save his children, he'd do it. He was an experienced pilot and he knew he was going to get blown out of the sky, just like he was. What I'm saying is, I think the man would have been willing to commit suicide if he thought it might keep his family alive, especially if he knew he wasn't going to kill anybody else, much less the president.'

'But what makes you think anybody held a gun to his kids' heads?' Emma said.

'Two things, and I've already told you the first: my gut feeling that he wouldn't have done what he did if he wasn't forced.'

'Well, that's weak,' Emma said.

'The second thing is the fingerprint on the bullet box.'

DeMarco explained how Donny Cray's fingerprint had been discovered on the box of bullets used to kill Reza Zarif's family and the FBI's conclusion as to why the single fingerprint was there.

'So,' DeMarco said, 'one explanation for that fingerprint is that this yokel Cray sold Reza a gun just like the FBI thinks. But another explanation is maybe Cray was in Reza's house.'

'But what motive would Cray have?' Emma said.

'I don't know,' DeMarco said.

'And this other guy, the one who hijacked the shuttle. Did someone force him too?'

'I don't know,' DeMarco said again. He was getting tired of saying that.

He told her how questioning Youseff Khalid's wife had been a little tough since she didn't speak English, but he said he didn't see any evidence that the woman had been abused in any way and she denied – he thought – that she'd been used to coerce her husband to hijack the shuttle.

'Well, shit, Joe,' Emma said, clearly unimpressed with DeMarco's logic.

'Yeah, I know,' he admitted. 'But what *really* makes

me think there might be an honest-to-God conspiracy going on is not Reza Zarif or Youseff Khalid but the cabdriver who tried to walk into the Capitol with blocks of C-Four strapped to his chest.'

Mustafa Ahmed came from Pakistan thirty years ago, and twenty years ago he became an American citizen. According to newspaper reports, he wasn't known to have been involved in any political organizations, and he rarely attended his mosque. His only outside interest appeared to be soccer. He had bought an expensive cable package primarily so he could watch international games, and three times in his life he had taken vacations to attend World Cup matches. He had never married but he did have a large extended family, three siblings and a passel of nieces and nephews whom he reportedly spoiled rotten.

Following his attempt to detonate a bomb inside the Capitol, the FBI searched Mustafa's house and found a folder filled with literature – pamphlets and books and articles taken off the Internet – that were sympathetic to radical Muslim causes. All Mustafa's friends and family, people who had been in his house, said they had never seen such reading material in the place before and they had never heard Mustafa side with al-Qaeda politics. They all said the same thing. The only thing the man cared about was soccer, and he didn't have a political bone in his scrawny body.

Folks did admit that Mustafa was a very emotional man, one of those little mouse-that-roared guys who took offense easily and was always ranting and raving about something. And a month before he attempted to blow up the Capitol he lost a case in traffic court that he was felt was due to religious bias. His car had been broadsided by a white man, and the white man claimed Mustafa had run a red light. Mustafa swore the light was green, but the white judge sided with the other man, and a bailiff had to drag Mustafa out of the courtroom as he screamed curses at the judge, calling him a fool and a bigot.

Mustafa's friends admitted that he'd been outraged by what had happened but refused to agree that losing a case in court would have provoked him into doing what he did. The FBI discovered, however, that the court's decision had a profound impact on Mustafa's life. Mustafa's cab company was a loosely affiliated group of gypsy drivers, men who owned their own cabs, and the cabs were insured by the drivers, not the company. For whatever reason, Mustafa had missed a payment on his auto insurance and he didn't have the money to pay for the damage to his cab or the white man's car. So Mustafa hadn't just lost a case in court. He hadn't worked in a month, he had lost his means of earning a living, and he was being hammered on by collection agencies to pay his bills.

As with Youseff Khalid, the man who hijacked the

New York–D.C. shuttle, the FBI suspected that Mustafa had been helped by somebody. Somebody had given Youseff the plastic gun he had snuck onboard the plane, and somebody had provided the C-4 and constructed the bomb that Mustafa had strapped to his chest. The only reason the bomb didn't explode, the FBI explained, was that one of the wires connecting the dead man's switch to the detonator had somehow torn loose, maybe when Mustafa put on the raincoat he had worn over the bricks of C-4. But *somebody* had made the bomb, and it probably wasn't Mustafa.

With the two kids who had tried to blow up the Baltimore Harbor Tunnel, the Bureau knew for a fact that an al-Qaeda operative was involved. In the case of Mustafa Ahmed and Youseff Khalid they were convinced of similar organized terrorist involvement but as yet had no concrete evidence to support their theory. But when one took into account all the factors involved – the literature in Mustafa's house, his bitterness toward the judicial system, the sophisticated bomb vest, the depression caused by his financial problems – the FBI believed it had a pretty good case that Mustafa, with the help of some radical group, had the motive and means to blow up the Capitol.

But the *real* problem with all of this, DeMarco told Emma, was not Mustafa but the guy who had killed Mustafa.

His name was Rollie.

*   *   *

'Rollie?' Emma said.

'Right,' DeMarco said. 'His full name is Roland, but he looks like a Rollie and everybody calls him Rollie.'

Roland Patterson was a short overweight guy with bad feet who always looked puzzled. He was a security guard who screened people entering the Capitol and made sure they walked through the metal detector. And if the detector alarmed, Rollie would tell them to take the change out of their pockets. That was Rollie's job.

'I've never talked to the guy,' DeMarco told Emma, 'but I see him in the morning, about half the time when I go to my office. And right away you get a sense of him. The other guards will be sitting there bullshitting, and they'll be giving Rollie a hard time. He's just that kind of guy, the kind other guys are always teasing about something. And he always has this confused look on his face.'

What DeMarco meant was that if one of the other guards said, 'Hey, Rollie, go get us some coffee,' Rollie's brow would furl and he'd get an expression on his face as if he were being asked to make a number of extremely complex decisions. Where should he go for the coffee? What size cups should he get? Should he pay for the coffee or ask the other guys to pay? DeMarco had no evidence that Rollie was in any way stupid. He was just a guy who mulled things over slowly and took his time answering.

The other thing about Rollie was that he almost always worked near one of the Capitol's entrances, at a job where he could sit for long periods. Supposedly, Rollie had a partial disability, some problem with his feet that prevented him from walking the perimeter.

'The day Rollie killed Mustafa Ahmed, he did two things completely out of character,' DeMarco told Emma. 'First, he decided to take a walk when he went on his break. Normally, when it was time for Rollie's break, he'd go into this little room the guards used and have a snack and read the paper. But that day – and it was colder than hell outside – he decided to stretch his legs and walk around the building, and he just *happened* to stop and bullshit with the two guys guarding the West Terrace barrier. The second thing he did that was unusual was that he made a decision and he made it quickly.'

This was what really bothered DeMarco: Rollie, a guy who couldn't seem to decide what kind of doughnut to buy, assessed the situation with Mustafa in about five seconds and then pulled out his gun and killed him.

'I mean, that's what I don't get,' DeMarco said. 'The other two guards, they're scared shitless trying to figure out what to do. Here's this crazy guy walking toward them with enough explosives on him to blow the dome off the building, they've never been in a situation like this before in their lives, and they're probably thinking that if they shoot Mustafa they'll hit the C-Four and blow themselves to kingdom come. But not Rollie. Friggin' Rollie takes out his gun and blows the guy away.'

There was one other thing about Rollie, DeMarco explained to Emma. While everybody agreed that Rollie was a malingering slug, they also agreed he could shoot a pistol. When the guards had to pass their shooting quals, Rollie had no trouble at all. He was overweight, flatfooted, and not the least bit athletic, but he was a natural when it came to using a pistol.

'Hmm,' Emma said. 'Anything else?'

'Well, no, but when you look at the whole package, you've got a lot of stuff that doesn't make sense: an apparently apolitical cabdriver who suddenly decides to become a suicide bomber, and the guy who takes him out is the last person you'd expect to do it. It's just a puzzle.'

'And maybe a conspiracy,' Emma said, smiling slightly.

22

He sat watching the television set, amazed at what had almost happened.

A man had just tried to walk into the U.S. Capitol with an explosive device strapped to his body. They had pictures of the man – somehow, some way, in this country there was *always* someone with a camera or a cell phone nearby – and the pictures showed the man standing, his arms outstretched, and then the bullets striking his chest. Why didn't the bomb explode? he wondered.

But it was still amazing. Counting the man who had tried to crash his plane into the White House, there had been three attacks by Muslim Americans in a period of less than a month, and the last two had been only a week apart. The country was in an absolute frenzy. This man Broderick and his bill, his law – whatever they called it – it appeared he was going to succeed.

And if he did, the hatred would grow.

Maybe that was why the attacks had happened so close together: because Sheikh Osama wanted this law passed. But that could also explain the failures. Whoever was helping the American martyrs had rushed their planning or had not trained their recruits well or had not checked their equipment as thoroughly as they should have. But still, two attacks in seven days? That was phenomenal. They had never acted this quickly in the past.

He was embarrassed. He knew he had to move slowly and cautiously; unlike his brethren here in America, *his* identity was definitely known to the authorities. Still, it had been over three months since Baltimore. He needed to move more rapidly, particularly if his success could influence this law they kept talking about.

He and the boy had been to the refinery five times now, three times during the day, twice at night, and they still had one or more trips to make before they would be ready. The first visit had been the most dangerous. He had stopped the El Camino on a road that was not heavily traveled, and from which he could see the refinery, and then he had jacked up the vehicle to make it appear that he was changing a flat tire. But if a policeman had driven by, and if he had seen two Arabs, and if he'd realized the significance of the refinery, they could have been arrested on the spot. That did not happen, though; God protected them.

During the first visit, he and the boy studied the refinery for three hours. He took photographs with a digital camera with a long-range lens and used binoculars to study the markings on the various tanks and pipes. The refinery was *filled* with tanks and pipes; it was a forest of tanks and pipes. But the boy was very bright and he had no trouble at all memorizing the markings that were significant and tracing the routing of the pipes that were important.

The next two daylight visits, he'd dropped the boy off and told him to find the best spots to place the explosives, places not too close together, places where the charges would not be visible to someone passing by, places where he could hide when he attached the bombs. He told the boy it was particularly important that certain valves be destroyed so the valves couldn't be shut to stop the chemical from escaping.

He purchased bright-colored clothes for the boy, the type of clothes that teenagers his age wore: a sweatshirt that had the logo of a local sports team, baggy jeans, silly-looking tennis shoes. He made the boy turn the bill of the baseball cap around so it was pointed backwards, and when the boy did he couldn't help but laugh. Even the boy laughed, something that rarely happened.

And he told the boy, 'Don't sneak. Don't act like

you're skulking about. Act like a boy. Throw rocks, kick cans, run a stick along the fence. You're just a boy walking about, going wherever boys go.' On the last visit they'd been lucky enough to find a dog wandering near the refinery, and he tied his belt around the dog's neck to serve as a leash, and the boy had pretended to walk the dog as he looked for places to hide the bombs.

23

'So you wanna know about Jubal Pugh,' Patsy Hall said.

Hall was a mid-level supervisor at the DEA, and according to Barry King she was the DEA's expert on Pugh. She was in her early forties and had smile lines bracketing intelligent brown eyes, a trim build, and short-cut, no-fuss dark hair. She was wearing a charcoal-gray pantsuit, a white blouse, and a big gun in a holster on her hip. She was short enough – and the gun was big enough – that the handgrip on the gun was halfway up her rib cage.

Two minutes with Hall, and you knew you were dealing with someone who was bright, tough, stubborn, and confident. DeMarco bet that none of the men who worked for her had any doubt that she was the boss, and most of them, the ones with any brains, knew she deserved to be the boss.

'Jubal Pugh,' Patsy said, 'likes to—'

'Jubal,' DeMarco said. 'That name just cracks me up.'

'His full name in Jubal *Early* Pugh, Jubal Early having been a Confederate Army general who – Aw, never mind. At any rate, Jubal likes to wear an old slouch hat and he shaves about once a week. In the summer, he wears bib overalls, no shirt, no shoes, and he talks so slow you wonder if he's ever gonna finish a sentence. Your first impression would be that he's the brother of the guy who played the banjo in *Deliverance*. And you'd be totally wrong.

'Pugh sells meth; he's one of the top five dealers in Virginia. His territory also includes parts of West Virginia, Maryland, and Pennsylvania. I know he's killed people and burned their houses and intimidated witnesses to stay king of his little hill. I know all this, and I haven't even been able to arrest the bastard, much less convict him. And I've been after him for more than five years.'

Hall gave a little tug on her holster to readjust the pistol grip digging into her ribs.

'Jubal didn't go to school beyond the tenth grade, and he started out with a 1956 Airstream trailer and ten acres he inherited from his daddy. Today he owns *four hundred* acres. He's got apple orchards and gas stations and a muffler shop, and he makes cider for sale. He uses these businesses to launder his drug money.

He's not that smart, but he's smart enough to know what he doesn't know. He's got a good accountant, who makes sure he stays out of trouble with the IRS, and another guy who manages his legitimate businesses. And even though he's no Rhodes scholar, he hires people that are competent and then he micromanages the shit out of them so they don't screw up.'

'Isn't he some kind of white supremacist too?' DeMarco said.

Hall laughed. 'Yeah, Jubal's the head of a group called America First. And you know why he heads up this group? For money, pure and simple. His militia or club or whatever the hell it is never meets, but it has about three hundred dues-paying members. Jubal hired a kid from Shenandoah University to build him a Web site, and every month the kid writes a bunch of garbage about how blacks and Hispanics and whoever are taking over America, and every month a bunch of idiots send money, just small donations, but it adds up. The Web site cost Jubal only two hundred bucks to design and he makes a few thousand dollars a year off the loonies who support groups like his.'

'So why can't you nail him?' DeMarco asked.

'Do you know anything about meth?' Patsy Hall said.

'No.'

'Well, let me to tell you,' she said.

*　　*　　*

Methamphetamine is highly addictive, and the effects of the drug on the human body are devastating. Longtime users will appear twenty years older than their actual age, will have lost their teeth, and have open sores on their faces. And the drug doesn't simply affect the users. In communities where meth addiction is widespread, crime – theft and murder – tends to skyrocket.

Depending on purity and availability, a pound of meth can cost as little as six thousand dollars or as much as twenty thousand dollars, and the thing that makes meth particularly troublesome to law enforcement is that anyone can make it. Poppy flowers and coca plants and complex equipment are not required. To make meth – or *cook it*, as they say – most of the ingredients and equipment needed, things like rubbing alcohol and drain cleaner and lye and lithium batteries, can be found at your neighborhood hardware store.

The key ingredient in methamphetamine is either ephedrine or pseudoephedrine, chemicals found in over-the-counter cold medicines like Sudafed and Actifed and a dozen other brands used to unstop your stuffy nose. Meth cookers used to be able to walk into drugstores, buy all the Sudafed on the shelf, and then go home and cook up a few batches of speed for themselves and their friends.

But times had changed. Laws were now in place in an increasing number of states limiting the amount of ephedrine-based drugs that an individual can buy at one time. And consumers of these cold remedies are required to show the pharmacist a driver's license, and the pharmacist is required to record the name and address of the buyer. Then the pharmacies provide the narcotics cops with these names and addresses, and the narcos start watching those folk who seem to have a chronic case of the sniffles and live in shacks out in the woods.

So in the last few years, because of the difficulty of purchasing ephedrine in the States, Mexican cartels had become the primary manufacturer and distributor of meth because they were able to purchase ephedrine in large quantities – large being *tons* – directly from the nine foreign chemical companies who make the stuff. According to Patsy Hall, what Pugh had managed to do was get a Mexican connection to provide his ephedrine – a connection small-time local dealers didn't have – and then Pugh either sold the ephedrine directly to cookers or cooked the meth himself for distribution.

'What's all this have to do with your not being able to nail Pugh?' DeMarco asked.

'Right now,' Patsy Hall said, 'meth is a big problem on the West Coast and a growing issue in the Midwest. Because of the proximity to Mexico, places like California and Arizona are up to their necks in the shit. But here on the East Coast, the big drugs are still heroin and crack cocaine, and the DEA's budget and

manpower are primarily focused on the big cities where
most of the dealers and users live. What all that means
is I can't get the priority I need to nail an SOB like
Jubal Pugh who deals meth and lives out in the sticks.'

Hall tugged on her gun again; DeMarco guessed
she did that a hundred times a day.

'Someplace on Pugh's property is a meth lab,' Hall
said. 'And every day a bunch of cars and trucks and
tankers go onto his property. They deliver fertilizer or
insecticide or they drop off people who pick apples or
prune his damn trees or clear the brush on his land.
And because he has four hundred goddamn acres,
there's a dozen ways to get on and off his property,
and meth and ephedrine are not bulky items – we're
not talking bales of marijuana here – so the shit's easy
to hide.

'The bottom line is, I can't get the warrants I need
to search Jubal's place and all the vehicles that are
constantly going on and off his property because I don't
have the two dozen additional agents I need to follow
all these vehicles. And when it comes to distribution,
like most drug kingpins Jubal is personally three or
four steps removed from the actual deals. People he
trusts make the dope and give the dope to distributors, the distributors give it to dealers, and the dealers
sell it to the junkies. So when the cops actually catch
some tweaker with meth in his jeans, they can't get
that person to testify against Jubal because the tweaker's
never met him. Or they catch a dealer and he gives

up his supplier, and we get the supplier *but*, because he wasn't arrested for murder, the damn judge lets the guy out on bail and the next thing you know the guy has vanished into thin air or turns up dead or develops total amnesia because Jubal has most likely told him he's gonna die if he talks.'

'Sheesh,' DeMarco said, but Patsy Hall wasn't through with her rant.

'The other way we usually get guys like him,' Hall said, 'is we plant someone in his organization, an undercover cop or some lowlife we've caught who'll work for us to keep from going to jail. But Jubal's too smart to let that happen. Normally he only hires people he knows personally, but if he hires an outsider he does a background check on the guy on par with what the government does to issue a Top Secret security clearance.

'So,' she said, 'I know the guy is importing ephedrine, I know he has a meth lab someplace on his property, and I know he's doing all sorts of bad things – and I can't get him. But I'm *gonna* get him,' Hall said. 'I swear to God I will.'

DeMarco also asked her about Donny Cray. She knew Cray was dead but she didn't know Cray's thumbprint had been found in Reza Zarif's house.

'You're kidding!' she said to DeMarco.

'No,' he said, and told her the FBI's theory that Cray had most likely sold Reza the gun he used to kill his wife and kids.

'That's possible,' Hall said. 'I mean, that's the kind of thing Donny used to do before he started working for Jubal, but I'm still surprised. Pugh keeps his people on a short leash. He wouldn't like Donny having some kind of sideline enterprise that could land him into trouble with ATF.'

'Yeah, that's the same thing Barry King told me,' DeMarco said. 'But now let me ask you something that's gonna sound kinda strange. Do you think Pugh would be the type to get involved in these Muslim terrorist attacks that have been taking place lately?'

'What in the hell are you talking about?' Hall said.

DeMarco was somewhat reluctant to let Hall know what he was thinking. She was a law enforcement fed and would obviously be more inclined to accept the Bureau's version of events than his, but he decided he had to tell her. And he liked her and she seemed like someone he could trust. So he told her his suspicions about Rollie and the Capitol bomber and how some things about the attacks just didn't add up, but in particular how he couldn't accept that Reza Zarif had killed his family.

He concluded by saying, 'What I'm asking is this: Do you think Pugh is the type that would threaten to kill Reza Zarif's children to make Zarif crash his plane into the White House?'

DeMarco realized how ridiculous that sounded the minute the words left his mouth.

'Not for political reasons,' Hall said. 'Jubal couldn't

care less about politics. For money he might do something like that – he'd do anything for money – but what you're saying . . . Well, I just can't imagine Pugh getting involved in something so high profile. He'd know that the FBI and Homeland Security and God knows how many other federal agencies would be coming after him. I mean, *I* may not be able to get the priority to nab him, but those guys sure as hell could. No, for Jubal to get mixed up in this terrorist stuff, the payoff would have to be *huge*.'

'Yeah, but who would pay him?' DeMarco said.

'Hey, it's your theory not mine,' Hall said.

DeMarco was silent for a moment before he said, 'There's one other thing. The bomb the cabdriver had – it didn't explode. The Bureau said a wire came loose, but it's hard to believe with as much bomb-making experience as al-Qaeda has that they'd screw up like that. But maybe someone like Pugh would make that kind of mistake.'

Hall shook her head. 'I think you're totally off base thinking Pugh's involved in any terrorist stuff. I mean, he's fire-bombed other meth dealers' labs, I know that for a fact, but I just can't see him making a bomb out of C-Four with a dead man's switch. No. That's just way too high tech for Jubal. He's a bottle-of-gas-and-a-rag kinda guy.'

24

The First Amendment of the Constitution may dictate a separation between Church and State but the fact is, when preachers preach, their congregations listen to what they have to say and tend to vote and contribute accordingly. So when Mahoney got a call from a preacher he too listened, and the preacher he was currently listening to was none other than Cardinal Patrick Mackey, head of the archdiocese of Boston.

Cardinal Mackey had called to discuss a bill in the House having to do with health insurance. As the Catholic Church had its fingers in a number of hospitals in the Boston area, and as the bill might affect the profitability of those hospitals, Cardinal Mackey wanted to make sure that the speaker understood the cardinal's perspective on the matter. Mackey, of course, being a man of the cloth, believed in treating the sick and giving alms to the poor; he just thought such acts of charity should come through private donations and not through enterprises that funded the Church's many other endeavors. Mahoney thanked the good cardinal for his input and concluded the call by saying that a man named DeMarco would soon be visiting the fair city of Boston. Cardinal Mackey knew exactly what Congressman Mahoney meant and said he'd say a special mass for his favorite politician.

Mahoney picked up the phone to call his chief of staff and discuss the cardinal's concern. His chief, a diabolical genius named Perry Wallace, would help him decide if they should do what the cardinal wanted and, if not, how they would make it appear that it wasn't Mahoney's fault that the cardinal hadn't gotten his way. But before Mahoney could punch the button on his phone to summon Wallace, Wallace walked into the room.

There are two types of fat men. There are those who carry their added poundage well, men whose girth gives them an imposing stature and creates an impression of bull-like robustness. Mahoney was one of those men. Wallace was the other type of fat man. He just looked fat, his stomach flopping over his belt, his face bloated into a small white moon.

Before Mahoney could tell Wallace about the cardinal's phone call, Wallace said, 'Broderick's bill just passed in the Senate.'

'Shit,' Mahoney said.

'Eighteen of our guys voted for it.'

'Goddammit,' Mahoney said.

Now Broderick's bill would come to the House – Mahoney's House.

25

'You guys know where Rollie's at?' DeMarco asked.

DeMarco wanted to talk to Rollie Patterson, the U.S. Capitol police officer who had killed Mustafa Ahmed, but Rollie wasn't at his normal post. The two men he was speaking to – one black, one white, door guards who worked with Rollie – didn't answer his question immediately because they were busy admiring the backside of a female lobbyist who was passing through the metal detector.

'Why you asking?' the white guard finally said. 'They wanna give him another medal?'

The day after preventing the Capitol from being turned into rubble, Rollie had been presented with a medal. Meritorious something-or-other for valor. The presentation had been made in the House chamber, and Mahoney had personally pinned the medal on Rollie's stout chest. House members, the hundred or so who had bothered to attend the ceremony, had all risen and clapped their hands in tribute to Rollie's heroism.

'Nah, I just want to talk to him,' DeMarco said.

'Yeah, but who are *you*?' the black guard said.

'I handle media inquiries,' DeMarco lied. 'Got a question from some reporter that I'm tryin' to get answered.' Before the guards could ask another question – not because they cared, but because screwing with DeMarco was as good a way as any to kill time – DeMarco said, 'So is he here today or not?'

'No,' the black guy said. 'He's been off since he popped that guy. I guess havin' to stand up for all those pictures was hard on his feet.'

The white guy laughed.

Rollie, even after killing a terrorist, still got no respect.

Rollie had a small single-story home with a detached garage not too far from the Fort Totten metro stop in northeast D.C. DeMarco noticed that the mailbox was stuffed with envelopes, and three days' worth of newspapers were stacked up near the door. It appeared that Rollie was out of town and that's why DeMarco hadn't been able to reach him by phone.

DeMarco knocked on the door. No one answered. He knocked again and looked in the nearest window but couldn't see anyone in the house. It was beginning to look as if he'd wasted his time driving out to Rollie's place, but he walked around to the rear of the house, stood on the back porch, and looked in through the backdoor window, into the kitchen of Rollie's home. There were dishes on the table, and a carton of milk was sitting on the counter near the stove.

'Hey, whatcha doin?'

DeMarco turned and saw, peering over the fence that separated her house from Rollie's, an elderly white woman, bright-eyed as a robin. She was wearing an army fatigue jacket over a blue bathrobe, and there was a red stocking cap on her head, gray hair sticking out from beneath the cap.

'I'm looking for Rollie,' DeMarco said.

'How do I know you weren't planning to break into the house?' the woman said, then jiggled her eyebrows up and down.

DeMarco smiled. 'What would you have done if I had been?'

The woman smiled back and raised her right hand, which had been obscured by the fence. She was holding a revolver. She didn't point it at DeMarco, she just sort of waved it.

Jesus!

She laughed. 'Don't worry. It's not loaded,' she said.

'Good,' DeMarco said. 'So have you seen Rollie? I work with him, over at the Capitol. Been trying all day to get ahold of him.'

'No,' she said, 'and to tell you the truth, I'm kinda worried about him. The papers on his porch, you know.'

'You think we should call the cops?' DeMarco said.

The woman nodded, but then she said, 'Nah. Look under that flowerpot, the one with the dead plant in it. The key to the front door's there. We'll go in together.' Then she held up her gun again. 'And if there's anybody in there—'

'I thought you said it wasn't loaded.'

'I lied.'

DeMarco opened the door. Rollie's gun-toting neighbor – her name was Netty Glenn – was right behind him, which made him wish he'd let her go in first. Guns made him nervous.

The smell hit them the minute he opened the door.

'Oh-oh,' Netty said.

Though he was pretty sure he wouldn't get an answer, DeMarco called out, 'Hey, Rollie, you here? Anybody home?'

'Maybe you oughta wait here,' Netty said. 'I've seen lots of dead bodies.'

'What?' DeMarco said.

'I was a nurse in Vietnam.'

'Oh. Well, I'll be all right. I'll look with you.'

They found him in his bedroom, lying on the floor, fully dressed. His right hand was on his chest.

Netty made a *tsk-tsk* sound with her tongue and

shook her head. 'I told him that if he kept eatin' fried chicken every night of the week and didn't lose some weight, this was gonna happen.'

DeMarco looked around the bedroom. He didn't see anything out of place – other than a dead man on the floor with a waxy gray-green complexion.

DeMarco called the police using his cell phone. Netty said they should wait outside, but DeMarco said, 'Why don't we just take a look around first? You know, see if everything looks okay.' Netty started to say something, but before she could, DeMarco said, 'And maybe you oughta go home and put that gun away.'

'You got a point there,' she said.

After Netty left, DeMarco made a quick tour of the main floor of the small house. He didn't have time to go into the basement. He didn't see anything out of place – no sign of a struggle or a burglary – and was in fact surprised to find that Rollie was a fairly neat housekeeper. In the second bedroom, a room Rollie apparently used as an office, he looked at the papers lying on the desk, mostly bills Rollie hadn't gotten around to paying. He found a brochure for a paint-gun place, one of those places that latent homicidal maniacs go to, dressed in camo pants, and shoot each other with paint balls.

Actually, DeMarco had always wanted to do that. He thought it might be fun.

He looked through the drawers in the desk, using

his handkerchief not to leave prints, and found Rollie's checkbook. He ripped one of the deposit slips out of the back and put it in his shirt pocket.

There was a large metal safe in the room, about six feet high and three feet deep with a big combination lock. DeMarco tugged on the safe's door but it was locked. He guessed it was a gun safe, knowing of Rollie's interest in firearms, said interest being apparent because next to the safe was a bookcase filled with gun books and magazines.

He was turning to leave the office, figuring the cops would be there any moment, when he noticed something lying on the floor, next to the desk, as if it might have been blown off. DeMarco picked it up. It was a four-page pamphlet, printed on glossy paper, and appeared to be some sort of right-wing rant about how whites were becoming a minority in America and how they had to fight back. He looked around the room but didn't see any more literature like that. He thought of taking the pamphlet but then decided not to. Instead of putting it back down on the floor where he'd found it, he dropped it in the middle of Rollie's desk.

Netty Glenn was standing outside on Rollie's porch, smoking a cigarette.

'I don't usually smoke,' she said to DeMarco. 'Horrible, nasty habit. But dead bodies – they bring back memories.'

'I'll bet,' DeMarco said. He was thinking that this

was one interesting woman; he bet she'd been a looker when she was younger, like the nurses in the movie *M*A*S*H* – except she'd been the real thing.

As they were standing there, DeMarco noticed a big RV parked on the grass next to Rollie's house, on the side of the house he hadn't seen until now. He couldn't help but notice it because the thing was as long as a city bus.

'When did Rollie get that?' DeMarco asked Netty.

'Just last week, poor bastard. He was telling me – geez, I guess it was the last time I saw him – how he was already mapping out this trip he was gonna take out west when he retired.'

'That looks like a pretty expensive rig,' DeMarco said.

'He said it cost him forty-two five. It's used, but it's only got a few thousand miles on it. Ain't that life,' Netty said, flicking her cigarette butt away. 'A guy finally buys his dream machine, and the next thing you know . . .' She concluded by just shaking her head.

'Can I ask you something about Rollie?' DeMarco said.

'I guess,' Netty said.

'Was he some kind of racist?'

'Why you asking? Because he shot that Muslim guy?'

'No, not because of that. I saw this pamphlet on his desk from some white-power group.' Then, because DeMarco had claimed to be Rollie's friend, he added, 'I just never thought he was into anything like that.'

'Well, I don't know about any pamphlet,' Netty said, 'and I never heard him talk about stuff like that. But he was kinda scared. Every time a new family would move into the neighborhood – and if they weren't white, which they usually weren't – Rollie would say something to me about how he hoped we weren't gonna start getting a lot of crime and drugs in the neighborhood. But I never heard him goin' around sayin' nigger, nigger. Nothing like that.'

It took the cops about twenty minutes to get there, two cocky young guys in a patrol car. They told DeMarco and Netty to wait for them on Rollie's porch, then walked quickly through the house. They couldn't have spent more than five minutes inside the place. As one of the cops was calling for the medical examiner, DeMarco asked the other one, 'Will they do an autopsy on him?'

The cop shrugged. 'Not my call,' he said. 'But what would be the point, a fat guy with his hand on his heart?'

And rest in peace, Rollie.

26

Hydrofluoric acid is a chemical compound that exists as a colorless gas or as a fuming liquid. It is used to etch glass and clean brickwork and to make refrigerants and herbicides and pharmaceuticals. It's also used, in very large quantities, to make high-octane gasoline.

When hydrofluoric acid is released into the atmosphere, it has a propensity to form a toxic aerosol cloud that will drift for miles, and exposure to this gas can result in lethal damage to the heart, liver, kidneys, and nervous system. It blinds and it burns and it causes pulmonary edema. But the description of its effects he liked best was one he had heard on an American television show. The man on the show had said, 'It's a terrible death. It's one way you don't want to die. It just melts your lungs.'

The refinery on Lake Erie kept as much as eight hundred thousand pounds of hydrofluoric acid on hand.

The refinery had once been located on the outskirts of the city, but as the city grew it became surrounded by homes and schools and shopping centers and office buildings. Due to the huge lake and the thermal effects it created, there was almost always a breeze – and it blew primarily in the direction of a housing development in which mostly white people lived.

Another television show – they learned so much from American media that they didn't really need an intelligence-gathering apparatus – had described how vulnerable refineries and chemical plants were to attack – *terrorist* attack, as they put it. And they were. They were shockingly underprotected, considering what they contained, and the biggest weakness was not the physical security – the fences and cameras and alarms. The biggest weakness was the people who were paid to protect the facility.

The guards at this refinery dressed in dark blue uniforms and wore paratrooper boots and at first glance seemed quite impressive. Automatic pistols, Mace, oversized flashlights, and batons hung from their belts. But these men – and even some women – were laughable. Most were middle-aged, few had military training, and many had been rejected by police forces in the region because they failed to meet even the minimal qualifications required by local law enforcement. But more important, they had nothing to do. They occasionally conducted drills that disrupted refinery operations, but their primary function was to annoy the people entering the plant by performing perfunctory searches of backpacks and lunchboxes. Other than that, they *sat*. They sat all day and all night, waiting for something to happen, and they'd been sitting for so long doing nothing that they had long ago stopped expecting anything to happen.

'You see,' he said to the boy, 'how the guard never walks into that area. It's dark there, and muddy too, and he doesn't want to get mud on his boots.'

'I know,' the boy said.

27

Sunday morning, Mahoney sat in front of the television in his condo in an old bathrobe, drinking coffee laced with bourbon. He was watching Kevin Collier, the director of the FBI, do his best to scare the shit out of the American public.

Collier had always reminded Mahoney of a Boston terrier he'd once owned: pudgy, bulging eyes, a pushed-in snout – and the misconception that it was a mastiff instead of a creature whose head was barely a foot off the ground. Collier was telling Tim Russert that the Bureau believed there were several al-Qaeda operatives in the United States and that those operatives were identifying disgruntled Muslim Americans and trying to convince them to commit terrorist acts.

Collier assured the television audience, though, that as tough as his job might be, he and all his agents were doing everything they could to track these culprits down. He said his job would sure be a lot easier if the borders weren't so long and porous, but he was confident that General Banks of Homeland Security was doing the best he could, implying, of course, that if the customs agents who worked for Banks had done their job in the first place, none of these foreign terrorists would be in the country. When Russert asked Collier if he thought that Senator Broderick's bill would make his job easier, Collier said that indeed it would.

Then Russert said, 'As you know, Mr Director, Senator Broderick's bill is currently in committee in the House. My sources have said that the House does not appear to be moving as expeditiously as it could to bring the bill to a floor vote. What's your opinion on that?'

When Director Collier cleverly answered Russert's question by saying that he was just a cop and it was the speaker's job to pass the laws, Mahoney wanted to reach into the television set and strangle the bug-eyed bastard.

But Russert's sources were right. Mahoney *was* doing everything he could to keep the bill in committee as long as possible without making it obvious that he was the one directing the slowdown. He had assigned the bill to a committee chaired by James Brice, a Massachusetts congressman so firmly under his thumb that the man was practically flat. Mahoney's direction to Brice was to nitpick the shit out of the bill, question the placement of every comma and period, and then call in eighty-five experts to provide their opinions. A normal bill, Mahoney could have kept in committee indefinitely, but there was too much media focus on this one. Brice would do what he was told, but Mahoney also knew he could delay things for only so long.

The next day Mahoney arrived at the Capitol with the temperament of a scalded bear and called DeMarco up to his office to beat him up. DeMarco naturally thought this unreasonable. The FBI probably had five or six thousand agents looking into the terrorist attacks, maybe more. They had the manpower, the authority, the expertise, and all the right equipment. The Department of Homeland Security was assisting the FBI, and the NSA was probably bugging every cell phone call in America. The CIA was involved too, trying to find terrorist connections to the attacks overseas; knowing the CIA, they were most likely skulking around inside the United States as well. So if all those agencies and all their agents hadn't turned up any evidence of a conspiracy, how in the hell was DeMarco supposed to?

Mahoney's response to this well-reasoned argument was that all those federal agencies were firmly convinced that al-Qaeda was behind the recent attacks. The only guy that wasn't convinced was John Mahoney, but he wasn't about to stick his thick political neck out and say this to anyone who might actually be able to do something. He preferred to beat on Joe DeMarco, which he did by listing all the things that DeMarco had failed to do. He hadn't been able to show that Donny Cray had done anything more than sell Reza Zarif a gun, he hadn't found any concrete evidence that the men who had attacked their own country had been forced to do so, and he had absolutely no proof that the late Rollie Patterson was anything other than the hero that Mahoney had personally claimed him to be when he had pinned the medal on Rollie's chest.

'So, goddammit, what are you going to do next?' Mahoney asked.

'Well,' DeMarco said, 'I was hoping that maybe you could get them to do an autopsy on Rollie, see if maybe they can find something to show that he died from other than natural causes.'

Mahoney mulled that request over for a minute.

'Yeah,' he finally said. 'I can do that. I'll call the guy who runs the Capitol cops and tell him, Rollie bein' one of our own and having just whacked this terrorist, that they need to cut him up to make sure some al-Qaeda loony didn't shove a hypo into one of Rollie's veins. He'll keep my name out of it.'

'There's one other thing,' DeMarco said.

'What's that?' Mahoney asked.

'I also want an autopsy performed on Donny Cray. I want to make sure his neck really snapped in a car accident.'

'What do I look like, the governor of Virginia?'

Mahoney yelled. 'An autopsy on Rollie's one thing, but gettin' one done on Cray is way out of my jurisdiction.'

Nothing was out of Mahoney's jurisdiction. He just didn't want to do anything related to the attacks that might garner more media attention. He was getting enough bad ink for just knowing Reza Zarif and then dragging his feet on Broderick's bill.

'But,' he said, 'you're right. They oughta take a closer look at how that guy died. So you go figure out some way to make it happen.'

DeMarco didn't bother to argue with Mahoney; he knew from past experience that arguing didn't help. The speaker was motivated, above all else, by self-interest. The other reason he didn't argue was that he thought it possible his new friend at the DEA, Patsy Hall, might have the clout to do what he wanted done.

But before he saw Patsy there was something else he needed to do.

He needed to get some help.

DeMarco was sitting behind his desk, just about to pick up the phone to call Emma, when the phone rang. It's spooky when that happens.

'This is Mrs Drake from Senator Broderick's office. The senator would like to see you at eleven A.M.'

Oh, boy.

Broderick's office was located in the Dirksen Senate Office Building. DeMarco entered the senator's suite and identified himself to the receptionist/executive assistant nearest the door, a young lady with strawberry-blond hair and an accent that made him think of magnolia blossoms and mint juleps and Daisy Duke. He may have been hopelessly in love with an Italian adulteress from Queens, he may have been smitten most recently by a cute schoolmarm from Iowa, but there was something about blondes with southern accents that always gave his libido a jolt. The young lady picked up the phone on her desk, punched a button, and said that a Mr DeMarco was there. Five minutes later he followed two well-oiled hips down the hallway to an office.

The man in the office was not Senator Broderick. He was a tall slim black man in his early forties. He had a longish nose, short hair, and a goatee. His eyebrows were slightly arched and, combined with the goatee, this made him look like a handsome, dark, brooding devil.

The man didn't rise from his seat or shake DeMarco's hand. He pointed to a chair in front of his desk and said, 'Sit down, DeMarco. I'm Nick Fine, Senator Broderick's chief of staff.'

'I thought the senator wanted to see me,' DeMarco said.

'Fortunately for you, the senator doesn't know who you are, and I think it would be in your best interest if the situation were to remain that way.'

Now *this* pissed DeMarco off: getting jerked over

to the Dirksen Building by a guy who had used his boss's name to get him there. Most folks come a-runnin' when a senator says he wants to see them, DeMarco being no exception, but he might have ignored the call from Broderick's office if he'd known he'd been summoned by someone on Broderick's staff.

Before DeMarco could say anything, Fine opened a folder on his desk. 'Your personnel file is amazingly . . . terse. It says you're a lawyer, a GS-Thirteen, and have a House position called Counsel Pro Tem for Liaison Affairs. The file doesn't identify your supervisor, and your job description is a single paragraph of absolute gibberish, which makes it impossible to tell what you do. So maybe you could clarify that for me, Mr DeMarco. Exactly what does the Counsel Pro Tem for Liaison Affairs do?'

DeMarco's title, the one in flaking gold paint on his office door, had been Mahoney's invention and it *was* completely meaningless. In order for DeMarco to get paid by the federal government he needed to be a civil servant. But as Mahoney didn't want it known that DeMarco worked for him, he made up an imaginary function that had nothing to do with the Speaker of the House, devised an incomprehensible title to suit the function, and then forced his will upon some minor bureaucrat who was responsible for establishing legitimate positions in the legislative branch of government. The consequence was that DeMarco received a paycheck every two weeks, but, as Nick Fine had discovered, nobody could tell exactly what he did or for whom he worked.

In response to Fine's perfectly logical question, DeMarco said, 'I do exactly what my title says. I liaise for congressional affairs.'

DeMarco didn't think he'd ever used the word *liaise* in a sentence before.

Fine stared at DeMarco for a minute, stroking his goatee. 'Don't try being cute with me, DeMarco.'

DeMarco didn't say anything. He just stared back at Fine, all the time thinking he might be in a shit-load of trouble here.

'I've heard,' Fine said, 'that you've been asking questions about the terrorist attacks that have occurred in the last few weeks. What authority do you have for asking these questions?'

There was an old saying that Mahoney had introduced him to: *Tell the truth as often as you can. That way it's easier to keep track of all the lies you tell.* In keeping with this adage, DeMarco said, 'I'm basically an odd-jobs guy. If a member of the House wants something checked out, something he doesn't want to assign to his staff for whatever reason, and in particular something dealing with other government agencies, he may call me. In this case, a member asked me to find out a little more about the attacks.'

'Which member?' Fine said.

'I can't tell you that. I'll let the congressman – or congress*woman* – know that you're interested, and if he or she wants to tell you, he or she can.'

Fine shook his head. 'What you just told me is pure bullshit. If a member of Congress wanted to know something about the attacks, he would have called the FBI directly. The second thing is, there's virtually nothing that Congress does that doesn't deal with other government entities, so I find it difficult to believe they need someone like you to do their staff work for them.'

Since the half-truth didn't work, DeMarco decided to ask his own question. 'Why do you care who I'm talking to?' he said.

Fine smiled as if amused that someone of DeMarco's rank would be so impudent. 'Senator Broderick, as I'm sure you know, is spearheading America's war against radical Muslims. He's the only person in this government who's actually trying to do something other than *lament* the situation. And because the senator's bill is so significant, it's understandable that there's a lot of healthy debate over the issue. But it appears to me, based on the sort of questions you've been asking, that what you're trying to do is muddy the waters. It appears that you're attempting to develop scenarios related to these attacks that don't fit the evidence. I think your goal may be to mislead the American people regarding what really happened.'

Mislead the American people? DeMarco didn't have the power to mislead anybody. And who the hell had Fine been talking to? How did he know what sort of questions DeMarco had been asking?

'Look,' DeMarco started to say, but Fine didn't let him finish.

'I'll tell you something else,' Fine said. 'Getting a bill passed, any bill, is difficult. My job is helping Senator Broderick get this particular bill passed, and I don't like someone like you – someone with no authority, someone unconnected to any elected position – making my job harder.'

'You're way off base here,' DeMarco said. And sticking to his previous lie – a liar has to be consistent – DeMarco said, 'Some congressman was just curious about a few things. I'm not trying to screw up the entire legislative process, and I'm sure as hell not trying to mislead anyone. I'm just—'

'*Some congressman,* you say. It just occurred to me that the speaker has close ties with one of the terrorists' families. Are you investigating these incidents because the speaker asked you to? We know Mahoney doesn't support the bill.'

This was dangerous ground.

'The speaker hasn't asked me to do anything,' DeMarco said. 'I doubt if he even knows who I am.'

DeMarco got to his feet.

'We're not through yet,' Fine said.

'Yeah, we are,' DeMarco said.

'DeMarco, I don't know what your game is, but you *will* stop doing whatever you're doing. I'm not going to allow you to become an impediment to something as serious as this legislation. And if you don't tell me who you're working for, I'm going to talk to the Bureau and suggest that *you* become someone they need to take a hard look at. You may actually be committing a crime by interfering in a federal investigation. I may also have a quiet word with a man I know at the IRS and suggest your tax returns be audited. I noticed you have a home in Georgetown, and I'm trying to understand how you can afford it. I'm sure my friend at the IRS will be curious as well. And I'm definitely going to talk to OPM and suggest that they review your federal position and determine exactly what you do that warrants your current salary. That's just for starters. There are probably a dozen other things I can do to make your life miserable if you don't crawl back under the rock you came from.'

DeMarco had encountered a lot of staffers like Fine, guys who liked to throw their boss's weight around, but this guy was taking things to a whole new level. He was also a total asshole.

'Gotta go, Nick,' DeMarco said. 'Talk to you later.'

That sounded pretty good, like DeMarco wasn't at all concerned about Fine's threats, but the truth was that DeMarco was very concerned. He'd prefer that Fine not talk to the Bureau or the IRS about him. Those agencies worried him, but they didn't scare him. But OPM – the Office of Personnel Management – scared the hell out of him. One of OPM's jobs was establishing pay standards for civil service positions. They had these absurdly rigid rules that specified, more or less, what one had to do to merit a GS-13's salary, and one of those rules was that people in those positions usually had to supervise other people or as a minimum be a specialist with some clearly defined function. If OPM ever took a hard look at DeMarco's job, he'd be reduced from a GS-13 to a GS-3. And if that happened he *wouldn't* be able to afford the house in Georgetown, which was already mortgaged to the hilt.

As he was leaving, he encountered Senator Broderick himself. Broderick had his butt planted on the blond receptionist's desk, apparently just chatting with her. When he saw DeMarco, he stood up, smiled broadly, and stuck out his hand.

'Hi, Bill Broderick,' he said. 'And are you one of my fine constituents, sir?'

After all he'd heard about the man, DeMarco couldn't help but be surprised by Broderick's boyish good looks, his seemingly genuine friendliness, his average-guy demeanor. But his overwhelming initial impression was: *lightweight*.

In response to Broderick's question, DeMarco said, 'No, sir. I live in the District.' Then, and he didn't know why he did it, he raised his right fist in the air and said, 'No taxation without representation.'

The southern belle twittered; Broderick just looked puzzled.

Unlike the fifty states, the District of Columbia has no senators or congressmen representing it in Congress. So even though D.C. has a mayor and a city government, it is, for all intents and purposes, a federal fiefdom and Congress has extraordinary control, fiscal and otherwise, over what happens within its borders. This being the case, a frequently seen D.C. bumper sticker was NO TAXATION WITHOUT REPRESENTATION – but Bill Broderick was apparently unaware of this popular sentiment.

'Just kidding, Senator,' DeMarco said. 'I'm Joe DeMarco. I work over in the House. Pleased to meet you.' Before Broderick could say anything else, DeMarco winked at the secretary and left.

Broderick opened the door to Nick Fine's office without knocking, something that annoyed Fine no end.

'So what did he have to say?' Broderick asked.

'Nothing. He gave me some bullshit about a congressman being curious about some things related to the attacks, but he wouldn't tell me who or why.'

'Is he going to be a problem?' Broderick asked.

'No. He's just somebody's lackey. I suspect somebody over in the House is grasping at straws, hoping DeMarco will find something to keep your bill from moving forward. So I'll keep an eye on him, and maybe I'll make his life hell because I told him I would, but he's not going to be a problem.'

'I hope not, Nick,' Broderick said. 'Things are starting to come together in the House. I don't want anything gumming up the works, not at this point.'

'Yes, sir,' Fine said.

He hated having to call Broderick *sir*. He hated that almost as much as having to call him *senator*.

28

DeMarco may have played in a political arena, but he really didn't pay all that much attention to the other players. Fortunately, he knew people who did.

There was an alcoholic reporter at *The Washington Post* named Reggie Harmon who had been around forever. In the Senate, there was a guy he went to law school with, Packy Morris, who was chief of staff to the junior senator from Maryland. Packy breathed gossip instead of air and always seemed to know who was doing what to whom. But when the stakes were really high, and he wanted insight and intuition and not just data and rumors, he went to Miranda Bloom.

Miranda was older than DeMarco but younger than the speaker. Because she'd been blessed with a super-model's face, long legs, and a noticeable bosom, in her late teens she'd been a Miss America runner-up.

She could have married a golden quarterback from Ol' Miss, had a couple of gorgeous kids, and spent the rest of her life hosting parties and talking about how close she'd come to being princess for a year. But Miranda Bloom had been blessed with more than a good body and a lovely face. She had a wicked, devious, clever mind, and she put it to good use.

Miranda was a lobbyist and had been one for many years. She was in fact *the* lobbyist, the one desperate CEOs came to when they wanted legislation twisted unreasonably in their favor. And get it twisted, Miranda did. How she did what she did was something she could never have written down in a how-to book. There was no set formula, no consistent, identifiable set of rules. She operated by some deep inbred political instinct she couldn't have explained to anyone other than someone just like herself, of which there were none. But most important, from DeMarco's perspective, she knew every politician in town better than they were known by their lovers and their mothers; she *had* to know them that well to get them to do whatever she wanted done.

Miranda had been married three times that DeMarco knew of and had had more affairs than probably even she could remember. DeMarco suspected that one of those affairs had been with Mahoney, because once – when Miranda misstepped, when her marvelous instincts momentarily failed her – she did something that at best could have landed her in jail and at worst could have caused her to be disappeared, and the speaker sent DeMarco to help extricate her from the situation.

After being threatened by Nick Fine, DeMarco had decided he needed to talk to Miranda and he arranged to meet her in the bar of the St Regis Hotel located on K Street, close to her office. She was dressed in a white silk Versace blouse and a red St John suit that showed off her legs to their best advantage. A simple strand of pearls graced her long neck, and her earrings matched the pearls. DeMarco knew nothing about women's fashion, but he would have bet even money that the outfit Miranda had on – clothes, jewels, and shoes – was worth more than he made in a month.

DeMarco loved talking to Miranda. She reminded him of Mrs Robinson in *The Graduate*, not because she looked like the late Anne Bancroft but because she was delightfully jaded, world-weary, wise, and sexy. With the help of a good surgeon she had aged extremely well, so well you had to wonder how she could have ever been a runner-up to anyone in Atlantic City all those years ago. It was her voice, though, that DeMarco thought was her best feature: a deep southern accent combined with a cigarette- and whiskey-tinged purr filled with the promise of seduction. Her voice alone had probably corrupted more lawmakers than her clients' money.

'Tell me about Nick Fine,' DeMarco said.

'Oh, that poor boy,' Miranda said.

'What's that mean?' DeMarco said. He found it hard to imagine anyone feeling any sympathy toward the guy he'd just met.

'You know of course that he was chief of staff to the late Senator Wingate?'

'No, I didn't know that,' DeMarco said.

'Well, he was. He worked for Wingate for almost twenty years, started right out of college, but unfortunately for Nick, Wingate just lived forever and ever. It seemed like the man was *never* gonna die.'

'What's this—'

'Wingate, that glorious old bastard, promised Nick that when he retired – it never occurred to Wingate that he might actually *die* – the party would back Nick for his seat. He told Nick he was what the Republicans needed: their own brilliant, handsome, articulate black politician, one who might actually get a few African Americans to vote for the Grand Ol' Party. And twenty percent of Virginia's residents are black. Wingate, for the last five years, had all but guaranteed Nick his job when he moved on – or up, as it were.'

'But he didn't get it,' DeMarco said.

'No, he did not. When Wingate joined that great caucus in the sky, the party hacks decided they didn't like Wingate's choice of successor, maybe because of his race, but more likely because they thought Bill Broderick was a guy they could push around.'

'So why didn't Fine quit when Broderick got the job?'

'I heard he considered that quite strongly. I know he approached a couple of K Street firms and offered his services, and a lad like Nick would seem to be a real catch as a lobbyist. He's been on the Hill a long time, knows who's who, and has the brains to understand what needs to be done. Although I'd never hire him, I heard he got a few good offers, three times his current salary.'

'Why wouldn't you hire him?'

'Because Nick's one of those people that, if given the choice between battering you into submission and sweet-talking you into doing what he wants, he prefers to batter. Though he hides it most of the time, there's a deep mean streak in Nick. Maybe he feels, had he not been born black and poor, he wouldn't have been playing second banana to Wingate all those years. Whatever the reason, I just don't think he'd fit into our little club. We lobbyists don't go around *armed*, darlin'. We rely on our charm as well as our clients' money, and Nick, handsome and smart as he is, is for the most part devoid of charm.'

She said *chawm*, and DeMarco couldn't help but smile.

'I still don't get it,' he said. 'If he resented Broderick so much, why didn't he take a job at some think tank or a consulting firm? For that matter, why didn't he go home and start campaigning against Broderick?'

Miranda didn't answer immediately. She was making eye contact with a tall gray-haired man at the bar who was about as handsome as Cary Grant. She tipped her martini glass at the gentleman, then said to DeMarco, 'Well, what I heard was that Nick met with Cal Montgomery . . .'

Montgomery was the chairman of the Republican National Committee.

'. . . and with Rick Walters . . .'

Walters was the minority leader in the Senate.

'. . . and I think those boys gave Nick the ol' your-time-will-come speech and probably made him some kinda promise. You know, Virginia's other senator ain't no spring chicken either. But I'm just guessin', sugar, since I couldn't get any details from anyone.'

Which meant Miranda wasn't sleeping with anyone who'd attended the meeting.

'This bill of Broderick's,' DeMarco said.

'Now ain't that somethin',' Miranda said.

'How involved is Fine in that?'

'Totally, would be my guess. Broderick's had some incredible luck – if you can call the Capitol nearly gettin' blown up *luck* – but the guy who maneuvered that bill through the Senate was Nicky.'

'I can believe it,' DeMarco said. 'Is Broderick really the lightweight that he seems to be?'

'Yes and no,' Miranda said. 'I mean, the man's no intellectual giant, but he has one thing goin' for him and that's ambition: raw, unrestrained, unadulterated ambition. You'd never guess it to look at him, but he's one of the most power-hungry bastards you'll ever meet, and considering that he works with ninety-nine other power-hungry bastards, that's saying something.'

'What's he wanna be, president?'

'No. I mean, yes, of course he wants to be president, but that's not what motivates him.'

'What does?'

'Sibling rivalry.'

'You gotta be shittin' me.'

'No. Bill Broderick was the classic unloved and ignored middle sibling, and his two brothers were the apples of his daddy's eye. The oldest is not only a neurosurgeon, he's out there on the leading edge. And the other brother, the one on the West Coast, he's on the Hollywood A-list and has been invited to the White House a lot more times than brother Bill. I've heard that if you even mention his brothers to him, he gets this look on his face like he'd like to strangle you. This is the first time in his life, being a senator *and* in the middle of a national debate, that he's ever gotten more attention than those other two boys, and he's just lovin' it.'

When DeMarco saw Miranda glance over at the gray-haired matinee idol at the bar again, he thanked her for her time and tried to pay for the drinks, but she wouldn't let him. She pointed out that she spent more on shoes than he made in a year. As DeMarco was shrugging into his topcoat, she asked, 'Are you finally over that ex-wife of yours?'

DeMarco laughed, sat back down, and told her about his cousin getting arrested and Marie having the nerve to ask him for help. He concluded by saying, 'Yeah, I'm definitely over her.'

Miranda Bloom looked at him for a long moment with her marvelous, dark, seen-everything eyes. Then she reached out and patted his hand and said, 'Oh, honey, you are *so* not over her.'

29

Oliver Lincoln sat on the patio of his Key West home, flipping through a copy of *GQ*, drinking iced coffee. The soothing burble of a nearby fountain – he liked fountains; he had three on his estate – added to his contentment. A feature on Italian tailors reminded him that he needed to contact Rubinacci and schedule a fitting. Spring was just around the corner, and he needed a few new lightweight suits. The Naples tailor was so busy that if he didn't visit soon –

'I'm so sorry to disturb you, Mr Lincoln.'

Lincoln looked up. It was Esperanza, his maid.

'Mr Harris is on the phone. I know you said you didn't want to be disturbed . . .'

'You did the right thing, dear. I'll take the call. Thank you.'

Lincoln was always polite to his domestic staff and

he paid them well, and they, in turn, took very good care of him. Lincoln was not, however, happy that Harris was calling. Harris was a conduit, a human relay station, and the only reason he could be calling was because the client wanted to speak to Lincoln. And that meant Lincoln would have to leave his comfortable home and his lovely shaded patio with its bubbling fountain.

'What is it, Harris?' Lincoln said into the phone. He had no need to be polite to Harris.

'At eleven-thirty,' Harris said, 'Prudential is expected to be at seventy, Amerigas at thirty-two, Johnson and Johnson at fifty-six, Credit Suisse at fifty-eight, and Chubb at ninety-seven.'

Harris worked for a national brokerage firm, and if by some fluke a law enforcement agency happened to note that either the client or Lincoln had called the firm – or was called *by* the firm – that wouldn't be considered unusual. And whenever the client or Lincoln called Harris, they didn't call Harris's extension directly but went though a number used by the general public. And if someone happened to be tapping Lincoln's phone, they would have heard Harris give reasonably accurate predictions for five stocks for a particular time of day, but the five stock prices given equaled a ten-digit phone number – 703-256-5897 – assigned to a public booth, and the time given was the time Lincoln was to call the number.

But connecting with the client was annoying.

Lincoln would now have to drive to a public phone booth, making sure he didn't use one he'd used before or one too close to his house. And finding a functioning phone booth was no easy matter. The other thing that irked him was that the client had the audacity to presume that Lincoln would just drop whatever he was doing and make the call at the time specified. Well, considering what he was being paid, Lincoln had to admit that wasn't completely unreasonable.

He checked his watch. He had an hour and a half before he had to make the call. He took a shower and shaved, then dressed in fawn-colored linen-silk trousers, a whimsical Charvet sport shirt, and Spanish sandals. On his head he wore a white Borsalino straw hat and Persol sunglasses. He looked in the mirror and was delighted by his reflection.

Lincoln had been told before that he looked like a young Orson Welles. He was tall, six-three, and powerfully built. If he didn't watch his diet he could become quite obese – as Orson had in his later years – but he did watch his diet. He had sleek black hair, a handsome, somewhat arrogant face, and sensuous lips – appropriate, he thought, for a sensuous man.

There had been some rather ferocious two-legged predators who'd made the mistake of thinking that Lincoln, a man with style, was easy prey. The predators no longer walked the planet, but Lincoln did – shod in Spanish sandals.

He left the main house and strolled to the converted carriage house where he stored his cars. Which should he drive: the Porsche, the Jag, or the Mercedes SUV? The Porsche, he decided. It was too lovely a day to drive anything other than a convertible. He drove slowly down the long driveway toward the main entrance to his property, admiring his yard as he drove, and then waited patiently for the gates to open. Oliver Lincoln was a patient man.

He found a phone booth on the beach, one that wouldn't be too noisy, one where he could watch lovely young women walk by in their swimwear. At precisely eleven-thirty he made the call.

The client began speaking as soon as he answered the phone, before even confirming that it was Lincoln calling. Not only was that rude, it was also rather rash. The odds were high that Lincoln was the caller, but it was also possible someone could have dialed the number by mistake.

'We may have a problem,' the client said.

'Really,' Lincoln said, but he doubted that was the case. On the other hand, the client was not given to panic.

'There's a man,' the client said. 'He's some sort of investigator who works for Congress. I'm not sure who he works for specifically, but he's not a cop and he's not very high up the food chain. However, he's taken an abnormal interest in the . . . the recent events.'

'Such as?' Lincoln said.

'He's talked to the DEA twice about that idiot Cray.'

'So?' Lincoln said. 'Cray is dead and the FBI – according to *your* sources – are happy with the explanation for his fingerprint.'

'That may be, but I don't like the fact that he's asking questions at all.'

'Is there anything else?'

'Yes, he was the one who found the Capitol policeman's body. He apparently went to his home to question him.'

'But since the policeman's dead, I still don't see that we have a problem,' Lincoln said.

'He was also in Key West,' the client said.

'Oh,' Lincoln said.

'Yeah, I thought that might get your attention.'

'What was he doing here?' Lincoln said.

'I don't know. My source at Homeland Security just said he was down there.'

'Why was he at Homeland Security?'

'He was asking about the man from New York.'

The client meant Youseff Khalid, the man who had tried to hijack the shuttle from LaGuardia.

Lincoln didn't say anything for a moment. Then he asked, 'Is there something you want me to do, or is this call simply informational?'

'I want you to do something. I don't like this man's . . . persistence. And there's something else. I found out he was involved in wrapping up an espionage ring on the West Coast a while ago, but I couldn't get any details on what his role was. His name was mentioned only once in the press; then it disappeared like he was never there. What I'm saying is, this guy might be some kind of heavy hitter and I can't take that chance.'

'But what do you want me to do *exactly*?' Lincoln said.

'Neutralize him in some way. Incapacitate him. I don't care what you do, but do something to stop his meddling.'

'I'm not sure that's wise,' Lincoln said. 'You said he works for Congress. If somebody in the House assigned him to investigate, and if something were to happen to him, that could cause complications. All you have so far is a man without a badge asking questions, but he's not getting any answers other than those we want the public to have.'

'I don't want to take the chance, not at this point,' the client said. 'Do something.'

Lincoln could refuse, but to refuse would reduce his income. 'I think it's going to take about two hundred thousand to do what you want done,' he said.

'That's fine,' the client said.

That was the one thing Lincoln liked about the client: there was never any quibbling over money.

30

Their trips to the refinery at night were the most dangerous.

During the day, there were cars and people about, and trucks and vans were constantly moving around the area. A boy walking his dog in the open field on the west side of the plant wasn't particularly noteworthy, provided the boy didn't get too close to the perimeter fence. And a vehicle parked for a few minutes at some spot in which a man in a baseball cap appeared to be studying a road map or adding water to the radiator wasn't likely to give cause for alarm if the vehicle didn't stay there too long.

But at night it was different. The businesses closest to the refinery were mostly industrial, plants that manufactured things like tires and cardboard boxes and sheet metal, and most of these industries were open only during the day. The nearest restaurants and retail stores and homes were approximately two miles away, so there were few reasons for people to be in the vicinity of the refinery at night.

And on this trip the boy needed to walk the perimeter of the plant.

They were completing the final phase of their preparations. They needed to find a point of entry and then the safest route to the tanks and pipes containing the hydrofluoric acid. The refinery was well lit in some places, with huge overhead lights that shined down onto pumps and control stations that housed meters and valves. But other locations throughout the plant were less well lit because there was normally no need for people to go into these areas at night.

The perimeter of the plant was similarly well illuminated, particularly near the entry gates, and lights were placed every fifty yards or so along the top of the barbed-wire fence that surrounded the plant, but there were many places along the perimeter where the lights didn't overlap. So the boy had been given two tasks: find the best place to enter the plant and find a route through the plant to the hydrofluoric acid tanks that was mostly in the dark.

The refinery worked three shifts a day. They would plant the devices on the graveyard shift, which began at 11 P.M. and ended at 7 A.M. There were only about ten workers on this shift. He had read that these workers maintained the equipment, and their primary duty was to ensure, when the main work-force came to work the next day, that the refinery was fully functional and ready to operate. And he had seen only two guards on the graveyard shift, two middle-aged men who sat in a shack near the refinery's main entrance.

The graveyard shift. He liked that name.

'Son of a bitch,' Eddie Kolowski said, and pulled his glove back on. Every time he took off a glove to get a smoke, his damn fingers almost froze.

Before they'd assigned the new guy to their shift, when it had just been him and Billy in the shack, this job hadn't been too bad. He and Billy would sit there bullshitting, listening to the radio, nodding off when it suited them – and if he felt like taking a little nip, he'd take a little nip. But now they had the new guy, a little Mormon shit. He didn't drink, he didn't smoke, he didn't cuss. Eddie just *hated* the son of a bitch.

They were supposed to walk around the plant on a continuous basis, one guy always outside walking, while the other guy stayed in the shack to man the phones. In the summer, that wasn't so bad, but in the winter, when it was colder than shit out, when the damn wind just came screaming off the lake, him and Billy said, Fuck that shit. No way were they going to freeze their asses off, walking outside. But now with this new guy, they were afraid he'd rat them out if they didn't follow the procedure; he looked like the type that would. They figured after a couple of months he'd either quit – most young guys didn't last too long – or he'd figure out that there wasn't much point in just walking around in the dark, but for a little while they'd have to pretend they were playing the game.

There was one spot near the southeast corner of the plant where there was a good windbreak, and for some reason, maybe the chemicals they had in these pipes, the pipes there were hot. So Eddie, when it was his turn to patrol, always headed right for that spot and planted his ass on one of the hot pipes, and then he would sit there and take little hits from his flask and smoke until it was time to head back to the shack.

What the hell? Was that somebody standing there? The guy – he thought it was a guy, a little guy – was just standing there in a shadow between the lights. What the hell was he doing? Eddie waited a bit, figuring the guy was just some bum and he'd haul out his pecker in a minute and take a piss and move on, but the guy just continued to stand there. What the fuck?

Eddie thought about pulling the pistol out of his holster, but to do that he'd have to take off his glove again to unsnap the little metal button on the holster flap. Screw that. He pulled the flashlight off his belt and shined it right at the guy's face.

It was a kid. A short, scrawny kid with a big honker. Not black. Mexican or something else, and man, did he have a nose on him! He figured the kid would bolt like a scared rabbit when the light hit him, but he didn't. He just shielded his eyes with his hand.

'What are you doing?' Eddie asked.

'Looking for my dog,' the kid said.

'Your dog? At this time of night?'

'I live over there,' the kid said, and pointed vaguely behind him. 'My dog was barking, and when I looked outside to see why I saw him run off. He must have seen something, a raccoon or a possum, and he chased it. He came this way and I just saw him, here along the fence, but now I don't.'

'Well, he sure as shit ain't on *this* side of the fence,' Eddie said. 'Not unless he dug a hole to get under it.' Eddie shined his flashlight along the bottom of the fence. 'And I don't see no hole.'

'Yeah,' the kid said. 'Maybe he went back home.' Then the kid turned to leave, but before he did, he said, 'Thank you.'

Nice kid.

'Hey, what kind of dog was it?' Eddie said.

'A German shepherd,' the boy said. 'Be careful if you see him. He bites.'

Eddie thought the kid might have smiled when he said this.

*   *   *

It was his fault the boy was almost caught. He hadn't been watching the guard shack at all. He'd been watching a group of three workers who had left one of the buildings and were working on a pump on the north side of the refinery, and he'd been making sure that the workers didn't go to the other side of the refinery where the boy was. If they had, he would have called the boy on the cell phone he had given him. The boy had been told that if the cell phone vibrated, he wasn't to answer it; he was to come quickly back to the car. But he never saw the guard leave the shack, and that was inexcusably careless on his part.

'You did well,' he told the boy. 'Very well. The worst thing you could have done was run.'

He was extremely concerned that the guard had been standing where he was. Previously the guards on this shift had never left the shack near the front gate. And the boy said the guard had been sitting in the shadows, not walking where the lights were, so he hadn't been able to see him.

'You still think the southeast corner is the best place to enter?' he asked the boy.

'Yes. It's the shortest route to the tanks.'

'Well, the guards have changed their procedure since the last time we were here. We're going to have to come back a few more nights and watch them.'

The boy didn't say anything. He just nodded his head.

He loved this boy.

31

DeMarco needed Emma and he needed Fat Neil. He needed Emma because there was something he wanted her to do that he couldn't. He needed Fat Neil because he wanted to pry into the finances of a United States senator.

Neil was an old friend of Emma's, and DeMarco had used his services in the past. He called himself an 'information broker,' this bland euphemism meaning that if a client was willing to pay his outrageous fees and wanted information on a certain party or subject, Neil would tap into a vast network of contacts to obtain said information. And if he couldn't obtain the information legally, he would hack into computer networks or place bugs in boardrooms and bedrooms or do anything else necessary to satisfy a paying customer's desires. Neil worked for both the private sector and the U.S. government, and it was most likely because of his government work that he wasn't currently in jail. DeMarco assumed that he had worked for Emma on occasion when she was with the DIA, though neither she nor Neil had ever confirmed this.

Neil was a short, wide man with a big head and a bigger ego. His once-blond hair was thinning on top, but what remained he tied into a thin, shaggy ponytail that reached down past his collar. Neil had married not long ago, and DeMarco was surprised that Neil's new wife hadn't made him clip off the unsightly extension. Wives can't resist the urge to renovate their spouses, and Neil was ripe for major improvements. She was managing to get him to dress a little better, though, DeMarco noted. On all the other occasions when he had seen Neil, he had been wearing shorts, beat-up sandals, and a Hawaiian shirt. He must have owned fifty Hawaiian shirts. Today he was wearing a V-neck sweater, a nice pair of gray slacks, and cordovan loafers.

The meeting was being held in Neil's office because Neil, even though he was the one billing DeMarco for his time, didn't like to leave his desk. Emma, who was working for free and had come only as a favor to DeMarco, had been somewhat reluctant to attend. She said she was training Christine's dog to do its business outdoors, and she didn't want to disrupt the process. DeMarco immediately had a vivid image of

Emma wadding up the critter like a bedraggled furry sponge and mopping up the pee on one of her Persian rugs. Fortunately, Emma didn't like Bill Broderick's politics and had decided that DeMarco's problem took precedence over housebreaking Christine's mutt.

After they had assembled in Neil's soundproof, electronically impenetrable room – Neil was paranoid that there was someone out there as good as he was – DeMarco briefed them on the few facts he had and concluded by saying, 'So I have no idea if there's really some sort of super conspiracy going on here, but there are too many things that don't make sense.'

'Such as?' Neil asked. He'd been only half listening while DeMarco had been talking, busy taking something out of a box.

'Such as the following,' DeMarco said. 'First you have a guy like Reza Zarif killing his family, an act that's inconceivable to those who knew him. Then the guy whose fingerprint was found on the bullet box conveniently dies in a car accident before the Bureau can talk to him. Next there's Rollie Patterson, a normally indecisive slug who suddenly decides to take a walk around the Capitol in freezing weather and becomes some sort of take-charge Wyatt Earp when he sees Mustafa Ahmed. Rollie's actions, just like Reza's, were out of character and he too died, making it impossible for anyone to question him further. Oh, I almost forgot: Rollie had a newly purchased RV sitting in his driveway.'

'So you're assuming that this Rollie person was told in advance that Mustafa was going to try to blow up the Capitol and he was paid to kill him,' Neil said. Neil had finally managed to extract from the box whatever was inside it, but DeMarco couldn't see what it was.

'I'm not *assuming* that,' DeMarco said. 'I'm just saying it's a possibility. And although I don't have any evidence to support it, I think something similar may have happened with the air marshal who shot the hijacker. I think he may have been tipped off in advance that Youseff Khalid was going to try to hijack the plane, and just like Rollie he plugs the guy before he can do anything. Or confess to anything.'

'Is the marshal dead too?' Neil said.

'Not that I know of. I tried to see him when I went up to New York, but he wasn't home. He's one of the reasons I need some help; while I'm trying to track him down I need to get some other things moving.'

Now DeMarco could see what Neil had taken from the box. It was one of those games they give hyper-active ten-year-olds on car trips, the type where you try to get all the little BBs to roll into the proper hole. Neil was now playing with the game.

'I'll tell you another thing that's bothering me,' DeMarco said, speaking to the top of Neil's head as he tilted the BB toy back and forth in his hands. 'With the exception of Zarif's family, none of these three terrorist events resulted in anyone dying except the supposed terrorists. Reza was shot down before he could crash his plane into the White House, Mustafa's bomb didn't explode, and the shuttle hijacker was killed before he could do anything other than scare a planeful of people. If al-Qaeda's really behind these things, I have a hard time believing they're this inept.'

'So what do you want us to do?' Emma said, speaking for the first time.

'A bunch of things. The first thing I want Neil to do is find out who Broderick's biggest backers are.'

'Bastard,' Neil said, speaking to one of the BBs; then he added, 'Do you actually think Broderick could be personally involved in these incidents?'

'I'm not saying he is,' DeMarco said, 'but every-thing that's happened works in his favor. So maybe that's why someone is doing these things, to scare people and get Broderick's bill passed, and maybe that same person is backing Broderick financially.'

'I don't know,' Neil said, sounding unconvinced. 'Someone would have to *really* want that bill passed. I mean – Jesus, two kids were killed.'

'I've thought about that,' DeMarco said, 'and I can come up with a couple different motives. One is hate. Whoever's doing this hates Muslims and wants them treated like the Jews in Nazi Germany, little yellow stars of . . . of somebody pinned to their coats.'

'But why do they hate Muslims?'

'Hell, I don't know, Neil! Why are some people bigots? Why do some people become white suprema- cists? And, by the by, the guy Donny Cray worked for, some character name Jubal Pugh, heads up some white-power group and Rollie had some racist litera- ture in his house. So maybe the people doing this are just Muslim-hating white-power loonies. Guys like Timothy McVeigh who get a screwball idea in their head and start blowing things up.'

Before either Emma or Neil could object to DeMarco's logic – or point out the flaws in his logic – DeMarco said, 'Another motive could be money.'

'Money?' Neil said. 'How could anyone make money from this?'

'I don't know, but whenever a law is passed in Congress, some people make money and some people lose money. It's like a political law of physics.'

'But how could someone make any money by kicking out Muslim students?' Neil said.

'I just said I don't know, Neil! Will you put that damn game down and pay attention? What I do know is that we need to look for a money motive, particularly among anyone backing Broderick.'

'There's something else we should look for,' Emma said.

'What's that?'

'Expertise. If these events were not orchestrated by al-Qaeda, you need to look for somebody or some group who has the ability to acquire C-Four and fabricate a plastic gun. Somebody who has the experience, the contacts, and the organizational ability to plan these ops.'

'Good point,' DeMarco said. Then, sounding like the man in charge, knowing that no one was ever in charge of Neil or Emma, he added, 'So Neil finds out who's supporting Broderick financially, and sees if any of these people could have a hate or a money motive and if they have the expertise to pull this stuff off. He also pulls the financial records for Rollie and this air marshal who shot the hijacker to see if there's anything squirrelly there. I wanna know how Rollie paid for his RV. I'm going to get the autopsy results for Rollie and Donny Cray, and I want to check out this air marshal some more.'

'And what do you want me to do?' Emma said.

32

The problem, DeMarco had told Emma, was that he didn't know any Muslims. Not one. He hadn't been able to talk to Youseff's wife, in part because she didn't speak English and he didn't speak whatever language people from Somalia spoke. Not even knowing the name of the language they spoke in Somalia showed how ignorant he was. But the other reason he hadn't been successful questioning her was because he was a white guy and looked just like all the white FBI guys who had already questioned her.

The biggest weakness in DeMarco's conspiracy theory was that he could find no evidence that either Mustafa Ahmed or Youseff Khalid had been coerced to do what they did. He suspected in Reza Zarif's case that somebody – possibly the late and un-lamented Donny Cray – had held a gun to the heads of Reza's children, but he couldn't find anyone who had been killed or kidnapped or tortured to make Youseff and Mustafa do what they did. And one of the reasons he couldn't do this was because he couldn't get people to talk to him.

But Emma did know Muslims. And she wasn't a white man. DeMarco wanted Emma to see if she could find someone close to Mustafa Ahmed who might have been used to force him to strap on a bomb. They decided to focus on Mustafa because he had lived in D.C., whereas Youseff's family was in New York.

The first thing Emma did was call a man who knew a number of languages spoken in Muslim countries. He was an interpreter who worked at the DIA, his parents were from Pakistan, and he was a Muslim. His name was Zafarullah Nazimuddin, a name almost impossible for most of his coworkers to pronounce or remember. His American friends all called him Zafa.

Emma paid a gypsy cabdriver to borrow his cab for the day and then told Zafa she wanted him to pretend to be a cabbie, park at some of the stands where Mustafa used to wait, and talk to drivers who knew him. She wanted Zafa to find out as much as he could about Mustafa and identify the people closest to him. Zafa, being very bright, took less than three hours to accomplish his mission.

'Emma,' he said, 'everybody all says the same thing. Mustafa was a soccer nut, and the person closest to him was one of his nieces. The girl's an Olympic-caliber player, and she was given a scholarship to UVA. The guy kept a picture of her on the sun visor of his cab, a shot he took of her heading the ball into the goal, and he was always showing it to his pals.' Four hours later Emma was in Charlottesville, Virginia, lying to a sweet woman in student housing to find out where Mustafa's niece resided.

Anisa Aziz wasn't so much pretty as striking. She had an angular face, high cheekbones, a strong nose, and heavy eyebrows over intense black eyes. Her eyes radiated intelligence. She was wearing a T-shirt and sweatpants, and maybe it was the athletic wear, but Emma had the impression that this girl just *flew* down the field when she was playing. To Emma, Anisa had seemed unusually nervous when she answered her door and saw Emma standing there. Maybe that was because Emma was a stranger or maybe it was because she had been expecting someone official to come calling – someone from the FBI – because of what her uncle had done.

'May I help you?' she said to Emma.

'I'd like to talk to you about your uncle,' Emma said.

'Are you with the police? The FBI?'

'No,' Emma said, 'but I'm working with somebody in the government who doesn't believe that your uncle was a terrorist, somebody who believes he was forced to do what he did.'

'My uncle was the kindest man I ever knew.'

'I'm sure he was, Anisa, but then why did he do it? Why did he try to blow up the Capitol?'

Anisa hesitated before she spoke, but when she did, all she said was, 'I don't know.' She didn't look at Emma when she said this.

'Were you threatened in some way? Did someone tell your uncle that you'd be harmed if he didn't do what he was told?'

The girl shook her head. 'No. Nobody did anything to me. And I don't know why he did it. Now I have to go. I have a test to study for,' she added lamely.

Anisa started to close the door and, when she did, Emma saw a bruise on the inside of the girl's upper right arm; then she noticed a mark on her neck. The bruise on her arm could have been caused by someone grasping her arm, but the girl was an athlete and there could be other explanations for the bruise. The mark on her neck, though, didn't look like something you'd get from running into another player. It was an ugly red line, and it looked to Emma like a ligature mark made by something thin, not a rope or a cord, maybe a wire. Emma stopped Anisa from shutting the door.

'How did you get that mark on your neck?'

'Mark?' the girl said, as if confused, but her hand had moved unconsciously in the direction of her neck. 'I don't know what you're talking about.'

'Anisa, don't you want people to know the truth about your uncle?'

'The truth! It wouldn't matter what I said. You people think we're all terrorists, even people like me who were born here. I'm as American as you are,' she added, her dark eyes flashing, daring Emma to say that she wasn't.

'I know you are,' Emma said. 'And if you need help, if someone's threatening you . . .'

'I have to study,' Anisa said, and began to push the door closed. 'You have to go.'

'Okay, I will,' Emma said. 'But I want you to take this.' She handed the girl a card. 'On the front of that card is my name and my cell phone number. On the back is the name and phone number of a Muslim woman, a woman from Afghanistan who now lives in Maryland. All I'm asking is that you call that woman and ask her about me. She's expecting your call. After you speak to her, and if you feel you can trust me, call me. Please.'

Emma found a motel near the campus and checked in. She wasn't sure if Anisa would call her, but she wanted to be close by in case she did. She flopped down on the bed and lay there looking up at the ceiling – and her mind drifted back to Afghanistan, to a village on the slopes of the Hindu Kush, to the woman she had told Anisa to call.

Emma, four U.S. Army Rangers, and an interpreter had been choppered into the village. She and the men were all dressed like the villagers, Emma wearing a loose-fitting robe, a veil covering her face. Their mission was to talk to the village chieftain: a ruthless thug, an opium trader, and a man who had gained control of his small fiefdom by shooting his predecessor in the back but who, for the moment, was an American ally. This was in the days when Osama bin Laden was an American ally as well, helping the Afghanis fight the Russians.

They explained to the chieftain that the Russians were building an airfield in a valley approximately fifty miles from the chieftain's village – fifty *hard* miles through steep mountain terrain that could only be navigated by brave men and sure-footed packhorses. And when they got close to the airfield, they'd have to travel mostly at night, because the Russians would have helicopters in the sky looking for mujahideen warriors. But in a month, Russian troopships and helicopters would begin to use the airfield, and then men equipped with surface-to-air missiles and mortars, men hidden in the caves and rocks surrounding the meadow, could do significant damage.

'How do you know about this airfield?' the chieftain said. When he spoke he looked at the interpreter, never at Emma, even though he could tell that the interpreter was only telling him what Emma said. The chieftain was a man who found it unfathomable that a woman could be speaking to him about a serious matter like this.

Emma pointed upward and said through the interpreter, 'We have eyes in the sky. Satellites and spy planes.' She wasn't sure the chieftain knew what a satellite was, but she knew he'd be too proud to ask.

'And for doing this, what do I receive?'

'Missiles and mortars,' Emma said. 'And a chance to vanquish your enemy.'

The chieftain smiled. 'You can't eat missiles.'

'Three thousand dollars for going to the airfield,' Emma said. 'Five thousand dollars for every troopship you destroy and two thousand for every helicopter. In American dollars.'

That was an incredible amount of money for people in this part of the world, and Emma knew that the percentage the chieftain would share with his people would be minuscule. She also knew the chieftain would lie about how many aircraft he had destroyed, but that was irrelevant. The only thing that mattered was disrupting Russian operations.

The chieftain didn't say anything. He looked down at the map lying in the dirt and, with a cracked, blackened fingernail, traced the route to the meadow.

'*Three* thousand for a helicopter,' he said.

Negotiations completed, Emma had one of the Rangers contact their base camp to send back the helicopter and offload the weapons, but she was informed that there would be a six-hour delay for some unspecified reason. Weather, mechanical problems, Russian activity – it didn't really matter; it was out of her control. She went into the tent where her men were waiting and began to open a packet of what used to be called C-rations but were then called M.R.E.s – meals, ready to eat. She'd always suspected the name was some bureaucrat's idea of a joke. She was trying to open a can of peaches with the ridiculous little can opener that came in the packet when she heard a commotion outside the tent, a man shouting and people whistling and clapping.

'Henderson,' she said to one of the Rangers, 'see what's happening.'

Henderson was the ranking Ranger, and he and the interpreter came back a couple minutes later. 'They're going to stone a woman,' Henderson said. 'She committed adultery.' Henderson was a hardened combat veteran, but this was something that seemed to shock even him.

Emma sat there a moment, rubbing her eyes with the thumb and forefinger of her right hand. She knew she should do nothing. She was under strict orders not to interfere in local affairs, and in particular she knew her mission was to make an ally out of this particular chieftain. But she *couldn't* do nothing.

Emma rose and walked out of the tent. Behind her she heard Henderson say, 'Ma'am. Where are you going, ma'am?'

Emma ignored Henderson. She stood there looking at the scene in what passed for a village square. A woman was standing there, her hands bound behind her back, a terrified look on her face. A man was standing next to her, screaming to the mob that had gathered. Emma didn't know if the man was a religious leader, a judge, or the woman's husband. As the man was talking – raving, actually – she saw boys placing stones in baskets and cooking pots. The boys' eyes gleamed with anticipation.

Emma looked around for the chieftain and finally saw him. His butt was resting on the rim of the village well, and he was smoking a cigarette as he chatted casually with another man. At one point, he gestured toward the bound woman in the square and laughed and shook his head. Emma guessed that he was saying the Afghani equivalent of 'The dumb bitch, can you believe it?'

Emma turned toward the interpreter, a doe-eyed man with a receding chin, and said, 'Come with me,' and began walking toward the chieftain.

'Ma'am, you can't interfere,' Henderson, the Ranger sergeant, said. When Emma ignored him, he muttered, 'Goddammit all' under his breath, then said to his men, 'Get your weapons.'

Emma had been with the four-man Ranger unit for three weeks now, and when the unit was first assembled, the men had been told she was in charge. They hadn't been told her rank or what organization she belonged to, but the bird colonel who briefed them told them she was the *man*. The soldiers figured that the tall blond gal was from one of the spy shops and it was probably some kinda political thing that the army had to go along with, but they had a hard time believing that they were going into the badlands with a young good-looking woman leading their squad. They'd follow her orders, of course – they were Rangers – but what they really expected was that Emma would listen to their sergeant and do whatever he said. It didn't take them long to figure out that she was bright enough to ask for the sergeant's input, but in the end she was the one who made the decisions. Emma had, even then, all those indefinable qualities of leadership that inspire confidence and obedience and loyalty, and after only a short period the Rangers were accustomed to following her lead. But now she was doing something that the soldiers knew was wrong – or at least wrong from the perspective of their mission.

Emma strode up to the chieftain. He raised his haunches off the rim of the well and looked down at her; he was six-foot-six. Emma took the veil off so he could see her face – she *hated* that damn veil – and while looking directly at the chieftain, she said to her interpreter, 'Tell him I want him to stop this.'

She saw the rage forming in the chieftain's face; women didn't speak to him that way. He looked as if he might strike Emma, but he restrained himself. He said something the interpreter translated as 'This is a tribal matter. Go back to your tent, woman.'

Emma suspected that if she threatened not to pay

him or give him the missiles, he'd agree and then
stone the woman as soon as the Americans left. She
also knew she had to come up with some solution
that would allow the chieftain to save face. He'd kill
Emma and her men before he'd be humiliated by
her in front of his tribe.

Emma looked over her shoulder. The man who
had been speaking in the center of the square had
stopped. The condemned woman had slumped to the
ground. The villagers were all looking over at the
chieftain and Emma. Most of the villagers at this
point, even the women, held stones in their hands.

'Tell him,' Emma said to her interpreter, 'that the
American army wants that woman. Tell him we need
a . . . a cook.'

Henderson, who was now standing next to Emma,
said, 'Ma'am, you can't do this.'

'Tell him,' Emma said, ignoring Henderson, looking
directly into the chieftain's eyes, 'that we'll pay him
a thousand dollars for the woman.'

The chieftain looked at Emma, then over at his
people, then back at Emma again. 'The woman has
a daughter,' the chieftain said.

'Tell him we'll train the daughter to be a cook too.
We'll pay five hundred for her.'

'Jesus Christ, ma'am,' Henderson said.

When they returned to their base camp with the
woman and her daughter, the bird colonel in charge
chewed out Emma as only a bird colonel can, then

asked her what in the holy hell they were supposed
to do with an Afghani woman and her daughter.
Thanks to the Red Cross and to people Emma
contacted back in the States, a year later the woman
and her daughter were in America. The woman never
acclimated to her new country and, oddly enough,
seemed to resent Emma for what she had done. The
daughter, however, thrived and was now the assistant manager of a bank in Maryland. The daughter
would tell Anisa Aziz that Emma could be trusted.

But Anisa didn't call. The next day Emma returned
to Washington, D.C.

33

DeMarco made the mistake of telling Mahoney that he was going to Long Island to talk to the air marshal who had killed Youseff Khalid. It was a mistake because Mahoney said, 'Well, hell, since you're going up north anyway, stop by and see Flynn and have dinner with Father Mike.'

This meant DeMarco would now have to leave D.C. at the crack of dawn, see the air marshal in New York, then catch another plane to Boston – and have to endure the heightened security at three airports instead of two. After he met with Flynn and had dinner with the priest, he'd then have to spend the night in Boston because the last shuttle would have left for the day, and he would have to catch *another* early A.M. flight back to Washington with a hangover so bad his hair would hurt.

But, he had to admit, he was looking forward to dinner with Father Mike.

DeMarco had called Orin Blunt's home the night before, and when a man answered the phone he'd hung up. He wasn't going to ask the air marshal if it was okay to come up and see him. He'd just knock on his door.

And knock he did. The man who answered the door was holding a magazine in his hand and wearing a faded blue denim shirt, khaki pants, and boat shoes. He was about DeMarco's height but didn't have DeMarco's bulk. He had gray hair cut close to his scalp, small features, and the kind of eyes and face that poker players pray for; they gave away nothing.

When DeMarco showed Blunt his ID and said he wanted to talk to him about the shooting on the shuttle, Blunt stared impassively for a second and then invited him into his home. He didn't offer DeMarco anything to drink; he just pointed him at a dining room table and took a seat across from him.

'Why are you here?' Blunt said. 'The TSA review board has already given me a clean bill on the shooting.'

Blunt had placed the magazine he'd been holding on the table next to him. It looked to DeMarco like a catalog for power boats.

'Thinking about buying a boat?' DeMarco said.

Blunt just stared at DeMarco for a moment and then said again, 'Why are you here?'

'I want to know how you happened to be on the same plane as Youseff Khalid that morning.'

'I wasn't on the same plane as him,' Blunt said. '*He* was on the same plane as me. That's the flight I was assigned to that day, and if things had gone the way they normally do, I would have caught a flight out of Reagan to Chicago, and then from Chicago back to New York.'

'I've got calls out to people who will tell me if you requested that flight or if you traded flights with someone,' DeMarco said. And that wasn't a lie. DeMarco had asked his new buddy Jerry Hansen, at Homeland Security, to see if Blunt had had himself assigned to Youseff's flight but Hansen hadn't gotten back to him. But what he really wanted was to see Blunt's reaction to his threat – and there was none.

Blunt just said, 'That's good.'

DeMarco figured that maybe somebody had killed Rollie Patterson to keep him from talking because Rollie seemed like the type who would cave the minute a cop placed him in the hot seat. Orin Blunt, on the other hand, wouldn't talk if you put his nuts in a vice.

'I understand you're on leave and thinking about retiring,' DeMarco said.

Blunt nodded his head. 'Shooting that guy really shook me up. I don't want to ever have to do something like that again.'

'Yeah,' DeMarco said. 'I can tell you've really been traumatized.'

There were many individuals, businesses, and organizations that contributed to Mahoney – and most of these contributors Mahoney was happy, even proud to name. But there were some who filled the speaker's war chest that either Mahoney or the contributor wished to keep secret.

Bailey Flynn was one of these secret donors. Flynn represented several businessmen like himself who operated clubs where young girls danced barely clothed or not clothed at all. Mahoney, a true believer in the arts *and* the First Amendment, felt that these businessmen had a right to representation; he just preferred that places like Chucky's All Nude Revue not be prominently listed among his supporters. And although its mission was certainly loftier than Bailey Flynn's, the archdiocese of Boston also could not afford to be identified as a Mahoney booster. The Church's tax-exempt status might come into jeopardy if it were seen to be emptying its collection plates directly into the speaker's pockets.

And thus DeMarco's reason for going to Boston: to meet those who directed the dancers and those who directed the choir – and take from them envelopes that he never, ever, looked into.

DeMarco dispatched Bailey Flynn in short order. He stopped at a club in Revere, took a seat, and ordered a Coke; he needed to keep his alcohol level on empty before meeting with Father Mike. A few minutes later Flynn joined him. Flynn was sixty, tall and perpetually morose, as if he spent his days embalming bodies. While Flynn told DeMarco that 'those blue-nosed sons-a-bitches have ruined the Combat Zone in Boston, and Mahoney goddamn well better put a stop to that shit before the same thing happens everywhere else,' DeMarco watched a girl with tassels on her nipples dance with as much enthusiasm as people display on their way to the dentist. Five minutes later he was on his way.

The thing about Jesuits, DeMarco knew from experience, was that they weren't necessarily smarter than you but they were certainly better educated. Not only did these men go to college and spend several years in a seminary learning the priestly arts, they almost invariably had doctorates in more than one subject. And Father Michael Thomas Kelly was not only better educated than DeMarco, he was also smarter, but as he never made a point of this, there was no other man on the planet that DeMarco enjoyed dining with more.

DeMarco had never seen the priest in a Roman collar. Tonight he was dressed in a soft tan jacket made of something that looked like suede, a brown silk T-shirt that showed off his physique, and dark brown slacks that fit him perfectly. With the possible exception of Joe's cousin Danny, Father Mike was probably the handsomest man that DeMarco knew. If he ever tired of being a cleric, he could make his fortune as a middle-aged model.

Although Father Mike never discussed his job, DeMarco had always suspected that the priest did for Cardinal Mackey what DeMarco did for Mahoney. If the Church had some sticky problem – and it had had more than its share of late – and if the problem couldn't be handled through normal channels, Father Mike would be dispatched. DeMarco also suspected that beneath the thick layers of charm and wit and blarney there was a hard side to the priest that came out when called for.

Dinner began as it usually did with Father Mike: martinis, more than one. From there they proceeded to a bottle of white wine, followed by a bottle of red, followed by a snifter of cognac that was old and smooth and absurdly expensive. And between the martinis and the cognac they ate a meal that should have been added to the list of deadly sins.

During dinner, Father Mike talked. He talked about everything: sports, movies, books, and, of course, politics. His speech was filled with quotes from famous dead people and anecdotes about famous living ones, all of whom it seemed he'd met – the living ones, that is. And he was so skilled at the art of conversation that he made DeMarco feel as though he was actually contributing, though the reality was that DeMarco hardly spoke at all and didn't mind that he didn't.

At one point, DeMarco noticed a gorgeous woman in her thirties smile at Father Mike and he smiled back, a smile that almost certainly made the lady tingle all way down to her toes. DeMarco had no evidence whatsoever that Father Mike didn't strictly adhere to his vow of celibacy; oddly enough, he believed sincerely that he did. But how he managed to do so the way women threw themselves at him, DeMarco couldn't fathom.

Three hours after the dinner commenced, Father Mike drove DeMarco to a hotel near Logan Airport, stuffed an envelope into the breast pocket of his suit, and then mumbled something as he made a shoo-fly gesture in the air with his right hand. DeMarco suspected that he'd just been blessed – that a Jesuit had just asked God to keep a completely inebriated man from doing harm to himself as he staggered toward his bed.

34

They would have to alter the plan, but just slightly.

After two nights, he understood the pattern of the guards. One man, who appeared younger than the other two, left the guard shack at 11 P.M., 2 A.M., and 5 A.M. and patrolled for an hour. He patrolled erratically, never following a set pattern, but he tended to stay in areas that were well lit. The second guard began his patrols at midnight and 3 A.M. He would leave the guard shack and go to a small building fifty yards away, a building that looked like some sort of storage shed, and he would stay inside the shed for an hour and then return to the guard shack. The third guard, the one who had seen the boy, patroled at 1 A.M. and 4 A.M., and he either went to the spot at the southeastern corner of the refinery, where he sat and smoked and drank from a small flask, or he went inside the same maintenance shack where the second guard hid.

So the boy would enter the plant as soon as the first guard, the diligent one, returned to the guard shack. That would give him two hours in which to set the devices – twice as long as he needed. To enter the facility, the boy would dig a small hole under the fence. The ground was soft and the boy was small so it wouldn't take long. Because the third guard, the man with the flask, sometimes sat close to the entry point that they had originally selected, the boy would move the entry point fifty yards up the fence line to a spot that was almost as good. After the boy had installed the devices, he would exit by the same hole. If he had time he would fill in the hole with dirt, and if he didn't have time he'd place a piece of cardboard over the hole. The area around the facility was littered with debris; a piece of cardboard lying on the ground near the fence would not be noticed by anyone.

After the devices had been planted, the boy would wait near the refinery. He wouldn't even need to hide; he would sit in the dark until sunrise, and when it was light out he'd just walk about innocently, a boy on his way to wherever boys go. Then at seven-thirty – when the day-shift workers began to stream into the facility, when the children were on their way to school, when the nearby buildings began to fill up with people, when the roads were crowded with cars – the boy would walk up to the main gate of the plant, declare his love for God, and detonate the bombs.

35

It was a hassle for Oliver Lincoln to contact the client, but to contact the Cuban all he had to do was go to a restaurant in Miami and have a nice dinner. The restaurant was very popular and very expensive, and the Cuban owned it.

She sat down with him after he had finished his dinner. He knew, in spite of all the business he'd given her over the years, that she'd charge him for the meal. She was, he was convinced, the most miserly person he'd ever known. She made a good income off the restaurant and an even better income from her other job, but she lived in a fifteen-hundred-square-foot home in a middle-class neighborhood in Miami; she wore off-the-rack clothes; and she drove one of those homely hybrids that got about fifty miles to the gallon. Lincoln suspected that the woman had millions stashed away in a bank in the Cayman Islands – or buried in a can in her backyard – but he had no idea what she was saving the money for. Lincoln couldn't retire because he had such expensive tastes. The Cuban, on the other hand, could have retired years ago had she wanted to, but she didn't. She loved money – not the things money could buy. Oliver Lincoln simply couldn't relate to people like her.

The other odd thing about the Cuban was that she was a beautiful woman who seemingly had no interest in sex. He suspected she was near forty. She had a lush figure, a flawless light-brown complexion, and long lustrous black hair. Lincoln had certainly made the effort to bed her, but she refused to have anything to do with him in anything other than a business capacity. And because he needed to know about her for professional rather than personal reasons, he'd had her followed on a number of occasions. She may have had lovers when she was a teenager, but Lincoln had known her since she was twenty-five, and in all that time she had never dated or lived with anyone that he had been able to discover.

'I want a man either incapacitated or dead,' Lincoln said. 'If he had some sort of accident that put him in the hospital for a couple of months, that would be all right, provided there was no doubt that what happened was an accident. You can kill him if that's easiest, but you have to make certain that it doesn't appear that he was the target; he *must* be collateral damage. For example,' Lincoln said, 'if a bus were to plow into a crowd standing on a corner and he was part of the crowd, that would be acceptable.' Lincoln smiled when he said this; he didn't really expect her to run the man down with a bus, but she didn't smile back. She didn't have a sense of humor either. He would really find her quite tiresome if she wasn't so good at what she did.

'How much?' she said

That was always the first question she asked. No who or where or why or when, but always *how much*?

'Seventy-five thousand,' Lincoln said. Lincoln thought it appropriate to keep half of what the client was paying, and after she tacked on her expenses – and padded them – her bill would be close to a hundred thousand.

As if they were both reading from a script that they'd read from many times before, she said, 'Plus my expenses.'

'Don't I always pay your expenses?' Lincoln said.

'Last time, when I asked you to pay for my shoes, you argued with me.'

'Well, I thought that was rather petty of you, billing me for that item. It wasn't *my* fault that you got Mr Potter's blood on your shoes and had to burn them.' Actually, Lincoln had given her a hard time about the shoes because it amused him to do so. She always presented him with a written expense report detailing every dime she spent on a job, and he always pretended to study it carefully before he paid her. Afterward she would destroy the report while he watched.

'It was a job-related expense,' she said.

'If you say so,' he said, just to tweak her.

She glared at him for a minute, then said, 'When do you want this done?'

'Immediately, of course. Why do you think you're being paid so much?'

36

Upon his return from Boston, DeMarco's small brain trust once again assembled in Fat Neil's office to compare notes and report on what they'd learned.

Emma opened the meeting by looking at DeMarco's bloodshot eyes and saying, 'You look like hell.'

'Thank you,' DeMarco said, and proceeded to give his report. 'Autopsies on both Rollie Patterson and Donny Cray were inconclusive,' he said. 'Rollie had a fresh needle mark in his left thigh, which could have been used to inject some heart-attack-inducing substance into his body. The problem is that Rollie was allergic to everything on the planet except oxygen, and he self-injected to keep from sneezing himself to death. Bottom line, no toxic substances were found in Rollie's body.'

'Which means nothing,' Emma said. 'I can think of three or four things that could cause a heart attack and not leave a trace.'

DeMarco wondered if Emma had considered using one of those 'three or four things' on Christine's dog, but he didn't ask.

'As for Donny Cray,' he said, 'the ME's report noted nothing inconsistent with an idiot not wearing a seat belt and wrecking his car. The problem here is the ME. The guy who did Rollie's autopsy is supposed to be super good. The one who did Donny Cray's lives in Winchester, Virginia, and is primarily a pediatrician. Add that to the fact that Jubal Pugh is a violent character who lives near Winchester. There's the possibility, *if* Pugh's involved in this, that he might have influenced the ME's report.'

'Do you have any evidence that Pugh is involved?' Emma said.

'Absolutely none,' DeMarco said. 'Finally, the air marshal. I met with him, and it was like talking to a slab of granite. I know the guy's planning to retire soon and when I met him he was looking at a power-boat catalog. I think he was tipped off about Youseff being on that plane and paid to blow him away, but nobody'll ever get it out of him.'

'Did the air marshal ask to be put on the same flight as Youseff?' Emma asked.

'No. I had a guy at Homeland Security ask the

same question, and he was told that Blunt had been scheduled for three weeks to be on that flight.'

'All that means,' Emma said, 'is that if someone forced Youseff to attempt the hijacking, they just made sure he got on Blunt's flight.'

'I guess,' DeMarco said. The way his head felt, it was hard to make sense out of anything. 'What'd you get on Blunt's and Patterson's finances, Neil?'

'Nothing noteworthy, no large changes in either man's accounts, which in the case of Rollie is problematic because it leaves open the issue of how he was able to buy his new RV.'

'Both these guys could have been given a bucket of cash,' Emma said. 'And if Rollie was still alive, he'd say that he didn't trust banks and had been saving for years to buy his RV and had been hiding the money under the bed.'

'So in conclusion,' DeMarco said, 'I got shit.' He almost added: *and the worst hangover of my life, thanks to the Catholic Church*.

'I talked to Mustafa Ahmed's niece,' Emma said, 'a sweet girl named Anisa. She wouldn't tell me anything, but my gut says something happened to her. And I think she was recently garroted.'

'Garroted?' DeMarco said. 'You mean strangled.'

'Yes, with a wire, a garrote. There was a deep ligature mark around her throat. I gave the girl the name of a Muslim woman who would vouch for me, and I know Anisa called the woman a couple days later, but she never contacted me afterward. So to repeat what Joe just said, I got shit.'

'What did you learn, Neil?' DeMarco said.

In a cooler next to his desk, Neil kept Popsicles. He opened the cooler now and pulled a grape Popsicle from the box, taking his time in removing the paper. He just drove DeMarco nuts. As he sucked on his Popsicle, Neil gave his report.

'Let's start,' Neil said, 'with the good senator, William Broderick. If our assumption is that Broderick is paying somebody to cause these terrorist attacks, an assumption I personally find hard to accept, it would take a lot of money. So in the case of Broderick, I looked for cash outflows: large blocks of stocks liquidated, CDs cashed out, bank accounts substantially reduced, et cetera. I found nothing. The problem, of course, is Broderick could have sold something, like a home or a yacht, and put the cash from the sale in an offshore account or in an account under a false name, and I wouldn't be able to see it.'

'Isn't the property he owns listed on his financial disclosure statements?' DeMarco said. People above a certain rank and holding certain positions in government are required to file financial disclosure statements that identify investments and sources of income for the person and his spouse. DeMarco, however, wasn't of sufficient rank or importance to be required to file such a statement, so he didn't really know what was on one.

'No,' Neil said, in answer to DeMarco's question. 'Financial disclosure statements are designed, in theory, to see if government officials have sources of income that represent a conflict of interest. In the case of property, you're required to list assets "held for investment or the production of income." So a coal mine he'd be required to list, but he might be able to exclude a hunting lodge in Montana. At any rate, regarding Broderick, nada.

'Next, we have Mr Nicholas Fine,' Neil said. 'Although you didn't ask me to, I decided to take a quick peek at his data. Unlike his boss, Nick appears to be a very bright fellow, magna summa whatever from Princeton, which he attended on scholarship, not having a rich grandpa like Senator Bill. Financially, he's in okay shape, but he's not megabucks rich. His net worth is about two million, most of that being the equity in his home.'

'How'd he make his money?' DeMarco asked. 'The Senate gig doesn't pay that well.'

'Most of what he has came from real estate deals, buying low and selling high. Bottom line with Fine is that he doesn't appear to have enough money to finance the kind of venture we're talking about, and I saw no substantial financial activity in any of his accounts.'

'What about Broderick's big contributors? What did you get on them?'

'I was just getting to that,' Neil said. 'And because

the good senator's fans have grown significantly in the last two months, I want you to know that this took some effort.'

'You're gonna send me a bill, Neil, so just get on with it,' DeMarco said.

'Fine. I'll spare you the details, but I want you to know that this is why I charge so much. But since you don't care . . .'

'I don't,' DeMarco said.

'Kenneth Dobbler and Edith Baxter,' Neil said.

'*The* Edith Baxter?' Emma said.

'Who's Kenneth Dobbler?' DeMarco said.

Neil chuckled; confusion in others pleased him. 'We talked earlier about money motives,' Neil said. 'You asked: How could anyone make money if Broderick's bill was to become law? Well, Mr Dobbler has found a way.'

'Which is?' DeMarco said.

'The federal government, as well as state and municipal governments and private companies, spends billions each year doing background checks on employees. They look at credit reports, criminal records, scholastic history, et cetera, et cetera. Mr Dobbler has a company, a profitable one, that does such background checks. Now imagine for a moment if Broderick's bill were to pass and the government required that a background check be accomplished on every Muslim American. And keep in mind we haven't even defined what a Muslim American is.

One who practices Islam? Someone whose ancestors came from a Muslim country? Someone married to a Muslim?

'At any rate, according to my trusty almanac there are almost five million Muslims in this country. Now I have no idea how that number was obtained, and I'm willing to bet that it's low and out of date, but just for the fun of it, let's say we're going to do background checks on five million people. A background check performed on federal employees for a very basic security clearance can take up to eight hours. Now throw in the need to check people for overseas connections, connections in places like Saudi Arabia and Iran and Pakistan and you can triple the hours, which I think would be conservative. And then we'll assume that Mr Dobbler's company charges a mere sixty dollars an hour, which is less than most plumbers charge and, based on my experience, less than what other government contractors typically bill. But let's just use sixty bucks an hour for the sake of argument and multiply that number by twenty-four hours and multiply the product by five million people.' Neil paused. 'That's seven point two billion dollars. That's *billion*, with a B.'

'Holy shit,' DeMarco said.

'Oui,' Neil said. 'Even if Dobbler had to share a seven-billion-dollar contract with other companies, he'd still be looking at millions – maybe hundreds of millions – in profit.'

'But what makes Dobbler think he'll get the contract for doing the screening?' DeMarco said.

'Connections, of course, connections to people like Bill Broderick, to whom he contributes. But, to be fair, Dobbler does have extensive experience at this sort of work and his company is reportedly very good at what it does.'

'Yeah,' Emma said, 'but is Dobbler the sort of person who would have Reza Zarif's family killed to get a contract?'

'That I don't know,' Neil said. 'On the surface he just appears to be a shrewd businessman, not a criminal. But he does have the money motive that Joe was looking for.'

'What about Edith Baxter?' DeMarco said. 'Why's she supporting Broderick? I can't imagine that she's interested in some contract to perform background checks, and she sure as hell doesn't need the money.'

Even DeMarco knew who Edith Baxter was. She was the poster girl for American businesswomen. She'd been the CEO of three Fortune 500 companies, two of which she'd been brought in to save when the companies had been on the brink of bankruptcy. She was one of the big boys, commanding compensation packages – meaning salary and stock options and various costly perks – in excess of a hundred million a year. She'd had her picture on the cover of *Time* magazine twice and she was one of the people the chairman of the Federal Reserve called when he was looking for advice from the private sector.

Before Neil could answer DeMarco's question, Emma said, 'I think I know why she's supporting Broderick's bill, but are you sure about this, Neil?'

'Of course I'm sure,' Neil said, offended that his research would be questioned. 'She's the biggest financial backer that Bill Broderick has, and she hasn't been the least bit subtle about how she's been giving him money. And—'

'But why's she supporting him?' DeMarco asked again.

'Because of her son,' Emma said.

'Her son?'

'Edith was married once,' Emma said, 'and she had a son from that marriage. His name was Craig Devon; the boy kept his father's name. As you can imagine, with Edith's career, she wasn't a stay-at-home mom. I suspect she was around very little when her son was young, and when she and Craig's father divorced, he got custody of the kid and Edith paid child support. At any rate, Craig was in Madrid when Muslim terrorists blew up the trains. His wife and daughter, Edith's granddaughter, were killed, and Craig Devon lost an arm, both legs, and an eye.'

'Jesus,' DeMarco said.

'But he didn't die. They brought him back to the States and he was hospitalized for over three years, one operation after another, setbacks due to infection and transplant rejections and everything else that could possibly go wrong. When they finally allowed him to go home with his titanium legs and a hook for a hand and a patch over his eye and somebody else's liver, he took a pistol in his good hand and killed himself.'

37

Fat Neil didn't drink, at least he didn't drink beverages that contained alcohol. But Emma, after hearing about Edith Baxter's connection to Broderick, decided she needed a drink, so she and DeMarco left Neil's office and drove into Georgetown. Emma was quiet as they drove, still thinking about Edith and her son.

DeMarco cruised around for a while trying to find a place to park – it's easier to find a virgin in a whorehouse than street parking in Georgetown – until Emma finally snapped at him and told him to park in a lot, one that charged ten bucks an hour. Emma had a money-be-damned attitude when she wasn't paying.

They went to Clyde's, DeMarco's favorite bar on M Street, and took a seat, and Emma ordered a Ketel One martini. When the waitress asked what DeMarco wanted, he hesitated. After a night spent drinking with a priest, could his liver stand any more? Yes, he concluded; hair of the dog, he told himself, and duplicated Emma's order.

Emma sighed. 'I've met Edith Baxter. She's an incredible woman.'

'How did you meet her?'

'*Fortune* sponsored a most-powerful-women-in-business thing. They held it at the Four Seasons in Palm Springs, and Edith, of course, was the biggest name at the conference. It was a networking orgy, all these powerful women getting together, meeting each other, and hopefully in the future helping one another and the women they were mentoring.'

'And *you* went to this conference?'

'Yeah,' Emma said. 'It was the only thing like that I ever attended. The people who arranged the event wanted a few women from government but not just politicians. I was at the end of my career at the DIA, had no pressing assignments, and the secretary of defense made me go. It was kinda funny. They printed up a little brochure for the conference that gave the attendees' biographies. All mine said was that I worked at the DIA and everything else was classified. Anyway, I met Edith. She's incredibly intelligent, principled, tough, driven, courageous. For some reason . . .'

Emma may not have realized it, DeMarco was thinking, but she'd just described herself.

'. . . for some reason we took a shine to each other and had dinner alone one night. I really liked her.'

'From what I've read about her,' DeMarco said, 'even with what happened to her son, it's hard to believe she'd be supporting Broderick.'

Emma shook her head. 'Imagine you're a mother and your only son – a son you've probably neglected his entire life – is horribly disfigured. Then for months and months you watch him suffer as he recovers, knowing he'll never be the same again. And then he kills himself. Don't you think it's possible you might be driven almost out of your mind with guilt and grief and hatred?'

'I guess, but hatred for whom?' DeMarco said. 'Al-Qaeda? All Muslims? Lunatics who bomb trains?'

Emma plucked the lemon twist from her martini and nibbled off a piece. 'I don't know,' she said, 'but let's say Edith decided to do something to avenge her son. And being Edith Baxter, she thinks *big*. She thinks she's going to make life miserable for every Muslim in this country and she's going to deport every one she can who's already here and not allow any more to come in. She's going to do her best to make sure that no other mother experiences what happened to her son. No more towers collapsing, no more planes crashing into the Pentagon, no more subway bombings.

'And this thing with Broderick, this bill of his, maybe that's just the first step. Maybe the next step is . . . hell, I don't know. Maybe it's crippling economic sanctions against every Muslim government. Maybe it's getting the European Union to pass laws similar to what Broderick's proposing.'

'That's a hell of an ambitious plan,' DeMarco said.

'Edith made her mark in the world executing ambitious plans.'

'But Jesus, if you're right, she was an accomplice to killing a couple of kids.'

'There's nothing to show she's had anything to do with these terrorist attacks,' Emma said. 'All she's done is support Broderick. But Edith lost *her* kid. Maybe she considers what happened to Reza Zarif's family the price that has to be paid to get what she wants. Or maybe she . . .'

'What?'

'We're still missing something here – assuming that *anything* we've learned is connected to anything. If somebody is forcing these people to commit acts of terrorism, there has to be an organizer, somebody who's doing the detailed planning, arranging for the equipment. And neither Edith Baxter nor – and I'm guessing here – this businessman, Dobbler, has that sort of . . . of *field* experience.'

'Jubal Pugh?' DeMarco said.

'No. Pugh's too much of a bottom feeder. He's a *meth* dealer, for Christ's sake. If someone is orchestrating these attacks, it has to be someone a lot more sophisticated than Jubal Pugh. That doesn't mean that Pugh isn't involved, but there has to be someone else.'

DeMarco drained his drink. 'So what do you wanna do?' he said.

'I want to talk to Edith Baxter.'

'Why? Do you think she'll *tell* you she's behind all this stuff?'

'I don't know, but I need to see her.'

'Okay. You go see Edith and I'll go see Dobbler. I like money motives.'

38

The materials he needed hadn't arrived, and he was furious.

He should have received the C-4 and the radio receivers and the transmitter and the blasting caps two weeks ago. The planning phase was over. The boy was ready. But the material for the devices had not arrived, and he had no idea what was causing the delay or how long he'd have to wait.

The materials were coming from Germany to Mexico, then across the Mexican border into Texas, after which someone would bring them to him in Cleveland by car. He couldn't simply make a phone call to find out what had happened; they had to assume that all the lines were monitored by the NSA these days. The same with e-mail; they didn't know the limits of American technology. So they communicated the old-fashioned way, by sending letters written in code and waiting for a response the same way. And the letters didn't go directly to the recipient; they were mailed and then mailed again before reaching their destination.

If he had been in another part of the world – or had he not been an Arab – he could have picked up the C-4 easily, almost as easily as buying bread from one of the giant American markets – or *super*-markets, as they called them. Even their grocery stores were monuments to excess and decadence.

So he would wait. He would continue to mold the boy, to make sure his resolve stayed firm, although he wasn't particularly worried that the boy would change his mind. His only task at this point was to make sure he wasn't arrested and to plan, as best he could, for the next operation.

There was that other boy in Santa Fe he'd read about. The boy had received an appointment to the U.S. Air Force Academy, which most likely meant that he was very bright. But the Air Force Academy had a large fundamentalist Christian faculty and was located in Colorado Springs, Colorado, which had one of the largest evangelical churches in the country. The boy was harassed so relentlessly that he was driven from the academy, and when his father, not a rich man, tried to sue the air force, he and his son were humiliated by the government's lawyers. The last article he'd read about the boy in Santa Fe said that he was working in a movie theater, serving popcorn, while he tried to save up enough money to attend another college. Would that boy have the same fire in his belly as this boy in Cleveland? He wouldn't know until he saw him, until he looked into his eyes.

39

The Cuban didn't know where the subject was going.

She'd arrived at Reagan National two hours earlier, where she'd been met by a man named Jorge driving a Honda SUV with tinted windows. She didn't know Jorge. She'd asked a man she knew – someone she trusted about as much as she trusted anyone – to supply a driver who knew the city and would follow orders.

Except for the fact that he talked too much, Jorge was acceptable. He was ugly and he was big, six-three or six-four. He had a shaved head and a stupid-looking little strip of beard beneath his lower lip. He was wearing a black hooded sweatshirt – the sleeves pushed up to show off the tattoos on his forearms – baggy jeans, worn so low you could see the upper half of his plaid boxer shorts, and big unlaced

Timberland boots that were a hideous yellow color. Around his neck were four gold-plated chains and on his left wrist was a fake Rolex.

He had a brain the size of a cashew.

The good news was that he did what he was told without arguing and she liked his size. One disadvantage of being a five-foot-six-inch woman who weighed one hundred and thirty pounds was that she wasn't physically intimidating. Usually that was good but sometimes, particularly if you needed to control several people, it helped to have someone like Jorge around.

After he'd picked her up at the airport she told Jorge she wanted to see the subject's house, and just as they arrived at the address in Georgetown, a car pulled out of the garage. She looked at the driver and compared his face to the picture in her hand, one taken from a DMV file. It was him: DeMarco. She told Jorge to follow the car. The man stopped at a restaurant on Capitol Hill, had breakfast and read the paper, then forty minutes later got onto I-95, heading north. When he passed through Baltimore, the Cuban began to wonder just how far he planned to travel. Not too far, she hoped.

Then she had an idea, one that was easy to execute. Lincoln had said that he wanted this man either killed or severely injured in some manner where it would not be obvious that he had been singled out as the target. There were a lot of big trucks on the road, eighteen-wheelers, and today the highway was relatively clear so the trucks were traveling fast. She and Jorge were two cars behind DeMarco, and DeMarco was in the outside lane behind a big rig, a moving van. She told Jorge what she wanted him to do. She wanted him to pass the van and then cut right in front of it, so the truck driver would have to slam on his brakes. She was hoping the tractor-trailer would jack-knife and that DeMarco would be caught up in the accident. It wasn't a sure thing, but it was easy to do, and if she was lucky she'd be back in Miami tonight.

Jorge, it turned out, was a better driver than she would have guessed and he executed the move perfectly. He cut in front of the truck so closely that she was afraid that *they* were going to get rear-ended, but the trucker reacted instinctively and, just as she'd expected, he slammed down hard on his brakes. She watched in awe as the trailer began to move sideways and *swatted* a car in the inside lane that had been trying to pass the moving van. She saw the car go into the grassy median that separated the north and southbound lanes, and watched it flip over twice. And then the trailer tipped over, and a second later so did the cab. The cab and the trailer were now both on their sides skidding down the highway, throwing up sparks. The only problem was she couldn't see DeMarco's car and couldn't tell if he'd been caught up in the accident or not.

*   *   *

DeMarco was flipping through a stack of CDs he had balanced on his thigh. He was trying to find one by Norah Jones that he knew was in the stack. He loved Norah Jones. He wished she'd marry him. Not only was she beautiful, but since she'd won about a hundred Grammys, she'd be able to support him in the style to which he'd like to become accustomed.

And then he saw the brake lights flash on the big rig in front of him.

'Jesus Christ!' he screamed and slammed down on the brake pedal, CDs flying all over the car. He was sure he going to rear-end the trailer – the bumper of which would go right through his windshield and turn his face to bloody pulp – when the trailer began to swing over into the left lane of the freeway, hitting a car that was just passing the truck. DeMarco didn't see what happened to the other car because his car was now fishtailing, and he was struggling to control it, afraid he was going to roll over, but somehow, no thanks to any skill on his part, all four tires stayed on the ground. As he was fighting to bring his car to a stop, it barely registered in his mind that the eighteen-wheeler was now moving down the road on its side.

DeMarco's car finally stopped skidding and came to a complete stop. His car was now perpendicular to the highway, the front tires on the paved part of the road, the rear tires on the gravel at the side of the road. Once his car had stopped, he immediately spun

his head to the left, his eyes big as saucers, terrified
that somebody was now going to plow into the side
of his car. Luckily, the car that had been behind
DeMarco when the accident started had been a safe
distance back – not tailgating the way DeMarco had
been.

DeMarco sat there for a minute with his eyes
closed, his head on the steering wheel, breathing
heavily. He couldn't believe he hadn't hit the truck
or rolled his car or been smashed into from behind.
Traffic was already starting to back up on the freeway,
and four or five people had left their cars and were
now running toward the wrecked vehicles to see if
the occupants needed help. DeMarco's hands shook
as he undid his seat belt, then he slowly opened his
door and walked unsteadily over to the truck that
had overturned. He looked in through the front windshield of the cab and could see the driver was still
in his seat, lying on his side. The driver was okay,
not obviously injured, but madder than hell because
he couldn't get free of his seat belt or upright himself.
Another man was talking to the driver, saying that
he'd already called 911. DeMarco found out shortly
that the man in the car that had been sideswiped by
the trailer hadn't been so lucky. He was dead.

Four hours after the accident, DeMarco pulled into
a visitor's parking space near the front entrance of
Dobbler Security Systems, Inc. He had called Dobbler's

office earlier to say he'd been held up by an accident, and Dobbler's secretary had become completely
flustered, as if nobody, for *any* reason, was ever late
for an appointment with her boss. When he walked
into Dobbler's office, the secretary – a skinny woman
in her fifties with butterfly-frame glasses affixed to
a chain around her ropy neck – informed him that,
since he was late, Mr Dobbler had moved on to other
things and DeMarco would have to wait. As she said
this, she nervously twisted a Kleenex in her hands
and little flecks of paper crumbled into her lap.
DeMarco had the impression that the secretary was
perpetually cowering, as if people screamed at her
about two dozen times a day, and he could just
imagine Dobbler calling out from his office for a cup
of coffee and this poor woman's ass going straight
up, two feet off her chair.

He was finally ushered into Dobbler's office an
hour later. Three of the four walls in the room were
devoted to certificates and plaques and photos obviously intended to impress Dobbler's visitors with his
deep charitable commitment to the City of Brotherly
Love. There were testimonies from every fraternal
do-gooder organization in Philadelphia; pictures of
him posing with Little League teams he sponsored;
a newspaper shot of him dishing out Thanksgiving
turkey to a line of men who all looked like winos.

Dobbler in the flesh, however, didn't strike
DeMarco as a man with a large strain of human

kindness running through him. He was a big florid-faced guy in his fifties, and DeMarco knew the minute he met him that his complexion would go instantaneously from red to purple whenever anything upset him. He had short-cut dark hair, a meat-eater's jaw, and somewhat protruding dark eyes, as if his elevated blood pressure was slowly forcing his eyeballs out of his head. He was six-three, over two hundred and fifty pounds – the type who would crowd you in an argument and try to intimidate you with his bulk. He wore a white short-sleeved shirt and a cheap-looking blue tie with red stripes. DeMarco would have bet fifty bucks that Dobbler was wearing white socks and his shoes were plain black lace-ups, but he never got a chance to find out because the man never came out from behind his desk.

To get the appointment with Dobbler, DeMarco had almost told the truth. He said he worked for Congress and was doing a little legwork for a congressional committee that was interested in – and approved of – the type of work that Dobbler's company did. The nonexistent committee had tasked DeMarco to interview Dobbler, obtain a few facts, and report back. DeMarco began by saying that he just wanted to hear a bit about Dobbler's background, and after that he hardly had to say another word. It was clear that there was nothing Ken Dobbler preferred more than discussing his own achievements.

His beginnings were predictably Lincoln-like: born in a rustic backwater, surviving on table scraps, never wearing a thing that wasn't a hand-me-down. He had a passel of underachieving siblings, a saint for a mother, and a worthless bum for a father. The military saved him, he said. He enlisted right after high school, his brilliance was soon recognized, and he was sent off to college on Uncle's dime and turned into an officer and a gentleman. He had spent some time in military intelligence, he said, coyly refusing to tell DeMarco exactly what he did.

After twenty years in the army, he retired and launched his own company. The company started off by providing rent-a-cops for businesses in Philly, and he soon squeezed out the local competition and expanded into other cities. Next he ventured into building security systems and opened branch offices up and down the eastern seaboard. He began doing employee background checks for private companies and state and federal agencies five years ago.

'I have a bunch of retired guys working for me,' he said to DeMarco. 'FBI, people from OPM, ex-military, ex-cops. There's nobody that can do background checks on people better or faster than my guys. I've got the right computer systems, the right contacts, and the know-how.'

'I've heard,' DeMarco said, 'that you're a strong supporter of Senator Broderick's proposed legislation, the so-called Muslim Registry Act.'

'You're damn right I am,' Dobbler said, his eyeballs swelling. 'Broderick's the only guy in Washington who doesn't have his head up his ass about those people.'

'I've also heard that maybe one of the reasons you're supporting Broderick is if his bill passes, your company might get the contract doing the background checks on the Muslims.'

DeMarco got to see that he was right about Dobbler's face changing color. A flush started at the base of the man's neck and spread up his face toward his hairline like an out-of-control brush fire. 'Are you implying that I'm doing something *improper*?' he said.

'Oh, no, sir,' DeMarco said. He then gave Dobbler his best impression of a D.C. insider's smirk, added a conspiratorial wink, and said, 'We all know that's the way things work in Washington. One hand washes the other. We approve.'

'Well, I'm not washing any damn thing,' Dobbler said. 'I'm just supporting a politician I believe in.'

'Yes, sir, I understand,' DeMarco said. To change the subject, he asked, 'How many employees do you have?'

DeMarco left half an hour later without having come to any useful conclusion regarding Ken Dobbler. The guy was a pompous, self-satisfied, arrogant bully, but that didn't mean he was coercing innocent Muslims into committing acts of terrorism to help pass Broderick's bill.

He checked his watch. It was almost 5 P.M.: quitting time. He found the closest bar to Dobbler's company. He was hoping a few Dobbler employees might stop in for drinks and that he might get some information from people who were less impressed with Dobbler than he was with himself.

The Cuban was patient – like a hunter in a deer blind – but being trapped in a car with Jorge for almost eight hours was beginning to grate on her. Earlier in the day he had tried several times to start up a conversation, the dimwit probably thinking he might be able to charm her into having sex with him. She'd seen tree stumps that were more appealing than Jorge, but even if he'd looked like Antonio Banderas he still wouldn't have scored. Sex was simply not a priority for her. She finally told him to shut up, he was being paid to drive, not talk. So for the past four hours she'd sat in the car with him as he sulked, her only relief being when she sent him for food and coffee.

She'd been disappointed that DeMarco hadn't been injured in the accident on the highway, but not really surprised. It had been an opportunity and she'd taken it, but it wasn't an opportunity she had direct control over. Other opportunities would come along. They always did.

If all she'd been asked to do was kill the man, it would have been simple. She could have killed him from three hundred yards away with a rifle or from three feet away with a silenced pistol, just as she had done with Lincoln's researcher Jeremy Potter. She'd also been trained by one of the best in the business in the use of explosives, and she could have blown DeMarco into tiny pieces when he started his car or opened his door or answered his phone.

She'd killed politicians surrounded by bodyguards and crime lords so paranoid they rarely left their fortified homes. Killing a man who had no training or protection, and had no inkling that he was a target, would normally be no more difficult than swatting a fly. But to kill him in the way that she'd been contracted to do – without making it obvious that he was the intended victim – well that wasn't so easy, particularly in this country.

Like right now, he was sitting in a bar. If this had been Israel, she could have tossed a bomb into the bar and killed DeMarco along with a dozen others. The act would have been blamed on Hamas, and everyone would have thought that DeMarco, the poor schmuck, had just picked the wrong time and place to have a drink. But that wouldn't work here, not in Philadelphia.

So she'd wait until the right opportunity presented itself. It always did.

It didn't take DeMarco long to strike up a conversation with a Dobbler employee. He recognized the people in the bar who worked for Dobbler because they all had company ID badges on lanyards around their necks. When one man wearing a Dobbler badge started talking to the bartender about the Redskins' chances of beating the Eagles on Sunday, he surprised DeMarco by saying that the Redskins were going to kick the Eagles' green-clad butts. This surprised DeMarco for two reasons: the Skins' chances of beating the Eagles were practically nil the way Washington was currently performing, and most folks in Philly were rabid Eagles fans. In fact, the word *rabid* didn't come close to describing their fanaticism. For a man to stand in a Philadelphia bar and admit out loud that he wanted to see the Eagles lose was tantamount to a death wish.

But it gave DeMarco the opening he needed. He told the man that he was from D.C. and 'Go Skins,' and a bond was formed. They became two cowboys surrounded by heathens, standing shoulder to shoulder, waiting to be scalped, as they wished for the downfall of Philadelphia's favorite team. Before too long, DeMarco got around to asking about Dobbler. DeMarco told the guy – his name was Chuck – that he'd had an appointment with Dobbler and that Dobbler had blown him off after he'd driven all the way from the capital. Chuck's response to this complaint was that he wasn't surprised because Dobbler was a prick. Yep, Chuck was his guy.

Chuck confirmed what DeMarco already suspected:

Dobbler was ruthless, mean-spirited, tight-fisted, and cared more about his company than the people in it. Dobbler, Chuck said, would fire you if you looked cross-eyed at him. Chuck did mention one interesting thing. When Dobbler started up his company, there were four other security firms he was competing against. Three of these outfits went out of business because the buildings they were supposed to be protecting began to experience an unusually high number of successful break-ins. Dobbler went to the people who owned the buildings and said if they wanted to stop having their offices robbed and trashed, maybe they should hire somebody who knew what he was doing, so the companies did. The rumor was that Dobbler had hired the thugs who did the break-ins, but that was never proven.

When DeMarco asked Chuck if Broderick's bill was going to be good for business, Chuck said, 'Beat's the shit out of me. I'm on the security systems side. But,' he added, 'I like what Broderick's saying.'

40

Edith Baxter had three homes: an oceanfront mansion in Carmel, a four-thousand-square-foot 'cabin' at Lake Tahoe, and a penthouse apartment in Manhattan. Fortunately for Emma, Edith was currently in New York. The other two places sounded more fun to visit, but Manhattan was closer.

Emma didn't call ahead. She showed up at Edith's building and gave the doorman her name. Edith at first refused to see her. She spoke to Emma over the doorman's phone, said she remembered her fondly but wasn't feeling well enough for company. Emma hated to do it, but she told Edith the reason she wanted to see her had to do with her son, which in a way it did, but the half-truth bothered her.

The elevator doors opened into Edith's home – her apartment occupied the entire floor – and she was standing in the foyer waiting for Emma. She was shoeless, wearing faded jeans and a long-sleeved blue blouse. The last time Emma had seen the woman, Edith had been slim, but in the way that a person who eats a healthy diet and has a personal trainer is slim. Now she looked gaunt: hollow cheeks, corded neck, her jeans riding low on narrow, bony hips. The skin beneath her eyes was smudged gray from sleepless nights, and her hair – which had always been carefully styled and shaded an attractive honey-blond – was streaked with gray, the ends brittle and split, as if she hadn't visited her hairdresser in a couple of months. Her eyes, though, seemed the same. The strength was still there, the indomitable will, the extraordinary intellect.

Edith didn't waste time on small talk. She didn't even invite Emma farther into her home, beyond the foyer. She immediately said, 'What do you have to say about my son?'

'I wanted to say how sorry I was for you and that I wish there was something I could do to take away your pain.'

'Thank you, but I don't think you came here just to express your sympathy. You sent me a card. Why are you really here?'

'Edith, when I first met you, you struck me as being fairly liberal, or at least as liberal as someone can be who's held the sort of jobs you've held. You were particularly sensitive when it came to discrimination.'

'What's this have to do with—'

'This week I found out that you're a major contributor to Senator Broderick. I'd like to know why.'

Emma expected Edith to tell her it was none of her business, but she didn't. She said, 'Because he's the only politician in Washington who understands that we must act, that we must do something to fight those people. Is that why you're here? To try to convince me to stop supporting Broderick?'

'Not exactly,' Emma said. She paused before adding, 'Edith, I have reason to believe that the Muslims who committed these recent terrorists acts were forced to do what they did, and they were *not* forced by al-Qaeda or some other group of Islamic fanatics. I think these so-called terrorist attacks have been engineered to help Broderick's bill pass.'

'What? What are you talking about?'

Edith *looked* confused, but was she? During her career Edith Baxter had played boardroom poker for billions of dollars.

'What I'm saying is that Reza Zarif was forced to fly his Cessna at the White House because someone made him. And whoever made him was doing so, at least in part, to advance Bill Broderick's agenda. An agenda that you support.'

Edith studied Emma's face for a moment. 'Are you still with the DIA?' she asked. 'The last time I saw you, you told me you were retiring.'

Why had she asked that? Emma wondered. Was

she trying to figure out if the government was investigating her activities? Emma opted for the truth. 'I *am* retired,' she said. 'I'm not employed by anyone.' *Sorta*, she added mentally, as Mahoney would have done.

'Then I don't understand. What authority do you have for questioning me?'

'None. I'm here because I've always admired you and I want to make sure that you're not involved in any way with what's been happening lately.'

'That's absurd!'

Behind Edith, Emma could see a formal dining room table that would seat twelve. The table was piled with books and magazines and manila file folders. Emma assumed that Edith must have some sort of home office in her spacious apartment, probably a library too, and could only imagine that whatever Edith was working on had overflowed those spaces. But Emma was standing too far away to see the titles of the books on the table. She took a step toward Edith, hoping the woman would back farther into her apartment so Emma could get closer to the table, but Edith wasn't the sort to back up.

'Reza Zarif's children were killed, Edith. An eight-year-old boy. An eleven-year-old girl.'

'*My* child was killed!' Edith screamed. 'Do you think I give a damn if some terrorist killed his own children? I don't know what you're playing at here, but whatever it is, it's a dangerous game. If you were ever to say publicly that you think I'm doing something illegal, my lawyers would destroy you. And the fact that I support Bill Broderick shouldn't surprise anyone. Those people mutilated my son. They butchered his family and they drove him to despair and they killed him.'

'Which people, Edith? Your son's family died in Spain. No one in this country had anything to do with it.'

'You don't know that! We're at war with these people, all of them, everywhere. They'd kill us all if they could. They're all responsible, every last one of them. Now get out of my house!'

Emma refused the doorman's offer to get her a cab. She walked for half a block and then stopped and waited. Twenty minutes later a narrow-shouldered young black man wearing dreadlocks came in her direction. He was carrying a toolbox and wearing the cap and uniform of an AT&T employee. The young man's name was Bobby, and he worked for Fat Neil.

When Bobby reached Emma, she looked at him, and he nodded his head and continued on his way.

Emma took out her cell phone and made a call. Someone answered.

'Pictures of everyone going in and out of the building for the next twenty-four hours. If she leaves, follow her, but I don't think she'll leave.' Then she made a second call and gave Fat Neil another assignment.

41

DeMarco met Emma at her house in McLean. When he entered her home, he looked around for Christine's new pet and didn't see the critter, but considering the size of the thing it could have been hiding in a tea cup.

'Where's the pooch?' he asked Emma.

Emma shook her head. 'Christine took that animal with her to practice today. She put it in her *purse*. She put a little coat on it to keep it warm. I don't know what's gotten into her.'

'Did you ever train it to do its business outside?'

'Oh, yes,' Emma said, a small self-satisfied smile on her lips. DeMarco figured that Christine's dog had been subjected to some sort of military psych-ops technique. It had probably been brainwashed so thoroughly it sprinted for the door whenever it even *thought* of peeing.

'Hey, since it's so trainable,' DeMarco said, 'maybe you could turn it into some sort of miniature attack dog. Like if a robber snuck into your house, the dog could snap the guy's Achilles tendons in half. You know, hobble the bastard? Then when he's on the ground, it could sink its little fangs into his throat.'

'What do you want?' Emma said.

'To compare notes. To see what you got in New York.'

'The only thing I got in New York was the impression that Edith Baxter's gone off the deep end. She looked like she was . . . unraveling. But I asked Neil to do a little more research, and he found out some things.'

'Like what?'

'I saw a bunch of books in Edith's apartment and Neil discovered from a credit card statement that she made a sizable purchase from a bookstore in Manhattan. Neil hacked into the store's inventory records and found out that she purchased every book they had dealing with Muslims and terrorism and al-Qaeda.'

'So?' DeMarco said.

'Edith's doing research. If she was engineering the takeover of a rival company, she'd know everything there was to know about the company. And if Edith's initiated some sort of campaign against Muslims, she'd do the same thing.'

'Big deal, she bought some books.'

'She also hired a PR firm. They're the ones that have been producing Broderick's television ads. And based on the amount of money she's thrown at them, they're probably doing other things like direct mailings and phone polling. She's also engaged a lobbyist in D.C., and through him she's been making donations to a number of congressmen. The ones she's been giving money to are those who appear to be on the fence when it comes to the bill, and she's obviously trying to knock them over to Broderick's side.'

DeMarco shrugged. 'She's a rich person with a cause and she's doing what rich people do. If she was supporting the Sierra Club on some kinda environmental legislation, she'd do the same thing.'

'Neil also discovered that she sent a large check to a private security company.'

'A security company? You mean like Dobbler's outfit?'

'No, I mean like mercenaries. This outfit supplies people to augment U.S. forces in Iraq and Afghanistan. They provide protection for Iraqi politicians, Halliburton's operations, oil fields, any mission that the U.S. military's too thin to support. But they also work for people like Charles Taylor, that sweet fellow who used to be the dictator of Liberia. They're not choosy about their clients.'

'So what are they doing for Baxter?'

'I'm not sure. But we were saying earlier that if

Edith was involved in something like what you suspect, she'd need people with expertise. *This* company has the expertise.'

'Yeah, but do you think she'd hire them so openly? I mean, write 'em a check with her name on it?'

'No. That's the part that doesn't make sense. What did you find out about Dobbler?' Emma asked.

'A couple of interesting things but no smoking gun. He seems like a rotten guy who would do anything to get ahead, but I didn't learn anything that would lead me to conclude he's doing anything illegal. He told me he spent twenty years in the army and worked in military intelligence, whatever that means. His Web site says he retired as a colonel, so he had some rank, and he probably knows a lot of other ex-military types. If you add it all up, he'd have the experience to organize these attacks. The other thing is, according to a guy that works for him, Dobbler muscled out the competition in Philly when he first got started.'

'Muscled them out how?'

'He hired pros to break into buildings being protected by other security companies to ruin their reputations. Supposedly.'

'Huh,' Emma said. 'Well, as for him being in military intelligence, that covers a lot of ground, but he couldn't have been anyone of note or I would have heard of him. But I'll check out his record. One other thing about Mr Dobbler,' Emma said. 'He called Broderick's office after you visited him.'

'How do you know that?'

'I have Neil tapping his and Edith Baxter's phones.'

'Jesus, Emma, do you know how much Neil charges? There are *surgeons* who bill less than him per hour.'

'I'm sure the speaker's budget can handle it.'

That was true; the speaker's budget, only part of which was visible to the General Accounting Office, was bigger than the GNP of some countries.

'Anyway,' Emma said, 'he called Broderick's office. But because of the way their phone system is set up, Neil didn't know if he spoke to Broderick or Fine or someone else. On top of that, Dobbler and whoever he talked to were using STU-III phones.'

'What's that mean?'

'It means the call was scrambled – encrypted – and Neil doesn't know what was said.'

DeMarco shook his head. 'We just keep getting these little pieces, pieces that might mean something but we can't be sure. Did that girl ever call you back, Mustafa's niece?'

'No. So what's next?' Emma said.

'I dunno,' DeMarco said.

They sat there in silence a moment. Then DeMarco said, 'We have two things that are solid, or more solid than anything else. We have a fingerprint connecting Donny Cray to Reza Zarif, and Cray worked for Jubal Pugh, who, according to the DEA, is a white supremacist who kills people.'

'Yeah, but Pugh *can't* be the mastermind behind all this, Joe,' Emma said. 'That just doesn't wash.'

'Maybe not, but if he's involved, he may know who is.'

'Okay, but so what?' Emma said.

'Well, I think I have a way to nail Pugh based on something Patsy Hall, the DEA gal, told me.'

'Nail him for what?'

'Drugs. And if I can get him arrested for dealing drugs, that gives us the leverage to make him talk.'

'How would you get him for dealing drugs when the DEA hasn't been able to get him in five years?'

42

The Cuban watched the subject as he left the house in McLean. It was a beautiful place but she wondered how much the owner spent to maintain it. She thought it was foolish to own a home that size.

Before coming to the house, DeMarco had had breakfast in the same restaurant on Capitol Hill where he had eaten the morning he had driven to Philadelphia. He sat at the same table he'd used the previous time, and based on the way the waitresses greeted him, he was clearly a regular customer. This could be useful.

When DeMarco had been in Philadelphia, the Cuban had ruled out the idea of bombing the bar he was in, but a restaurant on Capitol Hill was a different matter. The country was in a complete uproar because of what these Muslims were doing, and . . . well, it was like the politicians said. It was only a matter of *when*, not *if*. No one would be surprised if a bomb exploded in a restaurant visited by congressmen and their staffs. Yes, if a better idea didn't occur to her, she might enter the restaurant while DeMarco was eating and attach a bomb to a nearby table.

There were two good things about the idea. First, DeMarco would be the apparently random victim of a terrorist attack and there would be no reason to think he had been singled out. Second, she'd have plenty of time to get away. What she didn't like was that she'd have to enter the restaurant and somebody might remember her. On second thought, why should she go into the restaurant at all? She'd make this fool, Jorge, plant the bomb for her. Yes, that would work. But planting the bomb wasn't the biggest problem. The biggest problem was that every cop in the country would be looking for her if she exploded a bomb on Capitol Hill, particularly because of what had happened in the last few weeks. So it was a viable option, but not ideal.

Her second option was to make DeMarco a victim during a robbery. Last night, after he'd returned from Philadelphia, he'd stopped at a small grocery store near Georgetown and bought a couple of things. Like most men, he didn't shop in bulk; he just bought whatever he needed on the spur of the moment, probably not even paying attention to the sales. So there was a good chance he might pop into the same store again this evening to buy something for dinner, and if he did, she'd walk in, a ski mask covering her face, clean out the cash register, and then execute the clerk and all the customers. She noted that in the grocery store where he shopped the windows were covered with advertisements, and a store like that wouldn't normally have more than two or three customers at any one time. She liked this idea better than bombing the restaurant. A robbery was a fairly mundane sort of crime, even if two or three people were killed; it happened all the time. The downside of this plan was that the store was on a fairly busy street.

There was always a downside when killing people.

She was mulling all this over as Jorge followed DeMarco's car. Where was he going now? She hoped he stopped at a convenience store, a 7-Eleven, some-place like that. She wanted to get back home. She hated being away from the restaurant for very long; she just knew her employees were stealing her blind when she wasn't there.

The subject drove over the Key Bridge, got onto the Whitehurst Freeway, and exited onto K Street. He drove to where 8th Street NW intersected K Street and started to make right-hand turns. He appeared to be looking for a place to park. He finally found one; then she and Jorge trailed slowly behind him in Jorge's car until he entered a building on the corner of I and 8th Street NW. There were flags over the building's entrance, and chiseled in stone above the entrance were the words DRUG ENFORCEMENT ADMINISTRATION. Lincoln had not told her why he wanted this DeMarco person killed, but she found it odd that Lincoln would be involved in drugs. Drugs were so . . . she didn't know what, but drugs just didn't seem like something a dilettante like Lincoln would be involved in. But for whatever reason, DeMarco was visiting the DEA and now she had a third way to kill him, one that she liked and one that she could execute immediately.

She could see DeMarco inside the lobby of the building going through a metal detector. There were two guards that she could see and a number of people were in the lobby, waiting for elevators or exiting the building. DeMarco cleared security and then waited for an elevator himself. After he had entered the elevator, she sat watching the lobby a bit longer and was pleased when a group of four people came out together. It was almost lunchtime. That was good too.

'Do you have a gun?' she said to Jorge.

'Chur,' he said, and flipped open the glove compartment and pulled out a chrome-plated automatic with an eight-inch barrel, the weapon as gaudy as the chains around his neck.

'How many bullets does the magazine hold?'

'Twelve,' Jorge said. 'Why? Wazzup?'

She ignored him and checked the D.C. street map

that she'd bought. The damn map had cost six dollars in a drugstore; even if Lincoln was paying for it, it was outrageous that they should charge so much. She found the location of the DEA building and then saw what she was looking for: a metro station. Even better, it was located only two blocks from where they were parked.

'Jorge, how would you like to earn twenty-five thousand dollars?' she said.

She'd almost said fifty thousand but decided that twenty-five sounded more realistic, a large number, certainly more money than Jorge had ever seen at one time, but not so big he'd think she was lying to him.

She *was* lying, of course. She didn't plan to pay him a cent.

DeMarco's talk with Patsy Hall had gone just the way he'd expected. She'd *loved* his idea. It was complex and was going to be difficult to execute, and she wasn't at all certain it would work – but she loved it.

He now waited with another couple on the fifth floor for the elevator to arrive. On the way down to the lobby, two other guys entered the elevator on the fourth floor. DeMarco checked his watch. It was ten after twelve and he guessed all the narcs were heading off to lunch, which made him realize that he was hungry too. He had a sudden craving for a

pastrami sandwich, one on that swirly kinda bread
that was brown and white. Maybe he'd have a side
of potato salad and a big pickle too. On second
thought, he'd skip the potato salad and have a beer
instead. He figured the beer and the potato salad
probably had about the same number of calories, so
that was a fair trade-off; the fact that the beer had
little nutritional value was irrelevant.

He was trying to remember if there was a deli
nearby but couldn't recall one. Standing next to him
was the couple who had entered the elevator with
him. They were both white and in their early forties,
and he guessed they were DEA agents. The man
anyway, he looked like an agent, an athletic, cocky-
looking guy. He reminded DeMarco of Michael
Keaton when he'd played a cop in that Tarantino
movie *Jackie Brown*. The woman, she just looked
tough, not bad looking but tough. If she was an agent,
he'd bet she had a great big gun like Patsy Hall and
she'd kick you in the nuts if you gave her any crap.
Or, of course, the couple could just be a pair of DEA
pencil pushers, but he didn't think so.

He turned and asked the man if there was a deli
nearby. The guy said he didn't know of one, at which
point the woman jumped in and said, 'For Christ's
sake, Mark, there's one right across the street. You
walked by it to get here.' They must be married,
DeMarco thought.

It was good manners that saved DeMarco's life.

He was following the couple when they left the elevator, but as he and the couple approached the exit, a FedEx carrier was entering the building and everybody did a little dance to get out of his way, and DeMarco ended up being the first one to reach the door. He started to walk through but then the habits his mother had drummed into his head from an early age took over. He pulled the door open and stepped back as he'd been trained by his mom to allow the woman who was behind him to pass through the door first – and that's when all hell broke loose.

Suddenly glass was breaking all around him, and the woman slammed back into him, and at the same time DeMarco felt a stinging sensation along his left side. An instant later there was a sharper pain in his right leg, up high, on the inside of his thigh. He either collapsed to the floor or the force of the woman's body being thrown backward pushed him to the ground. He was now on his back and the woman was lying on top of him; it registered in his mind that the woman's left cheek was missing but all he was thinking about was getting out of the doorway. As another bullet struck the woman's torso, DeMarco tried to push her off of him, to crawl out from under her, and that's when the woman's husband fell onto both DeMarco and the woman. He was now pinned down by the weight of two bodies. He could hear people screaming and more glass breaking and bullets

ricocheting off the lobby walls. And he could hear –
or maybe feel – bullets slamming into the bodies of
the couple lying on top of him.

The Cuban was confident that the incident would be
reported just as she intended. A couple of gangstas
had driven up to the DEA building and shot up the
place. Why they did what they did was anybody's
guess. Revenge over some recent bust? Retaliation
for the killing of a gang member? Who knows why
these crazy drugged-up kids do what they do.

She and Jorge had been parked in a loading zone
right across the street from the entrance to the
building. It was a fairly narrow street and the distance
to the door was less than twenty yards. She got into
the backseat and on her command Jorge was to
power down the windows and start shooting at the
security guards that they could see inside the lobby.
She told him she didn't care if he hit anybody; he
was just to shoot as many bullets as he could as fast
as he could.

Jorge, the idiot, didn't even ask how they planned
to get away.

What the Cuban had wanted was for DeMarco to
come out the door with other people, and he did.
She saw a man and a woman approaching the
doorway and DeMarco behind the couple, and two
other people, both men, behind DeMarco. Perfect.
But then a damn FedEx guy, a chunky black *hijo de*

puta, bounced up the steps, a box on his shoulder, and went into the building, momentarily blocking her view of DeMarco. Shit, she thought at first, but it turned out perfect: DeMarco was the first one to reach the door. He put his hand on the door, pulled it open, but then, goddammit, just as she was squeezing the trigger, he stepped back and allowed a woman to go through the door before him.

The Cuban hit the woman but she also hit DeMarco. She was *sure* she hit him. She was positive. And even if she didn't hit him with her first shot, the type of bullets she was using would pass right through the woman unless they struck bone. She saw the woman fall and she saw DeMarco go down under her and then she saw a man standing behind DeMarco fall. She fired five more shots into the pile of bodies and then screamed at Jorge to drive.

She directed him to drive one block and turn right at the next corner. He never even questioned her orders. He was high from the adrenaline rush of what they'd just done. As he drove he said, 'Oh, man, that was cool, just fuckin' *cool*! Did you see those windows *blow*?'

'Stop at the next corner,' she said. She could see the big red M for the Gallery Place metro station.

'What?' Jorge said.

'Stop the car!' she screamed

And he did – and she shot him in the back of the head.

She exited the car and closed the door and walked quickly but calmly toward the metro station. With the tinted windows in the Honda, no one could see Jorge's body slumped over the steering wheel. As she descended the escalator to the subway platform, she heard the cars behind Jorge start to honk.

43

Emma had known Doug Chamberlain for twenty years. He'd been a Green Beret, and then he'd trained special ops guys before he retired from the army. He now worked for Prescott Security, the mercenary outfit that Edith Baxter had hired.

'Why are you involved with these people, Doug?' Emma said.

Chamberlain looked away, embarrassed. 'Because of Maggie,' he said. Maggie was his wife. 'I got drunk one night, three years ago, and drove the car off the road. Naturally, I didn't get a scratch. Maggie broke her jaw. The insurance paid for the first surgery, but the docs screwed something up. She was in pain for a year. And it affected her mentally too; she was so depressed I was afraid she was gonna kill herself. Anyway, the HMO wouldn't pay for another surgery so I paid out of pocket to have her taken care of. She's had two operations now and might have to have a third. I've got two mortgages on the house and I've wiped out our savings.'

'I'm sorry to hear that Doug. But Prescott?'

Chamberlain shrugged. 'They offered the most money. And all I do is train the people they hire.'

There was nothing to be gained by pointing out that the people he trained provided protection for dictators who butchered their own people. So instead, Emma said, 'Did you find out why Edith Baxter hired Prescott?'

'Yeah. You remember the deck-of-cards thing in Iraq? Saddam and the other fifty-one bad guys we were trying to capture over there? Well, Edith had her own deck made up, fifty-two radical Muslims. She's offering a hundred thousand a head for the capture of these guys.'

'Their capture or their deaths?' Emma said.

'The contract says capture, but well . . . you know. The thing is, Prescott's just screwing her. Governments – ours, the Europeans, even the Saudis – have been after some of these guys for years. Prescott's chance of catching them is practically nil, but he's billing Baxter for the hours he's spending looking for them.'

'Is Prescott helping Edith do anything here in the States?'

'In the States?' Chamberlain said.

'Yes, anything to do with Muslims here in the U.S.?'

'Not that I know of. I can try to find out if you'd like.'

'Well, if you could, I'd appreciate—'

Emma's cell phone rang at that moment. The caller ID screen said it was Howard University Hospital calling.

44

The wound in DeMarco's side was less serious than the one in his leg, but it hurt like hell. He supposed the reason the one in his leg didn't hurt so much was because the doctor had given him a local anesthetic when they'd patched him up. He bet, after the drugs wore off, the hole in his leg was going to hurt too. But the doctor hadn't seemed very worried; he told DeMarco to stick around for a couple of hours so they could watch him a bit and then he could go home. DeMarco thought they should have kept him longer, but the way hospitals operated these days it seemed you could get shot twice and be home in time for dinner. They probably wouldn't have kept him overnight for anything less than a heart transplant.

Including DeMarco, four people were injured and

three were killed at the DEA building. The couple he'd walked out the door with were among the dead. DeMarco found out that the woman had been a DEA agent, but her husband worked for the Department of Agriculture and had just stopped by to take his wife to lunch. A security guard had also been killed. The FedEx carrier that DeMarco had dodged to get to the door had been shot in the side. He was alive but was expected to lose a kidney.

The other thing DeMarco thought about as he lay there in bed was the way he'd acted when the shooting started. All he'd wanted to do was get away from all the screams and breaking glass and flying bullets. He didn't think about *anything* other than saving himself, and he was embarrassed by that. He wondered how soldiers did it. He assumed that when soldiers were in a firefight, bullets zipping past their heads, they somehow managed to return fire. But DeMarco knew, even if he'd had a gun, the *last* thing he would have thought about was shooting back. He'd just wanted to get out of that doorway; that had been his only thought. If he'd been able to, he would have dug a hole right in the floor and climbed into it.

And when they pulled the bodies off him, his only thought had been, *I'm alive, I'm alive, I'm alive*. He could still hear the bullets hitting the body of the DEA woman who'd been lying on top of him.

Emma came into his hospital room. She didn't

have the worried, terrified expression on her face of a woman rushing to the bedside of a dying man, or at least one who'd just missed death by inches.

'Thank God you were just nicked,' she said.

'*Nicked?*' DeMarco said. 'I'd call the hole in my leg more than a *nick*.'

'I've already talked to the doctor,' she said. 'The one shot barely grazed your side, didn't even hit a rib. And the one in your leg was a through-and-through and just hit meat, nothing vital. Anyway, he said you can leave in an hour or so. They just want to make sure they didn't miss anything.'

'Yeah, I know,' DeMarco said. 'I can't believe they're kicking me out of here so fast. I mean, I haven't even tried to walk yet.'

'So get up,' Emma said, 'and see if you—'

'How is he?' Mahoney said, blowing into the room, topcoat flying behind him. He spoke to Emma, ignoring DeMarco as if he was comatose.

'He was just scratched,' Emma said.

'Well,' DeMarco said, 'I don't know if I'd exactly call the hole in my leg a—'

'He's fine,' Emma said. 'One shot grazed his side and the other just went through the meaty part of his leg, no big deal.'

'You know,' DeMarco said, 'that one shot, if it had been a little higher, it could have—'

'Shit, is that all?' Mahoney said to Emma. 'Hell, when you called and told me three people had been killed, I figured he'd been all shot up. I mean, you wanna see a *wound* . . .' and he started to tug up his pant leg.

'Nah, that's okay,' DeMarco said. He didn't feel like watching Mahoney and Emma, both combat veterans, re-create that scene in *Jaws* where Robert Shaw and Richard Dreyfuss compare their scars.

'So what the hell happened?' Mahoney said. 'The radio said it was some kind of drug drive-by thing, a couple of idiots who decided to shoot up the building.'

'Maybe,' Emma said. 'One of the people killed was a female DEA agent with an impressive arrest record. I talked to someone I know, and he thinks they may have been after her specifically. But he said the shooters could have been retaliating against the DEA in general for some friend getting busted or killed.'

'So you were just in the wrong place at the wrong time,' Mahoney said to DeMarco. 'What the hell were you doing in the DEA building anyway?'

Before DeMarco could answer Mahoney, Emma said, 'I'm not so sure I'd conclude that. The DEA agent or the building may have been the target, but it's also possible they were trying to get Joe.'

'Why do you think that?' Mahoney said.

'A witness got the license plate on the car as it was pulling away and the cops found the car less than two blocks from the scene, near a metro entrance. The driver had a bullet in the back of his head, and that's what bothers me. If a couple of gangbangers had decided to shoot up the DEA building, why would one kill the other? It's more like the driver was executed so he wouldn't talk. That's something a pro would do.'

'So maybe some drug lord hired a pro to kill the DEA agent,' Mahoney said.

'Maybe,' Emma said again, 'but I don't like the timing of this either. I mean, here we are, looking into these terrorist attacks, and Joe is coincidentally a victim in this supposed drive-by.'

'Huh,' Mahoney said. 'What have you guys found out that's worth killing you for?'

'I don't know,' DeMarco said, and he quickly filled Mahoney in on everything they'd learned, the biggest news being that Edith Baxter and Ken Dobbler were giving lots of money to Broderick.

Mahoney rolled all this around in his brain and said, 'Well, hell. You don't have shit.'

Mahoney, always the complimentary employer.

'But if they tried to kill Joe,' Emma said, 'maybe we're close to something and don't know it.'

'But what?' Mahoney said.

Emma just shook her head.

Mahoney shrugged back into his topcoat. 'I gotta get back to work,' he said. 'And you,' he said to DeMarco, 'since you only got winged, you need to get back to work too.'

Jesus, what did he have to do, get a leg blown off to impress these two? But then he thought, *I'm alive.*

45

'The guy's going to be out of the hospital in a day. A day!'

The client was furious, and Oliver Lincoln could understand why. He had been paid very well to execute a simple assignment, and he'd failed.

'Do you want me to try again?' Lincoln asked. 'No charge, of course.'

The client was silent for a minute, apparently thinking. 'No. If you try again it'll be obvious that he was the target of the DEA shooting. Just forget about DeMarco. It's time to execute the last part of the plan.'

'Are you sure?' Lincoln said.

'Yes. The bill's stuck in the House. That goddamn Mahoney.'

Lincoln had hoped it wouldn't come to this. He

was very good and very careful, but if he executed the last phase of the client's plan . . . well, every cop in the country would be looking for the people involved, and they'd be looking for years. But, he thought, the only way they could get to him was if the client talked, and that wasn't ever going to happen.

'You blew it,' Oliver Lincoln said to the Cuban. 'You were supposed to *incapacitate* the man. He was barely wounded.'

The Cuban was embarrassed; she'd failed only one other time during her career and that had been nine years ago. But she'd be damned if she'd apologize to Lincoln.

'You still need to pay my expenses,' she said.

'Well, I don't know,' Lincoln said.

'You *will* pay my expenses. Now, do you want me to try again or return the money you gave me? Minus my expenses, that is.'

'No, to both questions.'

'What?'

'No, I don't want you to try again, and no, I don't want you to return the money. It's time to take care of the target that you prepared for last month. The client wants that target eliminated now.'

'Is the plan still the same?' the Cuban asked.

'Yes. Nothing's changed.'

'If you're thinking that I'm going to accept the

payment you gave me for DeMarco for this subject,
you're a fool. We already negotiated the price for
that assignment.'

She was correct. Her fee for her next assignment
was much larger than the amount she'd been paid
to kill DeMarco, which was only appropriate considering the risk.

Lincoln said, 'Of course I'll pay the price we agreed
upon.' Then he smiled. '*And* I'll let you keep the
money from the last assignment as well, even though
you failed.'

'Why?' the Cuban said, immediately suspicious.
'Why would you do that?'

'So you'll sleep with me,' Lincoln said.

The Cuban didn't say anything; she couldn't tell
if Lincoln was serious or not.

Lincoln struggled not to smile. He knew the last
thing she wanted to do was have sex with him, but
would she for seventy-five thousand dollars? Exactly
how greedy was this woman?

The Cuban still didn't respond. She stared at
Lincoln's face, her eyes blazing, yet at the same time
he could tell she was considering his offer.

'No,' she said at last, but he could tell it just *killed*
her to say that.

'A hundred thousand,' he said. 'For one night.'

She cursed in Spanish. She looked at Lincoln, then
looked away, then back at Lincoln. He could tell she
couldn't make up her mind. But enough of this; he

had to get going. He had a date in an hour. 'I'm just teasing you,' he said. 'I'm letting you keep the money because the next assignment is so critical and because I've moved up the date. And because I like you.' What he didn't add was: *and because it's not my money.*

The Cuban's face was flushed, embarrassed that she'd actually considered his offer – and that Lincoln knew it. Finally she said, 'Well, I don't like you. And maybe I'll kill you one day for nothing.'

46

The materials finally arrived. Praise be to God.

A man, a Muslim, someone he didn't know, knocked on his motel room door at two in the morning. He'd been sleeping and he woke up, terrified that it was the police. He looked through the peephole in the door, and when he saw the man's face, his dark skin, his features, he was instantly relieved. He opened the door and the man, who never said a word, handed him a box and left.

The next day, a Thursday, he and the boy connected the C-4 to the radio receivers and the blasting caps. There was enough material to construct one more device than he needed, and he was trying to decide what to do with the additional material. He could keep it for the next operation or have the boy plant it somewhere in the refinery, but keeping the material would be dangerous, particularly when he was traveling, and he didn't want the boy to spend any longer inside the refinery than they had already planned. The longer the boy was inside the facility, the higher the likelihood that he'd be discovered.

And then he thought of a better use for the extra device – a humane use.

When the devices were ready, he told the boy that he would place the bombs in the plant the following Monday night, and detonate them Tuesday morning. He wanted to breech the tanks on a weekday, and he preferred Tuesday to Monday because so many of these people tended to take three-day weekends.

The boy simply nodded his head.

Oh, he would miss this boy.

And then the boy finally asked him the question he'd been expecting for some time. 'What will happen to my mother?' he said.

'She'll be fine. They'll question her for a while, but she won't be arrested. And we'll send her money, and with you gone she'll be able to live off what she gets from the government. And, of course, she'll have God's blessing for eternity because she will be the mother of a martyr.'

47

To get Jubal Pugh arrested, DeMarco needed the cooperation of four people. The first was Patsy Hall of the DEA. Since Hall wanted Pugh more than anything else on the planet, she'd been easy to convince. The second and third persons whose help he needed lived in Queens, New York. One was the district attorney of the county; the other was a gangster. He decided to visit the gangster first.

Tony Benedetto's home was a medium-sized two-story brick structure in Ozone Park. Most of his neighbors were working stiffs, but more than a few were mobsters. One of Tony's goons met DeMarco at the front door and frisked him. He told the guy to watch his side and leg because he'd just been shot but this information, instead of impressing the man, only caused the sadistic bastard to pat him down harder. When he felt the bandage on DeMarco's thigh, he made DeMarco drop his pants to make sure he didn't have a transmitter taped to his leg. The bodyguard finally finished and DeMarco pulled up his pants and limped toward the kitchen, the wound in his leg throbbing from the guy whacking it.

Tony was seated at his kitchen table, wearing a jogging outfit: a maroon sweatshirt that zipped up the front and maroon pants with white piping on the sides. He was sixty-eight years old and had big ears, a big nose, and dyed-black hair that didn't make him look younger, just silly. When a man is almost seventy, his hair shouldn't be the same color it was when he was twenty.

He was reading *The Wall Street Journal* and drinking Slim-Fast from the can. He saw DeMarco glance down at the diet drink and said, 'Hey, it works. I tried Atkins, but who can live without bread and pasta? So I have one of these for breakfast, one for lunch, and for dinner I eat like a normal person.' He studied DeMarco for a moment. 'You know, you look just like your old man,' he said.

DeMarco's father had worked for another gangster in Queens, a man named Carmine Taliaferro. Taliaferro and DeMarco's father were now both dead, Taliaferro of natural causes, Gino DeMarco from three bullets in the chest. Benedetto had worked with DeMarco's father and had replaced Taliaferro as the head hood in Queens after Taliaferro died.

'I'm also Danny DeMarco's cousin,' DeMarco said.

Now Benedetto smirked, making DeMarco want to smack the reading glasses right off his big nose. Benedetto obviously knew about the connection between DeMarco's ex-wife and his currently incarcerated cousin.

'Is that why you're here, because of Danny? Whatta you gonna do, bug me like Marie to get him outta jail?'

'I don't give a shit if he rots in jail,' DeMarco said, 'but I need him for something. And I need your help too.'

DeMarco told him his plan.

Benedetto finished his diet milkshake and rubbed his chin as he thought over DeMarco's proposition. 'I can't see that it has a downside for me,' he said, 'but why would the Queens DA go along?'

Good fuckin' question, DeMarco thought.

'Are you out of your damn mind?' Thomas Farley said.

Thomas Farley, district attorney of Queens, was five-nine and a little on the pudgy side, but a well-tailored suit disguised this flaw fairly well. His best features were his eyes and his hair. He had a lush mane of gray hair brushed straight back from a broad forehead and intense dark eyes that were perfect for a man whose job was prosecuting heinous criminals. His eyes transmitted his outrage at whatever he was pretending to be outraged about, and right now all that righteous fury was directed at DeMarco.

With DeMarco was Patsy Hall. She had flown up from D.C. to join DeMarco for the meeting.

'Look,' DeMarco said, 'you know as well as I do that Danny DeMarco is a goddamn weasel of a fence, but he's never killed anyone in his life.'

'I don't know that,' Farley said. 'And if he didn't commit the murder, he was an accomplice to it.'

'He was *standing* there when Vince Merlino shot Charlie Logan, and Merlino shot him because Logan was strangling him.'

'I don't know anything about Vince Merlino, but—'

'Bullshit,' DeMarco said.

'But if this Merlino guy shot Logan as you say, all Danny has to do is tell us that. Merlino will go to jail for murder two and Danny will plead out to a couple of years. He just has to do his civic duty and testify against Merlino.'

'You know if he gives up Merlino, Tony Benedetto will have him killed.'

Farley shrugged. 'Not my problem,' he said. 'Either Danny boy does the time for Logan's death or he gives up Merlino. Personally, I don't care who does the time, but somebody's going to.'

'Charlie Logan was an abuser with a violent temper. He knocked his wife and kids around before she divorced him. He beat up a guy at work; you guys arrested him for that. He was nobody's idea of a model citizen, and nobody gives a shit that he's dead.'

'I don't care if he was Satan incarnate,' Farley said, 'he was killed in my district. So unless you have something to say that I care about, I think we're through here.'

DeMarco looked over at Patsy Hall. He'd been hoping to convince Farley of the merits of his plan without having to use Hall to close the deal. In other words, he'd been hoping to get a politician to put aside his own self-interest and do something for the greater good of the country. He should have known better.

'Mr Farley,' Hall said, 'right now there's a Jamaican drug ring here in Queens. We're fairly close to wrapping this group up, but we're willing to give you total credit for the bust. This group, which your narcotics guys know very well, is a major distributor of crack cocaine, and they've killed more people than Vince Merlino and the entire Benedetto family combined. I think that's a pretty fair trade for Danny DeMarco.'

Farley studied Patsy Hall for a moment.

'And I – *we* – get the credit? I don't have to stand in front of the cameras with some fed next to me going on about how it was his guys who did all the work?'

'That's right,' Patsy said.

'And how many of these Jamaicans are we talking about?'

'Six for sure, maybe ten total.'

'How soon would this happen?'

'In a month, no longer than two. Right before you start running for reelection.'

Farley smiled at Patsy Hall; she smiled back.

DeMarco didn't smile. Patsy Hall didn't know it yet, but if his plan worked out she was gonna get screwed.

48

Danny DeMarco, the fourth and final person whose cooperation DeMarco needed, was on the other side of the glass in the visitor's area, talking into a phone. The son of a bitch hadn't shaved in a couple of days and was dressed in a jail jumpsuit, and he still looked like a million bucks.

Joe and Danny DeMarco looked alike; no one would be surprised to hear they were cousins. Both had full heads of dark hair, strong noses, good chins, and blue eyes. And Joe DeMarco was a good-looking man, handsome according to most. But next to Danny. . .? Well, it was all about millimeters. The millimeters of space between the eyes, the millimeters of difference in the length of the nose or the shape of the chin. Perfect symmetry versus near-perfect symmetry – that's all that separates the truly beautiful from the merely handsome. For example, if you placed a photo of Kirk Douglas next to one of his son Michael, taken when they were both thirty years old, there would be no doubt that the millimeters had favored Kirk. That was Danny and Joe DeMarco – and Joe was Michael, not Kirk.

And it wasn't just his cousin's looks that women – like Joe's ex-wife – found appealing. There was a sparkle in Danny's eyes that said he'd be *fun*, that life was his personal bowl of cherries and he'd happily share it with you. Most women, except for Marie DeMarco, it seemed, could tell that Danny was a short-term proposition, a guy who'd be great to spend a week with in Vegas but not someone who was going to be there for you when the doctor told you about that little lump in your breast.

'You understand?' DeMarco said.

'Yeah,' Danny said.

'And you understand this guy'll kill you if you fuck up?'

'Yeah.'

'And you understand you have to deliver? Giving it your best shot doesn't count.'

'Yeah. Do I have time to see Marie before I leave?'

An image of his ex-wife and his cousin immediately popped into DeMarco's brain, an image he tried his best to push aside. 'Yeah,' he said, 'but only because I have to do a couple things first. But your ass had better be on the first shuttle to D.C. in the morning. We'll drive over to western Virginia together, but in separate cars.'

'Who's gonna pay for my flight?' Danny said.

'You're gonna pay for your own fuckin' flight!'

'Yeah, okay, fine. Geez, you don't have to be so—'

'And I want you to bring clothes that make you look like the small-time guinea hood you are. Stupid gold chains around your neck. Loud ties. Shiny suits. Just the way you dress when you and . . . and her go out. Got it?'

'Yeah, but—'

'Just do what I tell you,' DeMarco said. 'And if you're not in D.C. tomorrow morning, Danny, I swear to God, I'll—'

'I'll be there, Joe. You got my word.'

DeMarco just shook his head. His *word*. Jesus.

'And Joe, thanks. I mean, I just can't believe you're doing this for me.'

'I'm not doing this for you, you asshole. Or for your wife. There's a whole lot more at stake here than you going to jail, which is where you goddamn well belong.'

49

Jubal Pugh lived at the northern end of the Shenandoah Valley, about ten miles from the city of Winchester, Virginia, and five miles from the West Virginia state border. The area around Pugh's farm was surrounded by apple orchards and low hills thickly covered with hickory and oak. Small creeks, no more than a couple of feet wide, seemed to be everywhere, cutting though the hillsides, running alongside the roads.

To Danny DeMarco, who rarely left New York City, the place was incredibly, hilariously rustic. He passed roads called Frog Eye Lane and Quail Run and saw at one point that he was less than ten miles from a place called Capon Bridge, West Virginia. He thought a capon was some sort of nutless chicken, but what did he know.

Following the directions given to him by his cousin, he found Pugh's farm – estate – whatever the hell it was. He could see a house sitting back in the woods, a good two hundred yards from the gate. The house was a big white clapboard place with two chimneys and a rooster weather vane on the roof. Or maybe it was a capon. There were half a dozen outbuildings near the main house – small garages or toolsheds – and a bunch of cars, six or seven vehicles in the yard in front of the house. Old broken-down cars appeared to be some sort of redneck collector's item; half the houses he'd seen on his way out to Pugh's had rusted vehicles in the front yard, up on cinder blocks, the tires missing.

Danny got out of his rental car, a crummy Taurus because he couldn't afford better. He walked up to the gate and gave a tug on the big padlock, even though he could see it was locked, then walked back to his car, planted his butt on the hood, and lit a cigarette. The DEA agent, that tough little cookie, had told him that eventually someone would come out and ask what he was doing.

Danny was wearing a camel-hair topcoat, a gray suit, a blue shirt with a big white collar, and a silk Versace tie that Marie had given him and that had cost more than a hundred and fifty bucks. He had on a pinky ring with a good-sized cubic zirconia stone, and on his feet were black Gucci loafers with tassels, the shoes already covered with a thin layer of dust just from walking from his car to the gate and back again.

Ten minutes later he saw a jeep pull away from the house and drive up the road in his direction. The jeep stopped on the other side of the gate and a man got out. The man was wearing jeans and scuffed-up work boots and, even though it was cold out, a plain dark-blue T-shirt. He was about six feet tall and not exactly skinny, but there was no extra fat on him either. His arms were corded with stringy muscles, the kind you get from doing real work and not from lifting weights to pump up for show. He had a raw, reddish complexion, as if his skin was permanently windburned, and hard high cheekbones, as if he had a walnut in each cheek. On his head was a dirty white baseball cap with the word PETERBILT emblazoned on it. Danny knew Peterbilt was a type of truck, not some kind of dick joke, but why the hell would anyone want to wear a hat like that? Lastly, Danny noticed the prison tats inked onto the knuckles of the man's hands, a bunch of stupid little x's, and he knew, without a doubt, that in the pen this huckleberry had belonged to the Aryan Brotherhood or some other Nazi fuckin' gang.

'What the hell do you want?' the guy said to Danny.

What a friendly bastard. 'My name's Danny DeMarco and I'm here to see Mr Pugh. Tell him I work for Tony Benedetto in New York and I have a business proposition for him.'

The man spat, the glob of saliva coming fairly close to Danny's right shoe. The guy had a mouth like a cannon. He stared at Danny for about thirty seconds, giving him his cell-block you're-my-bitch glare, then finally pulled a phone out of his back pocket and made a call. A minute later, he walked slowly back to the gate, spat again, and unlocked the padlock.

Jubal Pugh's once-red hair was beginning to turn an unattractive orange-gray color. He had small blue eyes under thick red brows, a long sharp nose with a small bump in the middle, and a weak chin that was somewhat hidden by a week's worth of grayish-red whiskers. He was not a handsome man. He was wearing corduroy pants and a long-sleeved denim shirt. On his feet were white socks and house slippers, fluffy, comfy-looking dark blue ones.

Pugh shook Danny's hand when Danny introduced himself, then sat down on a blue leather couch that was about ten feet long. He pointed Danny to a recliner that matched the couch; separating them was a glass-topped coffee table with legs the size of an elephant's. They were in a room that appeared to be Pugh's living room, filled with large expensive pieces of furniture. There was an enormous plasma-screen TV, and on the walls were paintings in ornate gilded frames. One portrait dominated the room, a picture of a stag in a forest glen with an enormous rack of antlers. Danny concluded that Pugh had spent a lot of money furnishing the room but didn't have the good sense to hire an interior decorator.

The hard case with the Peterbilt cap took up a position against the wall near the stag picture and crossed his arms over his chest. When he'd escorted Danny to Pugh's living room, Danny had seen an automatic – a walnut-handled .45 – sticking out the back of the guy's jeans.

Pugh studied Danny for a moment and his lips twitched briefly as if he was amused, by either Danny or his big-city attire. 'You told Randy you were sent here by a Mr Benny-Detto,' he said.

Jesus, the guy talked slow.

'Well, I don't know no Mr Benny-Detto,' Pugh continued. 'I don't think I know anybody in New York. Visited there once, though. Noisy, stinky kinda place, if you ask me, but lots of good-lookin' women, I'll give it that.'

'Yeah, more than you can say for Worstchester,' Danny said, 'or whatever the hell the name of that place is where I'm stayin'.'

Pugh smiled. He had small stubby teeth. 'That's *Winchester*, son, like the rifle, and I'm fond of the place.'

'Whatever,' Danny said. 'The reason I'm here is Mr Benedetto needs a meth supplier, a big one, and—'

'Whoa!' Pugh said. Turning to Randy, eyes wide with false astonishment, Pugh said, 'Can you believe this fella? He walks into a man's house, a man he don't even know, and starts talkin' about *drugs*. I got a good mind to call the sheriff.'

'Yeah, right,' Danny said, and saw Pugh's jaw clench. Maybe he should watch his mouth a little. 'Look,' Danny said, 'I know you don't know me from Adam, Mr Pugh. And I don't expect you to say anything in front of me because for all you know I could be a narc wearing a wire. So don't say anything. But before you toss me outta here, just listen to what I have to say.'

When Pugh didn't respond, Danny continued.

'Mr Benedetto is the *man* in Queens.'

'The man?' Pugh said.

'He belongs to one of the families that runs things in New York. He's mob, okay?'

Pugh shrugged his shoulders; he couldn't have cared less.

'There's a Jamaican posse in Queens that's about to go out of business. They deal crack and meth and grass. When this gang is wrapped up by the cops, which should happen in less than a month, Mr Benedetto's gonna move in and take over their action. But he needs somebody that's got a large-scale lab to supply the meth, not a small-time operation that some strung-out yahoo and his junkie girlfriend run outta their basement. And he doesn't want the lab close to home because if it's anywhere up near New York – New Jersey, Connecticut, any of those places

– it'll get sniffed out by either New York narcs or the DEA. That's what always happens. So he wants a guy out of the area to provide product, somebody who knows what he's doing.'

'Son,' Pugh said, 'I think you've been misinformed about a whole bunch of things. *And* you're insultin' me. I got a good mind to have Randy take you outside and rearrange your pretty face.'

'Yeah, well, let me show you something before you do that,' Danny said.

He picked up the briefcase he'd brought with him into the house, placed it on his knees, but before he could open it Pugh said, 'Hold on there . . . what'd you say your name was again?'

'DeMarco. Danny DeMarco.'

'Yeah, well, *Danny*, why don't you let Randy open that briefcase. Okay?'

'Sure,' Danny said, spreading his arms wide, palms out, not a thing to hide.

Randy took the briefcase from Danny and took it over to a side table and opened it. 'Nothin' but paper,' he said to Pugh. Pugh nodded, and Randy handed the open briefcase back to Danny.

Danny reached inside the briefcase, took out a manila file folder, and slid it across the coffee table toward Pugh. Pugh didn't touch it. 'In that folder,' Danny said, 'you'll find a copy of my NYPD arrest record. There's also a list of ten people that I did time with up at Altona. I did two years there for fencing stolen goods.'

And that was true.

'If you don't wanna call any of those ten guys, pick anyone you want who was up there from '95 to '97. Someone will know me – if they're white, that is. There's also a copy of a story from *The New York Daily News* saying I popped a guy named Charlie Logan – which I did. There's an article from yesterday's paper saying how they had to let me go because the witness recanted, which the old bitch did. There's another picture in there, also from the *News*, of my boss, Tony Benedetto. You wanna talk to Tony, his phone number's there, cell and home. You wanna make sure you're *really* talking to Tony and not some cop, call up anyone you know in New York and tell them to go to Tony's house in Queens and your guy can ID that it's Tony on the phone. And Tony's phones are bug free, because he pays to keep them that way.'

Danny stood up.

'If it's okay with you and ol' Randy here, I'm gonna leave now, Mr Pugh. But before I go I'll tell you what we're offering. We're offering to buy a million to a million and a half bucks' worth of product from you every quarter, provided you have a big enough operation to deliver that amount and keep on delivering. But we can't afford a shortage.'

Patsy Hall had told him to say *quarter*, not every three months, for some reason.

'Now, my boss knows all about you,' Danny said.

'He has two guys in the DEA that he pays to find guys like you. He knows you're smart and you're careful and you don't get busted. On the front cover of that folder is my cell phone number and the name of the place where I'm staying in Winchester. I'm gonna be there all day tomorrow since I know it'll take you some time to check me and Mr Benedetto out, but if I don't hear from you by the day after tomorrow, I'm movin' on down to South Carolina where there's another guy just like you.'

Danny drove back to his motel in Winchester, the whole time thinking that if Pugh didn't take the deal he was screwed. He was going to spend the next fifteen years in jail being . . . well, just screwed. There were times it was a liability to be so good lookin'.

He asked at the front desk if he had any messages and then flirted for a while with the cute chick behind the counter, a foxy little blonde with a good set of lungs. Inside his room, he turned up the heat and took off his suit and flopped down on the bed in his underwear, then used the motel's phone to call Joe's cell phone. He didn't know where his cousin was staying because Joe wouldn't tell him.

'It went okay,' Danny said. 'I thought the guy's eyes were gonna pop out of his head when I told him we wanted a million bucks' worth of shit every three months. So either I'll hear from him tomorrow or I won't, but he seemed interested.'

Patsy Hall had told Joe that Pugh normally did business only with people he knew, and when he did hire outsiders he did an extensive background check on them. But Hall also said that if the payoff was big enough, Pugh might do just about anything. So Joe had figured that Pugh might go for a deal that was worth five million a year if the people he was dealing with were known, successful criminals – for example, a guy like Tony Benedetto. All Danny could do at this point was hope that Joe was right.

'Good,' Joe said. 'Stay in your room tonight. If you have to eat, order a pizza. I don't want you going out. You'll just get drunk and in trouble.'

'Hey,' Danny said, 'I know what's at stake here. And I'm a pro.'

'You're a professional sleazebag. Stay in your room,' Joe said, and hung up.

Geez, the guy really hated him.

50

Emma was sitting on the couch in her living room, staring into the fire in her fireplace, feeling lonely and disgruntled. In her lap was Christine's rat-sized canine. Christine wasn't there because she was spending the night in Hartford with her mother, and as her mother was allergic to dogs, Emma had become involuntarily responsible for the care and feeding of the creature. Twice she'd put the animal into the toy-stuffed basket that Christine had bought for it, but it insisted on coming into the living room and jumping on her lap as if it were lonely too. It was odd, but there was something strangely comforting about holding the dog, with its warm body and its rapidly beating heart – although she imagined the same sensation could be produced by holding a fur-covered hot water bottle.

Emma was disgruntled because she'd wasted part of the day trying to learn more about the people who had shot DeMarco. Although he didn't seem to be worried for his own safety – which surprised her – and was satisfied that the shooters had been after the DEA agent who was killed, Emma still had her doubts. But after three hours of talking to people on the phone, in the end she learned nothing more than had been reported in the papers: Jorge Rivera, the driver who'd been executed, had been a small-time hood with links to a Hispanic gang. He certainly wasn't a contract killer, but he did have drug connections. Regarding the second shooter, the person who had most likely shot Jorge, the police had nothing. Cameras on the outside of the DEA building didn't get a clear shot of the person and the only fingerprints inside the car belonged to Jorge.

The remainder of the day had been spent with Fat Neil trying to find evidence that Dobbler or Baxter were tied in some way to the terrorist attacks. After five hours with Neil – nobody should have to spend five hours with Neil – they'd discovered nothing new. She did decide by the end of the day to focus on Dobbler and forget Edith for the time being. Edith was donating money to Broderick and every other organization and politician she could find with some sort of anti-Muslim bias, and she was paying Prescott's company to find radical Muslims around the globe, but everything she did was done openly, and nothing she was doing was illegal. She was obviously out of her mind with grief and guilt and doing everything she could to avenge her son, but Emma's gut told her that Edith wasn't involved in the attacks. She could only hope her gut was right. She also wished there was some way she could help Edith. It was terrible to see her in the state she was in.

The phone rang and the dog in her lap jumped as if it had been tasered. She hoped it was Christine calling.

'Hello.'

'This is Anisa Aziz. I'd . . . I'd like to talk to you.'

'Where,' Emma said.

'Uh, near the Rotunda? Is that okay?' Anisa said.

'I live in McLean,' Emma said. 'It'll take—'

'Oh. Well . . .'

'No, it's okay,' Emma said. 'I'll come to you. I'll be there in four hours. I'll meet you about ten-thirty.'

She hoped the damn dog didn't tear up the house while she was gone.

'There were two men,' Anisa Aziz said.

Emma was sitting with the girl on a bench looking out at a large terraced grass common in the middle of the University of Virginia's campus. At the northern end of the common, where they were sitting, was the Rotunda, a building designed by Thomas Jefferson that looks like the Pantheon in Rome.

'I don't know how they unlocked the door,' Anisa

said, 'but they broke into my room after midnight and put me in the trunk of a car. We drove quite a while, maybe an hour, maybe more; then they took me into a warehouse. In the middle of the warehouse was an office with glass walls. One of the men pointed a gun at me and then showed me a note written in English that said to take off my clothes. When I didn't right away, he slapped me. I thought they were going to rape me, but they didn't. They just tied me to a chair. Naked.'

The girl shuddered. It was a cold night, in the low forties, and all Anisa was wearing were sweatpants and a hooded sweatshirt that said UVA SOCCER on the back. Emma didn't think, however, that it was cold that had made the girl shiver.

'What did they look like?' Emma asked.

'One was big, at least six-four, and heavy. The other was maybe six feet, skinny but real strong. They both wore long-sleeved shirts and had gloves on their hands and ski masks over their faces.'

'What color were their eyes?' Emma said.

'Brown. Both of them.'

Blue would have been better. 'Could you tell if they were white? If they were American or from some other country?'

'No. They never spoke, not once.'

'Okay, then what happened?'

'Another man – he was wearing a ski mask too – he brought my uncle into the warehouse. My uncle could see me tied up naked inside the glass office. While my uncle was watching, one of the men, not the big man, the other one, the skinny one, came and stood behind me. He was holding two sticks with a wire connecting the sticks. He put the wire around my neck and began to twist it, to choke me, and I started gagging and my neck started bleeding. He stopped before I passed out. I looked up and the man with my uncle was talking to him. Then the skinny man strangled me again and I could see my uncle crying, begging for them to stop, and then my uncle and the man with him left the warehouse.'

Anisa stopped talking to keep herself from crying and closed her eyes for a moment.

'They left me alone for a long time, maybe five or six hours; then the skinny man came back. He showed me pictures of my mother and my little brother coming out of our house, and then he held up a note for me to read. It said if I talked to the police they would kill my mother and my brother. And me. Then . . . then he took off one of his gloves and he – he put his finger in me. After that he untied me and let me get dressed, and then he put me back in the trunk of the car and dropped me off near the campus. When I got back to my room, I tried to call my uncle, but he wasn't home. Then I turned the radio on and heard what he had done. And that he was dead.'

'I know this is hard for you, Anisa, but when the man took off his glove, could you see his hand?'

Emma said. 'I mean, could you tell his race from his hand?'

The girl started to shake her head, but then she stopped. 'Yes, his hands weren't real dark, not like a black man's or an Arab's. They were tanned, but he was probably white.'

'Good,' Emma said. 'Very good.'

'And there was something else. When he first took off his glove, I saw these blue marks on his knuckles, but only for a second. I think they were tattoos but I couldn't see a design and they might have been smudges of grease or dirt. I just don't know.'

'Can you remember anything else? The type of car they drove? If their clothes had any sort of distinctive labels on them, anything like that?'

'No. I'm sorry.'

She and Emma sat there in silence for a moment, then Anisa gestured with her head and said, 'Did you know they only give these rooms to seniors, the ones who the professors think are going to be somebody special someday?'

Emma nodded her head; she knew what the girl was talking about. On each side of the grass common were five 'pavilions' assigned to prestigious faculty members, and between the pavilions were fifty-four little student rooms called 'lawn rooms.' The rooms were built about the time Thomas Jefferson died and have no air-conditioning or showers. Yet in spite of their age, size, and lack of creature comforts, the lawn rooms are the most desirable dwellings on campus because only the university's most impressive overachievers are permitted to reside in them.

'What chance do you think a Muslim woman has,' Anisa said, 'of being picked to live in one of those crummy old rooms?'

51

Tim Crocker liked being a fireman.

He liked the guys he worked with. He liked putting out fires. He liked saving people and their homes. Hell, he even liked getting cats down from trees. What he didn't like was looking at people who'd burned to death.

The sight of a body – or in this case four bodies – burnt black beyond recognition, their heads turned into skulls, their mouths open from their last screams, their backs arched from their final struggles . . . well, he just hated it. And the smell. Every time this happened, he couldn't eat barbecue for a month.

The fire had started in a bedroom in an apartment on the third floor. Then the ceiling above the third floor unit had collapsed and two people sleeping on the fourth floor had dropped right down into the bedroom of the two people who'd been sleeping on the third floor. So he had four bodies – two couples – and the man and woman from the fourth floor were stacked on top of the couple from the third.

Crocker's guys had done a good job. They'd managed to put the fire out less than an hour after they got the alarm, and although three other units in the apartment building had been heavily damaged, no one else had died and they'd managed to save the building. It was the cause of the fire that was bothering Crocker. He wasn't the arson investigator but he'd been around a long time, and he was pretty sure that the fire hadn't been caused by a natural gas explosion or somebody who'd fallen asleep with a cigarette burning. There *had* been an explosion, though – strong enough to blow out a couple windows in the building next door – and Crocker thought that whatever had exploded had been attached to a container of something flammable. In other words, a damn incendiary device had gone off in this apartment.

So they weren't dealing with some semi-harmless firefly, some guy who got his rocks off watching buildings burn, or some schmuck trying to collect on the insurance. No, this was something else; he didn't know what, but whatever was going on it wasn't his problem. The cops and the arson investigator would have to sort that out.

'Hey, Chief,' a voice said.

Crocker turned. It was a cop, a young guy with ears like pitcher handles under his cap. Crocker wasn't a fire chief, but there was no point telling the cop that; the cops always called the senior fireman on the scene chief.

'You shouldn't be up here,' Crocker said. 'That floor you're standing on could give way.'

'I talked to the manager,' the cop said, 'and we know who three of these people are.'

'Yeah?' Crocker said.

'The couple from the fourth floor, their names were Sharon and Pat Montgomery. The gal was a teacher at some middle school and her husband worked at Macy's over in Arlington.'

Just a couple of ordinary people who had the bad luck to be sleeping in the wrong place at the wrong time, Crocker thought.

'Who owns this apartment?' Crocker said.

'A young gal named Jennifer Talbot. She was a secretary, and that's why I came up here. You're never gonna guess who she worked for.'

'Well, who is it?' Crocker said. He wished the damn cop would just get to the point and get out of here. He wanted to get away from the smell.

'Broderick,' the cop said.

'You mean *Senator* Broderick?' Crocker said.

'Yeah.'

Oh, boy, Crocker thought, and took out his cell phone. He needed to tell his boss what the cop had just said, but before he dialed, he asked, 'What about the fourth person, the one who was sleeping with Talbot?'

'We don't know yet,' the cop said. 'The manager, he said Talbot wasn't married and he didn't think she had a boyfriend, although he said she was one good-looking young lady.'

'Well, you guys need to figure out who he is,' Crocker said, 'because . . .'

Before Crocker could finish telling the jug-eared cop that they were most likely dealing with a homicide, another cop burst into the room, panting, like he'd just run up the stairs. His name tag said WILMONT.

'Artie!' Wilmont said to the cop who'd been talking to Crocker. 'We got . . . oh, man, you're not gonna fuckin' believe it!'

'Well, what is it?' Crocker said. What the hell was it with these cops? And what the hell were they all doing up here?

'I was down in the parking lot,' Wilmont said, 'looking around, and there was a car parked behind the car of the gal who owns this apartment. You know, blocking her in like she let whoever it was park there. Anyway, I figured maybe I could find out who the guy was, so I slim-jimmed the door open and checked the registration.'

'Well, goddammit, who is it?' Crocker said.

Within twenty minutes, a dozen FBI agents, two carloads of brass from the D.C. Metro Police, four guys from the Secret Service, and Tim Crocker's boss's boss were there.

Somebody had assassinated Senator William Davis Broderick.

52

Danny was going nuts; he'd been in the motel room eighteen straight hours. There wasn't a damn thing to watch on TV, the crummy motel didn't have pay-per-view, and he didn't even have a deck of cards so he could play solitaire. Not only was he bored, he was tired, so worried he hadn't been able to sleep all night. Joe had said that if this thing didn't work out he was going back to Riker's, and he knew Joe wasn't kidding. If Pugh didn't call today, he was fucked.

He turned on the television again. Something about some senator getting whacked. Who cared? He changed the channel and got *Wheel of Fortune* and that Vanna White broad. She'd been doing that show forever, smiling like she had lockjaw, turning over those letter blocks. She must *hate* those letters by now – and fuckin' Pat Sajak too. He wondered how old she was. She had to be pushing fifty, but he had to admit she still looked damn good. And these people they got for contestants. How the hell did they find three idiots every day that would jump up and down and scream every time they—

His cell phone rang. The phone was sitting on the nightstand next to the bed, and he grabbed for it so fast he knocked it to the floor. He rolled off the bed, landing hard on his knees, and scrambled for the phone. He answered it on the second ring.

'Yeah,' he said.

'Get on a land line. Call 540-432-2387. Got it?'

'No! Wait a minute! Let me get a pen.' Before the guy could say anything, he reached up and grabbed a pen sitting next to the motel phone. 'Give me the number again.' The guy repeated it, and Danny wrote the number down on his left forearm.

The caller had sounded like Jubal Pugh's snake, that skinny rat-bastard Randy with the prison tats on his knuckles. Thank you, Jesus. He waited a couple of minutes and then picked up the motel phone and called the number Randy had given him.

'Come on back out to Jubal's place,' Randy said. 'If somebody follows you, we'll know it.'

Shit, the guy could have told him that on the cell phone. 'Aw, relax, Randy. I'll be there in forty-five minutes. That's how long it took me to get there yesterday.'

He hung up and called his cousin. 'Joe, it's me. It looks like we're on. I'm heading out to Pugh's place right now.'

Joe didn't say anything for a moment. Then he said, 'You better make this work, Danny,' and hung up.

Jesus. Would it have killed the guy to say 'good luck'?

There wasn't anything for Joe to do but wait. And while he waited, all he could do was think about his ex-wife. Every time he spoke to his goddamn cousin, every time he looked at his goddamn cousin, he thought about her. He was sick of thinking about her.

His cell phone rang again. It was probably Danny calling back. With DeMarco's luck, Danny had gotten a flat tire driving out to Pugh's. But it wasn't Danny; it was Emma.

'Anisa Aziz called me late yesterday and I drove down to Charlottesville and spoke to her last night. I just got home. Anisa was abducted right before Mustafa tried to blow up the Capitol.'

'Jesus. Will she tell the Bureau?'

'No. I spent an hour trying to get her to change her mind, but she's terrified. And I don't blame her. The people who abducted her showed her pictures of her mother and her brother and said they'd kill them if she talked to the police. If the FBI gets some-body, she'll be willing to testify, but she's not going to go to them now.'

'Well, shit,' DeMarco said.

'She did tell me a couple of things that I wanted to pass on. She couldn't identify whoever kidnapped her and doesn't know if they were American or foreign-born because they wore masks and never spoke to her. The only thing she saw was that both men had brown eyes, one was six-four and heavy, and the other was about six feet and skinny. The skinny one might be white and he might have had tattoos on his knuckles, but she wasn't sure if they were tattoos or grease or dirt. When your cousin goes out to Pugh's place, have him look for guys meeting that description.'

'You're too late,' DeMarco said. 'Danny's already left for Pugh's. I'll ask him when—'

'Oh my God, Joe! Turn on your television. Broderick's dead!'

Randy was waiting outside Pugh's house when Danny arrived. He was wearing a black sweatshirt, and his pants and baseball cap were that brown and green mottled camouflage color. On his feet were black combat boots. These peckerheads who wore camo pants and combat boots scared the shit out of him; it was like they could hardly wait for World War III to start.

Randy patted Danny down and they entered the house. It was 9 A.M. and Pugh was in a white bathrobe bearing the name of a Hilton Head resort and wearing the same fluffy blue slippers he'd had on the last time Danny had seen him. He was at his kitchen table, squinting at a newspaper, reading glasses perched on the end of his long nose. There was something odd about Pugh in reading glasses. He reminded Danny of a drawing you might see in a children's book: a rat dressed like a person, wearing glasses.

Danny started to sit down at the table, but Pugh said, 'No. Go with Randy. He's gonna make sure you're clean and you're gonna change clothes before we talk.'

Danny started to protest, realized it would be futile, and said, 'Hey, whatever floats your boat.'

Randy led him to a bedroom and told him to strip, all the way. Danny resisted the urge to make some comment about Randy getting his thrills by looking at his ass. He resisted the urge because Randy looked like he might beat the shit out of him if he said something like that.

He undressed and handed Randy his clothes, and Randy ran his hands over the garments looking for electronics. When he was naked, Randy had him turn around once to make sure there wasn't anything taped to his back, then tossed him a pair of swimming trunks and a white T-shirt. Danny put them on, and Randy turned to leave the room.

'Hey,' Danny said, 'I gotta go barefoot here? You don't have shower thongs or something?'

'Shut the fuck up,' Randy said.

Back in Pugh's kitchen, Jubal pointed Danny to a chair and said, 'Okay, I checked you and your boss out. You're a punk, but your boss is the real thing. I'm interested. So let's talk details. How much product do you expect to get for a million and how will we arrange delivery and make the exchange?'

Danny shook his head. 'Not yet,' he said.

'What?' Pugh said.

'I need to see your lab first. I told you, we have to make sure you have a big enough operation to deliver the quantities we need. If we have an inventory problem, we'll lose the market.'

Patsy Hall had told him to say that too, because Pugh would like it to sound as if he was supplying brake linings to General Motors, not some hillbilly dealing meth.

'My operation's big enough, sonny. Don't you worry about that. I supply half the tweakers in Virginia and cover parts of Maryland and Pennsylvania too.'

'Sorry, Mr Pugh,' Danny said, sounding contrite and respectful, 'but if you don't have enough product to take care of some biker and his bitch, they'll just wait a day. But we can't take that chance.' Before Pugh could protest, Danny said, 'I'm not disrespecting you here. My boss told me before we make a deal, I gotta see your lab. We're talkin' a lotta money here, for you, five million a year, maybe more.'

Pugh looked at him for a second, then nodded.

'Go put your shoes on,' he said, 'but nothing else. Randy, give him some overalls and loan him a jacket so he don't freeze out there.'

Danny donned grease-stained overalls and a leather jacket that smelled of stale beer. His Gucci loafers looked pretty stupid with the overalls. When he returned to Pugh's kitchen, there was another man with Pugh, a big guy with a beard and a huge gut. The fat guy looked a little friendlier than Randy, like maybe he smiled once a year.

'You know what to do,' Pugh said to Randy.

Randy just nodded, then said to Danny, 'Let's go.'

What the hell did that mean, *You know what to do?*

The three men left the house and walked over to a shed that contained five ATVs – all-terrain vehicles that looked like four-wheeled motorcycles. 'Roll two of them out, Harlan, and make sure they've got gas,' Randy said.

'You gotta be shittin' me,' Danny muttered.

'You ride behind me,' Randy said to Danny. That was good, Danny thought; the other guy's ass was so big there wouldn't be room for two of them on his machine. 'And we're gonna blindfold you,' Randy said, and before Danny could say anything, Randy pulled a white rag out of his pocket, the remnants of a T-shirt, and tied it over Danny's eyes. Then he put a ski mask over his head, the eye holes at the back.

This wasn't good at all, Danny thought. This was just going to fuck up everything.

Danny didn't like it on the back of the ATV, unable to see, unable to anticipate the bumps and turns. The ATV had little bars next to the passenger seat for holding on, and he gripped them as hard as he could. The main problem was his feet kept coming off the footrests, and every time they did it upset his balance and he thought he was going to fall. They stopped riding after half an hour, maybe forty-five minutes. Patsy Hall had told Danny that Pugh owned three or four hundred acres. Maybe that's why it was taking so long to get to wherever they were going, or maybe Randy was driving in circles. Danny had no way to tell.

Randy helped him off the ATV and started walking him, holding on to his upper arm. 'Can I take the blindfold off now?' Danny said.

'No,' Randy said. 'You don't do a damn thing unless I tell you.'

They walked maybe fifty yards down what felt like a dirt trail. He tripped once over a tree root but Randy kept him from falling. Randy had a grip that could crush rocks. Finally they stopped and Randy said, 'Stand still a minute.'

Danny heard something being moved, he didn't know what, and maybe the sound of tree branches brushing against each other. Randy grabbed his arm again and said, 'We're goin' down some steps. Slide your feet forward until you can feel 'em.' Danny did, and with Randy still holding his arm they descended seven steps. Danny counted.

They stopped moving, and Randy said, 'I'm gonna take off the blindfold now, but you look straight ahead. If you look up or behind you, I'll break your neck.'

And as strong as the guy's hands were, he could probably do it.

The hood was pulled off Danny's head and the blindfold off his eyes. He was standing on the earthen floor of a room that was about the size of a one-car garage. Stacked against one wall was all kinds of crap, metal containers of denatured alcohol and acetone and stuff like that. There were also stainless steel tables, like the type you see in restaurant kitchens, and on the tables was a bunch of . . . well, lab shit, beakers and scales and rubber tubing and pots. God, the place just *stank*. He felt like he was standing inside a sweat sock that had been worn by Shaquille O'Neal for ten games in a row.

After a moment, Randy said, 'Okay, slick. You satisfied?'

'Not quite,' Danny said. 'I want to see how much ephedrine you have on hand.'

Randy led him over to a stack of two-gallon cardboard containers, like the type you saw behind the counter at Baskin-Robbins, containing ice cream. There must have been twenty containers. Randy popped the top off one of the containers and Danny looked inside. White powder.

'Okay,' Danny said. 'That's all I wanted to see.'

The fact was that Danny didn't know anything about meth. He didn't know if the equipment and chemicals he was looking at were really used for making meth, and he didn't know how much meth the equipment could produce. Nor did he know if the white powder had been ephedrine; it could have been baking powder for all he knew.

But he didn't need to know any of that stuff to do what he'd been asked to do.

53

Mahoney was at the Vietnam Veterans Memorial, but it hadn't been easy to get there.

Since Broderick's death, security for senior politicians had been ratcheted up to a degree not seen since 9/11 or maybe since World War II. Homeland Security's color-coded threat level was now at red, the only time Mahoney could remember its being above orange since the system had been invented. He guessed that if they could've come up with a color more alarming than red, they would have used it.

The president was in the White House but the vice president was somewhere else, not in Washington, and the Secret Service wouldn't divulge his location. The White House itself looked like it was under siege: armed men stationed every few feet, armored personnel carriers parked in the driveway and outside

the gates, guys with sniper rifles and rocket launchers
visible on the roof – and those were just the security measures that could be seen.

Cabinet members were under guard too, as if they
were actually more important than the figureheads
that most of them really were, and senior leadership
in the House and Senate were flanked by armed men
whenever they left their offices and were driven to
meetings in armored cars. Mahoney himself, being
third in line for the presidency, was being *smothered*
by his security, four guys so big they all looked like
they could have played on the line for Notre Dame.
And that was the problem. He *felt* smothered, and
he needed to get away, to someplace where he could
be alone and think.

He had them drive him to a restaurant on Capitol
Hill and made two of them wait outside, saying four
inside was just too many. Then, once in the restaurant, after he'd had a drink, he rose from the table.
The two remaining security guys rose with him but
he waved them back to their seats. 'I'm just goin' to
the head,' he said, 'and I can't pee when I'm being
watched.' This embarrassed them so much that
Mahoney was gone before they could move.

But instead of going to the restroom, he ducked
into the kitchen, borrowed a ski jacket and stocking
cap from one of the cooks, and boogied out the backdoor, the cap pulled down low on his forehead. Then,
feeling momentarily gleeful, he sprinted down the

alley – well, for a guy his age and size it was a sprint – and caught a cab to the memorial. The security guys were gonna be pissed when they caught up with him, but screw 'em; he needed some *space*.

So now he sat on a bench near the memorial, that stark black granite wall that lists the names of the fallen and mostly forgotten. There is no memorial in Washington that is more poignant than that simple wall. Mahoney, bundled in the cook's stained jacket, the stocking cap on his head, looked like a broken-down old vet who had come on a dismal day to mourn those who had fought beside him.

And Mahoney was mourning, just not for the men on the wall – although he had known several of them. He was mourning Bill Broderick – not because he had liked the man but because Broderick's death was having a horrible galvanizing effect on the passage of his damn bill.

An ordinary bill Mahoney could have kept in committee indefinitely. He could have bounced it from committee to committee until Congress recessed or until it died a quiet death. But not *this* bill. There was just too much media heat and too many congressmen feeling the heat. Two days ago, it had reported out of the committee, two Democrats voting for it. Mahoney then began to do what he could to delay a floor vote, hoping – though without opti-mism – that something would happen to give him what he needed to get folks turned around. But then

Broderick had to go and get himself killed, burnt to a crisp while screwing his secretary. The idiot.

Now practically every member of the House was screaming for Mahoney to bring Broderick's bill to the floor for a vote. They didn't scream directly at Mahoney, of course – they screamed via the press. And the press, at least the conservative press, was starting to make John Mahoney sound as patriotic as Benedict Arnold.

There was something else that irritated Mahoney. Before his death, Broderick had tried and failed to come up with a clever name for his bill, something like the 'Patriot Act,' a name that would make it sound as if the bill were really in the country's best interest. He had tried to get the media to latch on to a couple of different names, such as the Domestic Security Act or the Muslim American Validation Act, but these names were neither particularly euphonic nor sufficiently misleading. And no matter what name Broderick tried to give his proposal, the liberals insisted on calling it the Muslim American Registry Act, a name Broderick had hated because it focused attention on the most controversial aspect of his bill. But now the bill had a name. It was being called the Broderick Act.

Jesus.

Nor could any advantage be taken of the fact that Broderick had been diddling his receptionist the night he died. A tidbit like that might have been useful if the man was still alive, but to bring it up now would be considered by one and all as a despicable thing to rub into the face of Broderick's widow. So the press, in a rare act of decency, was pretending to accept the story given by Senator Broderick's aide Nicholas Fine.

Fine had said that the senator had attended a meeting with some constituents the night of his death – this story matched the lie that Broderick had told his wife – and Fine assumed that the senator had stopped by Ms Talbot's apartment afterward to give her some urgent task related to the meeting. Maybe, Fine said, Broderick had given her something he wanted typed up that very night or possibly something that he wanted her to get into the mail first thing in the morning. *Yeah, he was giving her something, all right,* the reporters thought, but they didn't print what they were thinking.

Then the last straw floated down and landed on the camel's back, prompting Mahoney to ditch his security so he could be alone. The FBI had discovered a note in Broderick's car, a note that had apparently been left there by the bomber. The previous night when the cop had opened the car to find out who the car belonged to, he hadn't seen the note. In fact, the cop had planted a knee right on it when he reached over to open the glove compartment to get Broderick's registration. But after the FBI arrived and began to examine the scene in an organized manner, the note was discovered.

The note was typed and unsigned but appeared to have been written by a Muslim American, one not particularly well educated. There were references to Allah, the Koran, and the worldwide Muslim brotherhood, and there was the implication that al-Qaeda had helped the bomber, a statement to the effect that wise men across the sea had aided his efforts but al-Qaeda was not mentioned specifically. In the note Broderick was thoroughly denounced as a godless infidel whose bill was proof that America had declared an unholy crusade against all Muslims.

So even though the FBI could not prove it – even though the FBI said *repeatedly* that they could not prove it – the public was convinced that an American Muslim was responsible for the death of a United States senator, a man whose character had already improved tenfold in the hours since his passing.

Mahoney thought about calling DeMarco but decided not to bother. Unless DeMarco could find something in the next forty-eight hours, the Broderick Act was going to become law.

'Mr Speaker.'

Mahoney turned his head. Aw, shit. His four security guys were jogging across the grass toward him, the Notre Dame offensive line for sure.

They'd found him fast. These guys were good.

54

'They blindfolded me,' Danny said.

'Son of a bitch!' DeMarco said, glaring at his cousin.

'Hey! It wasn't my fault. I did what you wanted. I got 'em to show me the lab.'

Patsy Hall said, 'Yeah, but for all you know, it wasn't even on Pugh's property.' She thought for a minute. 'Was the lab in a cave?' Looking at DeMarco she said, 'There're a couple small caves on Pugh's land. I snuck in there one night to check 'em out, but at the time they were empty.'

'You went onto Pugh's property by yourself, at *night*, and explored these caves?' DeMarco said.

'Yeah. I didn't have a warrant and I wasn't going to get any of my guys in trouble.'

Wow, DeMarco thought. Patsy Hall was something else.

Danny said, 'This place I was in, it didn't look like a cave. It was man-made. But it *was* underground. I could tell because we walked down these stairs to get in and the floor was dirt. But the walls weren't made of rock, like a cave. They were built out of railroad ties, like they dug the space out and reinforced the walls with the ties so they wouldn't collapse.'

They were in a conference room in Winchester where the DEA had a small field office. They all sat in silence, Danny worrying about his future, DeMarco annoyed at his cousin, and Patsy Hall thinking about Pugh, her lips set in a stubborn line. Hall got up after a moment and opened a file cabinet and pulled out a topographical map that included Pugh's land. She spread the map out on the table.

'How long were you driving around?' she asked Danny.

'Half hour, maybe forty-five minutes.'

'Well, which was it? Half an hour or forty-five minutes?'

'I don't know! They took my watch when they made me strip.'

'Shit. And how fast do you think you were driving?'

'Wherever we were going, it was pretty rough. I'd say less than fifteen miles an hour most of the time, but a couple of times Randy, that asshole, really opened the thing up. Scared the crap out of me.' Then he added, 'I mean, being blindfolded like I was.'

'But most of the time you were going less than twenty?'

'Yeah, I guess.'

Patsy scratched some numbers on the edge of the map. 'If it took you forty-five minutes at an average speed of twenty miles an hour, you would have gone fifteen miles. She looked down at the map and said, 'Shit, if you were traveling in anywhere near a straight line, you'd be off Pugh's property.'

Danny said, 'But we weren't traveling in a straight line. We made a lot of turns. I could feel them.'

'I know,' Patsy Hall said, shaking her head, 'but if you drove that long I can't establish that you were on his property.' She stood there a moment, studying the map, tracing a slim forefinger over the heavy black line that outlined Pugh's land. 'Could you feel anything or hear anything while you were driving?'

'Like what?' Danny said.

'Like was the vehicle going up and down hills?'

'Sometimes,' Danny said, 'but not big ones.'

'There's a train track on this edge of the property,' she said, tapping the map. 'Did you hear a train? Or other cars, like you might have been near a road?'

'No. No noises. It was quiet, like we were deep in the woods.'

'This is hopeless,' DeMarco said. 'Maybe we can set up a delivery right away and get Pugh when he delivers the dope.'

'That won't work,' Hall said. '*Jubal* won't be delivering anything. All we'll get is some mule who won't talk.'

'There was one thing,' Danny said.

'Yeah, what was that?' Hall said, obviously not expecting much.

'Right before we stopped, maybe five minutes before, we drove over something that went *bumpitty-bump, bumpitty-bump.*'

'*Bumpitty-bump*?' DeMarco said.

'Yeah, like we were going over logs or one of those whaddaya-call'em – cattle guards. It happened twice, right before we stopped. *Bumpitty-bump, bumpitty-bump,* then a couple minutes later, *bumpitty-bump, bumpitty-bump* again. Then, a couple minutes after that, we stopped.'

Hall studied the map. 'Here,' she said, pointing. 'This could be it. There're two creeks running through his place, small ones, no more than two or three feet wide. If I remember right . . . Wait a minute.' She went to the file cabinet again, the one from which she'd taken the map. She pulled out an accordion file folder and came back to the table. From the folder she pulled a stack of eight by ten black-and-white photographs.

'We did *one* aerial surveillance of Pugh's farm. I tried to get 'em to park a satellite over his place for a week, but they laughed me off.' She flipped through the photos, then stopped and studied one.

'Here. You see that? A little bridge made from logs, and here, about two hundred yards away, is another one. The two bridges are where these two creeks come close to each other and run parallel for a while. So if you're right about the time it took you to get from the second bridge to the lab, the lab's probably someplace within a quarter mile of the second bridge.'

'But which one's the *second* bridge?' DeMarco asked.

'Were you going uphill or downhill when you came to the second bridge?' Hall asked Danny.

'Uh . . . downhill,' Danny said.

'Then this is the second bridge,' Hall said, stabbing a finger at the topographical map. She looked directly at Danny, her eyes bright, and said, 'You're going to have to go in there tonight and find that lab.'

'Bullshit!' Danny said.

55

DeMarco put on the night-vision goggles. The trees in the woods were clearly visible, everything a greenish color. He'd never worn night-vision goggles before – or a military camouflage suit, combat boots, and a bulletproof vest either. And he wished he wasn't wearing any of those things right now.

Hall said she couldn't search for the lab with them. She and her guys – a bunch of DEA cowboys who *knew* how to shoot and sneak through the woods – couldn't go onto Pugh's property without a warrant, and they didn't have sufficient justification to get one. If Danny had been positive he'd been on Pugh's property it would have been different, but since he'd been blindfolded and didn't have a clue as to how far he'd traveled, it was impossible to state with certainty where the lab was. Then toss in the fact that the judge would have to accept the word of a convicted felon regarding its whereabouts, and there was no way Hall was going to get a warrant.

So DeMarco and his cousin were on their own. DeMarco didn't want to go with Danny to search Pugh's farm, but he didn't trust his flake of a cousin; he couldn't put the unveiling of a national conspiracy in the hands of a mafia fence.

Hall and another agent had driven them to the northern boundary of Pugh's four hundred acres in a black Jeep Cherokee. To reach that spot it had been necessary to go through two pieces of property not owned by Pugh, and Hall had to cut through two barbed-wire fences on the way. Cutting the fences didn't seem to bother her a bit, DeMarco noted.

'You're sure you know how to use a GPS?' Hall asked Danny a second time.

'Yeah, I'm positive. I got my hands on one once . . .'

This meant, DeMarco suspected, that one of Tony Benedetto's crews had stolen a crate of the instruments.

'. . . and I played with the thing for a couple of days,' Danny said. 'I know how to use it.'

'Okay,' Hall said, and she showed him and DeMarco the GPS unit she was holding in her hand. 'Here's the waypoint for where we are now, and here's the waypoint for the second bridge. When you get to the bridge, start looking for a trail or a path.

Look for tire tracks made by ATVs, places where the grass has been beaten down. Understand?'

'Sure,' Danny said.

Sure, my ass, DeMarco thought. Like his cousin was Davy Crockett instead of some fuckin' New York wiseguy who could barely find his way through Central Park.

Hall pulled a pistol in a clip-on holster out of one of the pockets of the black ski jacket she was wearing and handed it to DeMarco. 'That's a forty-caliber automatic. There're eight bullets in the clip. You shoot somebody, even in the arm, it'll put him down. Have you ever used a gun?'

'Yeah,' DeMarco said. And that was the truth. He'd once killed a man with a revolver. The man had shot at him and DeMarco had pulled the trigger of the gun he'd been holding out of sheer fright and amazingly hit the guy. But the total amount of time he'd spent with a pistol in his hands could be measured in minutes, and the number of times he'd fired one at another person was exactly once. He didn't bother to tell Hall this. He did ask, 'Is the safety on or off?'

The agent with Hall muttered, 'Oh, great.'

Hall shot a shut-up look at the agent and said to DeMarco, 'Give it to me.' He handed her the weapon, and she did something to it and handed it back. 'Now the safety's off and there's a bullet in the chamber. If you have to take it out of the holster, don't shoot yourself in the leg.

'Oh, and one other thing,' she said. 'There might be people working in the lab.'

'What?' DeMarco and his cousin said at the same time.

'Pugh's cookers work at night, but we don't think they work every night.'

'You don't *think*?' DeMarco said.

'That's right. Every couple of weeks Pugh buses in a bunch of people to do things around his place: clear brush, prune trees, whatever. These guys will stay on his property overnight in his barn, sometimes for a couple of nights. What we think is that five or six of the workers are really Pugh's cookers. They sneak off to the lab in the dark and stay there for a couple of nights and brew his meth, then they leave on the bus with the real workers when they're done. Anyway, Pugh had a bunch of guys come in a few days ago and they left the day before yesterday, so we're pretty sure they're not in the lab now. But be careful.'

Be careful, DeMarco thought. That was just great fuckin' advice. But he didn't say anything.

'So I guess that's it,' Hall said. 'We'll wait here for you. If you haven't found the place by dawn, come back here and we'll try again tomorrow night. And good luck.'

'Hey, wait a minute,' Danny said. 'Aren't you gonna give me a gun too? I mean, if there're guys in that lab—'

'No way,' Hall said. 'I shouldn't even be giving one to your cousin. The DEA's not supposed to go around arming civilians, and I'm sure as hell not giving one to a guy that's still under indictment for murder.'

'But—' Danny said.

'No,' Hall said, eyes like flint. 'If you're in danger, call on the radio and we'll come in and get you. But I hope we don't have to do that, because that'll really screw up our chances of getting Pugh.' Then she laughed and said, 'Unless he personally kills one of you.'

Yeah, that was *real* funny, DeMarco thought.

They didn't make bad time. The good thing about the woods on Pugh's property was that there wasn't a lot of brush or ground cover. They had to veer around thickets of trees a couple of times, but Danny, who was in the lead, brought them back on course. Maybe he really did know how to use the GPS.

It took them twenty minutes to reach the log bridge. The bridge spanned a creek that was two feet wide and had carved a shallow gully into the landscape. Leading to and away from the bridge was a trail created by vehicle tires.

'Which way,' DeMarco whispered.

Danny pointed.

'How do you know it's not the other way?' DeMarco asked.

'The GPS. The other little bridge, the first one we crossed over when I was blindfolded, is behind us. It's that way. So we go *this* way.'

DeMarco took off the night-vision goggles and looked around. There was no moon, maybe a dozen stars overhead that weren't obscured by clouds, and it was so damn dark without the goggles he felt like he was standing inside a closet. He didn't have any idea how the goggles worked, but he was damn glad they did, because if Pugh had someone standing guard, the guard wouldn't be able to see them unless he was similarly equipped.

'Okay,' he said, putting the magic goggles back on. 'Let's go.'

They walked down the trail about seventy-five yards and the trail forked.

'Aw, shit,' Danny said. 'Now what? You wanna split up or stay together?'

If Danny had been right about the time, the lab had to be within a hundred yards of the fork in the road. They had radios so if they split up and if one of them found the lab, he could let the other guy know. Nah, forget that, he thought; he didn't want Danny doing *anything* by himself.

'We'll stay together,' DeMarco said. 'We'll go that way a hundred yards or so and look around for an hour; if we don't find it, we'll come back here and go up the other road.'

'You're the boss,' Danny said.

They walked for a couple of minutes. Then DeMarco said, 'Okay, what are we looking for?'

'Well, shit, Joe, I don't know. There's a door in the ground around here somewhere, I think, and there's bushes or something coverin' the door. Probably the best thing to do is just walk around and *sniff*. The place I was in stunk to high heaven.'

DeMarco went left and Danny went right, noses probing the air like a couple of Italian beagles. He searched for any anomaly on the ground, anything that didn't look natural. There was nothing. He wondered if he should take off the night-vision goggles and use a flashlight, thinking it might be easier to spot something with the flashlight as opposed to the green color he was seeing through the goggles. They were at least half a mile from Pugh's house and he didn't think a flashlight beam would be visible from that distance. He was still thinking about using the flashlight when the walkie-talkie on his belt squawked, a burst of static that scared the crap out of him.

'What?' he hissed into the radio. Then he remembered and said, 'Over.'

'I found something. Over,' Danny said.

DeMarco looked around. He could see Danny fifty yards away and he jogged over to him.

'Look,' Danny said, pointing to the ground.

Cigarette butts, a lot of them, in an area underneath a good-sized oak. Most of the butts were contained in a rough three-foot circle of ground and DeMarco guessed that the guys who worked in the lab came out here to smoke so they wouldn't blow themselves up. They'd sit under the oak, puff their cigarettes, squash the butts out near the tree, and then go back to work. So the lab had to be fairly close, probably no more than fifty feet away, but DeMarco still couldn't see anything with the night-vision goggles other than a fluorescent green forest.

'Shit,' he said. 'I'm gonna use a flashlight.'

'You sure?' Danny said.

'No,' DeMarco said, and took off the goggles and turned on the flashlight. He walked around searching the ground with the flashlight for five minutes but still didn't see anything that looked like a door. Then he noticed something. The cigarette butts made a trail, a little Hansel and Gretel trail. The guys would be almost done smoking their cigarettes and they'd start back toward the lab, and on the way they'd drop their cigarette butts on the ground and grind them out with their feet. They couldn't just flick the butts away because they might start a forest fire. So DeMarco followed the butt trail, sweeping his flash-light back and forth, and then he saw it: a little ridge of dirt about four feet long, about an inch high, and the ridge was absolutely straight. There aren't many perfectly straight things out in the woods. He walked over and knelt down next to the little ridge and ran his hand along it.

'Here it is,' he said to his cousin.

They rubbed their hands along the line in the dirt, came to another intersecting line, and finally understood what they were dealing with. It was a piece of wood, four feet square. A half sheet of three-quarter-inch plywood. On top of the plywood was a shallow layer of dirt and three small shrubs. DeMarco couldn't figure out how the plants could grow in so little soil until he touched the leaves: they were artificial plants and they were glued to the piece of wood. On two parallel sides of the plywood sheet were small rope handles that had been covered with dirt. All you had to do was pick up the piece of plywood and move it to one side.

Hall had said the meth cookers worked at night. During the day, the door to the lab would be almost invisible, just another square of forest, a small plot of dirt and shrubs. From the air it would be *completely* invisible. The nights when Pugh's men manufactured the meth, they would simply remove the hatch covering the lab's entrance; maybe they'd just leave it off to provide ventilation for the space, or maybe a couple of men would put the hatch back in place after the cookers had entered the lab and those guys would stand guard and periodically remove the cover when it was time for the cookers to take a smoke break. When they finished working for the night, they'd put the cover back in place and hide the edges with a layer of dirt. The cover was simple, easy to remove, and, most important, almost impossible to spot unless you were right on top of it. DeMarco would never have found it if it hadn't been for the cigarette butts.

'Let's get this thing out of the way,' DeMarco said.

'What if there's somebody inside the lab?' Danny said.

'Then either we would have heard them or they would have heard us, all the damn noise you're making. Pick it up.' Danny and DeMarco took hold of the rope handles, raised the door, and saw the steps going down into an underground bunker.

'Hurry up,' DeMarco said. 'Get the pictures.'

Danny hustled down the steps. Using a digital camera, he snapped off half a dozen pictures of the equipment inside the lab, shoved the camera back into one of the leg pockets in his camo pants, and came back up the stairs.

'Let's boogie,' Danny said.

'We gotta put the cover back or they'll know somebody's been here. And if that happens they'll remove all the drugs and the equipment.'

'Right,' Danny said.

Master fuckin' criminal, DeMarco thought.

They put the cover back in place and brushed dirt over the edges.

'*Now* let's get out of here,' DeMarco said.

'You assholes hold it right there,' a voice said. 'You move and I'll put deer slugs into both of you.'

Aw, Christ.

DeMarco watched as a man stepped out of the woods, a tall guy with an enormous gut and a beard. Like DeMarco and his cousin, the guy was wearing night-vision goggles – and he was holding a shotgun. There must have been some sort of alarm system protecting the lab. Maybe the plywood sheet covering the lab's entrance had been alarmed, but DeMarco didn't think so. He hadn't seen any wires or contacts, and it had taken them less than five minutes to take the pictures and put the cover back in place. The man couldn't have gotten to the lab from Pugh's place that fast. No, more likely they'd tripped some sort of perimeter alarm, maybe motion detectors or cameras that could see in the dark. Whatever the case, this wasn't good.

'Now unzip them jackets real slow and hold 'em open. I wanna see if you're strapped.'

Shit. The gun Patsy Hall had given him was on his belt, on his right hip, and the guy saw it as soon as DeMarco opened his jacket. Seeing DeMarco's gun, the man said to Danny, 'Where's yours?'

'Don't have one,' Danny said.

'I pat you down and find one, bud, I'm gonna put a hurt on you.'

Danny didn't respond.

'Okay,' he said to DeMarco, 'toss the gun into the woods. Use your left hand, just your thumb and one finger. You point it at me and I'll blow your ass away.'

DeMarco did as he was told. He pulled the gun slowly from the holster and threw it away under-handed, and when he did the fat guy's head turned momentarily as his eyes followed the arc of the gun – and just at that moment, DeMarco saw Danny's arm move in his peripheral vision. Pugh's man, unfortunately, saw Danny move as well. Without any hesitation, he swung the shotgun barrel toward Danny and pulled the trigger. The shotgun blast was horrendous in the quiet night, and Danny was blown backward by the slug striking his chest.

'Jesus Christ!' DeMarco screamed. His cousin was lying on his back, not moving. DeMarco didn't see any blood, but with the night-vision goggles maybe blood wouldn't be visible. 'Goddammit, what in the hell did you shoot him for?' he said.

'He put his hand in his pocket. He was goin' for his piece.'

'He didn't have a fuckin' piece!' DeMarco yelled.

'Shut the hell up.'

DeMarco looked down at his cousin again. Like DeMarco, Danny had been wearing a bulletproof vest underneath his shirt but DeMarco didn't know what a deer slug was, much less how much penetrating power one had. But it apparently had enough: Danny still hadn't moved, and one leg was twisted under him in an unnatural position.

'Now who the hell are you?' the man said.

There was no point saying that he and Danny were a couple of guys who'd just gotten lost in the woods, not dressed the way they were. So DeMarco tried another tack.

'We're federal agents,' he said. 'You just killed a cop. The smartest thing you can do right now is put that shotgun down.'

'The hell you say.' He glanced down at Danny. 'Take the goggles off that guy.'

DeMarco hesitated. Then he knelt and pulled the goggles off Danny's head. Danny's eyes were wide open, unblinking, and his head fell limply back to the ground after DeMarco removed the goggles.

'Yeah, that's what I thought,' the man said. 'That's that New York wop that came to the house today. What were you two jack-offs doing, trying to rip Jubal off?'

'I'm telling you we're federal agents,' DeMarco said. Pointing down at Danny he said, 'He was under-cover.'

'Bullshit,' the guy said. 'Jubal checked him out good.' Before DeMarco could say anything else, he said, 'We're gonna go on up to the big house and have a little talk. You, me, and Jubal.' He motioned with his rifle. 'Move.'

'What about him?' DeMarco said, gesturing at Danny. 'Let me check to see if he has a pulse.'

The man laughed. 'Believe me, slick, he don't have no pulse. Now let's go.'

DeMarco looked down at Danny one last time – Jesus, what would he tell Marie? – and started walking, the man falling into place behind him.

They hadn't walked more than three paces when a shot rang out. DeMarco heard the man behind him grunt and the shotgun fired, the bullet or slug or whatever it was hitting the ground near DeMarco's right foot. Then another shot was fired, not the shotgun, and DeMarco turned in time to see Pugh's man fall to the ground.

Danny had shot the guy in the back. Twice.

DeMarco looked over at his cousin. He was sitting up now, holding a short-barreled automatic in his hand. Where the hell had Danny gotten a gun?

DeMarco kicked the shotgun out of the fallen man's right hand, knelt down, and checked for a pulse in his throat. Pugh's man groaned. Good. He was still alive.

Danny was now standing next to DeMarco, looking down at the wounded man and at the same time rubbing his chest where the slug had hit his vest.

'Do you know him?' DeMarco asked.

'Yeah,' Danny said, 'it's that Harlan guy who went to the lab with me and Randy.'

He started to ask Danny where he'd gotten the gun when Danny said, 'Oh-oh!'

'What?' DeMarco said, and Danny pointed. There were headlights coming toward them, probably ATVs, and they were coming from the direction of Pugh's house. The pistol shots Danny had fired hadn't been that loud, just a couple of pops, but the two shotgun blasts could have been heard back at the house. DeMarco hoped Patsy Hall had heard them as well, but they were closer to Pugh's house than they were to Patsy.

'Let's get the hell out of here,' DeMarco said. He tossed Danny his night-vision goggles. Danny put them on, and he and DeMarco started running.

As they were running, DeMarco couldn't help but think of the time that he and Danny, both thirteen, went into a mom-and-pop store in Queens and stole two bottles of beer. Danny had been his best friend back then. The Italian who ran the store, probably a guy as old as DeMarco was now, took off after them. The store owner didn't stand a chance. DeMarco and his cousin, they just flew down the side-walk that day – and right now DeMarco was wishing he still had that kind of speed.

The second thought he had was: *Now I owe the son of a bitch for my life.*

DeMarco and Danny reached the point in the barbed-wire fence where they'd entered Pugh's property, both of them panting from the run through the woods. DeMarco looked behind him; he didn't see headlights. Maybe Pugh's men had stopped to deal with the injured man, or maybe they were checking on the lab. When DeMarco had enough breath to talk he said to Hall, 'We found it. We've got the pictures.'

'Do you have the GPS coordinates for the lab?' she asked Danny.

'Oh, *shit*!' DeMarco said. He hadn't even thought about that.

'Yeah,' Danny said. 'I hit the waypoint as soon as we found the fake-plant door thing.'

'The fake-plant door thing?' Hall said, 'What are you—'

DeMarco explained, concluding with, 'You'll understand when you see it.'

Danny handed Hall the GPS and said, 'The lab's the fifth waypoint.'

'Good,' Hall said, her eyes shining. 'Goddamn good,' she said again. 'Give me the camera. I gotta get a warrant right away.'

DeMarco said, 'There's something else you need to—'

'Not now,' Hall said, and turned away.

'Danny shot a guy,' DeMarco said to Hall's back. 'One of Pugh's men.'

'What?' Hall said.

DeMarco started to explain but Hall interrupted him.

'We'll worry about this guy you shot later. Right now I need a warrant.'

She walked over to her SUV, opened the rear hatch, and took out a laptop. She placed the laptop on the hood of the car and said, 'Come on, come on,' while the computer was starting up. Holding a penlight in her mouth, she connected the camera to the laptop and then started typing. DeMarco guessed she was e-mailing the pictures to somebody and then listened as she started talking into her phone.

'This is Hall. I just sent you photos of Pugh's lab and the coordinates where it's located. Go get me a warrant. Show the judge the photos and tell him I have two witnesses, and that one of the witnesses took the photos and was in the lab. Tell him the witnesses can *definitely* put the lab on Pugh's property. And if the judge gives you any shit, any shit at all, wake up Gail Bradley back in D.C.

'While you're getting the warrant, I want Jorgenson and three other men in the chopper and I want the chopper over that lab as fast as it can get there. Tell Jorgenson to shine lights down onto the lab but don't land until I give the word. If Pugh's guys fire at him, he's to return fire. Tell him to blast their asses away. I want the rest of the team to meet me at Jubal's front gate. The team with me will round up Jubal and whoever's with him in his house. Get moving.'

Jesus, DeMarco thought, she sounded like George Patton.

Hall closed her cell phone and said triumphantly to herself, 'I've *got* the son of a bitch.'

When Hall walked off to talk to the DEA agent that had accompanied her, DeMarco said to Danny, 'Where the hell did the gun come from?'

'I brought it with me from New York. I disassembled it and packed it in my luggage. I thought I might need one down here, considering what we were doing.'

Goddamn airline security was useless, DeMarco thought. 'Then why in the hell did you ask Hall for one?' he said.

'Would have looked funny if I hadn't,' Danny said.

56

'The DEA's arrested Pugh,' DeMarco said.

'Yeah, but is that—' Mahoney said.

'And we got something else,' he said. He told Mahoney how Anisa Aziz had admitted to Emma that she'd been kidnapped before her uncle tried to blow up the Capitol. 'The girl said that one of the guys who kidnapped her had some tattoos on his knuckles, and one of the yahoos they caught at Pugh's place has the tattoos. The problem is, the girl never saw the guy's face.'

'So can you tie Pugh to the damn terrorist attacks or not?' Mahoney said.

'Probably not,' DeMarco said. 'I mean, not based on any evidence that the DEA has found so far. Hall's guys—'

'Who's Hall?' Mahoney said.

'The DEA agent in charge down here, the one who arrested Pugh. Anyway, Hall's guys will search Pugh's place and if they find anything that ties him to the attacks they'll let me know, but I wouldn't count on it. This guy Pugh, he owns four hundred acres, and it's gonna take a long time to search the place.'

'Goddammit!' Mahoney yelled. 'I don't have time for that. You gotta make Pugh admit he was involved.'

'I know,' DeMarco said. 'And this is what I'll have to do. . . .'

When he finished telling Mahoney what he planned, he said, 'Hall's gonna go nuts. She might even go to the press.'

'I'll take care of her,' Mahoney said.

'She's good people, boss.'

'Yeah, well, sometimes good people get screwed too,' Mahoney said.

DeMarco waited impatiently for Patsy Hall to get off the phone. As he was waiting, Danny walked over to him and said, 'I just finished giving a statement to the DEA guys and a lawyer. They videotaped it. They said they won't need me again until they start prepping for the trial. Any reason I can't go back to New York?'

'You better check with Hall,' DeMarco said, motioning toward the office where Hall was sitting, 'but as far as I'm concerned you can leave. But you better understand something, Danny. You're not done with this thing until those guys are in jail. You got it?'

'Yeah, but I'm okay with the Queens D.A. Right?'

'Yeah. You can go back to fencing for Tony Benedetto until they catch you for doing it.'

Danny shook his head. 'Look, man,' he said, 'it wasn't like me and Marie planned to fall in love. It just happened. One of these days, maybe you'll find it in yourself to forgive us both.'

DeMarco stared at his cousin for a minute.

'Go fuck yourself,' he said and walked away.

'I need to talk to Pugh alone,' DeMarco told Patsy Hall.

'Sorry,' she said, shaking her head sadly, as if she meant it. 'But I can't allow that. Anytime anybody talks to Pugh, I want his lawyer and our lawyer in the room.'

One of Hall's agents stuck his head into her office at that moment. 'Patsy, Dick Garner's on the phone. Line four. He wants to talk to you.'

Richard Garner was the top man at the DEA, and Hall was several rungs on the ladder below him. She had heard Garner speak a couple of times when he gave one of his sappy pep talks to motivate the troops, but she had never spoken to him.

'I didn't know catching Jubal Pugh was *that* big a deal,' the agent said.

Patsy Hall punched a button and picked up the phone on her desk. 'Mr Garner, this is Agent Hall.'

All DeMarco heard was Hall's side of the conversation, which consisted mostly of *yes, sir.*

At one point, while she was listening, she looked over at DeMarco.

'Yes, sir,' she said again. 'May I ask why? . . .

'Yes, sir,' Hall said one more time before hanging up.

Looking at DeMarco she said, 'Mr Garner says I'm supposed to let you do anything you want. You wanna tell me what's going on here?'

'Sorry, Patsy, I can't,' DeMarco said. 'At least not yet.'

Hall stared at him. 'You screw up my case against Pugh, and I'm gonna get a nightstick and beat you to death. I swear to Christ I will.'

Pugh was dressed in an orange jumpsuit. At DeMarco's request – at this point, all DeMarco's requests were being granted – the manacles were taken off Pugh's hands. They were seated in an office, not an interrogation room. DeMarco was seated behind the desk of whoever normally occupied the office; Pugh was in a chair in front of the desk. A DEA agent was posted outside the door, and the door was closed.

'Who the hell are you?' Pugh said. 'And why wasn't my lawyer allowed to be here?'

DeMarco didn't say anything for a moment. He just stared at Pugh's unshaven face. With his pointed nose and weak chin, Pugh reminded DeMarco of a badger or a wolverine – one of those critters that makes up for its lack of bulk with pure viciousness.

'I'm the guy who set you up, Jubal,' DeMarco said. 'I'm the guy that got Danny DeMarco and Tony Benedetto to cooperate with the DEA. And I'm the guy who'll make Danny DeMarco testify against you.'

Pugh didn't say anything.

'You're going to be convicted for manufacturing meth, and the judge is going to give you the maximum sentence permitted by the sentencing guidelines. He's going to do this because he'll be pressured by some people in Washington. Those same people in Washington are also going to promise to make him a federal judge with a lifetime appointment if he does what they want. So it doesn't matter if you've got the ghost of Johnnie-fuckin'-Cochran for a lawyer, Jubal, you're going to jail.'

Pugh blinked once.

'You're fifty-eight years old right now,' DeMarco said. 'If you're not killed in prison, you'll be seventy-eight or eighty years old when you get out. By then you'll most likely have prostate cancer or colon cancer or whatever diseases afflict old men. You'll be on death's doorstep when you get out of prison.'

Pugh blinked again.

'Now look around you,' DeMarco said. 'You're not in an interrogation room. There's no one-way mirror, no video camera in the ceiling, no tape recorder. It's just you and me.'

'Maybe you're wired,' Jubal said.

DeMarco shook his head. 'I don't want what I'm

going to tell you recorded.' He paused. 'If you can give me what I want, I can keep you out of prison. Your property's going to be auctioned off and your bank accounts are going to be frozen and all the money you have will be placed in the U.S. Treasury. But *you* get to stay out of jail – *if* you can deliver.'

'So what is it? What do you want?'

'I *know*,' DeMarco said, though he really didn't, 'that your people forced three American Muslims to commit acts of terrorism. I know your guys – Donny Cray and that asshole Randy with the prison tats on his knuckles – killed Reza Zarif's family, his wife and his two kids, and made him fly that plane at the White House. I know your people abducted Mustafa Ahmed's niece to force him to blow up the Capitol. Mustafa's niece *saw* the tats on Randy's hands. And I know your guys also killed the Capitol police officer who shot Mustafa, to make sure he wouldn't talk.'

'That's all bullshit.'

'No, it's not all bullshit, but if it is . . . well, then too bad for you, Jubal. You go to jail for twenty years. You see, you're a malignant piece of shit but right now you're a small problem. Because of what you've done, Muslims in this country are being persecuted and a very bad law is about to be passed. So right now, getting you to admit that al-Qaeda wasn't behind these attacks is more important than putting your ass in the slam.'

Pugh tried to keep his face immobile but his lips twitched. Like a badger in a cage, he'd just seen a way out.

'And we're pretty sure you didn't personally kill anybody,' DeMarco said, 'which is the reason you're getting a break, but you have to testify against the people who did.'

DeMarco didn't really know that Pugh hadn't killed anyone, but he was guessing that Pugh wouldn't have taken the risk. And even if he *had* killed someone – even if Jubal Pugh had pulled the trigger that had killed Reza Zarif's kids – DeMarco was telling Pugh that he could blame their deaths on the people who worked for him.

'Somebody has to swing for these crimes,' DeMarco continued. 'So you have to give the FBI enough information to convict your pals, Jubal. If you can't do that, no deal.'

'Is that it?' Pugh said.

'No. You also have to give the Bureau the guy who hired you. We know there's a middleman, an organizer, a guy who's been giving you directions. And we know someone very rich hired the middleman. We want those two people, Jubal. If you can't deliver the middleman you're of no use to us. As bad as you are, we really want the people behind these crimes.

'And keep something else in mind,' DeMarco said, before Pugh could interrupt. 'Why do you think this middleman came to you? He didn't pick you because he thought you were some sort of genius. He came to you because you're the perfect patsy. You're the head of a hate group, at least that's what your Web site says, and this guy chose you because if by some chance we figured out that these Muslims were being coerced, and if we traced it back to somebody, that somebody would be you. And Jubal – going to jail for manufacturing meth is one thing. But if you don't cooperate and we can prove you were an accomplice to murdering two kids, you'll get the death penalty.'

Pugh sat there, saying nothing, studying DeMarco's face.

'I want this in writing,' Pugh said at last. 'And I want the document looked at by my lawyer, so if I do what you want, you won't be able to screw me later.'

DeMarco nodded. 'We can do that. But I need to know, right now, the name of the guy who hired you.'

'I don't know his name. I only met him once. I tried to have him followed, but he lost my guy.'

'Bullshit,' DeMarco said.

'I'm telling you the truth,' Pugh said.

DeMarco rose from his chair. 'Then I guess it's adios, Jubal. You're no fuckin' good to us.'

'But I got a picture of him,' Pugh said. 'And a computer on my farm loaded with his e-mails.'

DeMarco sat back down. 'Give me some details.'

*   *   *

DeMarco ignored Patsy Hall as he left the DEA building. He ignored her pleas, and later her threats, to tell her what was going on. He walked a block, then stopped and sat down at a bus stop. For a couple of minutes he didn't do anything; he just sat there trying to collect his thoughts, then he pulled out his cell phone and made a call. He talked to Mahoney for approximately ten minutes.

57

The first thing Mahoney did was let everyone know that the so-called Broderick Act wasn't going to get voted on in the House that day. This caused the expected uproar, which he ignored, and then he left the Capitol while his brethren were calling their contacts in the media.

His driver dropped him off at the Justice Department. He could have requested the attorney general and the director of the FBI to come to his office, and most likely they would have. But he liked it better this way, because after he met with the two men he was holding a press conference – he'd already given his contacts in the media the time – and he liked the idea of posing in front of the attorney general's building.

Attorney General Simon Wall and FBI Director

Kevin Collier both shook the speaker's hand when he entered Wall's office, but neither was particularly effusive in their greeting. They knew Mahoney was being lambasted in the press and that his approval ratings had slipped when he refused to support Broderick's bill. Wall and Collier, in other words, didn't feel that they had to be nice to a man who might not be the speaker much longer.

Simon Wall was a lawyer, a political appointee, and close friends with both the president and the chairman of the Democratic Party. He had a seal's head: wet-looking, slicked-back dark hair and warm, liquid brown eyes magnified by the lenses of his glasses. He looked harmless – but he wasn't. FBI Director Kevin Collier, the man who looked like Mahoney's old Boston terrier, was Simon Wall's puppet.

Mahoney didn't like either man.

Wall and Collier took seats at a small round table, and Mahoney settled into the third chair and began to speak. 'Yesterday the DEA arrested a meth dealer in Winchester, Virginia, who is also the head of a white supremacist group. The guy who hijacked the New York shuttle, the cabdriver who tried to blow up the Capitol, and the son of my friend who tried to fly his plane into the White House were all coerced by this drug dealer's people. In other words, these recent acts of terrorism, which the FBI has pinned on al-Qaeda and three Muslim Americans, were really the work of a bunch of white-power nuts. In other words,' Mahoney repeated, 'you two guys, who jumped with all four feet on Bill Broderick's band wagon, are gonna look like a couple of idiots.'

Wall opened his mouth to say something, but Mahoney continued. 'Now I'm gonna tell you what really happened.' And he did. He told them what Jubal Pugh had admitted to DeMarco. When he finished he said, 'What you're gonna do is this. The FBI's gonna take charge of this shithead that the DEA's arrested, and you're gonna offer him immunity from prosecution provided he can give you all the people who were involved in this thing. I've already told the guy you're gonna do this.'

'What?' Wall said. 'You don't have the authority to—'

Mahoney rose to his feet. 'I gotta take a piss – if it's okay with you, Simon, I'll use the can here in your office – but in ten minutes I'm holding a press conference right in front of this building. I'm gonna explain to the media how we were about to pass a horrible goddamn law because of terrorist attacks that were really orchestrated by these racist pecker-heads and not by good Muslim American citizens, but, thank God, the diligent agents of the DEA *and* the FBI have uncovered the truth. This means you guys have about half an hour to figure out a way to put a spin on this that makes you look less stupid than you really are. Now, Simon, where's your shitter?'

A platoon of lawyers and FBI agents invaded Winchester, Virginia, and took charge of Jubal Pugh, his people, and all the evidence the DEA had gathered. Jubal's gang was placed in a federal lockup in Washington, D.C. Jubal himself was placed in a cell at Quantico and protected around the clock by the FBI.

The day after Pugh was taken to Quantico, Patsy Hall walked into DeMarco's office in the Capitol. How she'd located his office, he didn't know. She threw open the door, and it banged off the wall so hard he was surprised the frosted glass didn't shatter. DeMarco took one look at her – all hundred and ten pounds of her trembling with rage, eyes blazing so hot they could have started a forest fire – and he was glad they hadn't allowed her into the building with a weapon.

'You son of a bitch!' she screamed. 'I spent five years trying to nail that bastard, and you're letting him go. Letting him go!'

'I'm sorry, Patsy, but it's for . . . for the greater good.'

'Yeah, well you can kiss my ass for the greater good.' She paused a moment and added, 'You used me, you prick.'

With that she turned and left, leaving DeMarco feeling like hell.

*   *   *

The press ripped the late William Broderick asunder and praised Mahoney to the skies.

Those politicians who had resisted Broderick's efforts stretched their arms and patted themselves publicly on the back for their fortitude. Those who had sided with Broderick blamed the FBI for getting the facts all wrong. Hearings would be held, they promised.

The House voted on the Broderick Act – *everybody* was happy to call it by that name now – and the bill was defeated by ninety-five votes.

Mahoney was a happy man.

Surprisingly, so was Nick Fine.

The governor of Virginia, who couldn't run again because of term limits, appointed Fine to fill Broderick's seat until a special election could be held. The governor acted quickly and without consulting a number of people he should have consulted. The governor extolled Fine's virtues, spoke of his experience, and implied that having *two* African Americans in the U.S. Senate wasn't exactly stacking the deck. He said that if Fine had been in charge, Bill Broderick's vile proposal would never have seen the light of day.

Miranda Bloom, DeMarco's lobbyist friend, told him later that someone, name unknown, had made a substantial contribution to the University of Virginia. The donation came with a caveat: it was expected that the university would offer the governor

of Virginia a position on its staff, the university being
close to the governor's home and a place where he
had stated numerous times that he'd like to teach
when his days of government service were over.

58

And then it all fell apart.

The day before he planned to have the boy install the devices, the workers at the refinery went on strike.

He blamed himself for not having known that a strike was pending, but as the facility was more than a hundred miles from Cleveland, the local papers hadn't discussed the likelihood of a strike, nor was the plant of such significance that an imminent strike had made the national news.

These accursed people. Their greed was without limit. Even the lowest-paid workers at the refinery, the guards and the people who mopped the floors, lived better than people he had seen in Africa and Afghanistan and Palestine. They owned cars, often two or three. They lived with families of four in homes where a dozen people could have dwelt. They squandered their money on alcohol and pornographic DVDs – and they wanted more, always more.

The papers didn't say how long the strike would last. On one hand, a stoppage could work to his advantage. If the facility wasn't operating, security would be even more lax. And for all he knew, the security force was also on strike and had been replaced by temporary guards even less qualified than the existing ones. The problem was that if the refinery wasn't operating, he didn't know if there would be enough hydrofluoric acid in the tanks to cause the calamity he desired. He was not going to waste all the work he and the boy had done by blowing up empty tanks.

An Internet article he had read said there was talk of bringing in nonunion workers to replace those on strike, but it was uncertain if that would happen or when. Another article he read said that before going on strike the workers had conducted illegal slow-downs, *sick-outs*, they called them, and he didn't know what that meant in terms of chemical quantities on hand. No, he didn't like all the new variables caused by the strike. If they brought in different guards, they might follow different security procedures. And if they brought in replacement workers, the refinery most likely wouldn't operate at maximum capacity, which could mean less of the chemical would be released. He just didn't know.

It was God's will. He would have to wait until the strike was over or find a different target.

After all, what did it matter if he had to wait a month or two? It had taken more than four years of planning to fly the planes into the Towers. And there was another reason why waiting could be good. He didn't understand what had happened with this senator and his bill. It had appeared that the bill was going to pass in the American parliament or whatever they called it, when suddenly this senator was killed and the next thing he read was that the terrorist attacks were really caused by some madman, some drug dealer, and not by true believers. Now they were saying the law was *not* going to pass and, if anything, the government was now apologizing to Muslims for what it had been about to do to them.

So maybe waiting was good from that perspective as well. Let things return to normal, and then, when the tanks were destroyed – when thousands of people were killed, when dead schoolchildren were seen lying on the ground, when the wounded were shown blind and horribly burned – then the furor would begin all over again. And this time the whites would *demand* that this dead senator's law be passed and there would be no doubt who was responsible for the attack.

The real problem with waiting was the boy's mother. In the first few months after her husband's death she had been almost catatonic, and when he'd first met the boy, she was still in that state. But in the last week or so, she had started to come out of it and was beginning to take an interest in her son's life again. She knew the boy had stopped going to school, and when she first found out about this she hadn't said too much. But now she was beginning to nag the boy about his education.

He had told the boy to tell his mother that he had a job, a job at a factory where he sometimes had to work nights. Where the mother came from, it was not unusual for boys her son's age to have jobs, and she was so isolated from others of her kind and so ignorant of American norms that she accepted the explanation. To reinforce the lie, he gave the boy a small amount of money to take home each week to his mother as proof that he was working. But now she was asking questions. Where was this factory? What did he do? Did he have a future working there? And who was the man who called so often?

Again, had this not been America, had this been anywhere else in the civilized world, the boy, as man of the house, would have told the woman to mind her own business. But this was America. The woman thought she had the right to meddle in the affairs of men, particularly her son's affairs.

The best thing would be if the mother were to die, but in some way that would increase the son's bitterness toward his own people.

He would have to give that some thought.

59

Unlike with the two men who had tried to blow up the Baltimore Harbor Tunnel, Myron Clark didn't have to sleep-deprive Jubal Pugh to get him to talk. He didn't have to bring in his glowering six-foot-four partner to intimidate him either. All he had to do was turn on his tape recorder. Pugh knew the only way he was going to stay out of jail was if he told Myron Clark everything he knew.

In response to Clark's first question – How did he become involved in the terrorist attacks? – Jubal shrugged and said, 'Got a letter in the mail.' He said this like the letter had been a coupon flyer from a pizza place. 'The letter said I'd make two million bucks if I was willing to do a few things to support a patriotic cause. *And* there was five grand in cash in the envelope, just for meeting the guy who sent the letter. That got my attention.'

'And where'd you meet this *other* patriot at?' Clark asked.

'At a restaurant in Winchester,' Jubal said. 'The Waffle Shop. Guy called himself Mr Jones. Sounded like a highfalutin' bastard.'

Clark guessed that meant the man didn't have the dulcet tones of one raised in an Appalachian hamlet.

'Anyway,' Jubal said, 'the first thing he did was name the guy who supplies my ephedrine.'

'What?' Clark said.

Pugh explained. The man who supplied the ephedrine that Pugh used to make his meth was the head of a Mexican drug cartel and lived in Mexico City. Mr Jones told Pugh that he'd done some work for the cartel and if Pugh wanted to check on his background, all he had to do was call his supplier and ask him about a man named James Flint and the job in Guadalajara. He said the Mexican was expecting Pugh's call.

'But I also figured Jones was sending me a message,' Pugh said. 'He was telling me he could fuck up my meth operation any time he wanted.'

'Are you trying to say Jones *forced* you into helping him?' Clark said.

'Nah, I guess not. I'm just saying he had some leverage on me.'

'And did you contact this Mexican?' Clark asked.

'Yeah. He knew Jones, or James Flint, or what-ever his name is, and he said the man was someone I could trust.'

'So you became partners with a man you'd never met based on the word of a drug lord.'

'No, I became his partner 'cause he was payin' me two million bucks. And I did try to find out who Jones really was,' Pugh added. 'I had Randy take his picture. Randy was up at the counter, drinkin' coffee, and while I was talkin' to Jones, Randy snapped off a shot with my Kodak.'

Clark didn't bother to tell Pugh that the picture wasn't worth a damn.

'And later Randy tried to follow the guy,' Pugh said, 'but he was too slick for that.'

Clark refrained from commenting on the slickness quotient of Jubal or his boy Randy.

'So then what?' Clark said.

'Well, then he told me what he wanted me to do,' Jubal said.

Pugh said Jones gave him a broad outline of the plan and said he'd pay Pugh in installments following each successful phase. Pugh said he was impressed with Jones's thoroughness and negotiated for another half a million.

'I mean, I knew the shit was just gonna *fly* if I did what this fella wanted, and I figured another half million was only fair, considering I was taking all the risks.'

'Yeah, sounds like you were a real bargain,' Clark said. This guy Pugh, with his ferret's nose and his tiny eyes and his unshaven chin, was just repulsive.

Pugh said that after he agreed to work with Jones, they left the restaurant together. In the restaurant parking lot, Jones gave Pugh a laptop, a schedule specifying when he was to turn the laptop on, and told him to hide the laptop someplace where it wouldn't be found in the event that some law enforcement agency – like the DEA – obtained a warrant to search his house.

Pugh gave a little sniff. 'Like I was an idiot or something,' he said. 'And then you know what the bastard said to me next?'

Clark just shook his head.

'He said it was a damn good thing I agreed to do the job, because there was a rifle pointed at me, and if he took off his cap I'd have a third eye in my head. That actually kinda pissed me off.'

Pugh told Clark that after that one meeting, he never saw Jones again and all further communications were by e-mail, either that or through Jones's man Jack.

'Jack?' Clark said. 'Who the hell's Jack?'

'This foreign guy who worked for Jones.'

'Foreign guy? Where was he from? What country?'

'I dunno,' Pugh said. 'He spoke English but he had an accent, maybe Russian, somethin' like that. He seemed to think it was funny calling himself Jack.

He showed up at my place one day and explained he was just there to make sure things got done right. He was also the guy, by the way, who was gonna shoot me if Jones took his ball cap off at the Waffle Shop. Said he woulda killed me easy, bein' only three hundred yards away.'

'Wait a minute!' Clark said. 'Goddammit, what in the hell are you talking about?'

Ten minutes later, it all became clear. Jones, not trusting Jubal and his men to follow orders, had sent in someone he could rely on to oversee things. Myron Clark had figured that Jones selected Pugh because Pugh was willing to kill for money, because he had an organization already in place, and if things went wrong a racist like Pugh would be the perfect patsy to blame things on. But Clark had always found it hard to believe that Jones, particularly for an operation this complex, would have such confidence in Pugh's ability. So Jones had assigned a straw boss, a man to manage Pugh. Jones would send Pugh the e-mails and tell Pugh where to send his men, and Jack would be there to make sure they did what they were told to do. But all Pugh could tell him about Jack was that he sounded 'Russian or something, was white, and kind of a smartass.'

Physically, the description Pugh gave of 'Jack' was useless – blond hair, light blue eyes, 'sorta handsome' – but Clark left the interrogation immediately to let his boss know that Pugh had had some outside help, a pro, maybe Russian mafia, maybe someone with a military background, but somebody good enough with a rifle to shoot Pugh from three hundred yards away if Jones thought he needed to be shot.

'So how'd you do it, Jubal?' Clark asked. 'How'd you get these people to commit these acts of terrorism?'

Pugh said it was the same in all three cases. They told Reza Zarif, Youseff Khalid, and Mustafa Ahmed that people close to them would be killed if they didn't do what they were told. Pugh said he had no idea how Jones had identified the Muslims, but it was obvious that Jones had done a lot of research to find people with some sort of grievance that could later be considered a motive for doing what they did. All Pugh knew was that a target would be identified, and detailed instructions for how to capture the target and use his loved ones to coerce him were all provided by Mr Jones and his man Jack.

Pugh said Randy and two other men did all the work. One of those men was the late Donny Cray. The second person was the guy Danny DeMarco had shot, Harlan Rhodes. Danny had not killed Rhodes, and he was currently in a hospital in D.C. being guarded by federal agents.

'What about this guy Jack?' Clark asked.

'He went with 'em, but he didn't do any of the heavy liftin'. I mean, he never killed anybody or anything. He'd just make sure that Randy and Donny and Harlan knew what to do.'

According to Pugh, the day Reza Zarif tried to crash his plane into the White House, Randy and Donny Cray entered Reza Zarif's house at 3 A.M. wearing ski masks and they tied up Reza's family. Then Randy handed Reza a gun and a box of shells and told him to load the gun. When Reza refused, Randy lit a cigarette and said he was going to blind Reza's son with the cigarette if Reza didn't do what he was told. Reza loaded the gun. Then Randy explained to Reza what they wanted him to do and said if he didn't do exactly what he was told, he was going to make Reza watch while they raped his wife and children – including his son. Randy explained to Reza that Harlan Rhodes had a taste for boys, having spent some time in jail.

'Jesus,' Clark said. It didn't take much of an imagination to visualize the terror experienced by Reza Zarif's wife and young kids.

'Yeah,' Jubal said. 'Randy really spooked that Arab guy.'

'He was an American, you idiot,' Clark said,

'Whatever,' Jubal said. 'Anyway, Randy told the guy that after they raped his family a couple times each, they were gonna tie 'em all up and pour gasoline on 'em and burn 'em alive.'

But Randy said if Reza Zarif cooperated, and since his family couldn't identify Randy and Donny, they'd let Reza's family go. So they gave Reza a choice. He could either allow his family to suffer painfully before they died, or kill himself by flying his plane at the White House. Reza made the only choice he could.

'After that,' Pugh said, 'Randy followed the guy to the airfield and waited until he took off. Then he called Donny, and Donny killed them little ragheads.'

It took a lot of willpower for Myron Clark not to hit Jubal Pugh.

'What happened to Donny Cray?' Clark asked. 'And don't tell me he died in a car accident.'

Pugh said that when the FBI found Donny's fingerprint on the bullet box, Mr Jones sent Pugh an e-mail saying Donny had to go and told him how he wanted him to die. Because Jubal could be tied to Cray, Pugh agreed, though he felt bad about it.

'Donny,' Pugh said, 'could be a little ornery at times, but he'd give you the shirt off his back if you were a friend.'

'So how'd you kill this guy who'd give you the shirt off his back?'

Pugh said he had Harlan Rhodes snap Donny's neck and then he bashed the head of Donny's skinny girlfriend against the windshield of Donny's truck.

'That Harlan,' Pugh said, 'he looks fat, but he's stronger than a gorilla. Then him and Randy drove Donny's truck to a good spot, put the bodies in the front seat, and pushed it down a hill.'

'How did Jones know the FBI had Donny Cray's fingerprint?' Clark asked.

'Beats me,' Pugh said. Then he smiled, 'If I had to

guess, I'd say that maybe Jones has one of you Hoover boys on the payroll too.'

'Do you have any facts or any specific information that a member of the FBI was involved with this Mr Jones?' Clark said.

'Well, no,' Jubal said.

'Then shut the hell up about the Bureau being involved in anything, you ferret-faced shit.'

'Hey, I'm sor—'

'Now tell me what you did to get Youseff Khalid to hijack that airplane.'

Two hours later, Myron Clark thought he had the whole story. In the case of Youseff Khalid, and unbeknown to the FBI, Khalid had had a mistress, an African American woman named Athena Warner. Pugh's men waited until Khalid visited his mistress at her home in the Bronx and threatened to rape and kill her if Khalid didn't attempt to hijack the plane.

'His mistress?' Clark said.

'Yeah, I guess Jones followed him or something, found out that boy had hisself a piece on the side. I told you he researched these people good.'

'Where'd the plastic gun come from?' Clark asked.

'Jack. He gave it to Randy. Don't know where ol' Jack got it, but that was a pretty slick piece of hardware.'

In addition to threatening to kill Khalid's mistress, they showed Khalid pictures of his two older children, entering their respective schools, and said they'd also be killed if Youseff didn't attempt the hijack.

Pugh said that before boarding the plane in New York, Youseff was allowed to speak with his mistress so he'd be assured she was still alive, and Randy told Youseff the same thing he'd told Reza Zarif: since Youseff's mistress had never seen Randy's or Harlan Rhodes's faces, they wouldn't kill her if Youseff did what he was supposed to do.

'But they killed her, didn't they?' Clark said.

'Yeah, 'fraid so. And they had to rape her a little before they did. You know, so it'd just look like your ordinary big-city crime.'

Clark stood up. 'Jubal, we're gonna take a break now. I'm afraid if we don't stop for a minute, I just might break every bone in your face.'

They were keeping Pugh in a cabin at Quantico, and the cabin was in the woods on a piece of land that Clark wished he owned. The setting was so peaceful you'd never guess it currently housed a piece of human flotsam like Jubal Pugh. Clark took in the aroma of the pines and let the cold air blast his cheeks red, then he called a number and told an agent to get the details on Athena Warner's death. Following the call, he just sat there looking into the woods for five minutes. When he felt Pugh was safe from him, he went back inside.

'Okay,' Clark said, 'now tell me what you did to Mustafa Ahmed.'

'Who?' Pugh said.

'The cabdriver. The Capitol Hill bomber.'

'Oh, yeah. I have a hard time keeping all them sand niggers' names straight in my head.'

Clark took a deep breath and let it out slowly. 'I swear, Pugh, that if you don't show a little more respect for these people you killed, I'm gonna—'

'Hey, sorry. Didn't know they was friends of yours. And *I* didn't kill *nobody*.'

Clark just shook his head and made a get-on-with-it motion with his hand.

Pugh said the same ploy was used again: Mustafa and his niece were captured, and Mustafa was told to act like he was going blow up the Capitol or the girl would be killed, and if she talked her mother and younger brother would also die.

Then Clark realized what Pugh had just said.

'What do you mean, *act* like he was going to blow up the Capitol?' Clark asked.

'Jones said to tell those people,' Pugh said, 'that they didn't actually have to kill anyone. All that Youseff guy had to do was *try* to hijack the plane: you know, get the gun on board, wave it around. Same way with the cabbie. He just had to put on the bomb vest and show it to the guards. He was told the bomb wouldn't go off.'

Now it made more sense to Clark. If *he* was given a choice of either seeing his family killed or blowing up the Capitol and crippling the United States government, would he do it? He didn't know. But if the choice was only to sacrifice himself to save his family, it would certainly be an easier decision. So now he understood. In all three cases the Muslim Americans involved knew in advance they'd be killed before they could actually harm other people. Or maybe they didn't all know that they'd be killed. Reza Zarif certainly did; he knew his plane would be shot down. But it was possible that neither Youseff Khalid nor Mustafa Ahmed knew they'd be shot. Youseff had been told only that he had to attempt to hijack the plane, and Mustafa was told the bomb vest wouldn't explode.

'So why didn't your men kill Mustafa's niece?' Clark asked Pugh. 'They killed Zarif's family and Khalid's mistress.'

''Cause Jones said not to. He said not to hurt her at all.'

Clark figured that by *not* killing Anisa Aziz there was no way anyone could claim that Mustafa had been coerced to commit an act of terrorism, provided Anisa was too afraid to talk, which she had been. And in the case of Khalid's mistress, no one even connected her death to Khalid.

'What pissed ol' Randy off,' Pugh said, 'was havin' a juicy little college girl like her all tied up naked and not bein' able to poke her one.' Pugh laughed and added, 'He did tell me he got a little stinky-finger, though.'

Clark hit Jubal Pugh in the nose with the palm of his right hand. He didn't know if he broke Jubal's nose or not. He did know that he didn't care.

Myron Clark finished his initial interrogation of Jubal Pugh, Pugh answering the remaining questions with cotton balls shoved into his nostrils. Clark would question the man several more times in the days to come, asking the same questions over and over again to make sure Pugh's story didn't change, but right now he was briefing a senior agent named Merrill Fitzsimmons. Fitzsimmons was the Bureau's current point man on the terrorist attacks, the last point man having been fired because he'd failed – with five thousand agents at his disposal – to figure out that it was Pugh and not al-Qaeda who was behind the attacks.

'And you think Pugh's telling the truth about the Capitol Hill cop?'

'Yes, sir,' Clark said. 'Pugh's guys had nothing to do with his death or with paying him to shoot the cabdriver.'

'And the air marshal?'

'Same thing. Jones arranged that on his own.'

'And this guy Jack?' Fitzsimmons said.

'Pugh doesn't know who he is, just someone Jones assigned to make sure Pugh's guys followed orders. He's obviously somebody with a lot more discipline than Pugh's people.'

'And the senator, who the hell killed him? Congress is goin' nuts over that. We've got so goddamn many agents looking for Broderick's killer, we're hardly doing anything else.'

'Pugh says he doesn't know who killed Broderick and I believe him. Maybe it was this guy Jack or somebody else. I mean, Jones sounds like some kinda organizational genius. Killing Broderick, *if* he killed Broderick, could have been a separate operation.'

'Christ!' Fitzsimmons said. He looked for a minute as if he was going to take out all his frustration on Myron Clark, but he didn't.

'Well, sit Pugh down with an artist,' Fitzsimmons said, 'and let's see if we can get a lead on Jack.'

'Yes, sir,' Clark said, although he'd already arranged for that.

'And we'll talk later, Agent Clark, about you losing control with the prisoner.'

'Yes, sir,' Clark said again.

60

Mahoney had requested that the FBI brief two of his associates, Emma and DeMarco. Mahoney didn't tell the Bureau why they should brief these two civilians, nor did he explain their relationship to him, but at the present time nobody in Washington was refusing Mahoney anything. And Special Agent Merrill Fitzsimmons, the man assigned to brief them, acted unusually humble. At some point the Bureau would go back to being the arrogant, insular organization it had always been, but for the moment the egg stains on the agency's face were still all too evident.

Fitzsimmons was a tall lean man in his fifties with gray hair. He was soft-spoken, cool, and collected and had been with the Bureau almost thirty years. DeMarco could tell that Agent Fitzsimmons was a fellow who was normally quite pleased with himself.

Fitzsimmons told them everything they'd learned from Jubal Pugh and then said, 'As you know, Pugh met with a man who called himself Mr Jones in a waffle house in Winchester, and Pugh's boy, Randy, took a picture of the guy. Here's the photo.' Fitzsimmons pushed a button on a laptop sitting on the table in front of him, and a picture flashed onto a screen at the other end of the table. The picture showed a man with long black hair and a full black beard, wearing sunglasses and a Tampa Bay Devil Rays baseball cap. The only feature that could be clearly distinguished on the man's face was his nose, and in the picture the man was sitting against a plain white wall.

'We gave that photo to the wizards,' Fitzsimmons said. 'They stuck it in a computer and removed the hat and the sunglasses and the beard, and here's what they came up with.' Fitzsimmons tapped his laptop again and now, next to the bearded man in the baseball cap, was a photo of a handsome beardless man with short dark hair and full sensuous lips. The man's arrogance was apparent even in a picture.

'That's the man who met with Pugh,' Fitzsimmons said.

'So who is he?' DeMarco said.

'His name is Oliver Lincoln,' Fitzsimmons said, 'and I'll tell you more about him in a minute. But those photos, both of them, are useless in terms of evidence. Pugh's not in the first photo, the one where Lincoln's disguised, so all we have is Pugh's word that he met with Lincoln, and Pugh's word isn't worth its weight in shit. Plus the photo was taken with Lincoln up against an unadorned wall so we can't even use it to prove Lincoln was in the restaurant. As for the second photo, the one that shows Lincoln minus the beard. . . . Well, it was made by manipulating pixels, so it's not going to stand up in court either.'

'Can't that guy Randy corroborate Pugh's story?' DeMarco said.

'He could, but Randy's not cooperating. At all. He literally hasn't spoken a word since we arrested him. He reminds me of McVeigh.'

'What about Harlan Rhodes, the guy my cousin shot?' DeMarco asked.

'Rhodes is in a coma, and the docs are saying he's not going to come out of it.'

'Shit,' DeMarco said.

'But don't worry. The minute we saw that reconstruction,' Fitzsimmons said, 'we knew Lincoln was the guy who managed Pugh. We knew this because half a dozen agencies in this town have either hired Lincoln or encountered him when he was working for other people. And he is *exactly* the kind of guy who could have engineered these fake terrorist attacks.'

'I don't know what you're talking about,' DeMarco said.

'Lincoln's a fixer,' Fitzsimmons said. 'He's worked

for some of the biggest mining, oil, and pharmaceutical corporations in this country – although none of those companies will ever admit they hired him. *And* he's worked for the U.S. government, the military, and the CIA, on more than one occasion – and they won't admit they hired him either.'

'What's he fix?' DeMarco asked.

'Whatever you want,' Fitzsimmons said.

Then Fitzsimmons explained. Say you were a major U.S. oil company and wanted to drill a couple of wells in Chile, but the Chilean government wasn't cooperating. In comes Oliver Lincoln. Within a few months, the atmosphere in Chile has changed dramatically toward U.S. oil. To achieve this turnabout, some people were bribed or blackmailed or forced out of office. Some even died, usually in tragic accidents.

'He's very good,' Fitzsimmons said. 'He's a master at planning and organizing complex operations. He goes into a place and figures out where the pressure needs to be applied, who needs to be greased, and who needs to be removed. And he rarely does anything himself. He develops the plan, hires people to do what needs to be done, and directs the people he hires. Just like he did with Pugh. And he's one of those people who's completely at home, even in West Africa or South America or the new Russia. He's been doing what he does for over twenty years, and the array of contacts he has in governments – both ours and foreign ones – and among criminals is enormous.

'But here at home,' Fitzsimmons said, 'Oliver's a pillar of the community. Gives to charities, supports the arts, all that bullshit. He has a beautiful home in Key West, he drives beautiful cars, and he sleeps with beautiful women. He collects wine and rare brandies and antiques. He lives large and well, and his only motive for doing what he does is money.

'So,' Fitzsimmons said, sitting back in his chair, 'now it's just a matter of tying Pugh to Lincoln and then tying Lincoln to whoever paid him. And we will.'

'You might want to see if there's any connection between Lincoln and a man named Kenneth Dobbler or a woman named Edith Baxter,' Emma said.

'*The* Edith Baxter?' Fitzsimmons said.

'Yes,' Emma said, then she explained.

'How'd you people find out that Dobbler and Baxter were contributing to Broderick?'

'That's not important,' Emma said. 'Just check them out and you'll find the same thing we did.'

Fitzsimmons studied Emma and DeMarco for a minute, seeing them in a new light – and not necessarily liking it. But, because they were the speaker's friends, he restrained from lecturing them on the inadvisability of civilians meddling in criminal matters.

'At any rate,' Emma said, 'one of the things we

learned about Dobbler was that he was in military intelligence. I pulled his file . . .'

'*You* pulled his file?' Fitzsimmons said.

'. . . and found out that he spent a lot of time in South America, fighting the so-called war on drugs. So there's a possibility that he may have known – or used – Oliver Lincoln when he was in the military. And Edith Baxter, as you well know, ran multinational companies located in political hot spots all over the world, and she may have known Lincoln as well. I never thought Edith was the type to employ someone like him – and I still don't – but then I never thought she'd support Broderick's politics either.'

'Well, we'll check them out,' Fitzsimmons said, making a neat notation on the legal pad on his desk.

'The other possibility is that Broderick himself hired Lincoln,' Emma said. 'Broderick was an ambitious man, and everything Pugh did advanced his agenda.'

'But then why was Broderick killed?' Fitzsimmons said.

'I don't know,' Emma said.

'Well, right now we don't have anything to show that Lincoln or Pugh had anything to do with Broderick's death,' Fitzsimmons said. 'When that bomb went off, all Pugh's guys were down on Pugh's farm, getting arrested by the DEA. And Lincoln, as I just stated, never kills anyone personally and we have nothing at this point to tie him directly to Broderick. But if Pugh's telling the truth, there's somebody else helping Lincoln kill people, like that Capitol cop. It could be this guy Jack who directed Pugh's men or it could be someone else. Lincoln knows lots of killers. Or maybe – and we're afraid to say this out loud right now – but maybe some Muslim really did kill Broderick just like that note in his car said.'

Fitzsimmons gave them a small smile that was meant to reassure. 'So that's where we are right now,' he said. 'We're after Oliver Lincoln. We have a lot of leads to follow, and we're gonna get him.'

And DeMarco believed him. FBI agents are dedicated and competent and well trained, and there are a lot of them. And behind those agents is an enormous support network: a legion of computer geeks and wiretappers and accountants and crafty lawyers. They have laboratories filled with high-tech gizmos and psychologists who understand the workings of the criminal mind, and they have millions of dollars at their disposal. There was nothing Emma and DeMarco could do that the FBI couldn't do bigger, better, and faster.

Yep, the big dogs were on the hunt. The FBI would get Oliver Lincoln and whoever had paid him.

61

He couldn't just sit in Cleveland doing nothing while this cursed strike continued. And he had to get the boy away from the influence of his mother.

He decided he would take the boy with him and look at the young man in Santa Fe that he had read about, the one who had been driven from the Air Force Academy because of his faith. And they would look at other targets. There was a nuclear facility in Illinois he wanted to see, a chemical plant in Colorado that sounded intriguing, and a refinery in western Texas that was particularly attractive.

He told the boy to tell his mother that his company – the company he supposedly worked for – had decided that because he was so smart, they were sending him to a special school in – oh, Chicago. Tell her you might be gone for as long as six months, he

said, and be sure to tell her that you will continue
to send her what money you earn. The boy did as
he was told, and his poor heartbroken mother
accepted the story, but he could tell that afterward
the boy was upset. When he asked what was trou-
bling him, he said, 'My mother was very proud of
me when I told her I was being sent to a special
school.'

He nodded his head. 'I understand,' he said. 'I love
my mother too.'

The ex-cadet in Santa Fe turned out not to be suitable. He was still working at the movie theater selling
popcorn, and he could sense the young man's bitterness, but when he tried to talk to him, to tell him
he had heard about what had happened at the military academy, he could see that he was instantly
suspicious. He was just too *American*. He may have
been angry about what had happened to him, but
he could tell in just one short conversation that the
one in Santa Fe was likely to report him to the police.
The Americans may not have been willing to let him
fly their warplanes but he was still, for whatever
reason, loyal to them. He just couldn't understand
it; didn't he realize he would never be accepted?

So he and the boy from Cleveland moved on. They
visited the other places he wanted to see. The nuclear
facility was out of the question. The guards there
acted like guards, and it would be difficult to damage

the reactor in such a way that a catastrophe could be guaranteed. The refinery in Texas, however, which also used hydrofluoric acid, looked like a . . . what was that expression he'd heard? Yes, a walk in the park. The security at the Texas plant was even worse than at the refinery in Ohio, and the hydrofluoric acid tanks were within fifty yards of the fence line.

He made the boy call home every few days and tell his mother how well his training was going, and every time, for a few hours afterward, the boy would be depressed.

And every day he looked on the Internet to check on the status of the strike.

It couldn't last forever.

62

Special Agent Merrill Fitzsimmons had been with the Bureau for twenty-nine years – twenty-nine successful, decorated years. He'd been thinking about working three more years, by which time his youngest would have her master's. And he figured when he did retire, he'd be leaving at the top of his game and he'd have no problem at all landing a job as a consultant. Yep, with consulting fees and his pension, he'd be able to buy that Bayliner he'd always wanted.

But now he was thinking that maybe he'd pull the plug this fall. Debbie would have to get a loan to finish school – Christ, what the hell did she need a master's for anyway? – and he would kiss the Bayliner goodbye. The way it was going now, he'd be lucky to get a job as a greeter at Wal-Mart after he left the Bureau.

And it was all because of that fuckin' Oliver Lincoln.

Folks had initially been delighted when they'd pinned the terrorist attacks on Pugh and Broderick's bill had failed, but after four and a half months all the delight had disappeared. Now everybody – the president and Congress and every two-bit scribbler who wrote for a paper – wanted the people behind Pugh, and they began to crap all over the director of the FBI. *And* they wanted to know who killed William Broderick. He may not have been a hero anymore, but he had been a U.S. senator. So they dumped on the director and, as the old saying went, the crap flowed downhill – right onto Merrill Fitzsimmons.

Fitzsimmons was *drowning* in crap.

At first he figured it'd be a piece of cake. They knew Oliver Lincoln had met with Pugh. Pugh had even identified the guy's voice. Fitzsimmons figured, with all the resources at his disposal – they'd given him everything he'd asked for – that in a couple of weeks he'd have Lincoln's head mounted on his wall.

They had the laptop Lincoln had given Pugh, and the laptop had e-mails in it that supposedly came from Lincoln, and the e-mails told Pugh how to orchestrate the attacks. But they couldn't trace any of the e-mails back to Lincoln. The e-mails had been sent from public libraries, places where Lincoln didn't have to open up an account, and nobody at the libraries remembered seeing Lincoln on the days the e-mails had been sent. It was possible that Lincoln had never even been in the libraries; some nerd could have fixed things so it only *looked* like the e-mails came from libraries. At least that's what the Bureau's nerds said, those useless geeks, so the laptop turned out to be no help at all.

Lincoln's man Jack, the guy with the Russian accent who had helped Lincoln, was a dead end too. They showed Pugh thousands of pictures of possible suspects, but no one looked like Jack. Jack, whoever he was, had disappeared and might not even be in the country.

Same way with Lincoln's bank accounts. Lincoln had paid Pugh a couple million bucks, but there was no money trail from Lincoln to Pugh, nor was there any evidence that Lincoln had received money from someone to pay Pugh.

The waffle house where Lincoln had met with Pugh was another bust. None of the sixteen people who worked there – all of 'em with two-digit IQs – could say that Lincoln had ever been to the restaurant. They knew Pugh had been there because he was a frequent customer, but they couldn't remember him being there with a bearded guy wearing sunglasses and a baseball hat on the day Pugh said the meeting occurred.

'The man was wearing a Tampa Bay baseball cap,' Fitzsimmons said to the waitress who usually served the table where Pugh and Lincoln had sat. 'You can't see many of those around here.'

'Well, to tell you the truth,' the waitress said, lowering her voice, 'I always thought baseball was a game for pussies and I never pay it any attention. Now if the man had been wearing a Dolphins hat . . .'

The only satisfaction that Merrill Fitzsimmons had was tormenting Lincoln, but even that small pleasure had soured. The first time he met Lincoln in the flesh, he had to ring the bell at the gate to be allowed onto Lincoln's estate and then had to wait to be admitted, like he was a damn Amway salesman instead of a federal agent. And after the big wrought-iron gates had finally swung open, he and three cars full of agents had driven up the quarter-mile driveway to Lincoln's mansion only to find Lincoln waiting for them, cool as you please, with his lawyer.

Now that had *really* pissed Fitzsimmons off. How in the hell had Lincoln known he'd been tied to Jubal Pugh? And how had he known the FBI was coming to his house that night? Obviously Lincoln had a source someplace in the government – in the Justice Department or Congress or right in the Bureau itself – and this source had given Lincoln so much warning that he had time to call his shyster.

And Lincoln's shyster was *good*. The man's name was Lamont Greene. He was very calm, very quiet, very businesslike – and as flexible as a rock. Every step of the way, he made Fitzsimmons jump through every legal hoop he could construct just to slow Fitzsimmons down. And when they questioned Lincoln – on five separate occasions – Greene had been there instructing his client to say nothing more than his name. When they asked Lincoln to take a lie detector test, Greene had laughed out loud, like that was the funniest thing he'd ever heard.

Fitzsimmons's only satisfaction to date was that his men had torn Lincoln's mansion apart during their search – they had just *ripped* the place up – and fuck Greene's threat to sue them for the damage they'd caused. Fitzsimmons worked for the United States goddamn government, and he didn't care if they doubled the national debt to settle with Lincoln. And, speaking of money, there was one other thing that made Fitzsimmons smile: Lincoln had to be paying Lamont Greene about six hundred bucks an hour. He could only hope the arrogant bastard would have to declare bankruptcy by the time they were done with him.

But after months of trying and thousands of man-hours expended by his agents, Fitzsimmons couldn't pin one damn thing on Oliver Lincoln. Lincoln had been too careful. He could find no connection between Lincoln and Kenneth Dobbler or Edith Baxter – or anyone else on the planet who might have paid Lincoln. He couldn't figure out who had killed Senator William Broderick or Rollie Patterson, the U.S. Capitol cop who shot Mustafa Ahmed. He couldn't even arrest the damn air marshal that had killed Youseff Khalid, even though he knew the marshal had been tipped off that Khalid would be on the plane that day.

Yes, retirement was beginning to look very, very good to Merrill Fitzsimmons.

63

'Well, Steve, there she is. Your new home.'

Steve. Jubal Pugh couldn't get used to that name. Nor could he get used to the fact that instead of residing on four hundred acres in the Shenandoah Valley he now lived in a trailer park in a place called Victor, Montana. Actually, it wasn't even *in* Victor but on the outskirts of Victor. All he knew was that he hated Montana, and he hated the trailer he now had for a home.

And he hated this goddamn marshal too. He thought a U.S. marshal would *look* like a marshal, like that actor Sam Elliott: tall and lanky with a handlebar mustache and cowboy boots. The marshal who escorted him to Victor looked like he should be selling life insurance. He had a pudgy build, a half-bald head, and he wore glasses, for Christ's sake. The only way you'd know he was a marshal was if he showed you his badge.

But until he could get back on his feet – if there was any way to get back on his feet – Jubal was stuck in Victor. And in some ways it was good that he was. He'd testified at Randy's trial, and the way Randy had looked at him . . . well, it was a damn good thing they'd moved him here. Randy had about a hundred cousins, and they were all just as mean as Randy. If they ever found out where he was. . .

'Well, Steve,' the marshal said, 'it's time to go meet your new boss.'

'A scrap yard?' Jubal Pugh said. 'That's the best job you could find for me?'

'Hey, it's not like you got a lot of skills, unless you consider making meth a skill. And you're gonna love your new boss,' the marshal added. 'He's this old Indian guy, big as a horse, and I've been told he just hates white people.'

64

On the first day of the lovely month of May, Mahoney woke up with his ass on fire.

Things had been relatively good in the speaker's domain since Broderick's bill had been defeated. He had won most of his political battles; laws had been passed, some good and some bad. Ali Zarif had survived his heart attack, and Mahoney had let the photographers take pictures of him and his old friend dining on fish and chips on Boston's waterfront. But this particular day he rose from his bed, annoyed that after four and a half months the only person who had been incarcerated for the deaths of eight people – including a United States senator – and a flagrant attempt to corrupt the legislative process was one Virginia thug: Randy White.

When he arrived at his office he called the director

of the FBI and asked him why he and all his minions hadn't made any progress arresting Oliver Lincoln and whoever had hired him. After listening to the director's blubbering excuses, Mahoney called the man a flaming idiot and told him that he was going to suggest to the president that a change in management over at the Hoover Building was overdue. After that he called the attorney general and told him the same thing. It was time the country got a new top lawyer since the one currently in the job didn't have the skills to catch a cold, much less indict one. He then poured himself a drink and sat there in his big chair scowling at an empty room, trying to decide whom to badger next. And when he couldn't think of anyone who actually had responsibility for solving crimes and catching criminals, he summoned DeMarco to his office.

At the time the summons was issued, DeMarco was lying in bed with the schoolteacher from Iowa. His friend from Key West had volunteered to take a group of kids to visit the nation's capital. She had never volunteered to lead one of these field trips in the past because she always suspected that chaperoning twenty twelve-year-olds would be a gigantic pain in the ass. But this year, when spring came, when the sap started to run again and the biological juices began to flow, she had an overwhelming urge to see a broad-shouldered Italian fellow she knew in Washington, and he, in turn, had been delighted to hear that she was coming.

The trip, however, hadn't turned out as well as they had anticipated for the simple reason that the twelve-year-olds were a full-time job, a twenty-four-hour-a-day occupation. During the day they had a nonstop schedule going to all the places the school had promised their parents that they'd take them. At night, once the kids were back at the hotel, it was then Ellie's job to make sure they did no harm: that they didn't smoke in their rooms, ingest illegal substances, or destroy hotel property that the school board would have to pay for. And, as some of the little shits were on the onset of puberty, it was also her job to make sure they didn't try to road-test the reproductive equipment that they'd been told about in the sex-ed class that half their parents had tried to ban from the curriculum. To make things worse, the male teacher who accompanied Ellie to Washington had caught a retching case of stomach flu the day after they arrived, and he spent most of his time either in bed or kneeling in front of a toilet bowl.

So it did not turn out to be the romantic rendezvous that she and DeMarco had envisioned. They never had one dinner alone in a fancy restaurant; they never went dancing cheek-to-cheek. DeMarco did go to Ellie's hotel room every night. He had to sneak in, of course, and, once together, they had a couple of drinks – Ellie actually needed several to restore her mood – and then they would hop into bed. About half the time their pleasures were interrupted, either by a kid calling to whine about something or by the hotel manager calling to whine about something the kids were doing. And every hour or so, Ellie would have to get out of bed, get dressed, and check to make sure that none of her charges had escaped and that they all were still breathing, if not asleep.

When DeMarco's cell phone rang he had been lying in bed studying the curve of the schoolteacher's rump. She was heading back to Iowa that afternoon. He had woken before her and had just been lying there hoping she would wake up soon. But then Mahoney's secretary called and told him to get his undersexed ass over to Mahoney's office.

'You need to do something to get this guy Lincoln,' Mahoney said, the moment DeMarco took a seat.

DeMarco's response was predictable. 'If the FBI can't get him, how in the hell can I?'

In response to this perfectly legitimate question, Mahoney got a crafty look in his eye. It was a look DeMarco had seen before, a look that said rules applied to other people, that rules were meant to be broken, that there were exceptions to every rule. And that was pretty much what Mahoney said.

'My guess,' he said, 'is that the reason the Bureau can't get this cluck is they're playin' by the rules. That's the problem with government organizations these days. Nobody's ever willin' to go out on a limb, to take a few chances. But you . . . ?'

Mahoney left the sentence unfinished but his meaning was clear. The reason Mahoney employed DeMarco, the reason DeMarco dwelt in a subbasement office instead of being a legitimate member of Mahoney's staff, was because Mahoney considered DeMarco's job to be unencumbered by the niceties of ethics and law.

'Well, shit,' DeMarco said. 'What do you expect me to do, plant evidence on the guy or something?'

Now had John Mahoney been a normal employer he would have said, *No, of course not. What sort of person do you think I am?* But Mahoney wasn't a normal employer; he wasn't even a normal human being. Instead what he said was, 'Now there you go, now that's usin' your head.'

'Mahoney,' DeMarco said to Emma, 'wants me to come up with some way to catch Lincoln, and he doesn't care how I do it.'

Emma, instead of acting surprised, nodded her head. 'Yeah,' she said. 'Something's got to be done about that guy. He can't be allowed to get away with this.'

Emma, unlike Mahoney – or, for that matter, Joe DeMarco – had rather high ethical standards. DeMarco, in fact, suspected that there were canonized saints who were less ethical than Emma. But here she was, apparently agreeing with Mahoney that when it came to Oliver Lincoln anything was fair game.

'Christ, Emma,' DeMarco said. 'It's like I told Mahoney. What can I do, plant false evidence in the guy's house?'

'No,' Emma said. 'That would be illegal. I have another idea.'

65

Emma's plan began with a series of digital photographs.

First she instructed Mahoney to direct the FBI to e-mail him the picture that Randy White had taken of Lincoln while Lincoln was sitting in the Waffle Shop in Winchester with Jubal Pugh. When the FBI asked Mahoney why he wanted to see the picture, he told them, 'Because I do.' Mahoney's secretary e-mailed the photo to Emma.

Emma then had a man fly to Key West and take a number of candid head shots of Oliver Lincoln. Her man then drove to Winchester and took a series of photos of the interior of the waffle house. And finally Emma obtained, from a source at *The Washington Post*, pictures of Jubal Pugh when he'd testified at Randy White's trial.

The FBI had used its wizards to identify Lincoln as the man in Randy White's original photo. Well, Emma had her own wizard. She had her wizard take all the photos and construct one showing Oliver Lincoln – still wearing his Tampa Bay Devil Rays baseball cap, a long-haired wig, a false beard, and sunglasses – sitting with Jubal Pugh at a table in the Waffle Shop. In the photo, a building across the street was clearly visible through a window near where they were seated. Emma, after studying the photo for a bit, made her wizard remove the sunglasses from Oliver Lincoln's face.

A week later, Emma now had the photograph the FBI *wished* they had: a photograph that placed a recognizable Oliver Lincoln with Jubal Pugh in exactly the place that Jubal said they'd met. The fact that the photograph was a fake didn't matter. Emma had no intention of giving the photograph to the FBI or using it to convict Lincoln for conspiring with Pugh. That wasn't the reason she'd had the photograph made.

They needed someone to run the sting against Pugh, and the ideal person was some government employee who had decided to go over to the Dark Side. They thought originally that maybe DeMarco himself might be the right man for the job but then ruled that out. The problem was that Joe DeMarco was related to Danny DeMarco, and since Danny had been the one who had set Pugh up, Pugh would be suspicious of anything anyone named DeMarco might propose.

They considered using DeMarco's friend Barry King at the DEA, but the truth was, even though DeMarco liked King, he just wasn't sure that his softball-playing pal had the ability to do what they wanted done. The other problem was that Barry would be a new face to Pugh, and Pugh might be leery once again of being set up by someone he didn't know.

No, they needed someone whom Pugh knew *and* someone who would have a legitimate reason for deciding to switch sides. They finally decided that the perfect person was Patsy Hall.

Patsy Hall had never been summoned up to the Hill before. People of her rank rarely were unless they'd turned whistleblower and had been asked to testify at some congressional hearing. The last time she'd been to the Capitol she'd come uninvited, to tell that bastard DeMarco what she thought of him for what he'd done. But now here she was again, and it wasn't to testify. It was to meet with the speaker of the House. Why the hell the speaker would want to talk to her, she couldn't imagine.

She walked into Mahoney's suite in the Capitol and was immediately taken to his office, no waiting at all. She'd seen pictures of Mahoney, of course, but the man in the flesh was more impressive than the photos. The photos captured his big white-haired head, the stubborn thrust of his chin, the powerful body. What they didn't convey was the twinkle in his eye or the way he blatantly checked out her figure when she entered the room. Nor did the photos capture the smell of bourbon on his breath when he grasped her small hand in his two big ones and said he was delighted to meet her.

'I know,' he said, 'that you're not too happy that this meth dealer, Pugh, ain't sittin' in a jail cell.'

Hall wanted to say *no shit*, but of course she didn't. All she said was, 'No, sir, I'm not.'

'And the fact is, we're not going to be able to put him in jail unless he commits some other crime. But what we can do, with your help, is get the man who hired Pugh, this Lincoln guy.'

'With my help?' Hall said.

'Yeah,' Mahoney said.

'What do I have to do?' Hall said, but she was thinking that if the Speaker of the House had wanted her to run around the National Mall dressed in a chicken suit, all he had to do was call the director of the DEA, that ass-kissing bastard Garner, and Garner would make her do it.

In answer to her question, though, the speaker surprised her by saying, 'I don't know.'

'What?' Hall said. 'You want me to do something to help get Lincoln, but you don't know what it is?'

'Yep,' Mahoney said. 'You see, I *can't* know, because

what my friend has planned isn't exactly – uh, orthodox.'

'I don't understand,' Hall said.

'Me either,' Mahoney said, and he laughed, and because she couldn't stop herself, she laughed with him. He was a lecherous old bastard, but he was charming.

'But what I do know,' Mahoney said, 'is that right now you're a GS-Thirteen and I know you're damn good at your job. And I know you've still got two girls at home, in high school if I remember right, and that you're on the road about half the time with this job you currently have. Whether you help me out or not, I've already told that brown-nosing boss of yours . . . what the hell's his name?'

'You mean Garner?' Hall said.

'Yeah, that's the guy. Anyway, I've already told him that because of your role in nailing Pugh's people, I'm disappointed that you're not a GS-Fourteen, maybe a Fifteen, and acting as the DEA's liaison with Congress. I got a feelin',' Mahoney said with a wink, 'that Mr Garner is very concerned that I'm disappointed.'

'Jesus,' Hall said. 'What do I have to do?'

'All you have to do is talk to a guy named DeMarco. I think you've met him.'

Hall's face must have conveyed her opinion of DeMarco because the speaker said, 'Yeah, yeah, I know, he wasn't exactly up front with you last time, but this time I promise he will be.'

'You don't have to bribe me with a promotion to get me to talk to him, Mr Speaker.'

'I know that,' Mahoney said, 'and it's not a bribe. I'm givin' your career a boost because I like you and because I'm impressed with all the knuckleheads you've put in jail *during* your career.'

Before Hall could say anything else, Mahoney said, 'You wanna drink? How 'bout a little Wild Turkey on the rocks?'

'Oh – uh, no, sir. But thank you for offering,' Hall said.

'Come on, Patsy, it's damn near quittin' time. The sun's practically over the yardarm.'

It was three-thirty.

'Well – uh, sure, Mr Speaker. Maybe just a small one.'

Mahoney rose from his chair and walked over to a cabinet, dropped two ice cubes into two glasses, and poured them both three fingers of bourbon.

'Let's sit over here,' Mahoney said, pointing to a couch. Then he winked at her and said, 'I can't see your legs sittin' over there behind my desk.' And again he laughed, and again Hall laughed with him.

She bet that when he was younger he was just hell on wheels, and it didn't appear that he'd slowed down all that much as he'd aged.

'Now, what are your daughters' names?' Mahoney said. 'I have three girls myself, you know. Man, were they a pain when they were in their teens, particularly my oldest one.'

Hall was just a little drunk when she met with DeMarco, but not so drunk that she was happy to see him. They met at Sam and Harry's on 19th Street.

'Would you like a drink?' DeMarco asked, as soon as she sat down.

'No. Mahoney already forced two drinks into me. I think he was trying to get into my pants.'

She wished immediately that she hadn't said that, even though she suspected it was the truth.

'Yeah, I wouldn't be surprised,' DeMarco said. 'But I'm not trying to get into your pants. I was just being polite.'

'So stop being polite and tell me what you want.'

DeMarco did.

'Jesus,' Hall said, 'are you *nuts*?'

'Probably,' DeMarco said.

'I could lose my job if I did this,' Hall said.

'You won't lose your job. Right now you're bulletproof. And unless something goes wrong, there's no reason for anyone to even know you were involved.'

'Something always goes wrong,' Hall said.

66

Patsy Hall had never been to Montana before, and the beauty of the place just overwhelmed her: the mountains, a cloudless sky like an inverted blue bowl over her head, the wide rivers cutting through the landscape. When she saw the rivers, she was immediately reminded of that Redford movie *A River Runs Through It*, and just like in the movie, there were men fly-fishing on the rivers. She didn't know if these guys ever caught any fish but they created the prettiest picture – the fishing line looping out behind them, then snapping forward, the fly landing on the water as light as a butterfly's kiss. And she loved the names: Bitterroot River, Sapphire Mountains, Anaconda Range. Maybe next summer she'd come out here with her husband and her girls, do a little fly-fishin' herself or take a rafting trip down one of those gorgeous rivers.

But that was next year. Right now her job was to con Jubal Pugh.

Pugh lived in a trailer park on the outskirts of Victor. His trailer was white with green trim and only a month old, yet it was already showing signs of neglect. Weeds were growing up around the blocks the trailer sat on, and a piece of sheet metal near one window was hanging loose. Hall knocked on the trailer door. She could hear a television playing inside, and when no one came to the door, she took out her gun, the big .40 caliber that was always digging into her ribs, and hit the door with the butt, hard enough to leave a dent in the metal.

The trailer door flew open. Jubal Pugh was barefoot, dressed in baggy grease-stained jeans and a white sleeveless T-shirt. Broad suspenders held up the jeans. In his hand was a Coors. He hadn't shaved in days and, judging by his eyes, the Coors in his hand wasn't his first.

Patsy knew Jubal liked his beer, but it looked to her like he'd gone considerably downhill since he'd left Virginia. She supposed that losing everything you owned and working in a scrap yard might have that effect.

'Why in the hell are you bangin' on—' Then Jubal recognized Hall. 'You bitch! What are you—'

'Let me in, Jubal.'

'Don't call me that. My name's Steve now.'

'I don't give a shit what your name is. Let me in.'

Pugh hesitated, but he finally stepped back so Hall could enter the trailer. It was worse than she'd expected, clothes lying on the floor and over the backs of chairs, beer cans and take-out food cartons scattered all over the place, unwashed dishes in the tiny sink. The man had definitely gone downhill.

'I don't know what the hell you're doin' here, you bitch, but the DEA—'

Hall executed the move so fast that Pugh was taken completely by surprise. She whipped a leather-covered sap out of the back pocket of her jeans and cracked it right across the bridge of Pugh's long nose. She didn't hit him all that hard, barely hard enough to break the skin, but Jubal's legs turned to jelly and he collapsed to the floor, landing hard on his butt.

Hall had wanted to do that for a very long time.

'Now, Jubal,' she said, looking down at him, 'I'm here to make you a proposition, one that's going to be very profitable for both of us, but you need to learn that I don't like being called a bitch. So quit being such a lousy host and offer me a beer.'

Pugh got up and walked unsteadily over to the small kitchen in the trailer and tore a sheet off a roll of paper towels. While he was dabbing the paper against his bleeding nose, he opened the refrigerator and got a Coors for Hall and another for himself. The one he'd been drinking had spilled when Hall had hit him. He handed her the beer and then fell into a fake-leather recliner and continued to press the paper towel against his nose as he glared at her.

Hall looked around for someplace to sit. There was a bench seat that wrapped around a small dining table and a built-in couch along one wall of the trailer. The couch appeared to be the cleaner of the two, so she sat there, took a sip of beer, and then leaned back and crossed her legs to give the impression that she was relaxed. 'Jesus, this place is a dump,' she said. She was still holding the sap in the hand that wasn't holding the beer.

'How did you know where to find me?' Pugh said. 'Those marshals said my location was secret.'

'Yeah, it's secret, all right,' Hall said, 'unless you work for the government and know who to ask.'

'So what do you want? You already ruined my life. I'm living in this shit hole and making about two hundred bucks a week. And since you can't put me in jail, there ain't a fuckin' thing you can threaten me with that'll make my life any worse.'

'You need to develop some listening skills,' Hall said. 'I told you I came here to make you a proposition.'

'What proposition?'

'You and me, Jubal, we're gonna blackmail Oliver Lincoln. We're gonna make him give us four million dollars, two for you and two for me.'

'What the hell is this?' Pugh said. 'You expect me to believe that?' Pugh pulled the paper towel away and tenderly touched his nose; the bleeding had stopped. He wadded up the paper towel and tossed it on the floor.

'Jubal, I tried for five years to put you in jail, and I know everything there is to know about you. But you – you don't know anything about me, so I'm gonna tell you a little about myself. I make about eighty grand a year, which isn't a bad salary unless you take into account that my dumb shit of a husband took out a mortgage on a house that's three times what we can afford, and then, after he gets the loan, he loses his job and hasn't worked since. So about three quarters of my salary goes to pay for a house we never should have bought in the first place, *and* I've got two daughters that are expecting to go to college in a couple of years. And while I'm dressing in clothes from Kmart, there's guys like you and Oliver Lincoln making money hand over fist. How much did you make last year, Jubal? Two, three million?'

'I don't buy that you're willing to risk jail time because you're a little short of cash,' Pugh said.

'First of all, I'm not a little short, I'm a lot short. But you're right, this isn't *totally* about money. Mostly, but not totally. You know what happened after I nabbed your ass? After the goddamn FBI made you that deal?'

'No.'

'Well, other than the fact that you didn't go to jail, my boss, this D.C. asshole, blamed me for you getting off. He blamed *me*! I didn't have a damn thing to do with the deal the Bureau cut you, but my boss was pissed because the FBI got all the glory, so he decided I was the one who'd screwed up. So even though I finally got the evidence to put you away, I'm no longer a supervisor and I'm working for some jackass who doesn't have half my brains. I might even get demoted. So I'm not a happy girl, Jubal. But I think two million dollars will make me happy, particularly if it comes from Oliver Lincoln.

'But enough talk about me. Let's consider your situation. You're livin' here in your double-wide—'

'It's not even a double-wide,' Jubal said.

'Whatever,' Hall said. 'It's like living in a coffee can. And this job you've got. A junkyard, for Christ's sake! But if you had two million bucks, you could get yourself a new identity, go live someplace nice, maybe even start making meth again.'

Jubal nodded his head unconsciously.

'How would we get the money out of Lincoln?' he said.

'All the FBI needs to put Lincoln in jail is proof that you actually met with him,' Hall said. 'If they had anything tangible, a good-citizen witness, a *decent* photograph of the two of you together, then they could use your testimony to nail him. Unfortunately all they have is that one crummy picture Randy took and your *word* that you met with him, and we both know what your word is worth. But what do you think the FBI would do if they had something like this?' Hall reached into her purse and handed Pugh an envelope.

Pugh opened the envelope and looked at the photograph that Emma had made.

'Where the hell did you get this?' he said.

'I made it,' Hall said. 'Actually, I got a computer geek that works at the NSA to make it for me.'

'What's the NSA?' Jubal said.

'A government agency that spies on Americans,' Hall said.

'But won't some expert be able to tell that this picture isn't real?'

'Probably not,' Hall said. 'The guy who made it doesn't run the one-hour photo place at the drug-store. But it doesn't matter. We're not planning to show that picture to some expert at a trial. We're just gonna show it to Lincoln.'

Pugh looked at the photo again. 'He doesn't have his sunglasses on in this picture.'

'Right,' Hall said, 'which makes it easy to identify him even with the fake beard.'

'But he never took off the glasses when we met,' Pugh said.

'Sure he did. You just don't remember – and Lincoln won't remember if he did either, when you met seven–eight months ago.'

'But Lincoln'll know this is a fake,' Pugh said. 'If I'd

had this kinda picture, I would have given it to the FBI when they arrested me.'

Hall shook her head sadly, the gesture conveying her disappointment in Pugh's ability to reason. 'Just get me another beer, Jubal,' she said.

Jubal struggled to get out of the recliner; recliners were made for drunks to pass out in, not to get out of once they were drunk. He went to his refrigerator, opened it, and said, 'There's only one left.'

'So? I'm your guest. Act like you have some manners.'

Pugh gave her the beer and collapsed back into the recliner.

'You didn't answer my question,' he said. 'If I had a picture like this, why wouldn't I have given it to the Bureau?'

'Because you're so sly,' Hall said. 'See, you're going to explain to Lincoln that you gave the Bureau that one bad photograph because you had to give 'em something to get your ass off the hook. But, clever bastard that you are, you kept *this* photo because you figured, when the heat died down a little, and if Lincoln didn't go to jail, you could use that photo to blackmail him. Oh, yeah, you're a very cagey guy, Jubal. *And* you have something else going for you: you have a witness.'

'A witness?'

'Yep. At the waffle house where you met Lincoln is a waitress named Sandy Burnett. Do you know Sandy?'

'Yeah. Ugly girl with bad teeth.'

'That's right, an ugly girl with bad teeth who's so much in debt that her landlord's about to evict her from the shotgun shack where she lives with her two kids. Sandy, for a very modest fee, will be willing to testify that she saw you and Lincoln together.'

'But why didn't she tell the FBI she saw us together when they questioned the people that worked at the waffle house?'

'Because of *you*, Jubal; because you told her not to. You gotta remember, back then you were the biggest badass in Frederick County, and she knew if she testified against you, your boys would kick the bad teeth right out of her head before they killed her.'

Jubal sat there a minute, rubbing his hand over his unshaven chin. 'I still don't buy that you'd be willing to—'

'Oh, for Christ's sake, use your damn head! Let's say you got caught trying to extort money out of Lincoln. *You* wouldn't go to jail. All you'd have to do is point the finger at me. You'd just say that nasty little Patsy Hall, a government agent, came to you with this scheme, and you thought you were really *helping* the government. You didn't know this bad DEA agent was trying to blackmail Lincoln. And it would take the FBI all of two minutes to find out that I flew out here. Do you understand now, Jubal? The best thing that happens is you get rich; the worst thing that happens is I go to jail.'

Pugh stared at Hall, scratching at the stubble on his chin. 'Shit,' he said. 'I wish you hadn't drunk my last beer.'

Hall was embarrassed to be seen in public with Pugh, but she wanted to keep him happy. They drove to a tavern in Victor of his choosing, and it was just the sort of place that she'd expect him to pick: video slot machines and pull tabs for ambience; glassy-eyed deer heads over the bar; neon beer signs on every square inch of wall space remaining. All the male customers wore baseball hats, and all the hats were emblazoned with some kind of slogan. CATCH AND RELEASE, MY ASS was a popular one.

They took seats at a table as far away from the jukebox and the pool table as they could get, and she ordered a pitcher of beer and poured a glass for herself and Pugh. Hall had always known Pugh wasn't a stupid man, and in spite of the amount of beer he'd consumed he continued to prove it.

'What's to keep Lincoln from killing me when I tell him what we want?'

'Good question,' Hall said. 'He just might try to do that. But you got two things goin' for you, Jubal. The first is that Lincoln would have to find you. Remember, you're in the Witness Protection Program.'

'Yeah, but you found me.'

'Yeah, but I work for the government. Lincoln doesn't.'

'What's the other thing?' Pugh said.

'I'm bringing in a team, private security guys,' Hall said, 'and they're not gonna let him kill you. I'll tell the team they've been contracted by the Witness Protection Program to – well, protect you. I never thought I'd say this, but keeping you alive is suddenly very important to me. And that reminds me. I was gonna pay the security guys out of what we took from Lincoln, out of the four million. That's kinda stupid now that I think about it. We'll ask Lincoln for four and a quarter. He can afford it.'

Hall and Pugh sat there in the bar another hour going over the details. Pugh was getting very drunk – but he was still thinking.

'Why do you need me at all? Why don't you just send Lincoln the picture and pretend it's from me?'

'Because,' Hall said, 'the picture isn't enough. I need the picture *and* the threat of you testifying against him. So *you* have to talk to Lincoln. You have to tell him that while he's living like a king in Key West, you're stuck here in Cowflop, Montana, livin' in a trailer, and you don't like it one damn bit.'

Patsy Hall told Pugh that, as Lincoln was under continuous FBI surveillance, Pugh was going to FedEx Lincoln a package containing a disposable cell phone and the photo. The FBI might be tapping Lincoln's phones and opening his mail, but they wouldn't be able to stop the FedEx package from getting through.

'Lincoln's a clever guy,' Hall said. 'He'll find some

way to call you without the FBI watching. And when he does, you're going to convince him that you're serious.'

Pugh sat there awhile, drinking silently, mulling over all that Hall had told him. He seemed to come to a conclusion, because he nodded his head, lit a cigarette, and commenced staring at Patsy Hall's breasts.

'What say we get a six-pack and head back to my place,' Pugh said, and gave Hall what she supposed was his version of a seductive look.

'Get serious, Jubal,' Hall said. 'I'd be more likely to have sex with a cucumber. Now, are you in or out?'

Hall didn't feel guilty at all for what she was doing to Pugh. Maybe she should have, but she didn't. Emma's plan wasn't to blackmail Lincoln, nor was it to use the phony picture to have him arrested.

Emma's plan was to arrest Oliver Lincoln for murdering Jubal Pugh.

67

A half hour ago Oliver Lincoln had spoken to Pugh. Now he was sitting on his veranda drinking champagne – he wasn't celebrating, he just liked champagne – and looking again at the photo he'd received that morning, the one that showed him and Pugh sitting together in the restaurant in Winchester.

One of the things Lincoln prided himself on was his ability to keep his emotions in check. No cursing, no screaming tantrums, no kicking over chairs and tables when things got sticky. No matter how complex a job might be, no matter what last-minute changes had to be engineered, no matter how much pressure the authorities were putting on him, he always kept his head – and, he liked to think, his sense of humor. But this, this demand from Pugh . . . well, it made him *very* angry.

This redneck was ruining his life. The one poor photograph that he'd taken had been enough for the FBI to consider him a prime suspect in the terrorist attacks. The good news was that Pugh's original photo hadn't been enough for an arrest. The bad news was that the investigation was tearing him apart. His lovely home had been ransacked, he'd paid his lawyer three hundred thousand dollars to date, and, because he was being watched so closely, he couldn't set up any other jobs to bring in more income. He had just turned down a very lucrative job in Nigeria, a simple thing related to ensuring the outcome of an election.

And now he had a demand from Pugh for $4.2 million. The odd number puzzled him, but it didn't really matter. He didn't have anywhere near that much money, at least not in the United States. He had money in offshore accounts, but if he tried to access those accounts the FBI might catch him, and then they'd start badgering him all over again about the source of his income. At a minimum they'd notify the IRS, and the taxman would kill him with penalties on back taxes or, even worse, send him to jail for tax evasion. To pay Pugh – not that he had any intention of paying Pugh – would mean he'd have to sell his home.

The photo. Was it real or not? It certainly looked real, but then King Kong swatting biplanes out of the sky also looked real. No, it had to be a fake. In the photo he wasn't wearing his sunglasses and he was *almost* sure he hadn't removed them the day he met with Pugh. He could get an expert to examine the photo, but ultimately that would be a waste of time and money. The photo was irrelevant. Jubal Pugh had to be eliminated.

He couldn't have Pugh hanging over his head for the rest of his life like some rusted sword of Damocles. Whether the photo was real or not, whether the witness existed or not, Pugh had to go. If the FBI ever managed to get any real evidence tying him to the terrorist attacks, Pugh would testify against him, and Pugh would be the last nail in Lincoln's legal coffin.

But he did need to confirm that the photo was fake. If it wasn't, he needed the memory card from the camera and he needed to know if other copies existed. He also needed the name of this supposed waitress witness. And the fact that he needed to know these things was *really* too bad for Jubal Pugh.

He raised the champagne flute to his lips and noticed for the first time that there was a slight chip in the rim. Now *that* was vexing. The flutes had been made to his personal specifications by a glassblower in Venice and the man was now dead. Those FBI . . . apes! They must have damaged the glass the last time they searched his house.

Take a breath. Take a deep breath.

Pugh had said he wanted the money in two weeks. If the man had had any brains at all he never would have given Lincoln that much time. Finding Pugh wouldn't be a problem; he could do that with a single phone call. The primary problem was convincing the Cuban to take the risk, which meant it would take a lot of money, money he would have to pay out of his own pocket, money he didn't have on hand. He might actually have to sell a few of his possessions to raise the money for her fee. Yes, Jubal Pugh made him very angry.

Lincoln hit the button on the house intercom. 'Esperanza, sweetheart, can you please tell Juan to pull the Porsche up to the door. I'm going to Miami. I'm in the mood for a lovely Cuban dinner, a nice *polla a la barbacoa* with *negros dormidos*.'

'Are you insane? What are you doing here?' the Cuban hissed.

'Relax. If they'd connected me to you, you'd have been arrested or questioned by now.'

'You're an idiot to come here,' she said.

'Sticks and stones. If you'd returned my phone call, we could have met somewhere else.'

'I'm not talking to you. Finish your dinner and leave.'

'Two hundred thousand,' Lincoln said.

The Cuban stared at him for a moment, then she blinked, then she blinked again – and Lincoln had the image of an old-fashioned adding machine, the lever going down, the machine going *ka-jing* as the Cuban added two hundred thousand dollars to her hoard.

She sat down with Lincoln and snapped her fingers at a waiter.

'Bring me and Mr Lincoln a Calvados,' the Cuban said, and then added, 'Put both drinks on Mr Lincoln's bill.'

68

Emma assumed that when Lincoln received the black-mail demand from Jubal Pugh, he would try to kill Pugh. He wouldn't, however, do the killing himself.

'Lincoln had somebody kill Rollie Patterson,' she'd told DeMarco. 'And maybe that same person killed William Broderick.'

'And maybe tried to kill me too,' DeMarco said.

'Yes,' Emma said. 'You got lucky.'

Emma's plan was to catch the killer that Lincoln sent to murder Pugh in the act of killing him, hopefully before he succeeded. The killer, to avoid a long jail term for attempted murder, would give up Lincoln, and Lincoln, in return for a reduced sentence, would give up whoever had paid him to organize the terrorist attacks. The other thing that Emma figured was that Lincoln's killer wouldn't just shoot Pugh with a rifle from three hundred yards away or blow up his mobile home. He *could*, but Emma didn't think he would. Lincoln needed to know if the photo Pugh had sent him was a fake and he needed the name of the witness that could place Lincoln and Pugh in the restaurant together. To get that information the killer would have to torture Pugh, and while he was being tortured, they'd catch the killer. But they might have to let Pugh get tortured for just a little while to make the case, which didn't bother Emma at all.

Yes, it was a pretty simple plan: one killer after another falling over like a row of dominoes. However, neither Emma nor DeMarco thought it was going to be easy. And something that neither of them said out loud was that keeping Pugh alive wasn't as important as catching the person who tried to kill him – or succeeded in killing him.

DeMarco had never been involved in anything resembling a military operation, but he was involved in one now. And Emma was the general.

The same day Patsy Hall mailed the photo to Oliver Lincoln, DeMarco, Emma, and four men arrived in Victor, Montana. The four men were ex-military, men that Emma knew, and they were professional bodyguards. Usually their clients were celebrities worried about lovesick stalkers or wealthy people visiting countries where kidnapping was a cottage industry.

Emma introduced the men to DeMarco as Bob, Stan, Harry, and Stew. They didn't look alike, yet at the same time they did. Stan and Stew were both short and stocky and had weight lifter's muscles. Bob was tall and rangy and bald. And Harry was just sort of average – average height, average build. The thing that made the men look alike was their eyes, eyes that said they'd been to hell and back when they'd worked for Uncle – and they weren't afraid to make the trip again.

And Emma's guys came well equipped. They had binoculars and night-vision goggles and .22-caliber pistols machined for silencers. They had sniper's rifles and radios and bulletproof vests. They were a mini-militia; they were ready for anything.

Patsy Hall had told Pugh to tell Lincoln to send the four million to a post office box in Harrisburg, Pennsylvania, in two weeks. Jubal had asked why she wanted to give Lincoln so much time and she explained that Lincoln would need that long to round up the money. She didn't tell him the real reason was so Lincoln would have time to plan Pugh's murder. Hall would then pick up the cash, telling Jubal it would be best if she made the pickup because (a) she was a trained government agent and (b) Lincoln had never seen her. Jubal, being the trusting guy that he was, wanted to know what was to keep Hall from absconding with his half of the money and leaving him to rot in Montana. Hall explained that if she did, all Jubal had to do was place an anonymous phone call to the DEA and tell them that a certain unpopular agent had suddenly become very rich.

Hall introduced Pugh to his security detail over the phone. She told him Stan was the man in charge as Emma figured that Jubal – being the redneck that he was – wouldn't like it if a woman was responsible for his safety. So Pugh thought that four people were protecting him, not six; DeMarco and Emma stayed out of sight.

After four days of watching Pugh, DeMarco was about to go out of his mind from boredom and he had grooves in his hands, arms, and neck from scratching at bug bites. He didn't know what kind of bugs they were, but they were vicious little bastards. But if sitting around doing nothing and getting eaten alive by insects bothered Stan and his crew, DeMarco couldn't see it. These guys, you could drop them into a swamp at night and they'd stand there in the water, never moving, while leeches vacuumed out their blood.

DeMarco was teamed up with Stan and Harry; they had the day-shift watch, from six in the morning to six at night. Emma was on the back-shift watch with Bob and Stew, because she figured Lincoln's assassin was more likely to come at night. When Jubal went to work at the scrap yard, they followed him then hung around all day while Jubal ripped parts off cars. DeMarco figured working in a scrap yard had to be a pretty boring job; it was definitely a boring job to watch.

After Jubal finished work, usually about four every day, he went to his favorite bar and drank beer for three hours, then went back to his trailer and drank more beer. Stan had instructed Jubal not to change his routine in any way. Emma had told Stan to tell Jubal this. She wanted to give Lincoln's killer every opportunity.

Emma figured that the killer would watch Pugh for a couple of days, then break into his trailer at two or three in the morning and start ripping out his fingernails. He might try to snatch Pugh and take him someplace to talk, but it seemed more likely that the killer would take him at his home. Emma and her guys spent a lot of time looking for anybody who might be watching Pugh, but didn't see anyone, and this Emma found disconcerting. Stan and his guys were too good to miss somebody following Pugh, and she started to wonder if Oliver Lincoln had decided he didn't need to kill him.

Emma said later if they hadn't all been sexists, including her, they never would have blown it the way they did.

On their eighth day in Montana, DeMarco sat with Stan in a clump of weeds on a small hill watching

Jubal work in the junkyard. Stan, pro that he was, kept searching the surrounding area with his binoculars, and every hour or so he'd talk to Harry on the radio to make sure nothing was happening on the side of the junkyard that Harry was watching. DeMarco mentioned to Stan that sitting in the weeds was maybe a good way to get bitten by a snake, which earned him a what-a-wuss look from Stan.

Jubal was currently taking the mirrors off three cars that had just been towed into the junkyard. DeMarco figured side-view mirrors were probably a pretty hot commodity in the junk business, as people were always ripping off their mirrors when they didn't pay attention going in and out of their garages. At least that's the way DeMarco had ripped the mirror off his car three months ago.

About 11:30 A.M., they saw Jubal wipe his hands off on a rag he kept in his back pocket and walk toward the main office to eat his lunch. Ten minutes later, a Ravalli County sheriff's car drove into the junkyard. DeMarco figured the cops probably came to places like this fairly often to check on stolen cars being stripped for parts. He picked up his binoculars and looked at the cop. She was wearing a peaked hat, sunglasses, and a brown uniform. Around her waist was a wide black belt with all the usual cop stuff on it – handcuffs, radio, nightstick, Mace, and gun. DeMarco figured a skinny man, a man with no hips, would have a hell of a time keeping the belt from falling down around his ankles with all the crap there was on the belt. But this cop, she had nice hips. A nice ass too. She didn't seem to be having any trouble keeping the belt up.

Fifteen minutes later the cop left.

DeMarco pulled a can of Coke out of his knapsack – he was getting pretty tired of drinking warm Coke – and checked his watch. 'Looks like Jubal's taking a long lunch break today,' he said.

'Yeah,' Stan said.

Yeah. DeMarco had tried talking to Stan but gave up after a couple of days. It was as if the guy was saving his voice for something; maybe he and his pals were some sort of lethal barbershop quartet.

Half an hour later, Stan said, 'Something's wrong here.'

'What?' DeMarco said. He'd just seen something that looked like a centipede, and he'd been checking the weeds to make sure there wasn't another one around close enough to crawl up his pant leg.

'I said, something's wrong here,' Stan said. 'This guy's never taken this long a lunch break before, and his boss, he's *always* outside walkin' around, doin' something.' Stan was silent a minute, then picked up his radio. 'Harry,' he said, 'is everything okay on your side?'

'Yeah, haven't seen a thing. But why the hell is this guy still inside the office?'

'I don't know, but I don't like it,' Stan said. 'I'm going down there.'

Emma, DeMarco, and Stan were standing in the parking lot of the motel where they were all staying. Harry was making a phone call.

'Emma, I'm sorry,' Stan said. 'I just never figured, in a place like this, that she'd impersonate a cop. I never figured it would be a *she*. Jesus, I fucked this up. I don't know what to say.'

'I never thought it would be a woman either,' Emma said. 'She's probably been watching him for a couple of days, and if we hadn't had mental blinders on, we would have seen her. Son of a bitch!'

'And, Jesus, she just shot the shit out of him,' Stan said. 'He sure as hell told her whatever she wanted to know.'

When Stan had entered the junkyard office, he saw the owner first, the Indian who owned the place. He had a single bullet hole in his forehead. He'd been lucky. Jubal had also been shot in the head, but before that he'd been shot half a dozen times in both knees with small caliber bullets. The killer had used a silenced weapon, probably a .22, and it looked like she'd just kept shooting Jubal in the knees until he told her everything she wanted to know.

As soon as Stan saw the bodies, he called Emma, then called 911. Calling 911 may have been a mistake because it was three hours before the cops would let

Stan go. He didn't tell the cops that he and DeMarco had been watching over Jubal or that they'd seen the killer. All Stan told the cops was that he'd come to the scrap yard to get a part for a car and that just as he'd driven into the place he'd seen a sheriff's car leaving.

'What do you think Jubal told her?' DeMarco said.

Before Emma could answer DeMarco's question, Harry walked back to the group. He'd been using a pay phone near the motel office. 'She didn't kill the cop. They found the patrol car, and the cop was inside the trunk, gagged, in her underwear, out cold. She'd been hit on the head, hard. Right now she can't even remember her own name.'

'Could you identify her?' Emma asked Stan.

'The killer?' Stan said. 'Yeah, no doubt about it. I got a good look at her.'

'I saw her too,' DeMarco said. 'But in profile and she was wearing sunglasses. So—'

'No!' Emma said. 'You can *positively* ID her. And don't you dare say otherwise. When we catch her we're going to say we have two eyewitnesses who saw her walk into that office in a cop's uniform, and that nobody went in there again until Stan found the bodies.'

'Got it,' DeMarco said. 'But what do you think Jubal told her?'

'I *know* what he told her. He told her the picture was a fake, that Patsy Hall had the picture made by some NSA guy, and he told her the name of that waitress in Winchester. I've already called Hall and told her that we blew it . . .'

'Oh, man,' DeMarco said. 'I'll bet Patsy was pissed.'

'. . . and I called someone to go pick up that waitress and hide her and her kids until we can figure out what to do next.'

'Do you think Hall's in danger?' DeMarco said.

'I don't know,' Emma said. 'Maybe.'

'So now what?' DeMarco said.

Emma didn't say anything. The four of them – Stan, Harry, DeMarco, and Emma – just stood there in the motel parking lot like a small group of friends trying to decide where to go for lunch. Or maybe like friends who had just eaten a very bad lunch.

'What will Lincoln do?' Emma said. DeMarco could tell that she was talking to herself, thinking out loud, playing a game of chess with Oliver Lincoln two thousand miles away. 'He could kill Patsy, just to eliminate a threat. Same with that poor waitress. Or he could have Patsy snatched and tortured and make her give up the NSA guy who made the picture.'

'But Patsy will say you made the picture,' DeMarco said.

'But Lincoln doesn't know that,' Emma said. 'Lincoln knows only what Patsy told Pugh. So Lincoln will think – assuming he can even get to Hall – that the best thing that will happen is she'll give up the name of the NSA guy that made the picture, which he now knows for sure is fake. But then what? Does Lincoln go after the NSA guy? Does he try to kidnap and torture *him* and get him to hand over all the files he used to make the fake picture? No, it's just too much. It's just too hard.

'Plus Lincoln thinks Patsy's just a blackmailing cop, not someone trying to put him in jail. He'll think that once she hears Pugh was tortured and killed, she'll be too scared to come after him again.'

Emma kicked at the parking lot asphalt with the toe of her boot and chewed her lower lip for a moment. 'Lincoln's not going to do a damn thing at this point,' she said. 'With Pugh dead, there's no solid connection between him and the attacks. And Lincoln now knows the picture's a fake. Certainly an expert could either prove that or make a good enough case to put doubt in the mind of a jury. So, Lincoln's just going to wait and see what happens next. I would if I was him.' Emma paused, her brain spinning, looking for a way to recover from their failure, then she just shook her head in disgust and said, 'Shit!'

'Maybe we can use Hall for bait,' Stan said. 'You know, get her to spook Lincoln somehow and when he takes a shot at her. . . Well, I swear, Emma, we won't—'

Before DeMarco could object, Emma said, 'No. I'm not putting her and her family at risk. Or at any more risk than they already are.'

DeMarco looked over at Stan. 'Are you sure you

got a good look at that woman, the shooter? I mean, she was wearing a hat and sunglasses, and you saw her for only a few seconds.'

Stan stared at DeMarco. As Stan was wearing sunglasses, DeMarco couldn't see his eyes, but he didn't have to see Stan's eyes to know that Stan was pissed.

'I said I *saw* her,' Stan said to DeMarco. 'When she stepped out of the car, she looked straight at me. You would have noticed if you hadn't been worried about bugs crawling up your leg. Then, when she turned to go into the office, I saw her in profile.' Stan paused before he said, 'If I saw that broad again, I'd recognize her.'

'Okay,' DeMarco said. 'Then I think we have maybe one chance – and it's a long shot – to tie Lincoln to this woman.'

'What's that?' Emma said.

'Well, Lincoln had to talk to this woman. Maybe he contacted her by phone or by e-mail or through a middleman, but he's been under continuous surveillance by the FBI ever since Pugh was arrested.'

'Ah,' Emma said.

69

As he and the boy traveled about the country – it was truly a beautiful land, so rich and so green – they spoke often of martyrdom.

Where he had been before – places like Afghanistan and Iraq and Indonesia – it was easy to find martyrs. Men and women, boys and girls, husband and wives, fathers and mothers – there were many willing to give their lives for their faith. But here in this country, even among the devout, it was difficult to find people who were truly committed. The men in Baltimore, they had said they were willing to die, but he could tell they hadn't been. They were willing to *murder* but not to die.

But the boy, he *believed*.

They had discussed many times what the Koran

said about those who died in the service of God, and the boy could quote the words flawlessly, the words that promised that a martyr would be married to fair females with 'wide, lovely eyes.' The boy always blushed when he said that, which made him laugh.

It was a shame that the boy would still be a virgin when he died.

But they spoke of more than what the Koran said about martyrdom. This was an intelligent child, and they discussed the strategic value of martyrs, how they were the most powerful weapon they had in their battle against the infidel. It was in these conversations that the boy became the most animated. He grasped completely the *terror* that the martyrs caused, particularly in this country.

He was sure it would be written later that an impressionable teenager had been brainwashed by an evil man. And he wondered himself at times if the boy was willing to die simply because he was depressed by what had happened to his father and the realization that whatever dreams he once had would never be fulfilled. But he didn't think so. He was convinced that this boy believed. He had the *true* faith.

He talked also of his own death. He said that he too would die a martyr and he would most likely die in this country, far away from his wife and sons. He said he was looking forward to that day – he could hardly wait for that day – but he had been commanded by Sheikh Osama to postpone paradise until all his tasks were done.

'You're the lucky one,' he told the boy.

70

Catching Jubal Pugh's killer turned out to be fairly simple.

The hard part was trying to explain to the FBI and the marshals in the Witness Protection Program what Emma, DeMarco, and four retired Special Forces guys had been doing in Montana in the first place. Once they got past the point of the FBI screaming at them to come clean, and Emma screaming back that watching Pugh wasn't a federal crime, they finally got around to talking about the person who had killed him.

Stan hadn't been kidding when he said he'd gotten a good look at Pugh's killer. They sat him down with an artist, and in a couple of hours the artist produced a sketch that Stan said was spot-on. They showed the sketch to DeMarco, and he said, Yep, that's her, but the fact was that DeMarco had gotten a much better look at the woman's ass than her face. If they had asked him to describe her *ass* to the sketch artist, he was willing to bet he could have done just as good a job as Stan did with the face.

The FBI then showed the sketch to all the agents who had been keeping Oliver Lincoln under surveillance the last four months, and two of the agents said the woman in the sketch owned a Cuban restaurant in Miami, and ten days before Pugh was killed Lincoln had visited the restaurant and had a long talk with the owner over a glass of brandy.

The owner of the restaurant was Bianca Teresa Elena Castro, no relation to Fidel. Ms Castro had entered the United States on a raft made out of two-by-fours, canvas, and tires when she was fifteen years old. Her mother was a hooker, and good old Mom had put young Bianca out on a street corner when she was thirteen; Bianca told immigration officials that she had been forced to have sex with all the men on the raft in order to be allowed to go with them. After spending two years in a camp near Little Rock, Arkansas, the girl was released into the custody of a woman who claimed to be a cousin but who actually ran a brothel near Jacksonville, Florida. Between the ages of seventeen and nineteen, Bianca was arrested twice for prostitution but never did jail time. After that she dropped off the face of the earth insofar as official records were concerned, until she was twenty-six, when she applied for a business license to open her restaurant. The Bureau examined Bianca's finances and concluded that she lived well within her means, all of her income apparently coming from the proceeds of her restaurant.

Then the FBI did the sort of the thing that it is very good at. Agents started looking at surveillance tapes of people going into the Miami International Airport in the ten days prior to Jubal Pugh's death. After looking at a lot of tape and talking to a lot of people, they could prove that Bianca had entered the airport six days before Jubal Pugh died and purchased tickets under the name Maria Hernandez. Bianca – Maria – had then taken a plane to Spokane, Washington. Thirty agents descended on Spokane, showed Bianca's picture to car rental agencies, and found a kid at an off-terminal lot who remembered Bianca because 'she was one fine-lookin' piece.'

Records showed that Bianca used the Maria Hernandez ID to rent a car. Mileage logs for the rental car showed the distance she traveled was consistent with a round-trip from Spokane to Victor, but this was not conclusive. Next the FBI looked at motels in and near Victor to see if Maria Hernandez had rented a room. No joy. So the FBI platoon started questioning motel clerks and maids and found one young clerk who recognized Bianca's picture. He said the woman paid cash when she checked in and used the name Elena Mendoza. She never showed him an ID or used a credit card, but the clerk was positive that the picture of Bianca Castro was Elena Mendoza. He remembered her because 'she was hot!' – young men out west being fairly consistent in both their appreciation and their description of members of the opposite sex.

Gotcha! the boys from the Bureau said. They had two eyewitnesses who saw Bianca in a deputy sheriff's uniform enter the junkyard office at the time Jubal Pugh was killed. They had statements from those witnesses that no one had entered the office after her or before the bodies were discovered. And they had proof she'd traveled to Victor and had stayed there. Yep, they had more than enough to arrest and convict Bianca Castro for the murder of Jubal Pugh, and they hadn't even started gathering whatever evidence they might find when they searched her house.

The first FBI agent who interrogated Bianca didn't realize it, but he said one thing that was pivotal in getting Bianca to give up Oliver Lincoln. Actually, he didn't really interrogate her – he made a speech. In his speech, he laid out all the evidence against her and told her she was going to get the death penalty for killing Jubal Pugh and the Indian who owned the scrap yard. He added, 'I'd suggest you hire a very good lawyer.'

Bianca concluded that there was no way she was

going to waste her money on a lawyer. She knew the FBI had her cold for killing Pugh, but they couldn't get her for killing Rollie Patterson. Most important, they had no evidence at all that she had planted the fire bomb under the bed of Senator William Broderick's mistress. She wished she hadn't popped the guy who owned the scrap yard, but when it came to Jubal . . . hell, he was a drug dealer who had been involved with the fake terrorist attacks and the deaths of at least eight people. No one cared about him. And she was *so* glad she had just knocked out the cop in Montana instead of killing her as she'd originally planned.

So she told the FBI she was willing to deal. No more than twenty years in prison, she said, and she had to be eligible for parole in ten. Twenty years was plenty of time for killing Jubal and one junkyard Indian. But in addition – and this she said was a deal breaker – the government had to agree not to touch her assets and allow her time to move her money into long-term investments before she went to prison. If they didn't agree to that they could threaten to throw her in jail forever, and she still wouldn't tell them a thing.

The Cuban was forty-two years old. If she served twenty years, she'd be sixty-two when she got out of prison, younger than that if she could get paroled. Her mother was still going strong at sixty-seven and her grandmother had been ninety-two when she died. Bianca came from a line of long-living whores, and her greatest fear had always been being old and poor. So she'd take the twenty years, provided she got to keep her money.

The FBI agreed to Bianca's terms – and she gave them Oliver Lincoln.

71

Nick Fine – Senator Nicholas Fine – beat them all to the punch.

Fine found out that Oliver Lincoln was going to be arrested long before the FBI placed the handcuffs on his wrists; he found out as soon as Bianca Castro gave him up. And as soon as he did, he called a press conference.

Fine looked very good standing behind the lectern, dressed in a gray suit, tall and lean, devilishly handsome with his arched brows and his perfectly shaped goatee. The cameras loved him – as did more than a few female reporters.

Fine told the assembled news hawks that he had just come to a 'very disturbing realization.' He said that after he was appointed to fill William Broderick's seat in the U.S. Senate, he eventually got around to looking at how much money was available in Broderick's war chest. Well, Fine said, he was shocked – absolutely shocked – to discover that Broderick had vectored approximately eight million dollars to an account in the Cayman Islands. The fact that the money had been sent to an offshore account – well, that just smelled of 'monkey business,' he said.

'Ladies and gentlemen,' Fine said to the reporters, 'just two days ago I discovered that the account in the Caymans belonged to a man named Oliver Lincoln.'

A reporter's hand shot up. 'How were you able to find out that the account belonged to this man? I thought that's why people put their money into offshore accounts, so nobody could figure out who the money belonged to.'

Fine chuckled. 'A United States senator is not without influence, sir. I simply called up the president of the bank and told him that I very much wanted to know the name of the owner of the account. I don't remember my exact language, but I may have hinted that it would be a grave mistake for the bank to, ah, annoy me.' (The bank president later admitted that he did indeed tell the senator the name of the account holder, believing it was, in this very, very special case, in the bank's interest to ignore its normal disclosure policies.)

'Anyway,' Fine said, 'the name *Oliver Lincoln* tickled something in my memory. I remembered when

Senator Broderick attended one of his first Senate Intelligence Committee meetings he asked me who Lincoln was, and I said I didn't know. And I didn't. As aide first to Senator Wingate and then to Senator Broderick, I didn't attend all Intelligence meetings, because some of those meetings were limited to the principals, depending on the classification level of the subject matter. After that, I remember Senator Broderick asking me to provide him with the minutes from past Intelligence Committee meetings, some going back as far as ten years. I didn't question why he wanted to see them. He was, after all, my boss.

'I was just trying to decide what to do with the information I'd obtained when I was informed, this very morning, that the FBI had arrested Oliver Lincoln as the mastermind behind the terrorist attacks. I also found out that Lincoln has a history of carrying out complex operations, sometimes to help criminal cartels, and other times, unfortunately, to aid the American government, in particular the CIA. And that's why Senator Broderick had wanted to look at past meeting minutes, so that he could research Lincoln's past.'

The reporters started to buzz like angry bees around a ruptured hive. A dozen voices called out, which Fine ignored.

'I believe—' he said. Then he paused and repeated himself to increase the drama. 'I believe – and I've told this to the FBI, and I say this with great regret

– that William Broderick, in order to pass his bill, a bill as you all know I never personally approved of, paid this man Lincoln to orchestrate these terrorist attacks so American Muslims would get the blame.'

Whoa! the reporters cried. Why the hell would Broderick do that?

Fine said it was fairly obvious: Broderick was determined to make a name for himself in politics. He figured the best way to do it was to get his bill passed, and the best way to do *that* was by creating an atmosphere of fear and xenophobia caused by a series of terrorist attacks supposedly perpetrated by Muslim Americans.

But then why was Broderick killed? a reporter asked.

Fine shook his head. 'My answer to that question, sir, is that I do not know.' It was possible, Fine said, that a disgruntled Muslim had indeed killed Broderick just like the note found in his car had said. That would be ironic but also fitting. But it was also possible, Fine said, that there had been some sort of falling out among thieves, that Oliver Lincoln had killed Broderick for some reason. 'I just don't know why Senator Broderick was assassinated,' Fine concluded. 'That's a mystery the good men and women at the FBI will have to unravel.'

'One last question, Senator. Why on earth would Broderick have left records showing money going from him to this account in the Caymans?'

Fine hesitated. 'Well,' he said, and paused again as though struggling for words. 'I hate to say this, but Bill Broderick was not the smartest guy I ever met.'

72

Nick Fine had cut the legs right out from under Oliver Lincoln.

Lincoln was sitting in his cell, on the lower bunk, dressed in a plain white T-shirt and a pair of too-short jeans. On his feet were flip-flops. Above Lincoln, another man lay on his bunk, staring at the ceiling, doing nothing. The man was a child molester named Martin Cole. The first day they placed Lincoln in the cell with Cole, Cole had been sitting on the lower bunk. Without saying a word to Cole, Lincoln had pulled him off the bunk, dragged him over to the foul-smelling, shit-splattered toilet in the cell, and bashed out two of Cole's teeth against the toilet bowl. He then instructed Cole to move himself – and the mattress he'd been lying on – to the upper bunk, and he further instructed him that whenever Lincoln was in the cell, Cole was to lie on the upper bunk, doing and saying nothing.

Oliver Lincoln was a very angry man, and Martin Cole had been taught a lesson that many others had learned before him: Lincoln may have appreciated the soft and finer things in life, but there was nothing soft about him.

As it had done with Bianca Castro, the FBI had laid out its case against Lincoln. It had Bianca willing to testify that he had paid her to kill Jubal Pugh. Based on that testimony, they would then build the box around Lincoln, which would be constructed like this: Jubal Pugh had given statements prior to his death that a man named Mr Jones had paid him and directed him to coerce Muslim Americans to commit terrorist acts, the results of which had been the deaths of a number of people, two of them children. One of Pugh's men took a photograph that the FBI had used to identify Lincoln. Previously, the photo had been of questionable value as evidence, but since Bianca had testified that Lincoln had ordered her to kill Pugh, the FBI now had the link between Pugh and Lincoln that it needed. So, as a minimum, the FBI could send Lincoln to jail for life for Pugh's murder – and the murder of the poor man who ran the junkyard where Pugh had worked. But now, thanks to Senator Fine, the FBI could put the bow on the package: it could convict Lincoln for being the mastermind behind the terrorist attacks. All the

Bureau had to do was to get him to admit that he'd worked for Broderick.

But he wouldn't.

'Nick Fine hired me,' Lincoln said.

'You're lying,' the Bureau responded. 'You know that in order to save your rotten ass you gotta point the finger at somebody, and you knew if you pointed the finger at a dead senator you'd be screwed. So instead, you lying bastard, you've decided to accuse Nick Fine.'

'I'm telling you it was Fine,' Lincoln said.

'Can you prove it?' the Bureau said.

And that was the rub. He couldn't prove it.

As a minimum he was going to spend the rest of his life in jail. His days of Rubinacci suits and champagne were over. He might be able to avoid the death penalty – the case that he'd organized the terrorist attacks wasn't airtight, but it was tight enough that he'd never see the outside of a jail cell again.

On a glorious day in mid-June, Mahoney met with Emma and DeMarco at Emma's house. It being Mahoney, DeMarco knew there was some selfish reason for this. Mahoney may have been in the neighborhood for some other purpose – a lot of wealthy Democrats lived in McLean – or he may have been on his way to Dulles to take off on some taxpayer-funded boondoggle. All that DeMarco knew for sure was that Mahoney had selected the location because it was best for Mahoney and not because it was convenient for anyone else.

Emma, DeMarco, and Christine – and Christine's dog – were sitting on the patio, drinking lemonade and enjoying Emma's garden, which was in full bloom. When Mahoney arrived, the first thing he did was charm the pants off Christine as well as any philandering, chauvinistic, lecherous male can charm the pants off a lesbian. He took Christine's little dog from her hands, held it up like a campaign-stop baby, bussed it on the head, and proclaimed the animal to be the cutest little bundle of fur he'd ever seen.

'What's his name?' Mahoney asked, correctly identifying the dog's gender. He must have spotted the minuscule organ hidden amid all the hair.

DeMarco immediately swiveled his head to hear what Christine would say.

Christine looked at DeMarco, smiled slightly, then said, 'It's Jo-Jo. I had a dog named Jo-Jo when I was a little girl.'

'Well, he's just as cute as a bug's ear,' Mahoney said.

Christine excused herself by saying that she had to practice. As she walked away, Mahoney, oblivious to the daggers that Emma was looking at him, admired Christine's legs and backside. He flopped down on the chaise lounge that Christine had vacated and said to Emma, 'You got anything to drink around this place?'

'Oh, for Christ's sake,' Emma muttered. But she got up and said, 'What do you want, bourbon?'

'With a wee bit of ice, that would be lovely,' Mahoney said.

When Emma returned with Mahoney's drink – and a bottle of bourbon that she placed on the patio table next to him – he said, 'So you guys think Fine set this whole thing up?'

'Yeah,' DeMarco said. 'I never considered him for one simple reason. He didn't have the money. Somebody had to pay Pugh and Lincoln big bucks to do what they did, so I figured it had to be Dobbler or Edith Baxter or even Broderick. But not Fine.'

'But it turns out he did have the money,' Mahoney said.

'Yep. He had access to all Broderick's contributions. In other words, Fine did exactly what he accused Broderick of doing, but he set it up so if something went wrong, it would appear that Broderick had organized the whole thing.'

'So what was Fine's motive?' Mahoney said.

'I think at first it was money,' DeMarco said. 'This is all conjecture, but I think Fine's the guy that sucked Dobbler in. If Broderick's bill had passed, Dobbler would have gotten a contract worth a few billion, and I think Dobbler would have given Fine his cut. I think, in the beginning, Nicky Fine said, "Screw it. These white bastards won't let me be a senator, and I'm sick and tired of working for chicken feed."

'So I think what happened is this,' DeMarco went on. 'The two guys in Baltimore tried to blow up the tunnel, and Fine, not Broderick, came up with the Muslim registry idea. He talked Broderick into launching his bill, and then he tells Dobbler how they can both get rich if the bill is passed and convinces Dobbler to give him a bucket of cash to grease the wheels.

'He knows, however, that two guys *trying* to blow up a tunnel won't be enough. So Fine, who knew about Lincoln – he lied to the media when he said he didn't – hatches the idea to coerce Muslims to do things like fly planes into the White House and paid Lincoln to execute his plan.'

'But why did he have Broderick killed?'

It was odd, DeMarco thought, but Mahoney appeared completely relaxed as he asked his questions. Maybe it was the bourbon, but he didn't think so.

'To get the bill passed,' DeMarco said, in response to Mahoney's question. 'Broderick's bill *almost* had the support it needed. It had already passed in the Senate, it looked like it might pass in the House, but there you were, gumming up the works. Fine figured he just needed one more little thing to get it over the hump: kill Broderick and turn him into a martyr. Remember, all Fine wanted at this point was the money he'd make off Dobbler. But then Fine thinks, Why not go for the whole enchilada? Why not replace Broderick in the Senate? The Republicans almost gave him the job when Wingate retired, so Fine cozies up to the governor of Virginia and in return for appointing him to fill the Senate seat, he gets the governor a teaching job at UVA. Or, for all we know, maybe Fine gave the governor an even bigger payoff.'

'But then the bill doesn't pass because you nailed Jubal,' Mahoney said.

'Right,' DeMarco said, 'but Nick Fine still got the consolation prize. He got to be a U.S. senator.'

'So why can't they get to Fine through Dobbler?' Mahoney said.

'Because Dobbler would have to admit he was in collusion with Fine to rig a government contract. Dobbler's gotta be madder than hell right now, about all the money he invested to get Broderick's bill passed, but he's not gonna incriminate himself by pointing the finger at Fine.'

'Well, dang,' Mahoney said, and rattled the ice around in his glass. 'So you got any ideas for how to get Fine?'

Well *dang*? What was with Mahoney?

'No,' DeMarco said.

'How 'bout you, hotshot?' Mahoney said to Emma. 'You're the one who always comes up with cute ideas, like letting that Cuban gal kill that yokel so the Bureau could get to Lincoln.'

Emma stared at Mahoney like she wanted to throttle him, either for the hotshot tag or for implying that she had deliberately allowed Pugh to get killed. Mahoney, however, was oblivious to Emma's stare. Partly he was oblivious because he was Mahoney, and partly he was oblivious because after he made the remark he reached over and picked up the bourbon bottle to refill his glass.

'No, I don't,' Emma said. 'I was hoping – for once – that you might use your influence to get the FBI to take a harder look at Fine. I'm sure a statement to the media would be too much to ask for . . .'

'You got that right,' Mahoney said.

'. . . but you could at least sit down with the Bureau in private and tell them what you think.'

'I already did,' Mahoney said, surprising both DeMarco and Emma. 'But I don't have a lot of confidence in their nailing him, particularly now that the bastard's so popular. The polls are showing he'll get Broderick's seat when they hold the special election in Virginia.' Mahoney laughed. 'I heard the other day that Oprah's gonna have him and the guy from Illinois on her show at the same time. Anyway, bottom line, the Bureau's gonna walk on eggs around Fine. There's no way they're gonna take him into a room and whack him with a rubber hose until he talks.'

'So that's it?' Emma said. 'Fine gets a seat in the United States Senate after everything he's done?'

'Yeah, I guess so,' Mahoney said, his tone incredibly laid back.

For some reason, and DeMarco couldn't understand why, Mahoney was not at all upset that Nick Fine wasn't going to go to prison for his crimes.

Emma must have been having a similar problem with Mahoney's nonchalant attitude. She sat there studying him for a minute, biting her lower lip as she thought. Then she said to Mahoney, 'Are you thinking that—'

'Yep,' Mahoney said.

Thinking what? What the hell were they talking about? DeMarco wondered.

Mahoney tossed the bourbon remaining in his glass down his throat. Then, with some effort, he rose from the chaise longue. 'I gotta get goin',' he said. But before he left, he winked at DeMarco and said, 'Don't worry. I think things are gonna work out just peachy.'

74

He and the boy bowed their heads in prayer and gave thanks to God. The strike had finally ended.

It would take a week to get back to Cleveland, and then they would have to spend at least one more week making sure that nothing at the refinery had changed and verify that the facility was back in full production.

He would have the boy write the letters on the way back to Cleveland, because there would be little time for writing when they returned, and though the boy was a good thinker, he was a poor writer. It would take him some time to write the letters, which had to be in his hand and using his own words.

The first letter the boy wrote would be to his mother. He would tell her that he loved her and not to be sad for his death. He would tell her that he did what he did to avenge his father and because he believed in God and God's path and God's promise to the faithful who died for Him.

The second letter he would address to the president of the United States. He would say in that letter that he did what he did to avenge his father *and* all Muslims throughout the world who had suffered at America's hand. He would say that as long as America supported the Jews in Palestine and refused to accept the true faith, more Americans would die – and more Americans like him would help them.

Because he was afraid the letter to the president would be held up by underlings, he would send a copy of that letter to the FBI office in Cleveland and one to this man Mahoney, the speaker of their parliament.

He would mail the letters for the boy on his way out of Cleveland.

75

Bianca Castro was in the prison library, looking at yesterday's papers, checking on how the markets were doing. Not great but not bad. She shoved the papers into the bin and walked back into the stacks to find a book she wanted, a book on real estate investing.

She had never dabbled in real estate. She didn't know that much about it. She had always stuck with blue chip stocks and index funds, and right now she had a ton of dough in ten-year CDs, since she wouldn't be needing access to her money any time soon. And since she had the time, she figured she might as well educate herself on real estate investing. Another thing that interested her was the futures market, but she didn't know much about that either, just that futures were extremely risky but the payoffs could be huge. Maybe the library had some books on that subject too, but she doubted it. Most of the books in the damn place were lawbooks. All these women, most of whom could barely read, were always trying to find something on which to base an appeal.

She was running her fingers along the spines of the books when she heard a shoe scrape the floor to her right. Two bitches, both of them Hispanic, were coming toward her. She didn't like the expression on their faces but she wasn't too worried. The fourth day she'd been at the prison she'd demonstrated, in a particularly brutal fashion, that she wasn't a person you wanted to mess with.

The two women stopped a few paces from her. There was barely room in the narrow aisle between the bookshelves for the women to stand abreast, and there was no room at all for one of them to maneuver around behind her. But then she heard a noise, and she glanced over her shoulder and saw a third woman, also Hispanic, coming down the aisle from the other direction.

'You remember Jorge Rivera?' one of the women said.

'Who?' Bianca said. 'Who the fuck is Jorge Rivera?'

Then she remembered: the driver she'd used in D.C.

'He was my cousin,' the woman said, and she pulled a shiv out of the waistband of her jeans, a toothbrush handle filed to a lethal point.

The Ukrainian had used a glass cutter to cut a neat circle out of the hotel room window. Now all he had to do was wait for the water taxi to come across the river.

On one side of the Elizabeth River, in Portsmouth, Virginia, was a waterfront complex called Portside that had concession stands and hotels and an open area for outdoor concerts. Directly across the river, in Norfolk, Virginia, was a larger waterfront shopping area called Waterside, and it was filled with retail stores and places to dine and drink. A small water taxi for foot passengers and bicyclists traveled between Portside and Waterside every half hour. The Ukrainian was on the Portsmouth side of the river.

Both Portside and Waterside were currently awash in red, white, and blue. There were balloons, bunting, and banners everywhere in honor of the American holiday called Fourth of July. The Ukrainian had heard there would be a fireworks show that night, and he wished he could have stayed to see it. He liked fireworks and he liked celebrations. He would have bought a glass of beer and flirted with long-legged American girls. 'Hi, my name's Jack,' he would have said to them, and they would have gotten drunk together and watched the fireworks exploding over the river.

Unfortunately, he wasn't going to be able to stay for the fireworks; he would be miles away before the show started.

He checked his watch, and even without the binoculars he could see the water taxi loading on the Norfolk side of the river. Several men in white uniforms, maybe five or six, were walking onto the ferry together. He knew there was a large navy base in the area and he was guessing that the men in uniform were naval officers, and considering who they were with, they were probably admirals. He placed the binoculars to his eyes. Yes, there he was, surrounded by admirals. The goatee, he thought, made the black man look more like a saxophone player than a politician.

The Ukrainian waited until the boat was halfway across the river before he picked up the rifle.

Mahoney later said to DeMarco, 'The moral of the story, son, is never fuck over a man who plans assassinations for a living.'

76

DeMarco put his feet up on the rail of the deck and looked out at the lake. It was still light out at eight-thirty in the evening, and hot too, but a nice breeze coming off the water made the heat bearable. The surface was getting a little choppy now, but earlier in the day the lake had been as flat as a pane of glass.

He was a little tired from having spent most of the day outdoors, in the sun, waterskiing a good part of the time, and it felt good just sitting there. No, it felt *great* just sitting there, particularly considering that only yesterday he'd been in his basement office in D.C.

Yesterday he'd received two phone calls, and it was in part due to the first call that he accepted the invitation he received in the second call. The first call had been from his ex-wife, wishing him a happy birthday, a week after the event, and thanking him, for a second time, for what he had done for his cousin Danny. That wouldn't have been so bad except the call ended with: *You know I still love you.* He didn't slam the phone down when he heard that, he just placed it gently in the cradle and sat there a minute with his eyes closed, wishing the woman would move to a different planet.

When the phone rang the second time he almost didn't answer it, thinking it might be Marie calling back because he'd cut her off. But it wasn't Marie, it was Ellie. The first words she said were: *Have I got a deal for you.*

The boy would enter the refinery that night at 1 A.M. All the devices, except for one, were ready.

He would drop him off and wait for him to install the bombs, and as soon as he was back outside the refinery fence, the boy would call on his cell phone. Then he would wish God's blessings on the boy and leave. He wanted to be far away when people started dying.

He called the boy over and had him try on the vest, a vest sports fishermen used that had many pockets. The C-4 was in a pocket over his heart. He had never told him how hydrofluoric acid killed; he'd implied, without lying, that people breathed the gas and simply died. But this was better. When the materials had arrived and he saw there was enough material for one extra device, he decided the boy would wear it. The Americans would still be able to identify him because of the letters and DNA, but this way he would die a painless death and kill whoever was standing near him.

'Is your spirit ready for the journey?' he asked.

'It is,' the boy said.

Oh, this child! He kissed him on the forehead and said, 'Let's pray together until it's time to leave.'

Eddie Kolowski was late and he was drunk. Son of a bitch. He'd gone to a wake for a guy he'd been in the navy with, and shit, next thing he knew, it was midnight and he was three sheets to the wind. He knew he oughta slow down, some cop was gonna pull him over for sure, but even at the speed he was going, he wasn't gonna get to the refinery until one, maybe one-thirty. If it had been just him and Billy on the shift, bein' late wouldn't be a big deal, but with that little Mormon shit still there – why in hell hadn't that kid quit yet? – he might get reported. Son of a bitch.

Have I got a deal for you.

Ellie said her rich aunt was going on vacation for a couple of weeks and she wanted somebody to house-sit her fancy place on Lake Erie. And as she was through with the summer class she'd been teaching, and as she'd have access to a water-ski boat and her aunt's Mercedes, and as the house was stocked with steaks and booze, she decided to accommodate her beloved aunt – and she just wondered if DeMarco could get away for a few days to join her.

DeMarco had immediately called the speaker's office and confirmed that Mahoney was still in Boston and had no plans to come back to D.C. anytime soon. He was on a plane that afternoon and waterskiing the next day.

Ellie was in the bathroom getting ready to go out. She wanted to have a few drinks at this place downtown and dance. DeMarco didn't really like to dance all that much, but for her he'd pretend that he did. He'd stand there like a tree, firmly rooted to the earth, move his arms a little, and she'd dance around him like he was some sort of thick Italian maypole.

He looked down at the paper lying on the deck at his feet. Mahoney had been right about Fine – and about Lincoln.

Oliver Lincoln admitted immediately that he was responsible for Nick Fine's death. A number of African Americans had taken to the streets as a result of the senator's assassination and they were demanding that the government find the white racist who had killed him. Lincoln said he didn't want anyone to get hurt because of Fine, but his main reason for confessing to Fine's murder was that he didn't want the bastard turned into a hero and a martyr. He said again it was Nick Fine who had paid him to orchestrate the terrorist attacks, not that simpleton Broderick.

When asked how he had arranged to have Fine killed, Lincoln said it was pretty simple. He knew several assassins; that was the business he'd been in. He gave an old friend a letter to mail to one of them, and had his friend transfer money from one of his hidden bank accounts to the assassin. The FBI had not found all his offshore accounts and since he was never going to get out of prison, what better use did he have for the money? After the hit, he instructed his pal to pay the assassin the other half of his considerable fee, including a rather generous tip for both the assassin and his friend.

When asked if he had paid someone to kill Bianca Castro, Lincoln said no. He just had his friend mail a letter to a relative of Jorge Rivera.

But DeMarco didn't care about Fine or Lincoln or Pugh or any of them now. He was going dancing with a schoolteacher.

He stopped the car, the truck, whatever it was, a safe distance from the refinery.

It was out of his hands from this point forward. Even though he did not need to say it again, he told the boy, 'Don't enter the plant until the young guard returns to the building by the gate.'

'I know,' the boy said.

'And put the first device on the tank. You *must* plant that one. If you're caught while you're inside the facility, detonate the bombs. Not as many will die, but on a night like this a lot of people will still be on the streets, drinking in bars, sleeping with their windows open.'

'I know,' the boy said again. He seemed impatient to be on his way.

He was thinking that if the boy had to detonate the bombs prematurely he would shut the car windows and drive as fast as he could, but he might die too. So be it.

There was only one thing left to say.

'Go with God.'

The boy nodded his head, his eyes luminous. He opened the door and exited the vehicle. In one hand he held the short-handled shovel that he would need to dig under the refinery fence. In his other hand was the satchel that contained the bombs.

Eddie had made good time – it was only twelve-thirty – but by the time he punched in and changed and got to the guard shack, he was going to be almost two hours late for work.

Oh, shit! Was that a car stopped on the road up there? Was that a fuckin' cop? He tapped the brakes and slowed down. He still couldn't make out if it was a cop car or not, and that's when he realized that he'd been driving with his lights off ever since he'd left the bar. Half the time, that's the way cops caught drunks: the drunk would forget to turn on his lights. Eddie reached down and turned on his lights when he was fifty yards from the car parked on the side of the road. Thank God, it wasn't a cop. There was no light bar on the car. Then, as he blasted past the car, he caught a young guy in his headlights holding a backpack and something else.

It took him a couple of seconds to realize what he'd seen: it was that guy with the puke-green El Camino. He hadn't seen the car in maybe six months. The last time was before the strike. Yeah, he'd seen it maybe three times before the strike, always at night near the plant. He'd noticed the car because his worthless brother-in-law had owned an El Camino. Only an *idiot*, which his brother-in-law was, would buy one. Eddie always figured: You wanna car, buy a car; you wanna truck, buy a truck; but for God's sake don't get something that thinks it's both.

There was something else bothering him about what he'd just seen, but he didn't know what it was.

He finally got to the gate and Billy let him into the refinery and gave him this where-the-fuck-you-been look as he drove through the gate.

The bar had an outside deck and a disc jockey that played rock-and-roll oldies, the kind of music DeMarco liked. Fortunately, for the moment, the guy had picked something slow, an old Roy Orbison song.

He held Ellie close and she felt good. He wished the
guy would just play slow dances the rest of the night.
He didn't look like such a doofus dancing slow *and* he
got to hold a beautiful woman in his arms while
he danced.

He was sweating a little – Ellie was sweating
more because she moved more than just her shoulders when she danced – and the breeze coming off
the lake felt great. There was a funny smell that came
with the breeze though. Maybe it was coming from
that big ugly facility he'd seen on the way to the bar.
Whatever, the breeze felt good, funny smell or not.

He looked over the top of Ellie's head and saw
another woman dancing that reminded him of Emma
– tall, short blondish hair – and he wondered how
Emma was doing with Edith Baxter. Emma had told
him she was going to save Edith. She had a brilliant
psychologist friend in New York, a woman she'd once
lived with, and Emma and the doctor were going to
see Edith whether Edith liked it or not. Emma figured
Edith was such a formidable personality that her
friends – she had no relatives left – were afraid to
force her to get help. Well, Emma was pretty formidable too, and she was determined to make Edith
get some help before she killed herself.

And while Emma was off doing good works,
DeMarco was dancing with a pretty woman, and he'd
spend tomorrow zooming around Lake Erie in a fast
boat. He really got a kick out of driving that ski boat.

'You wanna head on home?' Ellie whispered into his ear. She sounded both tired and sexy at the same time.

'You bet,' DeMarco said.

'You're late,' the little Mormon shit said to him, as soon as he stepped into the guard shack. 'And you're drunk.'

Eddie was still trying to get his belt buckled, the belt that held the gun he'd never fired and the can of Mace he'd never used. Finally, he got the damn thing through the hole in the belt; if he didn't lose some weight he was gonna have to get a bigger belt.

'Shut up,' he said to the Mormon kid. Before the kid could say something else, he said to Billy, 'I saw something funny tonight, on the way here.'

'Oh, yeah,' Billy said.

'Yeah, this El Camino.'

'El Camino. You mean one of them cars that's—'

'Yeah, one of them weird Chevys. My dickwad brother-in-law, he owned one. Anyway I seen this—'

'Billy, it's your turn to patrol,' the Mormon kid said.

'Shut the fuck up!' Eddie said. 'I'm talkin' here and it might be important. Anyway,' he said to Billy, 'I seen this same car parked around here, two–three times before the strike.'

'On *our* shift?' Billy said.

'Yeah, but there's something else. I saw this kid gettin' outta the car, and there's something about this kid, this little scrawny hook-nosed kid, but I just can't put my finger on it.'

'Have you seen the kid around here before?' Billy said.

'I don't know,' Eddie said. 'There's something about him, but I can't remember what. And when I saw him tonight, I think he was holding something in his hand, but—'

The Mormon kid said, 'You say you've seen this car, this . . .'

'El Camino,' Eddie said.

'You've seen it near the plant a few times on *our* shift?' the Mormon kid said.

'Yeah, that's what I just said. Clean out your ears!'

'We should call this in,' the Mormon kid said.

'No way!' Billy said.

'I dunno,' Eddie said, talking more to himself than the other two guards. 'There's just something about this kid.'

'We should hit the button,' the Mormon kid said, and Eddie looked over at him. The kid's eyes were all bright, all lit up, like he'd just seen Jesus.

'Are you outta your goddamned mind?' Billy said.

There really wasn't a button, it was just an expression. *Hitting the button* meant they'd make three phone calls. The first one would be to the foreman of the guys working in the plant, telling him there was a potential security problem and to get his guys assembled in case they had to evacuate the plant. The second call was to one of the big bosses. But the third call went to the sheriffs. The company had a deal with the sheriffs that if they had a potential security problem on the backshift, the sheriffs would send some patrol cars, lights flashing, sirens blaring, and they'd start searching the plant with the guards. The last thing Eddie wanted was to be talkin' to some boss – or some deputy – smelling like a damn brewery, then telling them that the reason he'd hit the button was that he'd seen something funny, but he didn't know what.

Goddammit, what *was* it about that scrawny kid he'd seen next to the El Camino?

'If you even *think* we have a potential security threat,' the Mormon kid said, 'the *manual* says you're supposed to hit the button.'

'Aw, shut the fuck up,' Eddie and Billy said at the same time.

Maybe he'd just patrol with Billy but *really* patrol. Just walk around a little and check things out. Plus the walk was a good idea, it'd sober him up some.

'I'm making the call,' the Mormon kid said.

'You touch that phone, and I swear to God I'll break your arm,' Eddie said.

77

DeMarco got out of bed, trying not to wake Ellie, who was a shapely mound under the sheets, one tanned leg sticking out. DeMarco smiled. He was a lucky man.

He went to the bathroom, took a quick shower, and put on shorts, a faded Redskins T-shirt, and flip-flops, and then made a pot of coffee. He looked out at the lake through the kitchen window and then up at the sky. Perfect. The lake was flat and the sky was cloudless. It was going to be another good day to go jettin' around in Ellie's aunt's boat.

He went outside and got the paper, then took the paper and his coffee out onto the deck. He wished *he* had a big house with a deck on a lake. He slipped the rubber band off the paper and saw the headline: TERRORIST ATTACK FOILED AT LAKE ERIE REFINERY.

'Jesus Christ!' he said out loud, then read the article.

Last night, security guards at the Sheffield refinery on Lake Erie foiled a terrorist attack that could have resulted in hundreds and possibly thousands of deaths. According to FBI spokesperson Jerome Hickson, the terrorist was a fourteen-year-old American Muslim from Cleveland named Javed Khan, who is now in police custody.

At approximately 1 A.M., Khan dug a shallow hole under the refinery's security fence, entered the refinery, and attached three explosive devices to tanks and pipes containing hydrofluoric acid. According to Dr Matthew Trace, a professor of chemistry at Ohio State University, inhaling even small amounts of hydrofluoric acid can be fatal or cause permanent damage to organs.

Khan also had a fourth bomb attached to his clothing. The FBI believes that Khan had intended to wait until refinery workers were entering the facility on Tuesday morning, and then he would have gotten as close to the refinery's main gate as possible and exploded all four bombs simultaneously, including the one on his person. By doing this he not only would have released the hydrofluoric acid to the atmosphere but would also have killed or injured numerous refinery workers and made it more difficult for the refinery to deal with the catastrophe. It is unclear how many people would have died if the bombs had been detonated, but experts said that if the acid had been released, it could have affected people as far as ten miles away from the refinery.

Two security guards, Edward Kolowski and William Horton, were making a routine patrol of the refinery's perimeter when they saw Khan crawling under the security fence. He had already planted his explosives and was attempting to leave the facility. When Khan was captured, the remote control for detonating the bombs was in his jacket pocket, but because Kolowski and Horton seized the terrorist as he was crawling under the fence, Khan was unable to reach the remote. Had he been able to reach it, the FBI believes that he would have exploded the bombs at that time, killing the guards and himself and releasing the acid to the atmosphere. The FBI spokesperson stated that Khan had an accomplice, a man driving a pale green Chevrolet El Camino; all law enforcement agencies in the area are looking for the vehicle.

Mr Hickson noted that the possibility of terrorists attacking refineries has been a concern for some time and that Congress has held hearings on the subject. John Tolliver, plant operations manager for the refinery, stated that such concerns have been overstated and last night's events showed that refinery security procedures were effective. Tolliver said, 'We have state-of-the-art security equipment at our refineries, but our primary line of defense is highly trained, alert security personnel like Ed Kolowski and Bill Horton.'

The Cleveland Plain Dealer discovered that Javed Khan's late father, Ishaq Khan, had been detained by the FBI approximately a year ago for possible links to al-Qaeda and speculated that Khan may have been carrying on his father's work. Attempts to contact Khan's mother . . .

Wow, DeMarco thought. He wondered if he and Ellie had been in any danger. Damn good thing those security guys had been on their toes. Yep, he was a lucky man, he said to himself again, and turned to the sports page to see how the Nationals were doing.

Author's Note

The vulnerability of chemical plants and refineries to terrorist attacks is real and has been the subject of various television shows and congressional hearings. The potentially lethal affects of hydrofluoric acid on humans is also real, and the statement that the chemical 'can just melt your lungs' was taken from a transcript of the PBS show *NOW*.

I was also amazed that as late as April 2007, while I was still writing this book, and twelve years after the bombing of the Alfred P. Murrah Federal Building in Oklahoma City, there was a bill in the House (HR 1680) proposing, finally, to increase controls and make it more difficult for terrorists to buy ammonium nitrate fertilizers. It's possible that the bill will have passed by the time this book is published – but *twelve years*!

Lastly, I must confess that I took a little literary license with the DEA building in Washington, D.C. The DEA does have an office for its Washington Field Division located on the fifth floor of a building on I Street NW – and the building is located a couple of blocks from the Gallery Place metro station as described in the story – but the building does not have DRUG ENFORCEMENT ADMINISTRATION chiseled over the building's entrance. Instead it says DEPARTMENT OF VETERANS AFFAIRS. For what I'm sure are some very good reasons, the DEA tends not to mark its office locations very well, and I had a heck of a time finding one of their other buildings located in Arlington, getting some funny looks from a security guard when I . . . but that's a different story.